Bulletproof Soul

Michelle Buckley

Bulletproof Soul

Michelle Buckley

Urban Books
6 Vanderbilt Parkway
Dix Hills, NY 11746

ISBN 1-893196-16-X

First Printing May 2005
Printed in Canada

10 9 8 7 6 5 4 3 2 1

*This is a work of fiction. Any references or similarities
to actual events, real people, living, or dead, or to real
locals are intended to give the novel a sense of reality.
Any similarity in other names, characters, places, and
incidents is entirely coincidental.*

This is dedicated to all the women in the world with
unbreakable hearts . . .
indestructible spirits . . .
and bulletproof souls.

Acknowledgments

Thanks to God Almighty for blessing me with a gift He saw fit for me to share with others. May I continue to use it to glorify Him by making a difference in the world.

To my parents and biggest fans. You've always believed in me, even when I didn't believe in myself. Thanks for encouraging me at a young age to believe I could be and do anything I wanted to be and do (you were "write")!

To Gertrude Spurgeon, my grandmother and other "momma." There is no better example of female grace. I feel blessed to have your blood running through my veins.

To my brother, Stan, his wife, Kristen and my niece, Faith...my not-so-subtle reminders that you can't take yourself or life too seriously.

Much love to all my other kinfolk who constantly remind me of the importance of family: R.A., Reggie and Georgette Session, Nicole and Jay McIlveen, Erma Washington and Belle Doxey, Gloria and Charles Sanders, Marguerite and Linda Waller, Barbara and Jessica Garrett, Robin and Curtis Drapeau, Faye and Flip Smith, Julia Buckley, Tonya and Carl Bass, Kevin and Herman Buckley, Deann King, Elizabeth Hubbard, Penny Barnes, Anna Mae Woods, Moses Woods, and the entire Woods family.

Thanks to my friend Marguerite Jordan, who was there when the seeds of this book took root. And thanks also to other friends whose support has meant a lot: Carla Rainey, Michelle Keller, Deborah Garrett, Aretha Shepherd, Monnette Wilson, Teresa Clay and Deidre Fisher.

A big thanks to the supreme Iyanla Vanzant, Dawn Marie Daniels, Rashena Lindsay and author, Monica Jackson who set in motion a series of events that led me down this path. And a SUPA DUPA THANK YA to author, Donna Hill, my agent, who took the time out of her busy writing career and schedule to find my first book a home. I only hope I'm able to help others along the way as she has helped me.

To model, Candace Franklin, and Kansas City photographer, Maurice Fields, whose cover shot proves he can work mad magic with a camera—thank you. And thanks to Kevin Jones of TEMAC Solutions, Inc., in Houston, Texas for the bangin' website (www.michellebuckley.com). You're all aces—what a team!

To St. Luke's, my first church family. Thanks for the support. You've been there for as long as I can remember. I feel blessed to know ya!

To Carl Weber, my publisher and mentor . . . thank you for believing in me and teaching me so much about the biz. And to my editor, Martha Weber, your patience and guidance helped make my first publishing experience truly a joy!

And finally to the media, book lovers and booksellers everywhere—I appreciate you taking a chance on me. God bless you all!

Michelle

ONE

Like many women in America, I feel like I'm under attack.

More often than I care to admit, I feel like I'm under fire, like I have a friggin' target on my back. A target that makes people, particularly men, think I'm an easy mark. Or to be more precise, particularly men I just happen to fall in love with.

Hmmmm . . . Love? What a joke! P-E-Z. Romantic PEZ.

That sums up the bulk of my love relationships. That's the not-so-sweet truth about my numerous romantic entanglements. Like PEZ, my relationships have been tiny, bite-sized morsels of excessively tart nothingness—easy to swallow, but ultimately unfulfilling and unsubstantial. Too much exposure to them over the years has caused atrophy and decay—not to my teeth, but to my heart, my psyche.

Surely disease and death are just around the corner. At least that's what I used to think before I met the man I thought I would spend the rest of my life with—the man whom I had been totally in love with, devoted to and fooled by for three years.

What an idiot I'd been. What we once shared had long vanished and I'd been stuck in Candyland a while, drowning in sweet, sometimes semi-sweet, and very often downright sour indulgence. But now I was in Candyland . . . dying.

Most recently death has come into my life in the form of a lost love, a love that I'm constantly trying extremely hard—and, might I add, unsuccessfully—to forget. In my most recent efforts to forget about this unforgettable love otherwise known as Sebastard, I mean Sebastian Gamble, I have also managed to forget where I am . . . who I'm with . . . and how I friggin' got here.

Baaaammmmmmmmm!

1

"Tha hell?" I screamed, shooting straight up. "What's goin' on?"

What was a 250-pound, tattooed, half-naked hairy creature doing jumping into a hotel bed beside me? I said a silent prayer before peeking under the worn, dingy and slightly tattered covers.

Thank goodness for small favors. At least I was fully dressed. That was an extremely encouraging sign.

Dagnabit, Lacy Eymaleen Foxx! What on earth is his name?

For the life of me, I couldn't remember the name of the extremely hairy creature lying in bed beside me, but I was a reporter. I was determined to figure it out. I searched the room for clues. My investigative abilities failed me. Clues evaded me like the plague.

Was his name James? Steve? Martin? Rashon? I couldn't remember. Baby, darling and sweetheart always worked well whenever name recall failed. But as difficult as it was for me to remember his name, it was even harder for me to remember why or how I'd ended up in bed with him in a cheap, fleabag hotel.

There wasn't much I remembered about last night except for it was my birthday. One of the few other things I remembered was finishing off a bottle of Alizé Bleu by myself. And I don't even drink (much). At least not anymore, not since my alcohol-filled lose-all-control college days, which ended six years ago.

My problem was obvious. Once again, I had forgotten a simple yet powerful key life principle. When it comes to things like liquor, food, sex and relationships, moderation is the key…especially when it comes to love.

Eventually, it started coming back to me in bits and pieces. No more drinking and going home with folks for the sole purpose of trying to forget about my ex-fiancé. The ex-fiancé who had once been the love of my life, but was now simply and less than affectionately known as Sebastard, Jerkface or Ratboy, depending on the day of the week.

"Me hairy creature, you Jane," The Creature said.

Or did he just say, "Hey, what's happening?"

"And you are?" I asked with an attitude. The Creature laughed. I didn't.

"Quit playing, baby."

He obviously can't remember my name either.

"We didn't . . . you know . . . did we?" I asked, afraid of completing the thought.

"Nope. You passed out before anything could happen. I know last night was your birthday, and I thought we could celebrate it properly this morning," The Creature said as his version of a sexy grin overtook his face.

Unfortunately, I couldn't keep my version of a pained grimace from overtaking mine. "I really have a lot to do today. I have to get going," I said while leaping out of bed like a hurdler.

"You sure? Well, give me your business card before you leave. Don't forget I promised you an interview with my boss."

His boss? Who was that? I couldn't remember. I took a chance.

"Who? Nelly? Fine, I'll give you my number. Tell him he can call me anytime."

"Nelly? You mean Lionel, don't you?" The Creature asked.

Lionel Richie? Father of Nicole Richie, star of TV's *The Simple Life*. Okay . . . bet.

I jammed my size ten feet into my size nine shoes, and before The Creature could blink, I combed my hair, grabbed my coat, threw him a business card and dashed for the door.

"Ciao bello," I said while walking to the door.

Shoot, I still can't remember his name. With that revelation, I blew The Creature a kiss and was gone. What a way to start the week! I now had another reason to hate birthdays and Mondays.

Despite the bright sunlight, it was at least ten degrees below zero outside, and I shivered all the way to my car. Januaries in Missouri are awful, and how had I chosen to keep warm? By cuddling up with a man, name unknown—or should I say name unremembered?

What had I been thinking? All the details of the previous night finally came back to me. I was working—covering Lionel's bazillionth comeback tour on my birthday, no less— when I saw *him* with *her*. Luckily, the two of them didn't see me. After the concert, I headed to the nearest bar, determined to drink myself into oblivion. After drinking a full bottle of Alizé, I was, to put it bluntly, ripped, and fortified with enough liquid courage to hit on The Creature, who I knew casually. He was a roadie from out of town who worked with a lot of R&B artists when they performed in Kansas City.

He was the ugliest, hairiest thing on two legs, thus his nickname. But he was nice and seemed harmless enough, hence my decision to return with him to his hotel room with the intention of erasing some painful memories.

Let's just say my plan didn't work! But, at least I got an interview with Lionel Richie out of it. Hmmm . . .

How I longed for my early days as a reporter. I was born to be a journalist. I have an insatiable sense of curiosity, or nosiness as my best friend calls it, and I absolutely love to write. Until about a year ago, all I ever wanted to be was a hard-hitting journalist. Protector of the public trust, watchdog of the truth . . . blah, blah, blah. Once, I actually believed the people had a right to know—a right to know which politician was screwing which businessman, because the people were usually getting screwed by both.

But then there was the matter of my brief stint in jail a little less than a year ago. Somewhere in the hallowed halls of justice is a file with my name and prison number on it, the

4

result of a contempt charge for not revealing a source when I blew the lid off a major corruption scandal involving a prominent businessman. There went the people's right to know, along with my previously pristine criminal record.

If I sound a little bitter, that's because I am. Now, I believe the only right to know the people have is whether Will Smith and Usher prefer boxers or briefs, and what was up with Lenny Kravitz's one-time relaxer. Yeah, I sold out. I took the easy road and I'm not a bit sorry. I don't regret it for a single, solitary second. Truth is, I believe there is something respectable about entertainment journalism. Journalists like *Sister2Sister's* Jamie Foster Brown, radio's Sybil and Wendy Williams, and *Access Hollywood's* Shaun Robinson have turned entertainment journalism into an art form. And while I wasn't on their level yet by any means, a sistah was well on her way.

Since switching from hard news to entertainment and society news, my professional life had become a lot easier. And I always promised myself the switch would be worth it when I hit the big time and jumped from *The Metro Tribune* to *Élan Live*, an Internet site and cable TV network conglomerate that was a knock-off of the popular *E! Entertainment*.

Thirty minutes after leaving The Creature, I walked into my condo and headed straight for the shower—that is after I checked my messages.

There were none from Jerkface.

I stepped into the shower and shivered like I always did when I felt the cold water cascade down my warm body. Jerkface always hated taking showers with me. He always said the only time he wanted to take a cold shower was when he wasn't with me, not when he was. But I loved cold showers. I loved the way the water invigorated me, made me tingle and come alive. Just like he once had.

After more than twenty minutes in the shower, I stepped out and dried myself off. As I did so, I examined myself closely in the mirror. My thick, medium-length, soft-black hair—thanks to Clairol #1N—was pulled back into a ponytail. Bangs framed my slightly square face. My slanted, light brown eyes were red from too much liquor, but they were still captivating. I looked more like a young hoochie of eighteen than an established woman of twenty-eight.

My five-foot-seven-inch, shapely size twelve body made me look thick, but not too much so. It was obvious I'd put on a little weight during the three years I'd lived with Jerkface. I skipped the freshman fifteen when I went away to college, but I was starting to make up for it now, years later.

My grandmother attributed my ever-expanding boobs and backside to "the steady sex weight gain hex." She blamed it all on the performance of my "wifely duties" during the time my ex-fiancé and I lived together. And by "wifely duties," she didn't mean cooking and cleaning.

The Native American side of my heritage was undeniable and becoming more apparent as I got older. I inherited my high, pronounced forehead, prominent cheekbones and white-girl thin lips from my great-grandmother on my mama's side, a full-blooded Ojibwa Indian, born in Michigan, land of the Ojibwa tribe.

Based on what I'd heard all my life, Eymaleen Polk was a sturdy, beautiful, self-educated, independent and stubborn woman who was ostracized by her tribe and her family—a mother, father, two brothers and a twin sister—when she nixed plans for an arranged marriage set up by tribunal leaders. She opted instead to marry my great-grandfather, Frederrick Hale, a fun-loving African-American sharecropper. As a youngster, I reveled in stories about my great-grandparents, who eventually migrated from Detroit to Kansas City. I was extremely proud of the fact that their rebellious blood ran through my veins.

I scooped some Body Shop Nut Body Butter into my hands and rubbed it all over my mole-dotted, mahogany-colored skin, then walked through a light perfume cloud of my signature scent, Donna Karan's Cashmere Mist. The grandfather clock in my living room struck the hour of eight. I had to get to work, but at the rate I was going, it would be ten o'clock before I rolled into the office. After an extended search for the perfect I'm-late-but-don't-even-think-about-looking-at-me-funny outfit, my phone rang. Fearing it was my boss on the other end of the line, I formulated a believable story as I looked for the portable phone in "the sty" — yes, as in pig — the name bestowed upon my condo by all who knew and loved me.

"Hello?" I said into the phone on the fourth ring.

"Dang, Lace. What took you so long?"

"What do you want, Sebastard? I mean Sebastian."

There was a long pause. "I just wanted to know if I could come by and get the rest of my things."

The mere sound of his voice irritated me. "Do whatever tickles your fickle pickle," I said.

"Not only do I want to come and get my things, but I think we need to talk."

"Haven't we talked enough? I'm not interested in rehashing things with you. Come get your things tonight. I'll make sure I'm not here. We won't even have to see each other."

"Maybe I want to see you," he said.

"Why? So you can throw that light, bright, almost white stripper girlfriend of yours in my face all over again?"

"Are you gonna harp on that forever? I admit it. I made mistakes. So did you. We both did. No one is perfect, that includes you, but after all this time, I still love you anyway. I probably always will."

"Whatever, Sebastian," I said with total disdain.

Suddenly, always didn't seem very permanent. He'd broken my heart once. He wasn't about to get a second chance.

"No, I'm serious. I still love you. I will always love you and I think— "

7

Click.

What a perfectly good waste of blood and vital organs. I wasn't trying to hear his nonsense. I had better things to do, like get to work. What had I ever seen in him? It was ironic his last name was Gamble, because I'd gambled on him and lost. Our last year together had been like hang gliding beneath a Boeing 747. The noxious drama that fueled our relationship kept me woozy and light-headed, but I held on for dear life and tried not to get in the way, for fear of being obliterated. Now, I was sorry I'd ever met Sebastard, let alone lived with him for three years.

In truth, I didn't really regret being with Sebastian. That distinction was reserved for one man. He was the only man in my life I truly ever regretted being with. He was Chuck Skinnard, otherwise known as Tiny Dick, Big Asshole, whom I was with shortly before I met Sebastian. Chuck had not developed psychologically beyond high school, and as a result he basically drank too much, smoked weed too much and screwed around too much with way too many women, including, at one time, a good friend's wife.

He was an angry little man a sad excuse for a human being, and he pretty much hated everyone, including — deep down — himself. I suspect a lot of his problems were the result of the inadequacies he felt as a man because he was so short and had such a small nub of worthless manhood, which I unfortunately had the displeasure of experiencing for five minutes during a lackluster round of sex. Was he sad? Yes. Pathetic? Yes. No longer my problem? Thank God, yes! I fooled around with TDBA for two weeks too long before meeting Sebastian.

As I finished getting dressed, I kicked myself for the umpteenth time when I thought of my ex-fiancé. My ringing phone pulled me out of my wish-I-could-forget-the-past state.

"Sebastian, look . . ."

"Sebastian? Honey, please. "

A smile spread across my face when I heard the voice of Marsha Turner, my best friend, who was an investigative reporter for *The Tribune*. "Hey, Marsh, what up?"

"I need you to do me a favor, Ace. A friend of a friend set me up tonight on a blind date with some guy named Patrick Nance. I need you to cover that Greater Kansas City Youth Center shindig at Union Station tonight because I don't want to drag my date to it."

"I'm not in the mood for that 'we are the world' nonprofit mess."

"Puhleeeeze!" Marsha pathetically begged. "I forgot all about my assignment and it's too late to cancel my blind date."

"All right. But you owe me big."

"Thanks. It starts at six, and your perpetually tardy self better be on time. It will be fun. I promise you won't be sorry."

Too late. I already was.

TWO

I didn't see Marsha at work all day. By the time I arrived at the Greater Kansas City Youth Center Gala, it was nearly seven o'clock and I had already missed the "aren't we great" pat on the back speeches.

The location for the Youth Center affair couldn't have been better. Kansas City's grandiose, refurbished Union Station was one of the last monumental train stations built in America in the early 1900s, and only New York's Grand Central Station surpassed it in size. Having the Youth Center Gala there sent a strong, upbeat message to the community.

The Greater Kansas Youth Center, popularly referred to throughout the area as the YC, had a good reputation in Kansas City. It was started in the mid-1950s by a handful of concerned, inner-city parents who wanted their kids to have positive activities to participate in and a safe place to hang out after school and during the summers. Located in the center of the city, the YC was considered a 10,000-square-foot beacon of hope for the inner-city kids who participated in its programs. Youth Center activities included choir and band, crafts, sports and scouting. Also available to YC members were drug and alcohol avoidance programs, homework tutoring, computer training, cultural outings and mentoring and life skills programs. There was even a 20-bed living area for troubled youth who couldn't function in their home environments.

The kids who attended the YC didn't have to pay to participate. Instead, they were awarded scholarships funded by private donors and the city. I'd donated money to the YC for years, and according to their latest direct mail piece I'd received, about 5,000 kids between the ages of five and eighteen were members. Some of the area's wealthiest residents, both black and white, supported the YC by either serving on its board or giving regularly of their time, money and talents.

Finding willing sources for my YC story wasn't hard. I chose two outgoing youngsters that regularly hung out at the Youth Center. Best friends, Trey Jenkins and Shequita Bell were decked out in over-sized jeans and colorful Youth Center sweatshirts. Both Shequita and Trey lived in the inner city, but it was obvious they both had what it took to break away from life in the hood.

I had read several times about 17-year-old Shequita in our newspaper. She was a common fixture in the sports section. She was an accomplished gymnast who started taking gymnastic lessons at the age of eight at the YC. She was a member of the Center's Tumbling Prancers, only the baddest black gymnastics team in the country. During the past five years, the Tumbling Prancers had performed throughout Europe and the United Stated. I'd seen them perform numerous times. They were amazing, and Shequita had been one of the group's lead gymnasts for years.

I'd heard that Kansas City's professional gymnastics team was sweating her, trying to recruit her to join them once she graduated from high school. But Shequita had her sights set on winning Olympic gold before joining them and going pro.

In addition to Shequita, my other interview source was Trey, a 17-year-old mocha-colored Adonis. Trey was his high school basketball team's captain, and he'd been on the honor roll since second grade. He too frequented our paper's sports section.

If my younger brother had lived past the age of sixteen, I imagined he would have been a lot like Trey—outgoing, handsome and intelligent. My brother Gary and I had been very close. His wild, impetuous ways always got us into trouble, but my quick wit and smart mouth always got us out. The thing that bothered me most about his death was that I wasn't with him when he really needed me. He and his friend Rayce were shot after somebody stepped on somebody's foot or somebody tried to talk to somebody's girl at some stupid club they shouldn't have even been able to get into.

I didn't understand it all then, and I still didn't, some ten years later. I was two years older than Gary when he died. I always felt like I should have been the first to go. I always felt like his death was my fault though I wasn't even there. I was off at the University of Kansas when I should have been protecting my little brother. I could have saved his life; at least that's what I thought.

But others consistently pointed out to me that what happened to Gary most likely would have happened sooner or later given his somewhat wild personality. Despite that, I was in intensive psychiatric therapy for five years after his death and the soon-to-follow accidental death of my mother.

Gary had always said the North Kansas City 'burbs we grew up in were too safe and too boring for him. That's why he always hung out with his boy, Rayce. The hoodlum. Rayce? What kind of people name their son after a verb? I always knew Racye was trouble. He and his gangsta friends added a sense of excitement to Gary's boring suburban life.

It was too much excitement, as it turns out, for both Gary and my mother.

Mama died of an accidental prescription drug overdose shortly after Gary and Rayce were killed. Throughout my life, things had been a bit unstable because my mother suffered from bipolar disorder, a form of depression, with intense highs and lows. After my brother's death her depression seemed to get worse.

Whenever I think about Mama, I subconsciously rub the watch my father gave her on their wedding night, which I have worn since she passed. My father and I are the only ones left.

"Yo, yo, yo, Li'l Miss Reporter. You a'ight?" Trey asked.

"Yeah, Trey. I'm fine. I'm sorry. Let's get started. Now, tell me. What is it about the Youth Center that keeps the two of you coming back?"

"Mr. T.," Shequita said simply.

"Mr. T.?" I asked, thinking of the 1980s gold-adorned, muscle-bound, mohawked African-American action hero.

"Yeah, Mr. T. is the baddest dude on the planet next to Shaq," Trey said.

"So, tell me about this Mr. T."

"His real name is Wynnton Trust, and he's the one that got us interested in the YC in the first place. He's a volunteer. Because of him, I don't drink or smoke. He's got me hooked on basketball and sports instead. I go to the YC to shoot hoops and hang out, but there are all kinds of things for kids like us to get into," Trey said.

"Yeah, there are arts and crafts projects, photography, talent shows, field trips, sports, dance and gymnastics. You name it, we do it!" Shequita said enthusiastically.

Their excitement was contagious. I was proud of Kansas City. I was proud of the support we were giving these kids. I made a mental note to increase my charitable contributions to the YC by one hundred dollars for the year.

"Tell me this. Why did you two join the YC in the first place?" I asked.

Trey looked away when I asked the question. His face, and in fact the entire room, seemed to dim. Shequita took his hand in hers and spoke quietly.

"That's something Trey really doesn't like to talk about. You see, his dad doesn't live with his family," Shequita said.

"My dad's a punk. Don't nobody even know where he is."

"His oldest brother and sister are drug dealers and they're hooked on crack, and his mother works three jobs to take care of him and his younger brother and sister."

"I don't get to see Moms much. When she's home, she's usually too tired to talk, help me with my homework or do stuff with. But next summer, I'm gonna get a job and help her out. That way she'll only have to work one job. I'll miss the YC, but a man's gotta do what he's gotta do," a hurting Trey said.

These kids were breaking my heart. Forget about increasing my charitable contribution to the YC by one hundred dollars, I was going to increase it by two hundred dollars. I reached for Trey's other hand but he snatched it away.

"So, Shequita, tell me why you joined the Youth Center."

"I originally joined 'cause I wanted to be a Tumbling Prancer. That was nine years ago. I keep coming back 'cause of all the friends I've made. Plus, I like all the exciting things I get to do. Another reason I come to the Youth Center is to escape."

I felt another sad story coming on, and mentally prepared my pocketbook.

"See, unlike Trey's dad, my father lives with my family, although sometimes I wish he wasn't around. He and my mom fight all the time. He's even hit her a couple times. All they do is argue, argue, argue. It's like they don't love each other no more."

What do you say to young kids with impressionable minds who are carrying the weight of the world, not to mention the sins of their parents on their shoulders? I'm sorry you're having such a hard life? Everything will be okay? I know where you're coming from?

Well, I didn't know if everything was going to be okay, and I couldn't even begin to imagine where they were coming from. Words seemed inadequate, especially from someone like me.

"So, tell me, you two, what's so special about this Mr. T. you were talking about earlier? Where is Mr. Wonderful?" I asked, eager to lighten the mood.

Was it my imagination or did the light in the room increase as the smiles returned to their faces?

"You wanna meet Mr. T.?" Trey asked.

"Sure. I have to meet the man who has inspired my two new best friends," I said. Shequita laughed. "You'll love Mr. T.," she said. "He's so nice and funny. We call him our earth angel 'cause he keeps us out of trouble. Plus, he's really, really cute."

"He also has a mean jumper. He's a'ight for an adult," Trey said.

Now there's a ringing endorsement.

The two of them grabbed my hands and led me around the room for nearly five minutes before we finally found Mr. T. Cute didn't even begin to describe him. He looked like he had just stepped out of the pages of *Esquire*.

"Mr. T.! Mr. T.!" Shequita said while waving at a darkened shadow that slowly approached us.

Wynnton Trust walked with the aplomb of an African king. Strong. Proud. Confident. An aura of quiet strength enveloped him like a trusted old friend guarding a well-kept secret. Through his clothes I could detect the outline of a massive chest, broad shoulders, dense arms and muscular legs. He had deep chocolate, silky smooth skin, a chiseled jaw and deep dimples. He was bald and had a beautiful set of full lips that easily stretched into a picture-perfect smile. A perfectly shaped goatee framed his sexy mouth.

The genetically gifted Mr. T. looked like basketball star Jason Kidd, only darker and a thousand times sexier. He was a six-foot tall hottie—a walking, talking, thinking, breathing romantic encounter waiting to happen, and the moment I saw him, I fell head over Nine West heels in lust with him.

"So, this is the infamous Mr. T.? You know you have quite a fan club. I'm glad that I'm finally getting the chance to meet you. I've heard a lot of good things about you and the YC," I said.

Why am I rambling?

"And you are?" his sexy confident voice asked.

"She's a reporter for *The Metro Tribune*," Shequita said. "Her name is Lacy Foxx. Isn't she cute?"

Am I blushing?

"Nice meeting you. Call me Wynn," he said, shaking my hand.

How 'bout I call you fine?

His handshake was firm yet gentle. Marsha swore by the belief that you could tell what a man would be like in bed by examining the way he shook your hand. Firm. Gentle.

Hmmm . . . a simple handshake had never turned me on before.

I was glad I wore my form-fitting, two-piece black crepe Calvin Klein suit with red piping. Mr. T. was wearing pleated black pants, a black turtleneck and a neon turquoise jacket. He looked scrumptious and smelled of Giorgio Armani's Acqua Di Gio.

"While I was interviewing Trey and Shequita about the Youth Center, they just couldn't stop talking about you, so I thought I'd interview you to see what all the fuss was about. That is, of course, if you don't mind."

"I hope I can live up to your expectations," Wynn said.

"I'm sure you will."

Why am I blushing again? Did I ever stop?

Normally, no matter how overwhelmed I get, it's nearly impossible to tell. I've never been left speechless nor do I ever act fidgety. That's one of the first tenets I learned as a reporter. Never let 'em see you sweat. But this blushing thing was really starting to bug me, and unfortunately I couldn't help it.

"So, shall we have a seat?" Wynn asked. I hugged Trey and Shequita, told them good-bye, then followed their idol to an empty table located in the back of the room. I couldn't take my eyes off of him, but I hoped everyone in the room didn't notice.

"To be honest, I don't like doing interviews," Wynn said while pulling out a chair for me. "I'm not exactly a media darling. I've been hurt . . . burned by the media in the past."

"I'll be gentle with you. This will be painless," I said through a goofy smile.

Once we settled into our seats, I pulled out my trusty reporter's pad and readied my pen. "This won't take long. I just have a few questions. Tell me, how did you become involved with the Youth Center?"

"The YC has been a part of my life ever since I was a young child. I was a Youth Center member from the time I was eight until I was fifteen. When I was finally old enough to work, I chose to work at the Youth Center. I worked there every summer while I was in high school."

How admirable, I thought, glancing at my steno pad's blank page.

He continued. "When I was eighteen, I started college but was still really involved with the Youth Center. During my freshman year, my cousin, Abram, started running the YC, and he asked me to help him out as a volunteer. I did, and I've been helping him out ever since. He's in L.A. now taking care of his sick mother. It looks like he'll be there all year, and until he returns, I'm kind of running things at the YC."

"Impressive," I said, not so impressively.

"The YC was my world of firsts," Wynn said. "I won my first basketball tournament there, made my first clay sculpture there, learned how to swim there, performed in my first talent show there, got my first job there and kissed my first girl there."

After that, I heard nothing else, as I imagined being the first person to ever kiss his magnificent mouth.

He rambled on. I drifted.

"Ms. Foxx? Ms. Foxx? Ms. Foxx? Do you have any more questions?"

How long had he been finished? How long had I been staring? I hadn't written down a thing he said in my reporter's pad.

Never let 'em see you sweat.

"Yeah. I have just a few more questions. Why are places like the Youth Center important to Kansas City?"

This time I was going to write down every word that crossed his luscious lips.

"The need for organizations like the Youth Center is stronger than ever before. The world is really a harsh place. Before our kids can realize their true promise and potential, they are being threatened by negative forces that the generations before them never even dreamed of having to face at their age."

Amen. Ain't that the truth?

"If we adults don't take a more active role in the lives of our nation's young people, forget Generation X. They'll be known as Generation Wrecked. Drugs, drive-bys, teenage sex, pregnancy, AIDS. It's crazy! These kids need a place they can go and take charge of their lives. That's what the Youth Center offers. Hope, a future, choices."

Did I mention the brother was deep? I looked at my pad. *Nothing.* "What volunteer opportunities are available for people in Kansas City who may want to get involved with the Youth Center?"

I didn't even bother with my pen or pad.

"We need positive role models. People can get involved on either a long-term or short-term basis. As volunteer coordinator, I have an upcoming project that is near and dear to my heart. We're having a career fair in three weeks. I'd love it if you would stop by and talk to the kids about being a reporter."

"Me? Uhmmm, I don't think so. I get asked to participate in so many things, I kind of have a policy. I'm not taking on any new projects for a while."

"Oh, come on. You're just the kind of woman we need to expose our young people to, especially our girls. In the short time you spent with Trey and Shequita, it was obvious you won them over. You made an impact."

"Well, let me think about the career fair thing, okay?"

"I hope you'll really think about it. Some of Kansas City's African-American heavyweights are participating. There's a city councilman and an attorney. Willena Hughes, a top area doctor; Deanna Moore, a black syndicated radio talk show host; award-winning architect Marshall Resse; Darnella Smith, the owner of a black-owned engineering firm; and Tamerek Landon and Khalil Quest of 2Tuff, a local positive rap group."

"That's pretty impressive. But can we just concentrate on the interview? I'm almost finished. I just need to ask you a few more questions for the article. For attribution purposes, I need some background information."

Look at me . . . lying. I was just being nosy. I wanted this information strictly for personal reasons. I prayed that he didn't see right through me.

"Name?"

"Wynnton Clarence Trust, the second. My friends call me Wynn."

"Age?"

"Thirty-two."

"Occupation?"

"I'm the volunteer coordinator for the Greater Kansas City Youth Center. I also run my own company."

"Address?"

"5912 Gaylord Road."

"Home and work phone numbers? Our fact-checkers may need to do some follow-up."

"My home number is 555-4242. My number at the YC is 555-3704."

"Marital status?"

"Divorced with a son, Édonte. He's six years old and lives with me. He's a member at the YC. He's running around here somewhere with the Youth Center's assistant director, Voncile Ford."

Preferred sexual position? Okay, enough was enough. I hadn't said that out loud, had I? I must not have because he didn't look at me as if I were from another planet. Instead, he stood, extended his hands and helped me out of my seat.

"I hope you change your mind about the career fair. It's exactly three weeks from today. I really and truly would like to see you there."

I really and truly would like to see you naked and served on a platter, I thought to myself. "We don't always get what we want," I said playfully instead.

"True, but maybe I'll get lucky. Here, take my card. I'm at the YC most days."

"How's that possible? Didn't you say you run your own company?"

"Yeah, it's a computer software company that I started with a couple of brothas back in college. I used to work pretty hard at it, but now my partners pretty much run things. I just sign the checks and sit around looking good at board meetings."

"Must be nice," I said while trying hard not to roll my eyes.

HNIC, huh? Yeah, right. I wasn't impressed. I was tired of men who were always trying to give themselves juice, trying to make themselves sound bigger and more important than they really were.

"Give me a call if you change your mind about the career fair," Wynn said.

"I won't change my mind."

"To be honest, I'm not surprised that you're turning me down."

"Why? What do you mean?" I asked.

20

"You reporters are all extremely biased in your coverage of the inner city. When you get the chance to see how things really are, you're not interested. That's why I hate doing interviews. I thought you'd be different."

"Contrary to what you think, we're not all out for your blood. You don't know me, and you can't blame me for problems you've had with other reporters."

"What a typical response. But what else would I expect from a bougie, it's-all-about-me self-centered ghetto princess?"

What happened to the caring man I had just interviewed? Why had this rude alien life form taken over his body? And more importantly, who the heck did he think he was talking to? Someone who cared a lick about his opinion?

"Look, I got what I wanted. There's really nothing else to say, except for I'm sorry you have such a deep hatred for the media, women in general, and me in particular."

"To have a deep hatred for you would mean I'd have to care about what you think, and guess what, I don't!" he said.

Why was he suddenly getting so ugly with me? "Angering the media isn't exactly a great public relations move."

"Is that a threat?"

"Call it what you want," I said in as controlled a voice as I could manage before turning on my heels and walking away.

THREE

The long drive home was spent thinking about Wynnton Trust, whom I couldn't get out of my mind. Trey and Shequita were right. He was the baddest dude on the planet, or at least in my jerk-filled world.

Too bad he also suffered from jerkitis and more than a touch of jackassidness.

I'd never in my life met a more arrogant man. So what if he had looks, brains, compassion . . . the whole nine? From what I could see, the only thing that kept him from being perfect was his attitude.

I racked my brain looking for other faults. I wasn't comfortable with the idea of a perfect man. Based upon my past experience, that would make him an anomaly.

Let's see . . . faults? Too muscular? Too accepting of his responsibility of raising his son? Too good looking? Too smart? Too compassionate? Too committed to the community? *Dagnabit!* I wasn't doing so well. I decided to dial a familiar number on my cell.

"Hello . . . " I heard Marsha's voice ask through the phone.

"Marsh, girl—"

"I'm gone, you're on." *Beep.* I hated that slight time delay she had on her answering machine message. I always fell for it. It always sounded like she was really on the other end of the line.

"I just encountered the biggest jerk I've ever met in my life. Don't get me wrong, though. He was a hottie with a BODY. His name is Wynnton Trust. The kids at the Youth Center call him Mr. T. He's a volunteer. Jerk had the nerve to call me a bourgeois, self-centered ghetto princess. Hmmm . . . Mr. T. I pity the fool who finds herself involved in a relationship with him. The man couldn't be more arrogant if he tried."

22

The phone beeped three times then hung up. I promptly hit the redial button.

"Hello . . . I'm gone, you're on." *Beep.*

"By the way, you should have gone to Union Station. The food looked great, not the same old rubber chicken crap they usually serve at those things. Anyway . . . where are you? You know I hate talking to this machine. You must still be on your blind date and you must be getting some 'cause it's after midnight. I hope you're having fun. Holla when you get in. Love ya."

I heard the three beeps and quickly pushed my phone's "end" button.

As I turned onto my street, I stopped thinking for a moment about how bad Mr. T. was and thought for a moment about just how truly bad I was. He wasn't the only one that had it all together. I'd turned out okay, and I managed to do it without bad manners and an attitude that reeked.

Here I was, just twenty-eight years old and considered a top, well-respected reporter for one of the largest newspapers in the area. I owned a beautiful, three bedroom split-level, Tuscan-style condo, for which I paid $100,000, a reasonable price for Kansas City. My home was filled with art and furnishings that would make any decorator worth his salt proud. So what if I drove an I-got-a-great-deal-on-this booger-green Dodge Neon, the Yugo of the 90s? I was a college grad with money in the bank and sex on the mind (most of the time). I was quite the catch, if I did say so myself.

When I walked into my condo, I was so lost in my thoughts that I failed to notice the silhouette in my living room.

"Hey . . . "

Tha hell?

I reached for and threw the first object I could find in the direction of the voice. Unfortunately, the object was my expensive, hand-carved mahogany Ashanti Akuba fertility doll. It promptly broke as it fell to the floor, after smashing into the skull of the person on the receiving end of my perfectly aimed throw. It was nice to see that my years as a Little League softball pitcher hadn't been wasted.

"Lace! What's wrong with you?"

"Sebastian?" I asked, turning on a nearby light. "I should be asking you the same thing!"

My ex-fiancé, Sebastian Gamble, was sitting on my custom-made raspberry leather couch, looking at me blankly as he rubbed his temple. He was wearing the full-length black leather coat and expensive designer jogging suit that I had purchased for him months ago for his birthday. He smelled of the Burberry cologne I'd also given him. Seeing him sorely reminded me of the fact that I was still paying for those three overly expensive items.

"Why'd you do that?"

"I thought you were a prowler," I said, defending myself.

"How many prowlers hang around on your sofa waiting for you to come home? Besides, didn't you see my car in front of the condo?"

"No," I admitted sheepishly. "What are you doing here?"

"You told me I could come by and get the rest of my stuff, which I can't find, by the way."

"Did you not see the POD in the driveway?"

"You put my shit in a POD?" he asked in disbelief.

"Portable on demand storage. Nothing beats it."

"That's messed up. It's *beyond* wrong. Have you ever thought about why I'm just now coming to get my things? Maybe I'm not ready to move on."

"That's too bad."

"You can insult me all you want, but we really need to talk. I'm tired of things being so tense and uncomfortable between us."

"Well, that's what happens when you cheat on your pregnant fiancée."

24

"Hold up! Hold up! Hold up! You got it wrong! You had lost the twins and turned your back on me long before I even gave Charron a second look."

"You no longer have to lie to me, Sebastian. I found her home phone number, her work number, her mama's phone number and her pager and cell numbers in your Blackberry way before I ever miscarried."

It upset me when I remembered how it felt knowing that another woman wanted *my man* to be able to reach her anytime, anyplace.

"Just 'cause I had her number—"

"Numbers," I said, correcting him.

"Just 'cause I had her numbers doesn't mean I used them."

"So, it's just a coinky-dink that you're with her now, huh?"

"You let your paranoia destroy ya. You let it destroy us."

"What destroyed us was the fact that you couldn't keep Li'l Sebastian in your pants. But what's done is done. If you're sincere about us being friends, you have to come clean. That's the only way the air between us will ever clear up. It's been months since you walked out on me. Don't you think it's time for you to admit the error of your ways and just apologize?"

"I'm telling you I have nothing to apologize for. I swear I never cheated on you when we were together. Not with Charron, not with anyone, not ever!"

I must have been really, really tired or losing my mind because I almost believed him. I walked back to my bedroom, stripped out of my work clothes and changed into an old, cropped tan sweater and a pair of black leggings. Sebastian stood silently in the doorway and watched. Not that I cared. Any feelings of modesty either one of us may have had around the other disappeared a long time ago.

As I brushed past him to walk back into the living room, my nipples stood erect. I had breasts like radar; they could track a man from miles away. As we returned to my couch, I hoped he wouldn't notice how perky they were.

He did. He couldn't take his eyes off of them. Under his steadfast gaze, they became volcanic mountains of mahogany-hued desire. I ignored their aching.

"Sebastian, I'm up here," I said, deftly turning his attention from my chest to my face.

"I see the girls miss me," he said while reaching in the direction of my chest. I grabbed his hands in mid-air.

"Don't play yourself. Still horny as ever, huh?" I observed with a reflective smile. "You were saying?"

"I was saying I didn't cheat on you. I wanted to marry you, but you wouldn't have anything to do with me after you lost the twins. I thought you wanted to be alone. You acted like you didn't want me around. After you miscarried, I prayed that you'd let me hold you, feel you, make love to you again."

"Thank goodness for unanswered prayers," I said snidely. He ignored me.

"We eventually stopped talking. We stopped being real with each other. When you lost the babies, that was the hardest time of my life."

Mine too.

My OB-GYN told me I miscarried because of a large fibroid cyst. I had an ectopic pregnancy. There was nothing anyone could do about it. My doctor said I'd never be able to carry a child to term. She was surprised that I had even been able to conceive. She predicted I'd never do it again.

That news was hard for a person like me to take; someone who felt she could do anything and everything. After the miscarriages, for the first time in my life I felt like a complete failure and unfortunately, I took it out on Sebastian. He was right. I coulda been more compassionate toward him.

And I woulda been, eventually.

I just needed more time. I had just lost two babies, for goodness sake. He shoulda been a little more patient. He

26

coulda been a lot more understanding. Didn't he realize there was a healing process I had to go through?

"I found this while looking for my things," he said, pointing to a large, plain metal box on the floor in front of the sofa. He picked it up. "Why do you still have all of this?"

"That's none of your business. Why were you going through my stuff?" I asked while trying to grab the box from him.

A few adroit moves later, he was on the other side of the room, rummaging through the contents of the box. "Sonograms, baby booties, coupons for clothing, lists of baby names, the necklace I gave you when we learned we were pregnant. What's goin' on? Why are you holding on to these things, Lace? It can't be normal or healthy."

"I'm not gonna bother explaining it to you. You won't understand. You didn't then and you won't now."

"Try me. I might surprise you."

"I doubt it."

"See, that was your problem. What did you think our relationship was? The Lacy Foxx Channel: All Lacy, All the Time? You weren't the only one that was hurting. I was hurting too, and I still am," he said. "I needed comforting and I needed to feel needed. I got sick and tired of turning to you and getting rejected. That's why I moved out and eventually turned to Charron."

That witch! What did he see in her anyway? We were nothing alike. I couldn't help but smile when I realized I'd answered my own question. Sebastian closed his eyes tightly and rubbed his temple. I reached for his face to take a closer look at the bump growing larger by the minute on the side of his head.

"Does your head feel as bad as it looks? Here, come with me. I'll get you some Tylenol and we'll put an ice pack on that nasty bump."

He followed me into the bathroom. I walked to the medicine cabinet and plopped onto the sink counter for a closer look inside. I peeked behind cough medicine bottles, boxes of Band-Aids, diuretics, facial creams, bottles of aspirin, cotton swabs and cotton balls before I finally found what I was looking for—a bottle of Tylenol hidden halfway between a bottle of multivitamins and birth control pills I no longer needed. I really had to clean out my medicine cabinet! I opened the bottle of Tylenol and shook out two pills.

"Here, take these," I said. I poured water from the sink into a paper cup and handed it to him. I then reached for the ice pack that was sitting in the back of the medicine cabinet. "I'll be back. I'm gonna go fill this with ice."

"Hey! I meant to tell you, our—I mean . . . your place is hot. What's up with all the color?" he yelled from the bathroom. "I thought you were like me. I thought you liked muted tones," he continued, obviously aware of the change in my condo's color, furnishings and decor. I neglected to tell him I'd redecorated my condo because I didn't want any reminders of him.

While the choice to redecorate had been a hasty one, I was pleased with the results. Our, no make that my condo, which had once been a monochromatic earth-tone pallet exercise in the understated—traditional, uncluttered, and quite frankly boring in its simplicity—had now been rejuvenated by a tasteful explosion of post-modern shapes and bold retro colors.

Still present were sentimental treasures including photos, bric-a-brac, and African and Indian-inspired art and photography. But now, thanks to the advice of a feng shui practicing interior decorator, these items were displayed amid a backdrop of soft burnt orange and yellow walls, odd-shaped leather furniture, an assortment of futuristic-looking tables, colorful rugs and pillows, and wall hangings in a variety of sizes, shapes and designs. A one-hundred-piece antique watch collection that had belonged to my mother, an avid antiquer, was beautifully displayed in the living room and considered the focal point of my decor.

When I returned to the bathroom, I sat on the sink counter and gingerly placed the ice pack against the knot on the side of Sebastian's head. He looked so pitiful, I thought he was going to pass out. But he didn't. Instead, he cupped my chin in his hand and kissed me softly, sweetly. When I tried pulling away, he held my face in his hands and kissed me harder. This time I didn't resist.

Finally, when we came up for air, I asked, "What about Charron?" His hands reached under my sweater. There was my answer. At that moment, I remembered how much I had once loved him, and I was suddenly swept away by my emotions.

I wrapped my legs around his and kissed him long and hard. He picked me up, carried me into my bedroom and laid me on my king-sized bed. My mind raced with reasons why we shouldn't do what was becoming inevitable.

Ex sex? I knew better. We both did.

There was no future in doing the do with someone from your past. Besides, even if Sebastian was telling the truth about not cheating on me, the fact that he was now about to cheat on Charron confirmed my suspicions that he had dog-like tendencies. But at that moment, I didn't care.

"Are you sure you really wanna do this?" he asked.

I responded by sitting up and removing his shirt, pants and briefs, and then my own. He smiled, kissed me then jumped off the bed and walked over to where I kept the condoms. I couldn't remember the last time we'd used one together.

Let's see . . . we had been broken up for two months. After I lost the twins, we lived together but grew apart for two months, and I had been pregnant for three months. Had it really been seven months since we last had sex? That was a record for me.

When Sebastian pulled out the "condom drawer," as we called it, he laughed. It was just as he'd left it. We had every flavor and texture imaginable.

"I'm feeling fruity and lubricated," he said.

He climbed back into bed, put on the condom and saturated my body with kisses. We soon found our familiar rhythm and a half -hour later, I felt a familiar explosion in my nether region that was not unlike a stampede of horses racing toward a never felt before freedom. I gasped for air as my sexual spirit, which had been reawakened, reunited with my earthly being.

I felt the muscular, sinewy hardness of Sebastian's chest above mine as our quivering bodies melded. After our respective visits to the bathroom, we fell asleep in each other's arms.

When I woke up the next morning, Sebastian was lying beside me, snoring gently. He was still as handsome as ever. He had beautiful, light brown, doe-shaped eyes, framed by long lashes. He was slightly darker than I, a candy apple caramel brown, but he wasn't as dark as Mr. T.

Hmmm . . . I hadn't thought about that snake for several hours.

I traced the contours of Sebastian's bulging biceps, chiseled chest, powerful pecs and washboard flat stomach. He had muscles for days, which he developed during diligent daily visits to the gym. He was a major workout junkie. He had even won a couple of local body-building contests. I think that's how he met Charron. She judged him in some contests and she worked as the manager of his gym. That was her legit job. At night she was a stripper, and from what I heard she was quite . . . uhmmm . . . gifted.

Sebastian had overripe lips that enclosed the most perfect set of straight, white teeth I had ever seen on a man, no doubt the result of having a mother and father who were both dentists. He was just over six feet tall and he had big hands, big feet and of course, the requisite other big body part. But he also had a big heart and a great big sense of humor, which I thought were his best qualities.

One of my biggest problems with Sebastian was the line of work he chose. He was smart, a college graduate. He majored in business at school in North Carolina, his home state. He could have done anything he wanted. He chose to be a firefighter. That's how we met. At the time I was doing a series of articles for *The Tribune* on young college graduates making loads of money who were employed in dangerous professions. Sebastian's goal was to make lots of money by the time he was forty-five so that he could retire and enjoy life while he was still fairly young.

But when we were together, I feared for his life every day. Before we met, he'd volunteered to help out in New York following the attacks on the World Trade Center. The whole time he was there, he says he was oblivious to the danger. He worked the devastating, war-like scene for three weeks. While in New York, he said he never even gave a moment's thought to the fact that some tower of debris could fall on him, crushing him, or that some smoldering fire could come alive, engulfing him and the numerous volunteers who worked alongside him.

By the time he returned, by all of his friends' accounts, he had changed. Once we got together, he refused to talk about the aftermath of the tragedy with me, but it was obvious he'd seen things no human being should ever see. And when we lost the twins, the horror and losses of September 11 seemed to haunt him all over again. He became quiet and aloof, and he threw himself into his work, taking unnecessary risks. He pulled away from me. We pulled away from each other. I was still desperately hurting from the loss of our two unborn children, and I feared losing him.

The fear I felt was a lot like a gallstone that wouldn't pass. In the pit of my stomach lay the fear of the unknown, the unseen, the uncertain. It was a fear that no amount of bile, antacid, stomach acid, laxatives or natural waste elimination could eradicate from my system.

But asking him to quit his job was not an option. I knew he wouldn't. I knew the job was about more than just money for him. While he was a young child, an uncle that he adored died in a fire. It was the result of an explosion at the manufacturing plant he had worked at for years. Sebastian wasn't on hand to save his favorite uncle, so instead he made a commitment to save the world, one fire at a time.

He was a man with a mission, a purpose. He was living his boyhood dream. In his eyes, he'd grown up to be a superhero like the Green Lantern, Batman, Spiderman, Superman and Captain America before him. The only difference was he didn't have superpowers. He was just a man. He was just a man with a big, warm, caring heart that saved scores of lives everyday, often at the expense of his own. He was just a man who wouldn't have it any other way.

While I was deep in thought, Sebastian rolled over and I greeted him with a big, goofy smile. "Mornin', sexy."

"Mornin'," he said. "Why are you looking at me like that? What's wrong with you?"

"I was just thinking about you and me and what coulda been, shoulda been, woulda been if I hadn't been so stupid," I said.

"Look, my coming here may have been a big mistake."

"Why do you say that? Having sex with me now is all of a sudden a big mistake? What's the matter? Feeling guilty for fooling around on Charron?"

"I should have known you'd take what I said the wrong way. I didn't mean it like that. It's just that I'm upset."

"You're upset? About what?" I couldn't imagine what he had to be upset about. We had just finished having the best sex either one of us had probably had in a long time.

"I know you probably don't remember this, but while we were making love, you yelled out a name a couple of times that wasn't mine."

"Yeah, I know, Tony the Tiger. Remember, that's what I used to call my bundle of joy 'cause sex with you is grrrreat!" I reminded him as I reached for Tony under the covers. He grabbed my hand and looked squarely into my face. I could see he was really hurting. Tears were gathering in his eyes.

One of the things I had loved about Sebastian was the fact that he was not afraid to show real emotion. He was the first man I'd ever been with who cried in front of me. It probably had a lot to do with the things he saw on his job. His vulnerability is what attracted me to him in the first place.

"The name you called out wasn't Tony. It was Mr. T.," he said. "At first I wasn't gonna say anything, but the more I think about it, the more it bugs me."

Suddenly, the idyllic tableau we had momentarily created was shattered. Had I really been fantasizing about that arrogant jerk, Wynnton Trust, while I made love to Sebastian? I honestly couldn't remember. I opted to play crazy.

"Quit lying, Sebastian."

The only thing was, we both knew he wasn't lying. I hadn't told him about Mr. T. How could he have known Wynnton Trust's nickname unless I called it out while we made love? How could I have been so careless?

"You know I'm not lying," Sebastian said defiantly. "So, who is this Mr. T. person?" he asked in a demanding tone while swinging around to look at me accusingly.

Who'd he think he was? We hadn't lived together for two months and hadn't had sex for seven. Wasn't I entitled to get on with my life? He sure had gotten on with his.

"Why do you care?" I asked in an acerbic tone.

"I don't! You can screw every Tom, Dick and Mr. T. you want for all I care. I have all the woman I want and need in Charron. At least she doesn't sleep around."

Low blow. So much for clearing the air between us.

"Yeah, not like her man," I said, spitting the words at him. "Besides, she wasn't all the woman you wanted and needed last night. As I recall, that was me!"

"Last night was a mistake that won't happen again," he said in a low, even tone while yanking on his clothes.

I couldn't believe I had made love to him and almost confessed to wanting him back. I'd been deceived, tricked, duped! Standing before me was Satan in a sweat suit, pure evil disguised as my ex-fiancé. The charming young prince I had just slept with had suddenly turned into the Prince of Darkness, Lucifer, Beelzebub, the Devil incarnate. I kept waiting for his head to start spinning. I kept waiting for slimy green projectile vomit to ooze from his tender lips. I waited and waited and waited. I studied him closely and waited some more. No vomit, no head spinning, just Sebastian and I together again.

"I'll send a mover over later to get my stuff out of the POD," he said before storming out of my condo.

What had I been thinking? Sebastian and I together again as a couple? Had I lost my mind? Hadn't I learned my lesson? Sebastian had caused plenty of psychological noise in my life once before. I had to be crazy to let him do it again. I knew that being a fool for love was just par for the course, but there *was* a limit. I believed that every woman was allowed only so many stupid points per relationship, depending on her tolerance level for crap.

If he doesn't call when he says he will, minus twenty-five points. More than twenty minutes late for a date? Minus fifty points. Cheap, shiftless and lazy? Minus seventy-five points. Ignorant, violent or crazy? Minus one hundred points. Doesn't support your goals, dreams, ambitions and aspirations? Minus one hundred and fifty points. Doesn't notice when you change your hairstyle, lose weight or grow a third eyeball in the middle of your forehead? Minus two hundred points. Lying, cheating, snake-in-the-grass? Minus three hundred points. Perfume on his person that ain't yours? Minus four hundred points. Acts like a jerk after you sleep with him? Minus five hundred points.

Last time I checked, I had used up all of my stupid points and then some with Sebastian. My fool-for-love days were over, and while my head knew it, my heart didn't.

After Sebastian left, I realized that what he said, he said out of pain. I know I would have felt awful if someone had done to me what I had just done to him. I toyed with the idea of calling him on his cell phone and apologizing, but my pride wouldn't let me. As I readied myself for work, I imagined I couldn't feel any lower than I already felt.

I couldn't have been more wrong.

FOUR

I pulled out of my two-car garage and headed north through my neighborhood. I lived in the pricey subdivision known as Brookside. Large, oversized oak and elm trees lined the subdivision's natty, well-manicured lawns. Thousand-dollar security systems and six-foot-tall wrought iron fences protected ample all-brick English Tudors and Dutch Colonials that were prefaced by winding, circular drives.

Located at the very eastern edge of the subdivision was condominium row, where dozens of yuppie and buppie wannabes—more yuppies than buppies—lived, including myself. My neighbors were a heterogenous mix of first and second generation college educated baby boomers and Gen-Xers who had made it.

Driving through my neighborhood usually lifted my spirits, but after my run-in with Sebastard, my mind was too busy reeling to enjoy the drive. Okay, maybe I was wrong for yelling out Wynnton Trust's name while having sex with Sebastian. And maybe I was wrong for jumping all over Sebastian when he confronted me about it. And maybe I was even wrong for sleeping with him in the first place.

But as wrong as I may have been, I refused to take all the blame for our unpleasant reunion. He was partially responsible for what happened. No, make that mostly responsible. Who told him he could come into my home and seduce me? He was verboten. He was seeing another woman. Heck, the fool was living with her and he was almost married. What was he trying to prove? We were through, history, kaput!

I alternately cursed Sebastian and felt bad about embarrassing him as I made my way onto Highway I-70. Usually, I dreaded the thirty-minute highway drive in rush hour traffic, and I could instantly tell this morning would be no different.

36

By the time I arrived at the office, I was a nervous wreck. I had almost been rear-ended twice, plus I had the unfortunate luck of getting stuck behind a Sunday driver who was going thirty miles an hour in a sixty-five miles per hour zone.

My long trek from the parking garage to my cubicle became more and more laborious with every step. *The Metro Tribune* was housed in a building that looked like every other old building in Kansas City. The decor was 1980's chic— unimaginative and mismatched. On each floor, there were rows and rows of over-decorated cubicles that reminded me of tiny, 13-foot by 10-foot carpeted jail cells.

The moment I stepped into my cell, the phone on my desk rang.

"What's up, girlie girl? I'm coming over!"

I smiled after hearing the familiar morning greeting. I stood and waved at my buddy, my best friend, my partner in crime, my ace boon coon, Marsha Turner, who was located on the other side of the newsroom.

Marsha had been my best friend ever since she arrived at *The Metro Tribune* a year after me. Every time I saw her, I couldn't help but smile. She was one of the few people I knew who really had it all together, and I loved her like a sister.

Truth is, I was a little jealous of the girl.

Marsha had beautifully dark and thick, shoulder-length, fly-as-hell, Senegalese two-strand twists. She was petite, smart, and a "real" journalist, with her Kappa Delta Zeta sorority loving behind.

The summer before her senior year at Howard University, Marsha, also a Kansas City native, got a hold of my name and she called me relentlessly, begging me to meet with her. She was looking for a job as a reporter and she had targeted me as her way in at *The Tribune*.

She made it her personal mission to make my life miserable until I agreed to meet her. After weeks of torture, I finally gave in. Marsha was sassy, irreverent, fearless, talented, beautiful, smart, funny and confident. She was everything I hoped I was.

During our first meeting, Marsha had me eating out of her hand. She had me wrapped around her little finger. We talked for an hour before I even asked her for writing samples. After two hours, she had finagled a recommendation for a summer internship out of me.

That summer was a blur of deep conversations, parties, shopping, men and sisterhood. By the time summer was over, Marsha had been guaranteed a job at *The Tribune* upon her graduation, and I had found a new best friend for life.

"What's up, Lace the Ace Band-Aid?" the amaretto-hued Marsha asked once she finally arrived at my desk.

Marsha had been delivering that same lame line for years, and I had just recently gotten to the point where I no longer cringed when I heard it. I never bothered trying to tell her that Ace made bandages, not Band-Aids. Besides, Lace the Ace Band-Aid sounded much better and much less crazy than Lace the Ace Bandage.

"FYI, the SOB has been looking for you. He's been mumbling about some deadline you missed on the Winter Blues & Jazz Festival. But forget that for now. Spill it, girl. I want to hear all about last night. I got your message about Mr. T."

"Then why didn't you call me back?"

"Because my date and I were busy, if you know what I mean."

"You are scandalous," I said, teasing her. "And speaking of scandalous, guess who I relived some old memories with in-between the sheets last night?"

"With who? Sebastard? Are you kidding? What was *that* like?"

"It was just like old times, that is until I called out Wynnton Trust's name. I don't remember doing it, but Sebastian claims I did."

"So, Wynnton Trust has you diggin' a brother, huh?"

"The only thing I'm diggin' is a ditch to throw his arrogant behind in."

"Yeah, right. Well, hurry up and tell me about him before the SOB shows up on the warpath."

The SOB was Steven Olin Bishop, our paper's pain-in-the-butt managing editor. He had serious issues. He suffered from Napoleon's Syndrome, which means to overcompensate for his small stature, five feet nine inches, one hundred and sixty pounds, he did everything big. He talked big (bragged). He dressed big (expensively). He lived big (owned huge homes and nice cars). And he hung out with Kansas City's big boys.

Despite his shortcomings, no pun intended, he was what they called a newspaper man's man. He'd been in the newspaper business for more than thirty years, and he could tell you about every major scandal, murder, etcetera in the area within the last century.

He pathetically lacked a life, and he was of the opinion that the rest of us should be willing to sacrifice our personal lives, all for the sake of a good story. Back when I was a hard-hitting journalist, I idolized him. But since becoming an entertainment reporter within the last year, I realized the unmarried SOB was just an unyielding, rigid middle-aged man who desperately needed some interests outside of work.

We in the newsroom fittingly gave him the moniker SOB because after all, he was one, *and* those were his initials.

The SOB suddenly appeared before I could share with Marsha any more details about my evening. He was a WASP in his early fifties. He had a slight build, a pointed nose and chin, and a receding hairline that sported a thin tuft of every-strand-for-itself hair, which awkwardly sat atop the middle of his elongated, bulbous head. His pale blue, saucer-like eyes were reminiscent of those belonging to the resident Whos from Who-ville, the town burglarized by Dr. Seuss's Christmas-stealing Grinch. Although the SOB wore expensive, top-of-the-line suits, he always had the disheveled look of a traveling salesman.

"Foxx, I want that Winter Blues & Jazz Festival piece on my desk in an hour, capisce? And Turner, don't you have a hostile takeover to get to?"

"Talk about hostile," Marsha said while walking away.

"Look, Foxx, I know you've been here at *The Tribune* for six years now, but you're starting to get a little complacent. I can't recall the last time you gave me a scoop. And being late on the Winter Blues and Jazz Festival piece, that is really unacceptable. I know things have been rough on you, what with you losing your twins and then your fiancé, but you've got to get over it. The paper really needs you." He gave me a fake, weak smile and walked away.

Your initials say it all, you cold-hearted SOB, I thought. That was one heck of a pep talk. Half hating him, half knowing he was right, I printed a familiar document and placed it in an envelope along with some of my recent press clippings. I addressed the large envelope without referring to my omnipresent stack of misfiled business cards. I knew the address by heart.

"Come on *Élan,* this time you have to notice me," I said in a half-whisper. After a short prayer to the job gods, my phone rang.

"Is he gone, Band-Aid?" Marsha asked through the phone.

"Yeah, thank goodness. So, you heard my news. What's up with you?"

"Everything's copacetic."

"Copacetic? This must be a C-word week."

"It is. How'd you know?"

"Because I've never heard you use that word before."

"What do you think I am? An idiot? A mome?"

"No, but I think you have the recessive gene which makes you a carrier," I joked.

Last week was an M-word week. To feed her constant need for self-improvement and exposure to new things, Marsha had the irritating but admirable habit of learning new words each week. And not only did she learn them, but she tortured everyone she knew by using them rather frequently and often incorrectly in conversation.

"Marsh, I can't talk now. The SOB just gave me an unreal deadline."

"Okay, but before you hang up, tell me, are you going to church with me and your grandmother on Sunday? We haven't seen you since the breakup. Sebastard is there faithfully right along with us every week."

"*You* only go to church 'cause you're trying to catch a man."

"It's not my fault church is to this decade what nightclubs were to the eighties and nineties."

"Am I the only person who thinks that prayin' for a layin' in God's house is gonna get you a one-way ticket to Hell?"

"Save the preachin' for Sunday. Are you going to church with us or not?"

"Not. Why would I want to go someplace where I have to constantly look at Sebastian? I have a lot going on, Marsh. I have to go. We'll talk later."

"We sure will. Adieu!"

The week before last was an A-word week.

FIVE

"A little flirtation goes a long way," Marsha said, reading the next day in the cafeteria from my horoscope, which predicted a four-star day.

"So does a bullet, and I need Wynnton Trust in my life like I need a bullet in my head," I said. "Now can I just eat my lunch in peace without you mentioning him?"

Marsha laughed. "I didn't mention him. Who said anything about Wynnton Trust? If you hate him so much, why are you so mad at him? Just because he called you a bourgeois, self-centered ghetto princess? And for the record, *have ya met yourself*? What he said was kinda dick, although he *is* right."

"Forget you, Marsh. I'm upset 'cause I know it's not true. At least not all of the time," I said, chuckling. "And I'm gonna prove it to him."

"Prove it to him?" Marsha asked. "Dream on. Why do you even care what this man thinks? There's more going on here than you're telling me, Ace."

"No, there's not," I said with a slight smirk. "Let's just drop it. Okay?"

"Okay, but before we do, tell me this, evil genius. How are you gonna prove he's wrong about you?"

"I'm gonna call him later and volunteer for his precious career fair. But it will have to wait 'til after my dream cruise to the Bahamas with my family."

"Speaking of living a dream, I have some great news," Marsha said.

"What is it?"

"The SOB just gave me the crime and drug beats. I've already phoned the captain of the city's drug enforcement team," Marsha said. "I'm going to accompany them on some busts this week. Isn't that great? Aren't you thrilled for me?"

"What's wrong with you? Crime and drugs? Are ya crazy? Can't you just interview the cops from the office after the busts?" I asked navïely.

Why did I have to go and ask her that? Marsha looked at me as if I'd made a wrong turn onto a one-way street. Didn't I know who I was talking to? Marsha feared nothing. She was raised in a household with only one girl and four boys. She learned at an early age that she either had to fight and protect herself or get the living daylights knocked out of her every day of her life until she moved out of her mama's house. The men in her family were mucho macho. I could only take them in small doses. Too much testosterone in one family, if you asked me, which, not surprisingly, no one ever did.

Marsha's grandfather, father and two of her brothers were cops. She also had a slew of cousins and uncles who were cops. At the age of five, they had her out on the range shooting guns. Nine millimeters, .22s, .38s, .45s. Heck, guns I couldn't even name, she was shooting.

Not surprisingly, Marsha was attracted to cops as well. For a few years she dated Joaquan, a cop who taught her Karate, Tae Kwon Do, Judo, all kinds of self-defense crap. He and the boys on the squad used to have tough man competitions, and no one was surprised when for several years, Marsha was the one whose name was engraved on the trophy.

After she won the last time, a fed up Joaquan dumped her.

While on the outside she may have appeared to be a petite, small, fragile flower, on the inside, Marsha was one tough female. She was stronger and more athletic than a lot of men I knew, both mentally and physically. The girl lifted weights three times a week, she ran five miles every other day and every single day she did aerobics in the gym at work. She even had my lazy behind doing Tae Bo.

"Not you too! You of all people should be supporting me, Band-Aid. A female reporter can cover the crime and drug beats just as well as any male reporter. I had to fight tooth and nail to get this assignment. What are women reporters supposed to do, relegate ourselves to the female reporting ghetto of the home, fashion, garden, society and entertainment sections?" she asked, not really caring to hear my answer.

Low blow.

Did I mention that Marsha was an ardent feminist and an EOW — equal opportunity witch? She could, and often did, put me in my place just as quickly as anybody else — friend, family or foe.

"That's what's wrong with society today," she said, continuing on her soapbox. "No one thinks a woman can do a job as good as a man. That's why we get less pay, even though we work just as hard, if not harder. I refuse to be treated like a second-class citizen. I refuse to give men, and in some cases women, the satisfaction of dictating what I can and can't do based upon my gender."

"Marsh . . ."

I shouldn't have tried to interrupt her. She was in full-blown Bad Mood Barbie mode. She got her second wind. "Plenty of women before us have bruised their heads on our patriarchal society's glass ceiling. It's time we started breaking through that glass ceiling because I, for one, have had it!"

Apparently Marsha thought I was overdue for a verbal beat-down. When she finished my thrashing, I didn't know if I should praise her or clock her. I chose to reason with her instead.

"Marsh, it's just that I care about you, girlie, and I don't want to spend all day every day worrying about you. If you're willing to put your life on the line for a job, that's fine. Go ahead. But don't expect me to be happy about it. When those idiots on the streets start shooting at everything that moves and shit that ain't moving, the fact that you're a woman won't mean a thing to a stray bullet!"

"Don't worry 'bout me, Ace. I'll be fine," she said with a smile before leaving the cafeteria.

I hated it when we disagreed. She was my best friend. We'd been through a lot together. But I just couldn't help the way I felt. I knew there was no way to bridge the chasm between us. Marsha would never back down. Unfortunately, she had a stubborn streak in her that she wore like a suit of armor.

Deep in her heart, I knew Marsha didn't think I was telling her not to cover the crime and drug beats because she was a woman, incapable of doing it. I was just plain scared for her. And while she wouldn't admit it, I think she was more than a little scared herself. The crime and drug beats were the most stressful beats at the paper. The reporter who normally covered them had just recently taken a six-month stress-related leave of absence. After covering breaking news on his beat, he always came back to the newsroom with some gory tale or another. He said riding with the drug enforcement team was like going to war every single day.

I didn't care what Li'l Miss Know-It-All Marsha said. She was entering dangerous territory. She was probably doing it just so that she could win some stupid award like a Pulitzer. Her naked ambition irked me. Like me, she was too doggone ambitious.

I knew if the SOB and other head honchos at the newspaper were going to let Marsha cover the crime and drug beats, they really believed in her work and had confidence in her abilities. Everyone knew that only the best could handle it, and in that sense I was thrilled for her. Yet, as I ruminated about Marsha's good fortune, I couldn't shake the ominous feeling of fear that was growing inside of me.

SIX

I made a conscious decision not to worry about Marsha, Sebastian, or Wynnton Trust until I returned from my five-day cruise to the Bahamas with my family. The trip was made possible thanks to my daddy, Harold Foxx, who for years had treated us to an annual family vacation. This time, my daddy, my Uncle Solomon, my grandmother and I were Bahama-bound.

The 900-foot long Bahama Mama cruise liner that was transporting us and three thousand other people from Miami to Nassau to Coco Cay and back, was an amazing, mammoth vessel. The cruiser, which was seven stories high, had an 18-hole miniature golf course, three movie theaters, two dinner theaters, seven nightclubs, a huge Las Vegas-style casino, three swimming pools, six whirlpools, four mid-sized dining rooms, a large three-story dining room encircled in glass, an Italian-themed, two-story solarium spa and gym, an outdoor cafe, a large children's play area and dozens of boutiques, gift shops and hair and nail salons.

It was my first time on a cruise ship and of course, out of the four of us, I was the one that got seasick. Through it all, my mother's mother, Hannah Hale . . . my Bibi . . . stuck by me.

When I was born, Bibi decided she wasn't having anything to do with the old-sounding word "grandmother," or any other cutesy derivative. According to Mama, while she was in the middle of labor with me, my grandmother made a big pronouncement that she wanted all of her grandkids to call her Bibi. She had read somewhere that Bibi was the Swahili word for grandmother, and in many other languages it was a common term of respect used to refer to elderly women. From day one, Bibi was a huge influence in my life, so no one was surprised when, at the age of two, the first word I uttered was Bibi.

Bibi, who had stepped in to take care of my father and me after my mama died, was my rock. My grandmother was an above-average-looking 70-year-old. She wore her shoulder length salt and pepper hair in a tight bun that helped keep the wrinkle-free skin on her face taut. She considered her bun the equivalent of poor man's plastic surgery.

Bibi had a medium build, and was five feet eight inches of extreme confidence and self-assurance. She was vibrant, hip and like no one else's grandmother I ever knew. She was the first civil rights/feminist activist that I had ever come in contact with.

Throughout my life, my grandmother schooled me on the value of hard work and the need for education. She taught me the importance of resisting the seven deadly sins—pride, envy, gluttony, lust, wrath, greed and sloth—most of which I still hadn't conquered. She also taught me to not be afraid of speaking my mind and standing up for myself and what I believed in.

During a time when a black woman's only career choices were to teach, work as a secretary or clean white folks' homes, Bibi was in a league all her own. She fought furiously to be one of the first Blacks to enter nursing school in Kansas City during the Fifties, and after she graduated, she had to fight even harder to get a job with a local hospital. In time, she proved herself and became the most popular nurse within a five-state area. Through her example, I learned that nothing could hold back a strong, smart, determined black woman.

My grandmother was like my best friend. I'd smoked my first cigarette with her—something I hadn't indulged in since—and I had my first alcoholic drink with her—something I'd indulged in more than I cared to remember. Not only did my grandmother introduce me to nicotine and liquor, but she also introduced me to the art of conversation and the enjoyment of the pursuit of knowledge. She wasn't the least bit interested in the interracial dating habits of my Ken and

Christie dolls, nor was she interested in how I'd mastered the jump rope. She was much more interested in being deep— talking about politics, sit-ins, marches, wars and medical breakthroughs. My "deep" conversations with my grandmother started when I was young and sparked my love of current events, a love that eventually lead me to a career as a reporter.

Considering our closeness, it was only fitting that Bibi was with me when my first bout of seasickness kicked in, which was a doozy. For the first three hours of the cruise, I stayed in the bathroom. Despite the pills I had taken to avoid getting seasick, I was dizzy and light-headed all morning. Fearing I'd be sick the whole trip, I toyed with the idea of flying back home once we reached our first port, Nassau, the next day.

By 9 o'clock that evening, I was feeling better. Around ten, Bibi and I ventured out. We headed toward the large glass dining room, where we found six buffet tables piled high with delectable-looking food that included a variety of fish, salads, exotic fruits and vegetables, pastas and weight-taunting desserts. Afraid that I wouldn't be able to keep much down, I ordered some soup and tea. My grandmother, on the other hand, made several trips through the buffet line.

"Bibi, am I spoiling your trip?" I asked after she returned from buffet trip number three.

"Glory be, no. Any time I spend with you is a blessing, even if you are throwing up all over the place," she said with a huge grin on her face.

"Hey, look. There's Daddy." I pointed and waved at my handsome father, who was sitting on the other side of the room. "Who are they?" I asked with a scowl when my father and two women waved back.

"LeAynne and Ruth. Didn't I tell you? It seems as if your dad and your uncle are quite the catches. While you were lying down in the room, I saw the two of them in the lounge and they were like melon magnets."

"Bibi!" I said, appalled at her tacky reference to the female anatomy.

"I guess the crazy, man-hungry women on this boat think your father and uncle have money. These silly women have been flocking to them all day. In particular, those two middle-aged women, plus another one that I don't see right now. Oh, there she is, on the dance floor with your uncle. Rachel. Glory be. Look at her, the old hussy, rubbing all up against him."

I followed my grandmother's gaze to the far left side of the dance floor. My fifty-something uncle looked dapper in a lightweight blue shirt and matching pants. He had the same gentle and kind face as my mama, his younger sister. He was tall and a little overweight. The woman he was dancing with was very attractive and looked to be in her early forties. I grew uneasy watching her grind against my uncle in a non-discreet fashion.

"I think I'm gonna be sick again," I said, uncomfortable with the thought of my uncle and father as mack daddies.

Just then, my daddy appeared at our table with his two lady friends in tow. "Hi, baby doll. How ya feelin'?"

My daddy, in all his mack glory and resplendency, was a handsome and pudgy man whose ethereal smile and charming wit helped mask the pain he still felt following my mama's death, all these years later. His broad shoulders were slightly slumped and his black hair was just starting to gray and thin, indicating his age. He had big, expressive eyes and a rather large nose that sat asymmetrically in the middle of his face. As we talked, I was embarrassed by the way he beamed at me. It was obvious he loved me. I was his little girl. I always had been and I always would be.

"I'm doing a little better. Are you having a good time?"

"Yeah, I'm having fun, baby," he said. He smiled a big, toothy grin at his female companions.

"So, who are your friends?" I asked, feeling my dinner rise.

"Honey, this is LeAynne Sanders and Ruth Jackson."

"It's nice meeting the two of you," I said to the women who both looked a lot older and a lot more haggard than my father.

"Are you the poor baby that has been sick all day?" a genuinely concerned Ruth asked while hugging me. I instantly liked her.

"Yes, ma'am," I said respectfully.

"I have some Dramamine in my room. Would you like some?"

"No, ma'am. I've already taken some. It's finally starting to work."

"Honey, we're going to go see *Ain't Misbehavin'*. They have a live theater show in twenty minutes. I know it's one of your favorite plays. Do you want to join us?" my father asked.

"No. To be honest, I'm still not feeling all that great. I think I'm gonna go back up to my room, get a good night's rest and try venturing out again in the morning."

"Okay then, honey. Let's meet down here for breakfast at eight."

"All right," I said, rising to my feet. My grandmother rose with me.

"Bibi, you don't have to go with me. I've spoiled enough of your fun. You go on and go with them. I'll see you later. Okay? Good night all."

"Good night," everyone said in unison.

The next morning, I woke up early, feeling much better. It was well after eight, and I knew I had missed breakfast with my family. Within an hour, I'd dressed and made my way to the ship's promenade deck. Once there, I found the cool breeze off the water, the beaming sun, and the clear blue ocean calming as I read a Walter Mosley mystery that I'd been anxious to read for months.

"The butler did it," a strong, dulcet-toned voice said from the other side of my book. I ignored the voice, hoping it would go away.

"I'm telling you the butler did it," the voice said again. This time, the man behind the voice closed my book, removed it from my lap, and replaced it with a dozen peach roses. I ignored them. So what if he was semi-charming?

"Excuse me! I was reading that!" I said, informing the stranger of the obvious.

A fairly attractive woman couldn't go anywhere without being harassed by a man. They acted as if it were their inalienable right to hit on us, no matter the time or place. Life, liberty and the pursuit of a woman! It didn't matter if the woman didn't want to be bothered. It didn't matter if she was married, a lesbian, blind, deaf, cripple or crazy. If the man wanted her, she was fair game. And if she insulted him and put him in his place, watch out! She'd be called everything but a child of God. She'd be made to feel like she had done something wrong, like she was the one with the problem.

Well, I, for one, was fed up. I was no longer going to allow men to invade my personal space in public. If I didn't want to be bothered, I didn't want to be bothered. Period. No explanation necessary. It was time for me to take a stand. If Mr. The-Butler-Did-It didn't leave me alone, he'd feel the brunt of my wrath.

Hell hath no fury like a woman who doesn't want to be bothered.

I looked long and hard at the arrogant stranger who had interrupted my solitude.

He wasn't particularly attractive. He'd obviously been swimming all morning, and his coarse hair was kinked into little nappy black balls. The fact that he wasn't carrying lotion with him was apparent because his dull, ink-black skin was covered with pockets of ash. He had a flat nose and bloodshot eyes. His only saving grace was his enchanting smile. No, he wasn't attractive, but I found his bravado and confidence both intriguing and appealing.

"Hi, I'm Levi Daugg from Brooklyn. That's D-a-u-g-g. And you are?"

"Unimpressed. Levi Daugg from Brooklyn, can I have my book back?"

"What a long name. What should I call you for short?"

"Not interested," I said.

"Great, you're beautiful and feisty."

"Levi, I can appreciate a brother tryin' to get his rap on, and while I don't mean to be rude, I'm not in the mood for socializing."

"So, what are you in the mood for?" he asked, situating his narrow behind into the chaise lounge beside me.

"Reading *alone*," I said, eyeing him suspiciously.

"Okay, I know when I'm not wanted. Just tell me your name and I'll give you back your book and be on my way."

"My name is Lacy Eymaleen Foxx. That's F-o-x-x," I said, reaching for my book, which was perched precariously on his lap.

"I'm-a-lean? How did you manage to get that as a middle name? It's cute, but it sounds so old-fashioned," he said.

"Eymaleen was my great-grandmother's name. She was a full-blooded Ojibwa Indian. They're known for their interesting names," I said, finding myself unwittingly drawn into a conversation with the persistent stranger.

"So, Ms. Foxx, you're not traveling alone, are you? If you are, couldn't you use a companion for the rest of the trip? Perhaps a bodyguard to help you fight off unwanted suitors?" Levi asked.

"You mean unwanted suitors such as yourself?"

"I may be unwanted now, but give me a chance. I'll grow on you. You'll learn to like me," he said.

"Fungus grows on things, and I haven't learned to like that. Besides, I hate to disappoint you, Levi Daugg, but I was taught to never talk to strangers, and you seem about as strange as they come."

"Me? Strange? I'm just your average, normal guy."

"Okay Mr. Average, Normal Guy. Where is your average, normal girl?" I asked.

"I'm traveling solo. It's just me, myself and I."

"You're not traveling with a wife or girlfriend? Or worse yet, with your boys?"

"What you see is all there is. How about you? Are you here alone?" he asked.

"No. I'm here with my family. We were supposed to meet for breakfast this morning, but I missed them. Now I don't know where they are."

"A woman as lovely as you shouldn't be alone. I'm gonna go clean myself up. Why don't we meet in the large dining room later for lunch?"

"I can't. I need to try to find my family. I'd like to have lunch with them," I said.

"If you don't agree to have lunch with me, I'm gonna jump," he said as he walked toward the cruise liner's railing.

I laughed. "You are trying way, way, way, way too hard."

"What can it hurt to have lunch with me, Lacy I'm-a-lean Foxx?"

Despite his looks, his confidence was sexy. And I did have to eat. Besides, I'd promised myself before my vacation started that I was truly going to unwind and be open to every experience that arose—that included sexy, confident, seemingly-into-me men.

"Okay, okay, fine. I'll see you in the large glass dining room in an hour."

"All right, it's a date," Levi said, rising from the chaise.

When I arrived in the dining room an hour later to meet Levi, he was already waiting for me at the door. I hardly recognized him. Homeboy cleaned up nicely. His nappy locks were replaced by a nice texturized fade. A pair of linen khaki shorts and a royal blue polo shirt covered key parts of his body. And the parts of his body that were showing were a far cry from ashy. His eyes were no longer bloodshot, most likely the result of him using a half bottle of Visine. As I approached him, his enchanting smile took over his face.

"I didn't expect you to come," he said.

"Why not? I told you I'd be here, and I am a woman of my word," I said rather coyly. He pulled out my chair and handed me another bouquet of a dozen roses. This time they were red. Brotherman was on his J-O-B. He was playing the chivalry role to the hilt.

"So, tell me, Levi. What is a man like you doing alone on a romantic cruise like this?" He let out a loud belly laugh.

"What's so funny?" I asked innocently.

"That sounded like a really bad pick-up line."

"But I wasn't trying to — "

"I know, I know. Unfortunately you weren't trying to pick me up. And to answer your question, I had been planning this trip with the woman I was going to marry. When she dumped me last month, I decided that I still wanted to come, so I did," he said.

"You were going to get married?"

"Yeah, it's still a little hard for me to talk about, though."

"Then let's not talk about it."

"So, what about you? Why aren't you on this cruise with your man?"

"I'm between men right now. Way between."

"It looks like today may be my lucky day."

"Don't count on it. Can we talk about something else?"

"Your wish is my command. So, what do you want to talk about?" he asked earnestly as he grabbed my hand and started rubbing it between his.

"I'd like to talk about how wonderful that food over there tastes."

"Oh yeah? Someone sounds like she's ready to get her grub on. Come on, let's do it to it," he said, offering me his hand as he stood.

A few minutes later, we returned to our table, our plates overflowing with baby back ribs, Norwegian salmon, seafood gumbo, sausage, and several different types of vegetables and salads.

After a few healthy bites of food, Levi spoke.

"So, you said you were traveling with your family. Where are they? I'd like to meet them. Any crazy, hardheaded brothers I should know about?"

"I haven't seen much of my family since we left Miami. My grandmother is probably stockpiling loot. She has probably moved into one of the ship's boutiques."

"And what about the rest of your family?"

"From what I hear, my daddy and uncle have been acting like major playas ever since they climbed aboard. The older, single women on the ship are under the misguided impression that since my daddy and uncle are alone on this cruise, they have some money. Boy, those women are seriously mistaken."

"Lacy, this may seem forward of me, but I'd like to spend the rest of the day with you—heck, the rest of the cruise with you—if you'll let me."

"But you don't know me. For all you know, I could be a major crook. I could knock you in your head, take all your valuables and leave you for dead, hidden behind some tree at the next port of call."

"That's a chance I'm willing to take," he said with a wink.

Yeah, but am I?

"Actually, I think I'd enjoy hanging out with you for a bit. My family sure won't miss me."

"Great, then it's settled. We better hurry up and finish lunch. We're scheduled to hit the Nassau harbor in thirty minutes."

"Have you ever been to the Bahamas? I did a little reading about the islands before I came, but I really have no idea what to expect."

"Neither do I. Let's just play it by ear, okay?" he said in his signature take-charge style.

Forty-five minutes later, we were strolling along the streets of Nassau. We spent the rest of the afternoon visiting Nassau's legendary straw market and every duty-free boutique and gift shop in the city, in search of inexpensive knick-knacks, the kind that say to the receiver "Ha ha, I went to the Bahamas and you didn't."

After we finished shopping, we had our pictures taken with the famous "marching" pink flamingos in the beautiful Ardastra Gardens then we had a leisurely dinner at one of the gazillion beachside restaurants located on nearby Cable Beach, ten minutes from downtown Nassau. After dinner, we had to rush back to the cruise ship because it was scheduled to set sail at ten.

"Lacy, I had a great time," Levi said while walking me to my stateroom.

"So did I," I said, stifling a yawn.

"Although we did a lot of walking, today was rather relaxing."

"Well, what would you expect from the place that invented the hammock?" I asked with a nervous laugh. "Relaxation is one of the things they're known for over here."

"I enjoyed myself so much today. Why don't we spend some more time together tomorrow?" Levi asked.

"I'd like that, but first I want to see what my family is up to. I've hardly spent any time with them."

"They can join us," he said.

"I'll see what they plan on doing in the morning and then I'll call you. What's your room number?"

"Why don't I call you? I usually get up early to go work out. Do you want to join me in the gym?"

I could barely suppress my laughter. "That's okay. I'll pass. Why don't you give me a call around ten? I should know what I'm doing by then," I said, turning my key in the door.

"Okay, I'll call you," Levi said, leaning in to kiss me.

"Good night, Levi Daugg," I said, placing my fingertips against his lips.

He kissed my fingertips lightly. "Good night, Lacy I'm-a-lean Foxx."

"Glory be, chile. It's almost ten. I haven't seen you all day. I thought you might miss the boat. Where have you been?" Bibi asked as she looked up from her worn Bible when I walked into the room. I peeled off my clothes and tumbled into bed.

"I was out seeing the sights with a friend," I said wearily.

"Someone you met here on the boat?"

"Yes."

"A man, I assume."

"Yes."

"And?" Bibi asked.

"And nothing. He's a nice guy, a great distraction 'til I get back home."

"And what's back home? Are you thinking about getting back together with Sebastian? You'll never find a man better than him. Mark my words."

"Bibi, please. You need to let that go. Sebastian and I are *never* getting back together. Why do you like him so much, anyway?"

"He reminds me a lot of your dad when he was courtin' your mama. Sebastian is a good man. You made a mistake by letting him go."

"Bibi, I've made mistakes before, and I'm sure I'll continue to make them."

"Is it possible that this guy you met on the ship could be a mistake?" she asked.

"Anything is possible. But like I said, he's just a distraction."

"So, does this distraction have a name?"

"Levi Daugg."

"Dog? There's an omen if ever I heard one."

"Not Dog, D-O-G. It's Daugg, D-A-U-G-G," I carefully explained.

"I don't care how you spell it. His name says it all."

"Well, Mr. Daugg wants to spend tomorrow with me. But I can dump him if you all would prefer doing something together as a family."

"Don't dump him on our account. I've met some church ladies and we're gonna tour the island together. Why don't the two of you come with us?"

"No thank ya. What are Daddy and Uncle Sol up to?"

"They're spending time with those three floozies they met. They're renting a sailboat and they're all going sailing."

"Great. That sounds like fun. By the way, Bibi, I don't think Ruth and LeAynne are floozies. They kind of remind me of Mama. They're so full of life."

"Oh, those two are okay. It's that doggone Rachel that hangs all over your uncle that I can't stand."

"I didn't get to meet her. She was the dancer, right?"

"Yeah, if you wanna call it dancing."

"Well, it sounds like everyone has plans. It looks like it's just gonna be Mr. Daugg and me tomorrow. Good night."

"Umphf . . . 'Night!" Bibi half-said, half-grunted from the other side of the room as she turned back to her Bible.

SEVEN

"So, what's the plan, Jan?" I heard Levi's voice ask through the telephone at ten on the dot the next morning.

"Good mornin' to you too."

"Are you going to make my day by telling me we can spend some time together?"

"You're in luck. I'm all yours," I said.

"If only that were true. Hey, I have an idea. Why don't I meet you in an hour on the promenade deck where we first met?"

"Okay, see ya then."

I was a little slow in getting ready. In typical CP time, I arrived at our pre-determined promenade deck site a half-hour late. I hung out on the deck for another thirty minutes in hopes that Levi would magically appear.

Disappointed that I'd missed him, I walked slowly to the main dining room, totally prepared to eat myself unconscious. "Excuse me," I apologized to the gentleman in front of me as I absentmindedly bumped into him while reaching for a plate.

"No problem," a familiar voice said.

"Levi? I'm glad I finally caught up with you. I'm sorry I missed you out on the promenade deck, but I've been running late all morning."

"Lacy . . ."

Was it just me, or were his eyes about to pop out of their sockets? "So, what do you have in store for us today?" I asked.

"We need to talk," he whispered. "There's something I need to tell you."

"Can you tell me while we eat?"

"That's just it. I can't eat with you, and I can't go ashore with you either."

"Why? Aren't you feeling well?"

"You see that lady over there? The one sitting in front of the waterfall looking at us? Uhmmm . . . that's my wife . . . Karen."

"Your what?"

"My wife," he said in a barely audible tone. "Karen and I are here on our honeymoon."

"I thought you said you were on this cruise alone. You told me that she broke off your engagement a month ago."

"When I saw you reading that novel on the deck, I couldn't take my eyes off of you. You were absolutely gorgeous, and at that moment, I wished like everything that I were single. That's why I told you that little white lie."

"If your wife is on this ship, how is it you managed to spend all day with me yesterday?"

"My wife has been seasick ever since we left Miami. This is the first time she's been out of our room in three days. This morning, right after I talked to you from the phone down the hall from our room, she told me she was feeling better. We're going ashore together after we eat. If you want to know the truth, I wish I were going ashore with you."

I was speechless.

"Lacy, don't hate me. If I had met you on this cruise before I married Karen, I wouldn't have gotten married. I guarantee you that."

"How stupid do you think I am? What kind of crap is that? That's supposed to make me feel better? My grandmother was right. A dog is a dog is a dog is a dog, no matter how you spell it," I said, shoving his plate of food into his chest. *Let him explain that to his blushing, beaming bride.* "You and your wife have a nice life."

I rushed out of the dining room, away from the sea of strangers having the time of their lives, and made my way to the ship's upper deck. By the time I found a quiet, uninhabited area, I was hyperventilating. It's not that I was mad at Levi, although I was—the snake! I was mostly mad at myself for being so quick to trust a total stranger.

Looking out across the ocean, my soul was immediately calmed. The tension flowed from my body as I surveyed the perfect, powder-white sand beaches, waving palm trees, brilliant blue water and the sky's huge, pillowy clouds. Suddenly Levi Daugg and his wife didn't matter anymore.

"Lacy? Is that you?" I heard a familiar voice ask from below.

"Bibi? I thought you were going ashore. Wait, I'll come down."

"I did go ashore," Bibi said, embracing me once I reached her side. "The old biddies I went ashore with tuckered out on me by lunch. They're asleep in their staterooms. Glory be. Can you believe it? It's like they're five thousand years old. Three hours on the island and they're exhausted. People like them give old folks like me a bad name."

"So, you don't have any plans?"

"Not really. Do you?"

"Nope. It turns out my friend on the ship was a mistake, a big one. He was married. Actually, he was a newlywed on his honeymoon."

"Forget about him. Your dad, uncle and their friends haven't left yet. They wanted me to find you to see if you wanted to join them. If you go, I'll go. They're sailing to Atlantis, you know, Paradise Island. After that, they said they might go on a submarine tour of some exotic sea gardens and go visit that underwater sea aquarium everyone around here keeps yapping about. And if you and I get restless, we can always throw the floozies overboard."

"Bibi! Do ya mind? Can you stop calling them floozies?"

"Just checkin' to make sure you're still among the land of the livin'," she said.

"Don't worry about me. I'm okay, really."

The rest of the day was spent enjoyably with my grandmother, my daddy, uncle and their women friends. Bibi and I spent most of our time observing the desperate women fawn all over my daddy and uncle. The all-day excursion was just what I needed.

My family spent the remaining days of the cruise rallying around me and my wounded pride. The floozies, old biddies and dogs disappeared from our world as quickly as they had appeared, and once again it was just the four of us against the world.

It wasn't the first time that my family had rallied around me in my time of need, and I would soon learn that it wouldn't be the last.

EIGHT

One evening, a few days after returning from the cruise, I found myself searching for Wynnton Trust's telephone number in my stash of misfiled business cards. After a lengthy search, I found his card filed under C for "Center" or "Cad," I couldn't remember which.

"It's a beautiful day at the Greater Kansas City Youth Center," a young, way-too-optimistic female voice said with glee into the phone.

"Hi, is Mr. T. there?" I asked tentatively.

"Yes, he is. Just one moment," the young voice said.

What would I say to him? *I know you think I'm a self-centered, don't-give-back-to-the-community, bougie princess, but really I'm not, and I want to prove it to you.* Was I insane? I thought about hanging up the phone, but before I could, I heard his soothing, deep voice on the other end.

"Hello, this is Wynnton Trust."

"Hello, Wynn? This is Lacy Foxx from *The Metro Tribune*."

"Oh. Hello."

Couldn't he at least pretend to be enthusiastic?

"I was wondering if you saw my article. What did you think?"

"It was fair. Accurate. It may not win you any awards, though."

"Look, I'm also calling 'cause I've been thinking about what you said. I'd love to participate in your career fair, but I can't because I'm facing a major deadline. I'll be here at work pretty late tonight."

"Thanks for letting me know you were at least considering it," he said.

"I wanted you to know that even though I can't come to the career fair tonight, I want to volunteer at the YC on a long-term basis. I have a great idea for a new program."

"I'm listening."

"I'd like to start a journalism program. I can get some friends from the paper and local radio and television stations to help. We can work with the kids on developing their own newspapers, radio shows and television news programs. It could do wonders for their communications skills," I said.

"It sounds like a great idea. Can you start tomorrow?" he asked.

"I guess so. I have tons of ideas on ways to develop the program," I lied. I'd only thought of the idea minutes before when I'd been put on hold. "Maybe we could get together after the career fair and discuss my ideas."

"Okay. Why don't you swing by the Youth Center when you can? How does nine o'clock sound?"

"That works for me."

"Do you know where we're located?" he asked.

"Off of Thirty-third and Owens, right?"

"Yep. See you tonight." Suddenly, there was a loud crash and crying in the background. "Mr. T.! Mr. T.! There's a fight in the rec room," I heard a police-informant-in-training report. "I really have to go," Wynn said. "Good-bye."

"Good-bye."

I hung up the phone, shell-shocked. *Tha hell?* What happened to my "no new projects" excuse? Why had I committed myself to developing a journalism curriculum for hundreds of kids? The things women did to impress men. I mentally kicked myself for agreeing to take on such an endeavor. Agree, nothing. It had been my idea! Here I was, I barely knew this man, and I was already trying too hard to impress him. I was trying to convince him he was wrong about me, trying to convince him that I was worthy of his acceptance. That was a bad sign. But of course, that was my problem, as well as the problem of a lot of other women I knew.

It was definitely a gender thing. We learned it as young kids. It was reflected in the games we played. At an early age, boys were taught to take, take, take. Look at sports for instance. Boys chased each other and took what they wanted — the football, the basketball, the soccer ball.

For girls, it was different. We played with dolls. We invited each other to tea parties. One lump or two? Give, give, give! We played teacher, nurse, wife. We nurtured, healed, gave. We wanted people, particularly men, to accept us so badly that we gave and gave until it hurt. We gave until we no longer remembered what we wanted, what we needed. "It's better to give than to receive," had become our motto . . . our creed . . . our mantra. And of course, the more we gave, the less we received.

It irked me that I was so quickly willing to give way too much of myself to a total stranger, all for his acceptance and his approval. Suddenly, I was mad at the whole male species and myself.

I needed to vent to Marsha. I looked all over the newsroom but couldn't find her. As I returned to my desk, I reflected on the fact that I hadn't seen much of Marsha lately, ever since she got the job covering the crime and drug beats. Come to think of it, I actually hadn't seen or talked to her much since her blind date with Patrick Nance, the night I met Wynn and slept with Sebastian. As it turned out, Marsha's blind date hadn't exactly been a love connection. She informed me a few days after her date that Patrick Nance was a short, light-skinned, overweight smoker. She couldn't fathom what possessed anyone to think he'd be perfect for her.

"What kind of vibes do I give off that make people think I'd be attracted to a troll?" she said at the time. "Promise me that you will never ever try to set me up on a blind date."

"You should so let me hook you up," I said. "I know exactly what you're looking for. It's the same thing we're all looking for. Someone that's tall, handsome, athletic, smart, sensitive, caring, passionate and of course, able to work it."

The fact that Patrick reminded her more of a gargoyle than a man didn't keep Marsha from taking care of her primal urges. How had she put it? Oh yeah. "It's amazing what liquor and a porno flick can do to put you in the mood."

I couldn't believe Marsha watched a porno flick, much less had sex with The Troll on their first date. But I kept my mouth shut. After my escapade with The Creature, who was I to question her judgment?

At one time, I had tried to talk to Marsha some more about Wynnton Trust, but before we even got started, she got a call from a source and was gone. That was before my cruise. I hadn't seen or talked to her much since.

The one time I did say more than "hi" and "bye" to Marsha was a few days earlier. She had been so upset. She was profiling a drug addict and had gotten really close to her source. From what I could tell, she'd gotten too close.

Her source, Zoretha Smalls, called her. She told Marsha she wanted to talk to her about something important. She had decided to give up the street life. No more trickin' and no more petty crime and drugs. She wanted to rid herself of all the unpleasant things and people associated with life on the streets, and she needed Marsha's help. But before Marsha could reach her, a couple of her low-life friends, if you could call them that, got a hold of her. They got Zoretha as high as a kite.

Free-basing, snorting, shooting . . . they did it all. When Marsha arrived, Zoretha was standing on the roof, naked and alone in the cold. She thought she could fly. She wanted Marsha to watch her fly. It turns out she couldn't fly, and Marsha couldn't write the story about her tragic death.

I was the only one in the newsroom that day not facing a major deadline, so I got the honor of writing about a life wasted. I interviewed Marsha for an hour. In a perfunctory manner, Marsha told me about what happened, but we never talked about how she felt. She clearly was avoiding that, and I was determined not to push her. I knew that when she was ready to talk, really ready to talk, she'd let me know.

The story I wrote about crack addict Zoretha Smalls was one of my best. It was one of the hardest articles I'd ever written. I gave Marsha co-writing credits because it was really her story. It turned out to be one of the best stories of my career, right behind my corruption articles, my series on dangerous careers and a series I did on sexual harassment. Zoretha's life story made all the national news wires and found its way onto the pages of every major and many minor newspapers.

Life sho' can be a mutha. One minute you're flying high; the next minute you're dead, either on the inside or the outside, emotionally, physically, spiritually, literally. I was suddenly depressed. I knew the best way for me to escape depression was to throw myself into my work, but I didn't have anything significant to cover. So, I did my monthly entertainment news roundup and recapped little stuff. Stupid stuff. New "Diddy Conquers New York City" predictions. Mind-numbing J-Lo, Janet, Whitney, Beyoncé and Ashanti relationship speculation. Unbelievable *American Idol Loser Becomes Big Winner* gossip. More *Desperate Housewives* accolades and more *Apprentice* and *America's Next Top Model* backbiting. It was the same old, same old. That interview with Lionel Richie was starting to sound good compared to this crap. I thought about calling The Creature but decided against it.

What I needed was a scoop. Something new, different and exciting about someone or something that was big and hot. I combed the entertainment calendars. Nobody big or hot was coming to Kansas City anytime soon, and I knew my chances of getting the paper to send me to Los Angeles or New York were slim. They would send me to junkets in both cities when the television season began, but that was months away, and I needed a scoop now.

I never got my scoop. I waited until the SOB left for the day before I sent my boring entertainment roundup article by computer to his office. I headed out of the building even more depressed as I imagined his colorful and not-so-nice editing comments staring me in the face from my computer screen in the morning. But that was tomorrow. I'd worry about it then.

A light snow had begun to fall when I arrived at the YC, fifteen minutes late. So much for making a good impression and showing Wynnton Trust he was wrong about me and my self-centered ways. But could I help it if my stockings had gotten a hellacious run in them? Actually, they got tired of running and had started skipping. I had to go ten miles out of my way to get to the nearest store.

Wynn was waiting for me at the front door when I drove into the Youth Center's parking lot. I flashed him a don't-hate-me-because-I'm-late smile and he responded with a stern, unsympathetic glare. He then grabbed my hand and guided me into the Youth Center's main building amidst dozens of yelling and laughing kids of all ages. My senses were instantly aroused by a high-energy, deafening and unintelligible roar.

The Youth Center looked like an old school both on the outside and inside. Immediately upon entering, to the left of the reception desk, I saw a large recreation room where more than 100 kids were involved in a variety of activities, including playing cards, ping pong, board games, checkers, chess and video games. At the very back of the rec room was a huge art studio featuring colorful paintings and sculptures created by the YC's young artists in residence. Hundreds of New Year's Resolutions written in child-like script were located on the walls of the art room and along every wall in the building.

"Are you ready?" I asked Wynn as he guided me through a maze of kids on the way to his office, which was located on the second floor, directly above the rec room.

From what I could see, down the hall from his office was a huge library where another fifty kids and their volunteer tutors were packing up. Also on the upper level were about a dozen classrooms and offices that overlooked a building adjacent to the main part of the center. That was the YC's 20-bed shelter, which also contained a huge pool.

"First I have to tell Voncile, the YC's assistant director, that I'm leaving, and then I have to call my mother to make sure my son is okay. After that, I'll be ready to go."

"Okay."

"Come on. I want you to meet Voncile. If we get your journalism program off the ground, the two of you will be working closely together."

"Great. By the way, do you think you could help me snag an interview with 2Tuff? Can you give them my number and let them know I want to do an article about them? I've heard them perform a few times. They're amazing."

"I can't wait for them to blow up and hit it big! I'll let them know you wanna write about them. You know, when they were younger, they both hung out here at the YC," Wynn said proudly. We walked in silence for a few minutes before arriving at our destination, the Youth Center's main office.

"This is where I spend most of my time, and this is the woman I spend it with. Voncile Ford, meet Lacy Foxx. She's the reporter who wrote the article in *The Metro Tribune* about the YC. She's gonna start volunteering here at the Youth Center," Wynn said with much fanfare.

"Uhmmm," Voncile said with disgust, not bothering to look up from the papers she was filing diligently into an already overstuffed file cabinet.

"I'm Perri with an I," said a cute, honey brown-colored girl with large, light brown eyes and dozens of tiny braids adorned with multicolored beads, as she peered from behind a desk.

"Hi, Perri with an I. I'm Lacy with a Y. Aren't you adorable?" I said as I bent down to pinch her cheeks. "Is this your daughter?" I asked the non-friendly Voncile.

"Yeah."

"Perri with an I, how old are you?"

"Two," she said, holding up four fingers.

"Vonnie, we're going out to dinner," Wynn said to Perri with an I's aloof mother.

Voncile looked at us just long enough to roll her eyes and suck her teeth in our direction. She was a pretty, light-skinned, stocky woman whose ugly attitude belied her good looks. With her slightly large head and even larger body she reminded me of one of my favorite childhood toys, a wooden, egg-shaped Weebil. Looking at her, I couldn't help but wonder if she lived up to the Weebil's catchy advertising slogan—if pushed, would she wobble but not fall down?

"Me go? Me go?" Perri with an I asked.

"Honey, you have to stay here with Mommy. If you're good, maybe I'll bring you back a special treat. How does that sound?" Wynn said, bribing her.

"Otay," she said, laughing. She ran to her mother and plopped down at her feet.

Wynn picked up the phone and from what I could decipher, he talked to his mom and son.

The Weebil observed me gloomily the whole time. After about ten minutes, Wynn and I left the room in silence.

"Voncile seems hostile," I said once we were out of her hearing range.

"She's dealt with a lot the last few years. It's made her a little bitter."

"So I see. With her attitude, is it good for her to be around the kids?"

"She's not usually like that. No offense, but you're most likely the reason she acted the way she did."

"Excuse me?" I asked. I wasn't in the mood for another of his verbal assaults.

"Don't take that the wrong way. It's just that Vonnie is very resentful of other young, successful black females. She's from a poor family and she had to drop out of college and give up a college scholarship a few years ago when she had Perri. She hasn't been able to return to college since. Plus, she has a bit of a crush on me and she hates seeing me go out with women such as yourself."

I wasn't even going to dignify that "women such as yourself" comment with a response. I wouldn't give him the satisfaction.

"So, where do you want to go for dinner? I'm really hungry," Wynn said while helping me into his midnight black Cadillac Escalade EXT.

I decided to test him. "How about 40 Sardines?" I asked as he closed my door.

40 Sardines was one of the most upscale restaurants in the area, and I suggested it just to see how he would react. To be honest, I wasn't even really hungry. But he was going to pay, literally, for the way he'd been treating me since we met.

"40 Sardines it is," Wynn said nonchalantly while climbing into the seat beside me. He turned the key in the ignition and within a few seconds we were on our way.

Sucker!

NINE

The restaurant, 40 Sardines, was located in Hawthorne Plaza, a suburban shopping area on the far south side of town, and although it was snowing heavily by the time we arrived, the wildly popular restaurant was brimming with customers. Considered one of Kansas City's "it" restaurants, 40 Sardines was situated in an understated stucco and beige brick building. Inside, calming shades of blue greeted diners, as did jazz music that floated invitingly from hidden speakers located throughout the restaurant.

Surprisingly, during our thirty-minute wait to be seated, Mr. T. and I actually got along. Once we were seated near the center of the restaurant, I decided to test him again. I ordered one of the most expensive and tasty entrees on the menu: a wood grilled centercut ribeye steak with roasted potatoes, chipotle and pistachio onion relish. Wynnton Trust didn't bat an eye as he ordered the equally expensive seared antelope with a root vegetable tart, chestnuts, black trumpet mushrooms and huckleberry sauce.

"In case you're wondering, the career fair went really well. I'm sorry the kids at the Center couldn't hear about you and your career. How about a personal overview?" Wynn suggested after we ordered our food.

"I've wanted to be a reporter for as long as I can remember. Well, actually, that's not entirely true. I've always wanted to be a writer. I remember being eight years old and while the other kids in the neighborhood were outside playing and having fun, I was inside writing misadventures for Curious George and Christie, Mattel's black Barbie. Can you say 'biggest nerd on the planet'?"

He smiled. God, he has a beautiful smile.

"I've always dreamed of writing the great American novel and selling it to Hollywood for millions so they could turn it into a blubbering, unrecognizable, wildly successful, highly commercial mega-hit mess."

He laughed. God, he has a wonderful laugh.

"I discovered early on I didn't have the patience for being a great American writer. My first stab at a manuscript was all of five pages. After that I got bored and restless. So, I decided the shorter the better. That's when I turned to journalism. I always received good grades in English, and I worked as a reporter on school newspapers in junior high, high school and college, and here I am. Although, hopefully not for long. I'm trying to get a job with *Élan Live*, a huge media conglomerate based in L.A."

Did I really sound as boring as I imagined I did? I changed the subject.

"So, when I interviewed you before, you mentioned you had a son. Tell me about him. What's his name? Édonte, right?" Wynn looked away. Suddenly, he seemed sad. Didn't all parents love to talk about their children?

"I was married to Édonte's mother . . . Jac . . . Jacqui, for almost four years. He's a lot like her," Wynn said as his voice trailed off and he stared into space.

It was the first time since I met him that I had ever seen him look sad, and dare I say vulnerable?

"I hope you don't mind me asking, but what happened?"

"My wife had an affair. A few days before our fourth anniversary, she came home, told me she was leaving me for another man, and then she left. Poof, the marriage was over like that, in the blink of an eye. The divorce was hard on Édonte. He and his mother were close, or so he thought. She walked out on us about two years ago, and after the divorce was final, we haven't heard a word from her. I don't even know where she is."

His voice hinted of desolate surrender. How does a mother just leave her child like that? I couldn't imagine. Actually, I could. When she accidentally overdosed following

Gary's death, Mama, in essence, did the same thing to me. She just left my father and me.

"What little family she has in town won't have anything to do with me or Édonte. I think they're embarrassed about what happened. Édonte is slowly but surely getting over it. Hanging out at the YC has really helped him. He has lots of friends, and I think he's developing some real potential as a photographer. Plus, he's learning to be responsible. He helps me out a lot around the Center."

"He sounds like a good kid," I said.

"He is. He's the best. You know what? It just dawned on me that you're *the* Lacy Foxx that used to cover the metro, business and government beats for the paper. I was a big fan of yours."

His praise rattled me, and I was surprisingly warmed by it, inside and out.

"The last metro piece I remember you covering was that big corruption scandal involving that multimillionaire and those politicians about a year ago. You went to jail for not revealing a source for your articles, didn't you? I remember the mug shot they printed of you in the paper. It didn't do you justice. What you did then was pretty admirable."

"Admirable and scary."

"Reading your articles got me through a tough time. They kept me distracted. Your articles were one of the few things I had to look forward to. That and taking care of my son," Wynn confessed.

I smiled. His kind words made me feel good. "Glad I could help," I said quietly.

"Why did you switch from business, government and metro news to society and entertainment news? You're too good for that. The stuff you cover now doesn't require a brain to write. You're wasting your time and your talent."

He had his nerve! He didn't know a doggone thing about me. Plus, he chewed his food with his stupid mouth open!

"Like you, I used to want to make a difference, back when I was a serious journalist. But for me, it didn't pay to care."

Oh and by the way, forget you and the horse yo' fine behind rode in on.

"I'm sorry. I didn't mean to offend you. It's just that—"

"Let's just drop it, okay?"

We ate our respective meals in silence. During the drive back to the Youth Center, we tried the conversation thing again. This time we kept it neutral. We talked about the weather (cold), music (he liked jazz, I liked neo-soul), our favorite author (Walter Mosley), his love of the macabre and my love of Shakespeare, and the journalism program I was going to soon start at the Youth Center.

As he was helping me into my car back at the YC, I invited him over to my place to talk more about my ambitious volunteer effort. Since we were both huge Walter Mosley fans, I also suggested we could watch a late night screening of *Devil in a Blue Dress* which I had on DVD. Wynn readily agreed. I'm sure it wasn't because he wanted to spend more time with me. I think he finally realized, as I did, that if we were going to be working together, we had to learn to get along, and it might as well be sooner rather than later.

TEN

When we arrived at my condo, I checked my messages, slipped off my plum wool blazer and offered Wynn something to drink. I apologized for not having any liquor and told him his only options were water and cranberry juice. I wasn't the least bit surprised when he told me he didn't drink alcohol. I fixed us two glasses of water with lemon and after taking them to Wynn, I excused myself and went to the bathroom. Once there, I called Marsha on my cell and left a message about how my date was going so far.

I returned to my living room and plopped in the movie. Wynn and I watched it in silence. There was Denzel in all his glory, having sex with his friend's girl, and all I could think about was how horny I was. And since Wynn Trust was the only man within shooting distance of my raging hormones, I turned to him and decided to bite the bullet.

"You know, I'm twenty-eight years old and I have neither the time nor the luxury to be shy nor coy. I'm used to going after what I want, and what I want right now is you. So, you can either kiss me now, or we can play games and you can kiss me later."

I puckered my MAC Diva-painted lips and closed my eyes. I hoped I would wow him with my directness and honesty. *No response. Nothing.* I peeked out from under my Moody Mauve shadowed eyelids. He didn't look impressed. It looked more like he was amused. I took matters, not to mention his face, into my hands, and I reached over and kissed him. He kissed me back halfheartedly then gently pushed me away.

"I know I'm irresistible, but someone needs to slow her roll," he said with a laugh.

"I pity the fool who finds you irresistible, myself included," I said, my tit for his tat. I inhaled deeply in preparation for round two of my assault.

"Whadayaknow? If I'm not mistaken, I think I'm being seduced."

"You think? Don't you know, Mr. T.?" I asked, leaning in to kiss him. Again he pulled back.

"Not you too. Please don't call me Mr. T. I get enough of that from the kids. Look, I appreciate being the object of your desire, but I ain't that easy. Okay, that's a lie. I *am* that easy. But don't you think this is a bad idea? I get the impression you don't like me much, and from my standpoint, the verdict is still out on you. Besides, if we were gonna do something, I'd like to be the one to initiate it, if you don't mind."

"Initiate away. And just to be clear, I'm not asking you to spend the rest of your life with me. The fact is, we're both human and we both have needs." Right then I started having second thoughts. In fact, my second, third, fourth and fifth thoughts kicked in, but I ignored them. I was a woman with something to prove, namely that he wasn't as repulsed by me as he thought. "And for the record, I never said I didn't like you. You'll do. You're a'ight," I said less than enthusiastically.

"I'll do? I'm a'ight? That's the best you can come up with?"

"Well, I've never thought about sleeping with anyone before on a first date, so you must be more than a'ight," I said, not feeling compelled to tell him about The Creature.

"Flattery will get you everywhere, although that was some pretty weak flattery."

"What am I supposed to do? Sing your praises? You'll excuse me if I don't break out in song. I'm a little tone deaf. If you don't want to do anything, that's fine. We don't have to. Really," I said, getting cold feet.

"Good, because I'm not into awkward casual sex."

"What I have planned won't be awkward or casual."

"I'm intrigued, but just answer me one quick question. If you've never done this on a first date before, why now with me? Why am I so . . . uhmmm . . . lucky?"

Suddenly, I felt common and cheap. I didn't have an answer for him, at least not one that I could articulate without sounding insane, so I kissed him. This time he wholeheartedly kissed me back. It was a tender, moist, warm . . . magnificent kiss.

"Don't forget who's runnin' things," he said with a big smile when we came up for air. Goodness, was he sexy or what? He was still a jerk, but a sexy one. He walked over to the television and changed the channel to BET. We watched in silent amusement an unimaginative, shake-your-thang, triflin' man video, and then one of my favorite oldies, "Next Lifetime" by Erykah Badu, started playing.

Wynn sauntered back to my couch, stood in front of me, extended his arms and helped me to my feet. I rested my cheek on his chest and we slow danced for the next three minutes in silence. He smelled good and his body was warm, hard, inviting. I could feel his heart beat faster and faster as we swayed slowly from side to side. I could also feel his manhood swell with every beat of the music and every gyration of my hips. It was all extremely intoxicating.

I was totally lost in the moment and wanted him badly. I soon regretted my agreement to let him control things. He was moving too doggone slow, so I decided to help him along. I gently moved his hands from my waist to my hips. He looked at me sternly.

"I thought I was supposed to be initiating things."

"You are," I purred seductively, "but you're taking a little too long for my taste."

"You know what they say. If it's good, it's worth waiting for."

"Well, in your case that remains to be seen," I said with a teasing smile.

"Ahhh, a sistah's got jokes," he said with a toothy grin. "Are you sure you want to do this? I'm really a good guy, but for all you know, I could be a freak."

"That's what I'm hoping for."

As far as I was concerned, I wasn't interested in having sex with his good-guy personality. You could throw a paper bag over his head and call him the Unknown Mean Comic for all I cared. The bottom line was, I was really horny and I had a point to prove. Stuck-up, bougie ghetto princess or not, the fact is, Wynnton Trust wanted me. There was no denying it.

I could feel his desire as he pressed up against me. I kicked off my three-inch high-heel, boff-me ankle boots and shimmied out of my skirt. I unbuttoned his red cotton poplin shirt and he slipped my beige Egyptian cotton blouse over my head and undid my Victoria's Secret Angel bra while the warmth of our mouths found each other like heat tracking missiles. We continued to kiss passionately as we made our way back to the sofa. He sat down and stretched out an inviting hand. I leaned over, kissed him on the mouth then left the room.

Safe sex sho' is a mutha, and it sho' don't do much for the mood.

I raced to the "condom drawer" and closed my eyes as I reached in.

Ah, chocolate and ribbed. Perfect.

"We can't forget this," I said to him when I returned, waving the colorful condom package. I tore open the package, straddled his body, and placed the condom on him. He kissed me and placed one of his hands in the center of my lower back. He used his other hand to guide himself gently inside of me.

Firm. Gentle.

With every movement of his body, I felt him grow. To accommodate him, I arched my back while spreading my legs farther apart. He showed his appreciation by burrowing deeper inside of me. He grew some more as he engaged my breasts with one hand and guided my hips with the other. As we found a comfortable, slow rhythm, he stretched out and flexed his long, lean, muscular body. I gasped. Was he still growing? I alternately tightened and relaxed my muscles. We moaned in unison as our entwined bodies took over and led lives of their own.

I closed my eyes, licked my lips and waited in anticipation for the sweet moment when our wetness would overtake us. I didn't have to wait long. Twenty minutes later, I felt his body shudder as he released his passion like a rocket headed toward some uncharted destiny. A few seconds later, I met him in orbit. Our lovemaking was like a kind of sexual alchemy. What could have been cheap and common morphed into something extraordinary.

Our sexual hunger satisfied, I fell against his hairless chest, exhausted but totally fulfilled. He enclosed his muscular arms around me. After a few minutes, I got up, went into the bathroom and returned with a warm, soft cloth that we used to cleanse one another. We made our way to the bedroom and drifted off to sleep. When I woke up a few hours later, I was, not surprisingly, ready for round two.

"I hope you're ready," I said, sliding my tongue into his ear.

"Ready for what?" Wynn asked groggily.

"Ready for another heapin' helpin' of my hospitality," I said, smiling broadly as I straddled him. "You know, this is black gold, Texas tea," I said while pointing to the lower half of my anatomy.

He laughed. "Well, maybe I'll have a taste of that Texas tea after I head for the hills," he said, reaching up to kiss my breasts.

"Sounds like somebody's a little bit freaky. I like that in ya."

"Oh yeah? So, tell me, is there anything in particular you'd like to do now, Ms. Foxx?"

What I wanted to do was have sex with him in every room in my condominium, and that is what we proceeded to do. The rest of the day—with the exception of some time devoted to me calling the SOB and feigning ill, and Wynn calling his office, the YC and his son—was spent making love. We did so on the living room floor, on the steps leading to my basement, on my bed, on my bathroom sink counter, on top of my car, in my office, and in the shower. Seven times in as many hours. I resigned myself to the fact that I would be sore for days when it was all over.

Sometime around six that evening, we lay in my bed, exhausted.

"I'm glad you like sex as much as I do, but what a surprise," I said in a feeble attempt to make the requisite after-sex chitchat.

"What do you mean?"

"Given our rocky start, who would have imagined us together?"

"I'm glad it happened. My fantasies and dreams needed detail and clarity."

"You fantasized about me?"

"I guess I fantasized just a little bit about getting you into the sack. But mostly I fantasized about converting you from your bougie, self-involved ways."

"You're not gonna start that mess again, are you?"

"Man, you're sensitive. I'm just kidding."

"You're a jerk," I said through a lopsided smile.

"I'm sorry you feel that way," he said with mock sincerity. "Look, I hope you know I didn't mean that stuff I said about you when we first met."

"Yes, you did."

"Okay, maybe I did. But you were right. My distrust of women and the media took over and I took it out on you. A little part of me had to test you out to be sure you were okay. You've proven with the article and your willingness to help out at the YC that you're committed to the community."

"So, what am I supposed to do? Jump for joy because I've received the Wynnton Trust seal of approval? Let's get one thing straight. I don't like playing games," I warned, lost deep in denial of the game I was playing myself.

"Neither do I. From this point on, no more games. Deal?"

"Deal. Okay, now I've got a question for you."

"I'm an open book. Ask me anything," he said.

"Does my honesty and aggressiveness bother you?"

"No. Why would you ask me that? Actually, it's rather refreshing. I'm used to conniving women who play a lot of games, who have ulterior motives. But you, you're different. A bit emotional and high-strung, but you're real. You know what you want and you go after it, but in a ladylike manner. You're direct, but not hard. And to tell the truth, I think you're a lot sweeter than you let on. Does that make any sense? You have style, class. You're definitely your own woman. And at the end of the day, all you can do is do you. Make no apologies for that," he said.

"I'm my own woman all right, but in case you haven't noticed, I'm also alone."

"Not anymore, you're not, sweetness," he said as he turned to me, kissing me gently on the forehead.

Although I was originally just trying to prove a point, I drifted off to sleep thinking I could really fall hard for this save-the-world Negro. Purely by accident, my AIDA Principles of Love Plan had gone into full effect. Borrowed by Marsha and me from the advertising world, AIDA stood for attention, interest, desire and action. It worked like this: first, I had to get the attention of my target, which I did during our first meeting when I sweated like a pig and rambled like a moron. If that didn't get his attention, what would? Second, I had to let my target know that I was interested in him, and I had to get him interested in me. I'd done that by volunteering at his precious Youth Center. He indicated his interest by agreeing to go out with me on a date. Third, I had to spark desire, which I did in a big way at least eight times throughout my condo. And finally, all of the above had to lead to action—

the desired action being marriage or a relationship that lasted longer than the time it took to fill my tank. In a few short weeks, I'd been through the "AID" part of my plan and it appeared that the final "A" would happen in due time.

ELEVEN

For every mistake and bad decision, there is a morning of regret afterward. My night (and day) of passion with Wynnton Clarence Trust, part deux, was no exception.

"Yesterday was a mistake," I said, greeting Wynn with the announcement the next day when I entered the Youth Center office for the first time as a volunteer.

"What? You didn't seem to think it was a mistake at the time."

I felt hopeless as I choked on the words I really wanted to say. "I got caught up. We both did. You were talking about your ex, I was thinking about mine, and we just kind of let things get outta hand." I didn't have the nerve to tell him I was just afraid of what I was beginning to feel for him.

"That's what a man likes to hear after the fact," he said sarcastically.

"I knew this wouldn't be easy. It's just that we now work together and . . . uhmmm . . . uhmmm . . . it was just one of those things. It shouldn't have happened and it won't happen again."

"I couldn't agree more," he said coolly before leaving the room.

"Looks like somebody's a ho," The Weebil said with a smirk as she walked into the office. "Do you always drop the drawers for just anybody?"

"What did you just say?" I asked in my fiercest Robert De Niro you-talkin'-to-me, ready-to-rumble tone. "Who you callin' a ho?"

Did I just say that out loud? How had I been reduced to this? Was I being punk'd? Was MTV's Ashton Kutcher lurking nearby, watching me on a small screen in the shadows? As I contemplated these questions and looked around for hidden cameras, The Weebil mumbled something under her breath and began tackling her never ending pile of files.

For the next few days, as I hung out at the YC after work putting together my curriculum, Wynn and I avoided each other. He and The Weebil were totally in charge, a fact that she didn't let me forget.

On Friday, I was scheduled to introduce my journalism program to the Youth Center's members. As I walked into the gym, just prior to my sign-up session, all YC staff members raised their right arms. The gymnasium fell silent. Sprinkled throughout the crowd were reminders of my brother. The members' young, eager, expectant faces forced me to fight back slow-building tears.

"We have a very special treat for you," Wynn's voice said over the intercom. "Most of you have met Ms. Lacy Foxx. She's a reporter for *The Metro Tribune* and she's going to start volunteering here at the Youth Center. She has a really exciting new program that she wants to tell you about. As she's talking, if you have questions, raise your hands. Okay, let's give Ms. Foxx a big YC welcome."

Wynn handed me the microphone and suddenly the gymnasium was awash in a deafening roar of clapping hands and stomping feet.

"How many of you read *The Tribune*?" I asked the overly excited group once they calmed down.

"I read the funnies!"

"I read the sports section!"

"I look at the pictures!"

Smart-aleck kids. I tried another tactic. "Who knows what a reporter does?"

"Reporters are always in other people's business," someone said.

"In a way, I guess that's true. But do you know why we're always in other people's business? To keep people like you informed. If there were a serial killer in the area, wouldn't you want to know? Or if Shaq were coming to town, wouldn't you want to know that too? Reporters have sources that tell them about these things long before it becomes common knowledge. And it's our job as reporters to pass that information on to the public."

Silence. Fearing I was losing the crowd, I pulled out the big guns.

"As an entertainment reporter, I get to meet a lot of interesting people."

"Like who?" someone asked from the back of the room.

"I've met Eddie Murphy, Martin Lawrence, the cast of *Eve* and *Girlfriends*, Michael Jordan, Samuel L. Jackson, Denzel Washington and Danny Glover."

"Ceeley . . . Ceeley . . . you sho' is uuugly!" someone wisecracked. A roar of laughter took over the room as I continued naming famous celebrities I'd met.

"I've also met Iyanla Vanzant, Oprah, Whoopie, Destiny's Child . . . "

"So who is the most interesting person you've met?" a high-pitched female voice queried.

"Who's the funniest?" someone else countered.

"Is Shaq really as tall as he looks?" a young boy in the center of the room asked.

"The thing you have to remember about all of these celebrities is that they're just like us. They put their pants on one leg at a time," I said.

"They're not like us," an older male voice interrupted. "They're getting paid mad money, and we ain't!" The immature crowd laughed.

"So, how did you get to become a reporter?" a young female voice asked.

"Yeah, tell us, 'cause I wanna meet some famous people too, " another young female voice said.

"I'm gonna be famous myself!" a young male voice yelled.

"To be a reporter, you have to love to write. You have to make good grades in English, and you need to be inquisitive."

"Inquisitive? What's that?" a little girl in front asked.

"It means nosy, stupid!"

"Hey, no name calling. Being inquisitive is more than just being nosy."

"Did you have to go to reporting school? Is it like Rib Tech?" someone wanted to know, making reference to the training institute prospective employees had to attend in order to work at Gates Barb-B-Q, Kansas City's world-renowned rib joint.

"I went to a regular college, KU, and my last two years were spent in nothing but reporting classes. Plus, I was an intern for the city's newspaper."

"What's an intern?" someone asked.

"It's someone who works for free," an older boy answered.

"That's not entirely true. I worked for the experience and college credit. A lot of college internships are paid internships nowadays."

"Good, 'cause I ain't tryin' to work for free!" a deep voice in the back of the room yelled.

"What do you like most about your job?" a voice to my left asked.

"I like the flexibility. I can come and go as I please. I meet a lot of interesting people. I feel like I'm actually helping people by keeping them informed. Plus the money isn't bad, and I get to travel."

"What don't you like about your job?"

"The deadlines. It's like when you're in school and you have to hand in your homework by a certain time. I hate that." Some of the kids in the audience moaned in agreement. "Now that you know all there is to know about being a reporter, if I offered a journalism program here, how many of you would be interested in signing up?"

Nearly every kid in the gym raised his or her hand. "If you're interested, come up front and sign up. We can take about thirty members per session."

I was immediately bombarded by kids of all ages. Thirty kids were signed up within minutes. An additional waiting list full of names had begun to circulate, but before everyone could sign up, The Weebil stepped up to the microphone and announced that a pizza party was about to start in the rec room.

The gymnasium cleared out quickly. That was just the beginning. From that point on, The Weebil made my life at the YC a living hell. For the next two weeks, she did one thing after another to sabotage me. On the night of my first session, she announced over the intercom a special viewing of a Martin Lawrence flick. Within five minutes, all of the Youth Center's members were plopped in front of the big screen television.

A week later, I searched high and low for important files on the computer that I had set up for my sessions, and I later learned from an office assistant that The Weebil had accidentally deleted them. But the straw that broke the camel's back occurred when she cancelled speakers for a special show-and-tell presentation I had arranged. That was it. I'd had it, and I was going to tell Wynn I wasn't putting up with it anymore.

"You better tell your pit bull, Voncile, to back off or I'm out," I said to Wynn somewhere near the end of my first month at the Youth Center.

"What's wrong? Can't take a little challenge?" he asked sarcastically.

"If I wanted a little challenge, I would have signed up for Outward Bound. I'm here for the kids, not to take abuse from some woman with a fractured ego. I know she gave up her dreams and dedicated her life to you—I mean the Youth Center—when she had Perri, but I refuse to take abuse from her 'cause she can't deal with her screwed up life."

"Calm down. What has Vonnie done exactly?"

"She's deleted important files from my personal computer. She has conveniently scheduled events for the kids during each of my sessions, and she repeatedly calls to cancel guest speakers I've invited to come talk to the kids."

"Those could all be considered honest mistakes."

"Honest mistakes my behind. We both know she's doing this intentionally. What's up with her anyway? What have I done to her? You know what, I don't even care. I don't want to know. I just want it to stop. You've seen what she's been up to. Why haven't you put a stop to it before now?"

"What exactly am I supposed to do?"

"You need to tell her to chill out. If you don't, I'll take my program elsewhere. I'll go to the Boys & Girls Clubs or the YMCA, or to some other youth group. I'm sure they'd be glad to have a program like this for their members."

"There's no need to threaten me."

"It's not a threat, it's a promise. I guarantee you that. Either she backs up off me or me and my program are out of here. And here's another thing for you to think about. Don't forget I work for a newspaper. One unfavorable article or editorial could wreak havoc with your reputation, funding and support."

"Is that all? Anything else you wanna say?" he asked, glaring at me. "Any other threats—I mean *promises* you want to make?"

"Nope. That should do it," I said before heading triumphantly out the door. I had no intention of ruining the Youth Center's reputation. I didn't mean to be so harsh with him, but I couldn't help it. My pride was beyond hurt.

I didn't see much of Wynn or The Weebil for the next few weeks, and that was fine with me. Within a short time, my journalism program took off. Every Monday, Wednesday and Friday evening after work, I headed straight to the YC for my thrice-weekly journalism sessions. My first group of kids were in the middle of their two-month long program. And since I'd been doing the sessions, which had become wildly popular, I'd even convinced Trey Jenkins to help out as my assistant.

I had the curriculum down to a science. During the first month, members of the Youth Center toured *The Tribune*, a local radio station and a local television station. I also invited different journalist friends to come in and make presentations to the kids participating in the program. During the second month, I would give the kids a chance to put together their own newspapers or hour-long radio or television news programs. For those who were really interested in learning more about journalism, I was going to connect them with sources for internships. It's like I was the belle of the ball. The kids liked me, I liked them, and everyone but The Weebil couldn't have been happier.

One night, shortly after a session, I had a moment alone with Trey.

"So, what do you think, Trey? Do you think we're on to something?" I asked as he copied handouts and I reorganized the room in a more feng shui-friendly arrangement.

"Yep, yep. Your journalism sessions are da bomb!"

"A lot of the success is because of you. The kids around here look up to you. And don't even get me started on the girls who just come to the sessions to flirt with you."

"You know my style. You know how I roll, how I do," Trey said, punctuating his comment with a big, toothy grin.

"No, I don't. How do you do?" I asked.

"A brotha ain't tryin' to get tied down. I'm just dippin' in this and that."

"You better not mean that literally. You are too young to be dippin' into anything. But if you are, you better be protecting yourself."

"Puhleeze I'm gonna be eighteen on November one-five. You betta recognize! Shoot, I'm grown. You know I'm gonna protect mine!" he said with a laugh. "Now it's your turn for the third degree. What's crackin'?"

"Ain't no dippin' goin' on here, if that's what you're asking."

"Whatever. That's not what Mr. T. said. Me and some of the fellas heard him talkin' to Ms. Ford about you when you first started volunteering here."

"Oh, yeah?" I asked, my interest piqued. "He was talking about me? And what did he say exactly?"

"Look at you, Li'l Miss Reporter tryin' to get information out of me."

"Come on Trey. Spill it!" I said, pinching his arm.

"Ouch! Hey, that's child abuse!" Trey said while rubbing his arm and laughing. "I'm turnin' you in to Child Protective Services."

"You can look forward to more of that if you don't start flappin' those gums."

"I can't tell you what Mr. T. said, man. I'll lose my playa's card."

"Trey . . ."

"A'ight. A'ight. But you didn't hear this from me. He was just tellin' Ms. Ford that he wished things had turned out differently between you two. He said somethin' about the two of you hookin' up, but things started moving too fast and you got scared."

"Really? He say anything else?"

"He said out of all the honeys he's gone out with, he never vibed with anybody like he did with you. He also said he was really feelin' you and that he hoped you'd quit trippin' and come around."

"Hmmm . . . " I said thoughtfully.

"So, what's up with the two of you anyway? From what I could see around here, I thought you couldn't stand each other. I don't think I've even seen the two of you talk," Trey said.

"It's a grown-up thing. It's complicated."

"By grown-up and complicated, you must mean it's whack."

BULLETPROOF SOUL

"Just finish copying those papers, Trey," I said as I turned my undivided attention back to rearranging the room.

TWELVE

I'd only been volunteering at the YC a short time but was fast becoming a ball of raw nerves. My encounters at the Youth Center with Mr. T. and The Weebil had taken a far larger toll on me than I suspected, and listening to hyperactive children all the time didn't help matters. I desperately need a colonic for my soul. What I got instead was an assignment I would never forget.

"Foxx, I need you to cover a fire," the SOB said, appearing out of nowhere at my desk one evening just as I was preparing to leave.

"Why me?"

"Ten reporters on the metro desk called in sick again today. It's mighty funny this coincides with labor negotiations."

I smiled in spite of my burgeoning workload. Those blue-flu staging rats were causing me a lot of extra work. "Fine, I'm outta here. Where's the fire?"

"Eighty-seventh and Newton. It sounds like a whole family died. According to the police scanner, the unit your ex-fiancé is in was first on the scene. Try getting an exclusive with him if you can."

That will happen in your dreams, I wanted to say, remembering my last painful encounter with Sebastian.

A short while later, I stepped from my car and thick, coal black smoke stung my eyes and embraced my lungs, daring me to breathe. The smell of burnt memories and belongings, charred wood and flesh assaulted me from all sides. Water from large, thick rubber hoses cut a translucent path through the smoke-filled sky. A strong gust of wind strew tiny pellets of ash against my face so hard that it felt like dozens of tiny daggers were stabbing at my flesh.

To add to the mind-numbing scene was a constant buzz of shouting voices relaying cryptic codes, and the shrill sound of sirens. I searched the chaotic scene for a fireman who wasn't fighting the life-altering wall of flames backlit by an ominous tower of smoke, a red-hot reminder of a family's life now gone.

"Ma'am, you're gonna have to move," a voice said from the other side of a dense wall of smoke.

"Sebastian?" I asked, recognizing the voice but unable to see the face and body it belonged to.

"Lace? What are you doing here?"

"I'm here covering the fire for the newspaper," I said. Slowly my eyes began to adjust, and after a few seconds I could make out his stoic form. "I need to do an interview with you. I understand that your unit was here first."

"Right now I'm in charge of this nightmarish scene and I don't have time to do an interview."

"Come on, Sebastian. You're not still upset with me because of what happened when we slept together a while back, are you?"

"What? My not wanting to do an interview with you has nothing to do with what happened between us," he said.

"Then what's the problem? Talking to the media is a part of your job. Admit it. You just don't want to talk to me. It's okay. I understand."

"You want a story? Okay, fine!" he said, grabbing me by the arm. He tugged on me so hard I nearly fell. We walked quickly toward one of the ambulances parked a few feet from where a house now stood in ruins. The ambulance's flashing lights altered my vision. All around me was indistinguishable. Everything was a blur of flashing lights.

"How is this for your stupid story?" Sebastian asked, ripping a black blanket off a nearby gurney.

The black dead eyes of a young child peered up at us. At least I think it was a child because of the small size of the skull. I couldn't tell for sure. The flesh of his or her face had totally melted away like the ebony wax of a black candle left burning too long. All that I could distinguish were the eyes.

They were eyes I'll never forget for as long as I live. They were eyes that stood wide open within a pool of molten flesh; eyes that reflected the horror of a life snuffed out prematurely.

"That's five-year-old Isaac. He was lying on the couch with his drunk father when his father fell asleep with a lit cigarette in his mouth."

I fell to the curb, my heart racing, my head in my hands while Sebastian continued.

"Isaac was the first to die. No, make that the second. His father was most likely the first to go. What about the rest of his family? What about his mother and two sisters? They could have been saved. They could have gotten out. They were all in the very back rooms of the house. But they never knew what hit them. There was no working smoke detector in the house. They never had a chance."

Sebastian stopped, closed his eyes, and relived the tragic scene in his mind. My heart ached for him and for young Isaac and his family.

"There's no reason in the world for anyone to not have a working smoke detector in their home in this day and age. We give batteries and detectors away for free at the fire stations," he said, shaking his head in disgust. "End of story, end of interview," he said with eyes as dead as Isaac's.

Before I could say another word, Sebastian vanished. I sat on the curb for thirty minutes, imagining happier times for Isaac, his mother, father and two sisters. I imagined Isaac as a joyous, beautiful child full of whimsy and curiosity. I imagined that Isaac loved animals and when no one was watching, he'd cross the street and play with the array of stray mutts who were there now, wagging their tails in ecstasy and salivating uncontrollably, anticipating his arrival.

I imagined that Isaac was smart and popular and loved by everyone who came in contact with him. The Isaac I created in my mind was the child I wanted, the child I once carried but would never hold. My ringing cell phone pulled me out of my Isaac-induced stupor.

"What's up, Lace the Ace Band-Aid? Where are you? Are you putting out that fire all by yourself?" I heard Marsha ask through the phone.

"That's not funny, Marsh. A family of five died here tonight, including some children."

"Uhmmm, sorry. I didn't know. How you doin'? You know you don't handle death well. Are you okay? Do you need me to come get you?"

"I'm okay. Sebastard is here."

"I'm on my way. The fire was at Eighty-seventh and Newton, right? Don't move.

I'll see you in a few."

Ten minutes later, Marsha was sitting beside me with her arms around me. It took me another ten minutes to realize it.

"Hey, girlie. Howyadoin'?" Marsha asked.

"Three kids all under the age of ten died here tonight," I said, not really answering her question.

"Ace, don't. At least not here. Let's go home and then we can talk."

I continued on as if she hadn't said a word. "How do you handle this stuff day in and day out? How on earth can you cover the crime and drug beats? How do you deal with all the death and hopelessness?"

"I'm not like you. I don't wear my emotions on my sleeves. I'm impervious to getting emotionally involved with the subjects I write about."

By impervious I think she meant immune, but I was too distraught to be sure.

"You don't get emotionally involved? Remember when I did that story about the crackhead, Zoretha Smalls, who thought she could fly? You were emotionally involved then.

You were so involved that you couldn't write the article about her death."

"I know, and ever since then I've vowed to remain distant from the people I write about."

"I remember it so clearly. When I interviewed you about what happened, you explained it so matter-of-factly. You gave me all the facts, but not once did you talk about how you felt."

"I remember too. You gave me a lot of love, girl. You gave me co-writing credit for the article. You never pushed when you interviewed me. You sensed that I'd talk about it when I was ready, which I still can't do. I never told you this, but I appreciated the way you respected my boundaries," Marsha said, squeezing my hand.

"A five-year-old boy died in that fire. His name was Isaac. Did I tell you when I was pregnant, I was sure I was carrying twin boys? I wonder what Isaac was like."

"You used to talk about losing the twins all the time. Do you still think about it a lot? Do you still think about them?"

"Yeah," I said softly.

"I'm your best friend, and although I was there for you during that time, I can't really imagine what it must have been like for you."

Words couldn't describe what it was like. It was the worst, most unimaginable thing—losing a child, let alone two. It was especially tough for a woman like me who had previously succeeded at everything I'd ever tried. To not be able to sustain life, give birth, the most basic of a woman's birthrights, was incomprehensible to me. I had never before felt like such a failure.

Learning to accept that it wasn't my fault was hard and it took me a long, long time. Apparently, it took too long for Sebastian. As is common for a lot of women, I simply had a fibroid cyst. Unfortunately, mine was extremely large and in the worst place possible.

When I lost the twins, I felt that maybe if I'd had more female checkups the mass would have been detected sooner. I felt that maybe if I'd eaten better, exercised more, or had sex less, things would have been different. Maybe then my body would have been better equipped to carry the twins to term.

"Earth to Lacy Foxx. Did you hear me?" Marsha asked, shaking me lightly. "Sometimes I think the last thing on earth I want is to have children."

"I know you say that, but I don't believe you."

"I know. Nobody wants to believe it. Whenever someone hears that a woman doesn't want children, they automatically assume something is wrong with her. Just because I'm a woman doesn't mean I have to want children. That's a responsibility I know I'm not ready to handle now, and I wonder if I'll ever be ready," Marsha said.

"How can you not want children?"

"More and more young, professional women are choosing lifestyles that don't involve kids. Besides, men go around proclaiming they don't want children all the time and that's okay for them. They don't need a reason. Why do I?" Marsha asked.

"Personally, I have yearnings, desires. I want a husband, three kids, the white picket fence, the dog in the backyard— the American dream. For me, it all spells security, and that's something I've had very little of in my life, thanks to Mama's issues."

"Wanting kids? That's fine for you. As for me, I like kids as much as the next guy, as long as I can give them back to their mothers at the end of the day. I ain't tryin' to have no rug-rats running around behind me calling me Mama."

"Don't you believe our future depends on the next generation that people like you and me need to raise?"

"Without a doubt, I believe that children are our futures, our tomorrows. They need love and nurturing, but I'm not the one. I think I'd be a horrible mother. I'm not the nurturing and loveable, perfect Claire Huxtable type."

"Who is?" I asked.

"Besides, who needs the crap associated with having kids? First of all, there's that pesky labor thing. Women going quote-unquote into labor? What the heck is that about?"

I laughed. "You're nuts. Giving birth is a labor of love, or so they say."

"It's hard enough trying to be a decent, moral person in this world, and the last thing I want to do is bring a child into this craziness. Every week some jacked up kid goes off the deep end and starts shooting up his parents or playground or classmates or total strangers. And don't get me started on adults. This world is whack and it will just have to do without my offspring, thank ya very much."

"Don't you believe it's up to our generation to raise and look after the next generation of our race, just like the generation before us raised and looked after us? You know, each one teach one. Noblesse oblige: to whom much is given, much is expected."

"Of course. I'm looking after my younger brothas and sistahs. I give every year to youth charities. I volunteer at youth organizations all the time. I speak at schools. I let kids shadow me at work. I'm a mentor. I do my part."

"Even though I can't have my own kids, one day I'll adopt some."

"Well, you go ahead and adopt on, my sistah. Now that we've settled that, can we get up outta here?" Marsha asked. "This cement curb is kickin' my gluteus maximus."

Was this a G-word week?

"I'm right behind you," I said.

We both laughed at the bad pun and rose simultaneously from the curb, our spirits jointly rising above the ashes.

THIRTEEN

I had just walked into my cell the morning after the fire when the telephone on my desk rang.

"Glory be. I swear I'm gonna kill that old coot!"

It was my grandmother, who had an irritating habit of always jumping right into whatever she had to say over the phone without first saying hello.

"Hi, Bibi. What has Mr. Harrison done now?"

"You wanna know what that old goon has done?"

Not particularly! Fearing that she would launch into a long, detailed harangue and knowing I was facing a major deadline, I cut Bibi off.

"I'll tell you what. Why don't I come over after work and we can talk about it then? Heck, if I have to, I'll even go talk to Mr. Harrison myself."

"You'd do that for me, baby?"

"Of course, in a heartbeat. I'll see you at seven o'clock, okay?"

"All right, baby. See ya then. You know what tonight is."

I hung up the phone, licking my lips. Wednesday night was Italian meal night at my grandmother's. I wouldn't miss that for the world. I was just an average cook, so needless to say, I ate over at my grandmother's house a lot. I felt my stomach growl in anticipation as I envisioned the tasty Italian dishes that would await me after work. Between all of my meals at Bibi's and my favorite soul food restaurants, the Peach Tree and Red Vine, it was a wonder I didn't weigh a ton.

I loved my grandmother dearly, but her problems with her crazy old neighbor, Mr. Harrison, were working my patience. They had been squabbling for years. Personally, I thought the two of them liked each other but were too old, too stubborn and too doggone proud to admit it. For the women on my mama's side of the family, that was nothing new.

I'd come from a long line of proud and stubborn characters that were larger than life. My grandmother, Hannah Hale, was no exception. She'd spent her twenties pining after a man who wasn't ready or willing to get married and settle down. My grandmother had my Uncle Solomon and my mama, Rebecca, out of wedlock by him. For five years, he promised he'd marry my grandmother, and when he finally got around to doing it, the stupid fool got hit by a bus and died, three days before their wedding day.

Everyone said Bibi was never interested in men after that.

Around 7:00, I walked into my grandmother's tidy home. I was immediately overcome by the inviting smell of food coming from her kitchen. Bibi was always cooking for some function or another. There was always an abundance of made-from-scratch pies, cakes, cookies and dinner rolls. She could southern fry a sponge and make it taste scrumptious.

Bibi never ate out, because according to her, no one in the city was as good a cook as she was. I had to bite my tongue to keep from telling her about the Peach Tree and Red Vine.

Bibi's best friend, Mrs. Mary Mack, was visiting, along with her persistently yapping and spoiled 16-year-old white toy poodle, Lammy. The dog was named after television's Lamont Sanford, son of crazy TV junk dealer, Fred Sanford. Mrs. Mack's husband had been a huge fan of the 70s show, *Sanford & Son*. Bibi and I felt sorry for the dog. It was blind, senile and should have been put out of its misery years ago.

Mrs. Mack, whose eyes, nose and mouth were trapped in a sea of fatty, ocher-colored flesh that had long ago lost its elasticity, was a quiet, overweight, genteel southern woman. She came from a family with money, and although she didn't have a dime now, she acted as if she were an heiress. She was a refined and regal lady, the kind who sneezed and yawned daintily with her hand over her mouth, even when she was the only one in the room.

It always amazed me that my grandmother and Mrs. Mack were such good friends because Bibi was outgoing, outspoken and hip, while Mrs. Mack was the exact opposite. She was quiet and reserved, always the lady. Despite their differences, I loved them both dearly.

Growing up, I ate over at Bibi's house quite a bit. A lot of folks did, including a lot of single men from the church who all wanted to snag the best cook in town. Bibi, bless her heart, never showed a lick of interest in any of them.

Although she never really had a man of her own, there were plenty of offers.

Back when she was younger, while other women her age cleaned white folks' homes, Bibi was working as the city's first black nurse. At the hospital where she worked, sexual harassment had become a way of life for her. My grandmother's claim to fame was that she could have been the mistress of dozens of prominent white doctors living within a five-state area.

Whenever they hit on her, she would kindly put them in their place and that would be that. They knew Hannah didn't play. Her experiences are what precipitated the award-winning series I did on sexual harassment in the workplace.

"Glory be, Lacy Eymaleen Foxx! Why do you come over here daydreamin', chile?" Bibi asked, attacking me while I hung up my coat.

"I'm sorry, Bibi. Did you say something?"

"No, but Mary asked you a question. Pay attention, chile."

I looked attentively at the overweight Mary Mack.

Mary had a Little Lam, Little Lam, Little Lam
Mary had a Little Lam, whose butt was really old
And everywhere that Mary went, Mary went, Mary went
Everywhere that Mary went that damn dog got to go.

"Yap!" the blind, stupid dog cried out as it ran into the side of Bibi's console television.

"Lay-cy!"

"Yeah, Bibi?" I asked, realizing I'd zoned out again.

"Mary asked you another question."

"Yes, Mrs. Mack?"

"Leave her alone, Hannah. Can't you see she's thinking about a man?"

Bibi grunted. "A man? Why would ya want to think about one of those if you didn't have to?" One reason instantly came to mind. Obviously Bibi hadn't had sex for a while. "So, who is he? Who are his people? Have you two had sex?" Bibi asked.

There were some things I didn't care to talk about with my grandmother, and my sex life was one of those things.

"Ignore her, Lacy. Your grandma's just a big ole heapin' pot of crazy. Who cares who his people are?" I smiled at Mrs. Mack for rescuing me. "I, for one, think it's sweet that you have a new love interest and you're having sex," Mrs. Mack said.

"Who said anything about love or me having sex?" I asked, irritated and not feeling so rescued after all.

"Uhmmm," Bibi grunted. "Neither of ya got the good sense God gave ya."

"A lot of men's ears in this town are gonna be burning tonight. Tell me, Lacy. What do you think about this new situation between your grandmother and her neighbor, Mr. Harrison?"

"Bibi hasn't told me the latest in her continuing saga," I said, trying unsuccessfully to hide my sarcasm.

"Oh, that's right. Glory be. Let me tell you what he's done now . . . "

Bibi started her story, totally oblivious to my disinterest in the subject. Thirty minutes later, she finished her rant, and by then I was lightly snoozing.

"Are you daydreaming again? Did you hear what I said, Lacy Eymaleen Foxx? You promised me you'd talk to him."

"I did, didn't I?" I asked ruefully. "Okay, Bibi. What do you want me to say?"

"Tell the crazy nut to stop waking me up at four o'clock every morning. Why is he building that stupid storage shed in the middle of winter anyway? I'm thinking of suing him again. Every morning I wake up to his hammering and sawing. It's a noise nuisance. Plus, the doggone fool is bound to catch pneumonia!"

"It sounds to me like you're concerned about his well-being," I said, teasing.

"Hog wash! The only thing I'm concerned about is my beauty rest."

"Hannah, it is his property, you know. He's entitled to improve it any way he wants," Mrs. Mack said, arguing in Mr. Harrison's defense.

"But so early in the mornin'?" Bibi asked, irritated.

"Hannah, last year you were upset with him because of the kind of trees he planted in his front yard," Mrs. Mack said. "And before that it was his chain-link fence and carport."

"Both were poorly constructed eyesores. The judge ruled in my favor."

"Yeah, after you spent three days in jail for contempt," I said.

Like grandmother, like granddaughter. That was one of the many things we had in common—a rap sheet.

"I don't need you two reminding me of all the things he's done to annoy me over the years. Personally, I think he intentionally tries to irritate me."

"Just remember what happened the last time you two went before a judge. He said the third time's the charm, and if he saw you two in his courtroom again, he'd impose an alternative sentence and marry you both," I said, laughing.

"I'd like to see him try," Bibi said. "So, are you going to go talk to Cyrus or am I going to have to do it?"

"I'm going! I'm going! Heaven forbid there be blood shed over his storage shed," I said, reluctantly donning my winter coat and gloves.

By the time I reached Mr. Harrison's front door, he was standing in the doorway, grinning. "I wondered how long it would take her to sic you on me."

"Hi, Mr. Harrison," I said, greeting the tall, lanky, Ossie Davis lookalike as I stepped into his home.

From where I stood, evidence of Mr. Harrison's decades-long marriage to the same woman was spread throughout the living room and could be sensed throughout the whole house. Their home definitely had a woman's aura and feel about it, even though his wife had died five years earlier.

Cyrus Everette Harrison was a handyman's handyman. I remember when I was growing up that he basically tore his house down and rebuilt it to look totally different, with his own hands. For years I had tried to convince my grandmother to hire him to build an addition on her house, but in her proud way, she refused.

"Lacy, it's so good to see you," Mr. Harrison said as he took my coat. "Here, have a seat. I'm making some tea in the kitchen. Want some?"

"No thanks. I can't stay long. It's getting late and we still haven't eaten over at my grandmother's house."

"Ah, your grandmother is a fine cook. I remember when she used to invite my wife and I over for dinner on Sundays. Speaking of your grandmother, why is she upset with me this time?"

"Mr. Harrison, I hope you know this is really embarrassing for me, but my grandmother sent me over here to ask you why you're working on your storage shed at four o'clock in the morning. Apparently it's keeping her from sleeping. And trust me, she can be pretty grouchy when she doesn't get enough rest."

"Well, no offense, but that must happen a lot. She's pretty much grouchy all the time. At least she is with me."

"I know, I know. The older she gets the more challenging she gets."

"Challenging? Ah, spoken like a truly loving granddaughter. Lacy Foxx, I don't care what you say. You look like you're freezing. I'm gonna go get you a nice, hot cup of tea. I'll be right back," Mr. Harrison said.

While he rummaged around in the kitchen, I surveyed his living room. On the walls of his home, in the form of dozens of photographs, lay the story of his life.

"You know, when I was a kid, I used to love coming over here. I loved looking at your photos," I yelled to him in the kitchen. "Your grandchildren and I used to make up stories about the people in these pictures all the time."

"My grandkids loved playing with you and Gary whenever you visited your grandmother," he yelled back. "I think they used to get on her nerves because they were always over there asking her when you and your brother were coming to visit."

"Well, the next time you talk to Andrea, Colin, Pascha and Samuel, please tell them I said hello."

"I will. They'll be glad to know you asked about them."

I stared at the photos. There were pictures of Mr. Harrison and his wife, his parents, his brothers, sisters, friends and other relatives. There were also pictures of his two daughters, Celia and Etna; framed obituaries for his wife and daughters, all of whom died of cancer; and photos of his five grandchildren, Andrea, Anitra, Colin, Pascha and Samuel. Colin and Pascha were both stationed overseas in the Army, Samuel was a doctor in Los Angeles, Anitra died of a drug overdose years ago, and Andrea, who had Multiple Sclerosis, lived in a nearby assisted living facility.

"I've been blessed to have lived an extremely full life," Mr. Harrison said, returning to the living room.

"I see. Your family is so beautiful. I've always thought so."

"Do you recognize your grandmother?" he asked, pointing to a section of the wall that contained several shots of a beautiful, thin, smiling woman.

"Actually, I didn't. She was so pretty back then."

"Your grandmother was a real looker. She still is. I think my wife was a little jealous of her beauty," he said while handing me a cup of tea.

"Your wife was beautiful too," I said respectfully. When his wife was alive, Bibi and Mr. Harrison had gotten along fine. Things had only deteriorated since his wife's death, and for the life of me I couldn't figure out what had gone wrong.

"Yes, she was. My wife was definitely beautiful."

We both sipped our tea, privately reminiscing about the good old days for a few moments before either of us spoke again.

"So, Mr. Harrison, back to why I originally came over. Is it too much to ask for you not to work on your storage shed at four o'clock in the morning?"

"I can't believe your grandmother told you I'm up that early working on that shed. I can barely see in the dark, and all the artificial lighting in the world can't help me. I need lots of natural light. I'm never out there until the sun comes up and nowadays, that's usually seven o'clock. And if I'm moving really slowly, which is most of the time, I don't make it outside until eight."

"But my grandmother said—"

"I've learned from experience your grandmother has a tendency to exaggerate."

Ya think?

"That she does," I said. "And you'd think I would have learned my lesson by now. I'll tell you what. From now on, I'll keep my big, fat nose out of your business," I said respectfully, rising to my feet.

"Lacy, I don't mind," he said sincerely while also rising.

"Well, I do. Mr. Harrison, so that I can get a moment's peace where Bibi is concerned, would you mind sitting down with her and calling a truce?"

"That woman would never listen to me."

"Please. It would make life a lot easier on all of us," I said as we reached the door.

"Okay, I'll try."

"Thanks for being so tolerant and understanding. Bibi can be a bear sometimes."

"Yep. She sure can."

"Oh, by the way, she also wanted me to ask you why on earth are you working on that storage shed during the middle of winter. She seems really worried that you'll catch pneumonia."

"She said that? She's worried?"

"Uhmmm, I don't think she used that word exactly," I said, distinctly remembering the words "doggone fool."

"Neither one of you need to worry about me. I'm as strong as an ox."

"All right, but you be careful, okay? Take care of yourself."

"I will. It was nice seeing you again, Lacy. Don't be a stranger."

Walking back to Bibi's house, I couldn't help but reflect on how attractive Mr. Cyrus Everette Harrison was for a man in his seventies. He was indeed the spitting image of the deceased and distinguished actor, Ossie Davis. Mr. Harrison's wife had been dead for five years and the handsome old devil needed someone to share his twilight years with. And Lord knows Bibi needed a man. Boy, I had some serious work to do.

"What did he say? What did he say? What did he say?" my grandmother asked before my foot crossed the threshold of her door.

"He said he has never worked on that shed before seven o'clock."

"What? Glory be. Is he callin' me a liar?"

"Nooo . . . just an exaggerator."

"I guess I could have misread my clock. My eyes ain't what they used to be."

"Bibi, why did you lead me to believe he's been waking you up?" I asked.

"He has been! I'll admit that he hasn't been waking me up at four o'clock. But whether he is waking me up at four or seven, the fact remains that he is waking me up."

"You and Mr. Harrison need to call a truce. You guys have got to work out some kind of compromise, because I can't keep butting into that man's business."

"You tell her, Lacy!" Mrs. Mack said, cheering me on.

"It's late and I'm exhausted. I'm going home."

"But you haven't eaten yet," Bibi said.

"I'm too tired to eat. I'll take a rain check."

"But I made all of your favorite Italian dishes," Bibi said in protest.

"I know. Why don't you give my portion to Mr. Harrison? He looks like he could use a good home-cooked Italian meal."

"Well, he won't get one from me. Not in this lifetime! That man will starve before he ever gets any of my cooking," Bibi said before storming off into the kitchen.

"It was worth a try," Mrs. Mack said with a wink as I shook my head and closed my grandmother's front door behind me.

FOURTEEN

"So, how goes it, Ace?" Marsha asked a week later as we hung up our coats while waiting in line to be seated at our favorite soul food hangout, the Peach Tree. I ignored her and tugged on my suit, which was way too tight.

"This way, ladies," our pretty, young hostess said. As we walked past a muted-toned mural depicting "Life on the Vine" during the 1930s, I proudly surveyed our surroundings. I loved visiting the Peach Tree with its deep brown and maroon colors, elegant oversized furnishings including a breathtaking baby grand, and authentic black and white photography from the early 1900s.

Walking through the restaurant toward our table, I felt the eyes of the restaurant's mostly blue-collar male clientele upon us. Marsha, who loved the attention, was shrink-wrapped in a long cranberry- colored skirt and matching cashmere sweater, which accentuated her usually non-existent bosom. I, however, felt extremely self-conscious and repeatedly tugged on my red wool DKNY double-breasted suit.

The Peach Tree was a fabulous restaurant located in midtown Kansas City's historic 18th and Vine area, a neighborhood that back in its heyday had been the jazz capital of the world. According to Bibi, in the early to middle 1900s, the area was known not only for its jazz, but it had one of the city's largest concentrations of African-Americans who frequented dozens of prosperous black-owned and operated businesses.

Bibi used to tell me about the proud, impeccably dressed and coifed Negroes going in and out of large, ornate, regal buildings and polished, freshly painted storefronts. All of those businesses were long gone, but the area was slowly being redeveloped. Now places like The Peach Tree and Red Vine restaurants, the Blue Room (a jazz club), the Negro League's Baseball Museum, the Kansas City Jazz Museum, and a few other long-standing businesses and organizations, like the Black Chamber of Commerce and the black-owned *Kansas City Call* newspaper, were banding together to revitalize the area.

At one time, Kansas City's first and only African-American mayor and mostly African-American city council had high hopes of returning the wonderful 18th and Vine area to its former glory. Thankfully, the Peach Tree was one of the area's successes, and I believed that frequenting the restaurant and stuffing my face with authentic soul food was the least I could do in the name of progress.

"So, how goes it?" Marsha asked again while we looked over our menus.

My mouth watered as I surveyed my favorite menu offerings of fried chicken, catfish, fried shrimp, macaroni and cheese, red beans and rice, sweet potato cornbread and corn on the cob. I felt like Judas betraying Jesus as I imagined what my grandmother would say if she knew I was eating soul food cooking that was as good as hers.

"How goes what?" I asked, motioning to our waitress. After we ordered, Marsha continued.

"Life at the YC."

"I've been volunteering there for a while now and I'm not even sure. I really like working with the kids, but the supposed adult role models are a trip, Mr. T. included."

"Things have been crazy. I can't keep up with you. I can barely keep up with myself. I need a drink," Marsha said, interrupting me.

"You know they don't serve liquor here, and you know I'm trying to give that up."

"Whatever. Okay, back to the Youth Center. With the fire and everything that's been happening with my new job, we haven't had the chance to really talk. Why are you all frowned up? Don't tell me! Mr. T. got a gander at your nasty bits, didn't he?"

"Ohhh . . . shhh. You sound like Bibi," I said, unable to look up.

"Look at you. Ya can't even look at me. He got more than a gander! You slept with him, didn't you? So, was he any good?" Marsha asked. She had a litany of tacky questions that I chose not to answer. "A'ight, a'ight, a'ight! Give it up. Let's hear all the gory details."

"Okay, you know I didn't attend his career fair, but we met afterwards for dinner. He took me to 40 Sardines and didn't even flinch when I ordered the most expensive thing on the menu."

"I know all that from your message. Give me some of the more intimate details."

"We talked for a while at the restaurant about our careers, his volunteering, our families and then we went to my place."

"Was 'the sty' clean?" Marsha asked.

"Yeah, for a change," I said with a laugh.

"Good, I guess there's a first time for everything."

"Now, here's the part you don't know about. We were sitting there on my couch, chillin', and the next thing I knew, we were doing the mattress mambo."

"What? I thought I taught you better than that. You are such a ho!"

"Takes one to know one. Don't forget you had sex with Patrick on your first date too. And to be clear, I am not a ho. I just have ho-like tendencies," I said, giggling.

"First Sebastard and now Mr. T.? Girl, who knew you had a randy streak?"

Great, an R-word week. I searched the far recesses of my long-term memory for rarely used words. I believed randy meant lustful, but I wasn't sure. "So, I'm asking you again. Was he any good?" Marsha queried, disrupting my inner word search.

"He was a'ight. I wouldn't kick him out of bed for eating pork rinds," I said.

"So, what are you gonna do now?"

"Nothin'. The next day, I saw him at the YC and told him we'd made a mistake. He agreed and that was that. He's pretty much left me alone ever since."

"Hmmm . . . So, you did what you always do, huh Band-Aid? You ran before you could get hurt. Just like you did with Sebastard. What's wrong with you? You want the security of a loving and committed relationship, but you never want to do the work it takes to make it happen. Why are you so timorous, so skittish when it comes to men?"

"In Wynn's case, we work together now. Who needs silly complications?"

"Well, I, for one, am proud of you. At least you got some. Two men in one month—that's a record for you," she said with more pride than I felt.

Make that two men and a hairy primate—almost, I thought, glad I'd neglected to tell her about my close encounter with The Creature.

"I just hope you know you ain't foolin' nobody. You slept with that man to prove a point, didn't you?"

"I don't know what you're talkin' 'bout," I lied.

Marsha rolled her eyes at me. "Don't front. Yeah, you do. You wanted to prove to him and to yourself that while on one hand he's repulsed by you, being the selfish, bougie ghetto princess that you are, on the other hand he's extremely attracted to you."

"Are you through analyzing me?" I asked.

"Nope. So, am I right?"

"Maybe."

"Great minds think alike. I would have done the same thing. Do you think he's figured out what you were up to?"

"Who cares?"

"So, what's with the games? That's not like you. You're usually a straight shooter when it comes to men," Marsha said.

"He had it coming."

"I'm not saying he didn't. It's just that games will get you nowhere fast. Take it from me. I know. My advice to you is to cut out the nonsense."

"Since it's official that he and I can't stand each other, that should not be a problem. Now, that's enough about me. Tell me what's going on with you," I said between spoonfuls of black-eyed peas.

"Patrick and I are going out again tomorrow."

"You're kidding! That makes how many dates now since you two met?"

"Twenty-five. But who's counting?" she said.

"You are."

"Okay, true, although I'm not sure how long it will last. He smokes and he's overweight and out of shape. You know I like my men athletic and active."

"He sounds like a 911 emergency medical call waiting to happen," I said.

"With all the sex we're having, I better brush up on my CPR," she said, chuckling.

"Speaking of . . . how is the sex?" I asked.

"Let's just say I'm thanking God for it every day. It's the best I've ever had."

"Really? Well, may you and your hot tail continue to be blessed," I said, holding up my glass of water for a toast.

"Let the church say amen!" Marsha said in agreement as we clinked glasses.

FIFTEEN

The next evening, I found myself in the library at the Youth Center moving a box full of items onto a high shelf. I was making quite a spectacle of myself. I was having a pretty hard time, which was obvious to everyone including Wynn, who finally took pity on me and offered to help. I was overwhelmed by his presence, although I worked hard to make sure he didn't know it. It was the first time we had been alone together in a room since I confronted him about The Weebil.

"Need some help?" Wynn's deep voice asked from behind me.

Just as the words "I don't need a doggone thing from you," were leaving my lips, the box toppled over.

Dagnabit!

"You were saying?" he asked smugly while bending down to help me gather the box's contents. "I'm not the enemy, ya know."

I clinched my lips together and glared at him. "You could have fooled me."

He smiled. "I keep hearing a lot of good things about your program. Word on the street is the kids love it."

"Smart kids. Smarter than some adults I know."

"Lacy, I know we got off on the wrong foot. I didn't know you well back then, but now I'm trying. I'm trying to get to know you better."

"What do you want, a prize? I took a lot of abuse from Voncile while you did nothing. You helping me pick up a few books and some papers isn't gonna erase the hard feelings that have festered because of our earlier issues."

"Why are you so angry? Did I miss something? Weren't we once intimate? Wasn't there once something between us? At one time, weren't you feelin' me like I was feelin' you?"

"Don't remind me. Yeah, there was something between us, albeit briefly."

"What is it with you? Why are you making this so hard? I'm trying to apologize for what's happened in the past. Can't you be gracious enough to accept my apology? Can't we call a truce? We're all going to be working together a long time. It would help if we could get along."

"You're right. I'm tired of fighting. We're all on the same team. We're all supposed to be here for the kids. We should be able to work together. Okay, truce," I said, shaking his outstretched hand.

"Now that we have that out of the way, can I ask you a little favor?"

"I should have known you wanted something."

"We don't have enough volunteers here to accompany the kids on an outing to the ice skating rink. We're leaving in a few and I was hoping—no, praying that you could help out."

"I'm not really feeling up to skating tonight," I said.

"What? You can't skate? Afraid I'll show you up?"

"This ain't junior high. That reverse psych mess ain't gonna work on me."

Wynn laughed. "Come on. Please say you'll help out. You don't have to do much. We just need another warm adult body there."

"Another warm adult body? Is that all I am?"

"You're forgetting I've seen you naked. In your case, you're another *fine* warm adult body."

"Compliments will get you everywhere."

"Yeah, but will they get you to the ice skating rink?"

"Maybe."

"Really? Great! Come on!" he said, grabbing my hand with his hand and my heart with his smile.

That evening at the ice skating rink, I discovered Wynn Trust wasn't the monster I'd made him out to be. We were two of only five adults chaperoning fifty kids, and watching him interact with the kids up close and personal, opened my heart to him in a way I would have never thought possible.

Also that evening, I learned some things about Trey Jenkins. He and Shequita Bell, the other YC member I'd interviewed, were no longer friends, although Trey was vague about the reason. Not only that, but I witnessed Trey get into a vicious fight with another boy who Trey claimed owed him $500. Trey didn't have a job, but it wasn't hard to figure out how a kid his age got his hands on that kind of money. I hoped for Trey's sake that he wasn't falling prey to his environment. I hoped that he hadn't turned to a life on the streets and started dealing.

I was surprised by the rage I witnessed in Trey. Gone was the nice, handsome young man I met the day after my birthday. In his place was a gnarling maniac full of enough hate and rage to fill a man well beyond his size and years.

On the way back to the YC, long after things had died down, the adult chaperones sitting in the front of the bus expressed concern about Trey's increasingly violent behavior. I wrote it off as a teenage phase. They, on the other hand, didn't seem convinced.

"The boy is hangin' by a thread," Vic, the only male chaperone other than Wynn said. "He's been expelled from school twice in the last few weeks for fighting. He's been kicked off the school basketball team. Not to mention he was arrested for shoplifting."

Although Trey was helping me out with my journalism sessions, he'd failed to mention any of this to me.

"And I've even seen him around the neighborhood smoking and drinking," a smallish woman in her sixties volunteered.

"Are we talking about the same child? Trey Jenkins?" I asked.

"Yes, Lacy. We're talking about Trey Jenkins," Wynn said solemnly, locking eyes with mine. "He is not the same kid he was when you first met him and Shequita at the Gala."

"Did the thought ever occur to you he needs—"

"What, Lacy? What does he need? What? Why don't you tell the boy he just got into a fight with what he needs? Why don't you tell his P.O. what he needs?" Wynn suggested cynically.

Trey has a probation officer?

"He needs a good butt whippin' if you ask me," Vic said, volunteering an answer.

After the Youth Center trip to the ice skating rink, I made a concerted effort to grow closer to Trey in hopes that I could help him. In addition to him assisting me with my journalism sessions, we ate dinner together regularly in the Youth Center's cafeteria, and during those times, he shared openly his dreams, hopes and fears. I also attended his weekly basketball games and helped him with his homework. He was like the little brother I once had but lost long ago.

My relationship with Wynnton Trust also progressed. We actually became civil and downright cordial to one another. With time, we became extremely close and our friendship soon blossomed into something much deeper.

In the six months following the trip to the ice skating rink, our relationship became a virtual whirlwind of activity. As the head volunteer of the Youth Center and the CEO/president of his own company, Wynn enjoyed numerous honorariums for his outstanding work in the community. He benefited from perks and creature comforts like those bestowed upon CEOs of major billion-dollar corporations. He received free tickets to concerts, football games, baseball games and other sporting events. Plus, there were invitations to upscale, swank galas and soirees, and at every event, I was there beaming on Wynn's arm. I felt like Cinderella who had stayed too long at the ball. But Wynn's ride never turned into a pumpkin, and I never lost my glass slippers.

When we weren't enjoying amazing new relationship sex—surreal between-the-sheets rendezvous every weekday and twice on Saturday and Sunday—we were hanging out with the who's who, doing the what's what of Kansas City. We even scheduled standing dates with Marsha and Patrick every Friday night, and throughout the week and on the weekends, we spent plenty of time with Wynn's son, Édonte.

As our relationship developed, I looked forward to seeing Wynn like a chocoholic looks forward to that next piece of chocolate. I faced each day like a junkie anticipating the next fix. Each moment was sweeter and more delicious with every mouth-watering, savory bite.

We called each other at work each day and saw each other at my home after work every night. We celebrated each other's joys, victories, triumphs, passions and loves and cursed each other's pains, failures and disappointments. Moonlit strolls, opulent shopping excursions, long weekend drives, romantic picnics, candlelit dinners, adventurous outings, passionate lovemaking sessions, and confessions of undying love became the order of the day.

Halfway through our whirlwind getting-to-know-each-other phase, Wynn met my family during one of Bibi's much-anticipated Italian meal nights. And while my daddy, uncle and Mrs. Mack were civil and gracious, the same could not be said for my grandmother. Bibi not-so-subtly insulted Wynn no fewer than a half dozen times by making it clear that she was sure Sebastian and I would eventually get back together as a couple.

Despite Bibi's disdain for our relationship, for six whole months, Wynn and I were awash in emotions and feelings that like caffeine injected into our bloodstreams, awakened our minds, bodies and souls. When we finally came up for air more than half a year after we'd met, we were hopelessly and shamelessly devoted to one another and very much in love.

******

"I hate living vicariously through you, Band-Aid," Marsha said one evening as we worked late. "What fabulous thing are you and Wynn doing tonight?"

"Probably dinner at my place. Pretty fab, huh?"

"What? Finally you two sound as boring as Patrick and me. But you still haven't been to his place yet, have you? You've been dating him for six months! What's he waiting for? What's he hiding? You should have Googled his behind a long, long time ago."

"Excuse me?"

"That or you can Lex Nex him. He's probably lying about his supposed business, or he's probably still married. Want me to give you the number of a good P.I.?"

"If Wynn is not being on the up and up, that will come out eventually. I'm not gonna Google him. I'm not running a Lexus Nexus search on him, and I'm not hiring a private detective. That spying crap is for the birds and for women who don't trust their men. I totally trust Wynn," I said.

"We're all naïve and blind at the beginning, girl. But as I recall, not too long ago you were a member of the women who don't trust their men club. Need I remind you of Charron's phone numbers you found in Sebastard's Blackberry?"

"Sometimes we're better off not knowing what we think we want to know. My days as Inch High Private Eye are over," I said.

"Let Wynn keep pulling the wool over your eyes if you want. When you've got a full-length wool coat, let me know, because I'm gonna want to wear it," Marsha said before walking away.

After Marsha left, I thought long and hard about what she said. I typed in and deleted Wynn's name several times on the Google search page, but I couldn't force myself to press enter. I was secretly relieved when the phone rang.

"Hey, sweetness. Get off that computer. I want you to join me and Édonte for dinner tonight at my place," Wynn said through the phone as if reading my mind.

His breezy, nonchalant invite pissed me off. He clearly didn't realize the importance of his invitation. "Okay, I'll be there," I said, trying to sound just as breezy. "What's for dinner?"

"You'll find out when you get here. See ya at seven."

Before I could ask anything else, Wynn hung up. I knew he wasn't listed in the phone book, and I had to look for my notes from our first interview in order to find his address, which pissed me off even more.

An hour later, when I turned onto Wynn's street, I was shocked. A winding road lined with towering trees provided a graceful approach to his three-story mansion.

Wynn greeted me with a kiss on the cheek when he opened his front door. "I'm glad you're here. My son isn't joining us. He just informed me that he'd rather hang out with his friend next door instead of his dad and his dad's old lady."

Still stunned by the expanse of his home, I didn't respond. Wynn didn't seem to notice as he opened wide the door to his residence. I walked past him and stepped into a parquet-floored foyer that had on its left a banquet-sized dining room that led to an eat-in kitchen, complete with state-of-the-art appliances and a large center island. To the right of the foyer was a magnificent living room.

I followed Wynn into the living room, which was replete with skylights, a vaulted ceiling and a double-sided fireplace. From what I could see, the living room was adjacent to a mahogany-paneled library with built-in bookshelves. At the back of the library, double French doors opened onto a balcony overlooking a tennis court, basketball court, in-ground pool, and beautiful flower garden.

"Want a tour?" Wynn asked, seeming somewhat embarrassed.

I didn't answer him as he led me to the level below. Located on that level was an exercise room, four bedrooms, two generous bathrooms and a den. Wynn then escorted me up a sweeping spiral staircase to the next level of luxury, where the master bedroom and bath took up a third of the floor. Two additional bedrooms with baths and a large office shared the top floor. Portal windows, a stucco exterior, a built-in entertainment center and other built-in, one-of-a-kind features added to the home's uniqueness.

The house hinted of a woman's touch. It was tastefully decorated with an interesting mix of textures, color schemes and feminine and masculine furnishings. As much as I hated to admit it, Wynn's wife, Jacqui, had exquisite taste, even if she was a cold-hearted tramp.

"So, what do you think?" Wynn asked when we returned to the living room.

Minus two hundred and fifty stupid points!

"I think I'm leaving," I said as I grabbed my purse and headed for the door.

"What? Where are you going?" he asked.

"I gotta get out of here."

"What? Why?"

"I had no idea you were living like this, Wynn. Whathahell?"

"You're mad at me because I'm rich?"

"No, I'm mad at you because we've been together six months and I feel like I don't even know you. Like I said, I had no idea you were ballin' like this. I feel really stupid. I didn't even know your friggin' address. I had to look it up in my notes from our interview!"

"There is no reason for you to feel stupid. Money makes people funny. I don't let just anybody know how I'm really living. When it comes to that, I'm pretty secretive."

"So I noticed."

"Particularly when it comes to women. I have a six month rule," he said.

"You have a what?" I asked.

"Because of my young son, I don't let just anybody come around. I can't have him getting too attached to women who may not be around long. Plus, I never reveal my true worth to a woman until we've dated at least six months. And for us, we've been dating exactly six months. Today is our six month anniversary, to the day."

The fact that he was aware of that and I wasn't impressed me, but not enough to keep me from being angry. "You, your six month rule *and* your six-month-to-the-day anniversary can kiss my ass!" I yelled as I walked to the door. I fiddled around with the door's locks but couldn't get the door to open.

I didn't care what he said. It had taken Wynn much longer than it should have to invite me to his house—rules or not! Until recently, he had always been vague about how he made his living, and while it bothered me, I pretended it didn't. I hid my true feelings because I didn't want him thinking I was a gold digger who was only after his money.

"Lace, just sit down a minute. Let me explain some things to you," Wynn said as he led me back to his living room. What he explained was the extent of his personal wealth and that of his family's.

"My dad is worth millions. So am I. My mom and dad came from working class, actually poor families from Little Rock. They grew up down the street from one another. My dad only had one older brother and an older sister. My mother had three brothers and two sisters. My dad loved going over to my mom's house because with all those kids around there was always something going on. To hear them tell it, they've loved each other since they were five. Disgusting, isn't it?"

"No, I think it's romantic," I said, warming up to him after hearing about his family.

"Anyway, my dad received a track scholarship from the University of Kansas and my mom followed him to Lawrence. After he graduated, they moved to Kansas City and got married."

The more Wynn talked, the more the inquisitive reporter in me took over and my anger began to dissipate. "How did he end up so successful?" I asked.

"With the help of some white friends from college, he started an automobile repair shop, Midwest Auto, and the business grew like crazy. Eventually he bought them out, and now it's all his."

"And your dad helped you get started with your business, right?"

"Yep. After I turned twenty-one, my dad gave my brother, my sister and me thirty thousand dollars each to see how we would manage our money. It was a test to gauge how well we would eventually run his company, once he was ready to give up the helm," Wynn said.

"And from the looks of things now, I'm guessing you excelled," I said.

"You know how I roll. I was the only one who managed to make my money grow. While I was in college, me and two computer-nerd friends started WebScape."

"I still don't know what your company does. Looks like I'm gonna have to Google you to get a straight answer. I was just about to do that tonight when you called."

"Really? You were going to do a background check on me?"

"Yeah, in this day and age, what choice does a woman have? Like you, a lot of men aren't exactly forthcoming. The truth is Marsha was pushing me into it, but I just couldn't do it. I thought anything you wanted to tell me, you'd tell me eventually."

"I know this has been tough on you and I'm sorry. I have been pretty secretive."

"Well, now that you're opening up, I want to know everything. You run this computer software company that specializes in information systems. Isn't that kinda vague? You sure that ain't code for 'I'm a drug dealer'? "

"Hah, funny girl. Everybody thought I was crazy investing $30,000 into the company. Plus, I had to work around the clock to get us some clients. And at the time, I didn't know anything about computers or computer programming. My boys had to teach me everything from scratch," Wynn said.

"But once you got the company's first client, your business grew, right?"

"Yep. We got a hospital software contract, then word spread and we got software development deals with some of the largest corporations in America. The company grew due to high-profile contracts, stock splits and a booming economy, and the rest, as they say, is history."

"Hmmm . . ." I said thoughtfully. "Wynn, you gotta promise me from now on you'll be more honest with me. We'll never survive if you hide important things about your life from me."

"You're right. No more hiding anything. I promise. Now, can we properly celebrate our six-month anniversary?" he asked as he stood, extending his hand.

I grabbed his hand and rose, smiling.

SIXTEEN

"We're gonna see the Mothership," Wynn said one rainy Saturday morning in early August during breakfast at his place.

"The moon is made of cheese," I said, countering catastrophically.

"What?" he asked, staring at me blankly.

A sly grin spread across my face. "I thought we were speaking in code," I said innocently.

"Even if we were speaking in code, what would that be code for?"

"Don't know, do ya?"

"There's one thing I do know. You're crazy."

"And that's why you love me, right?"

"That's not why I love you, sweetness," he said, throwing a Cheerio down my pajama top. "That's why."

"You are such a perv," I said, fishing out the Cheerio.

"What I meant was my brother asked me if we'd like to go to Sinbad's Slammin' Seventies Summer Jam Concert with him and his wife, Kim. It's next Sunday, the day after my birthday. Some of their friends backed out at the last minute."

"Are you kidding? Yeah, I wanna go! Who's performing?"

"You're the entertainment reporter. Don't you know?"

"No. You've had me a little distracted lately," I said as I climbed into his lap. He smiled.

"George Clinton is coming with the P-Funk All-Stars, and they're bringing the Mothership. Plus there's Funkadelic, KC & The Sunshine Band, Cheryl Lynn, Evelyn Champaign King, the Isley Brothers, Cameo, The Brothers Johnson and Natalie Cole."

"I'll see if the SOB will let me cover it, and then I'll be able to get backstage passes."

"That would be sweet."

"Hey, remember all of those great songs we used to listen to?" I asked as memories of the Seventies flooded my head.

"What do you remember about the Seventies? You weren't born until the late Seventies."

"My mama always filled the house with music. She loved Seventies R&B music and so did I. I remember it like it was yesterday."

"Man, those were the days. Who was your favorite group?" Wynn asked.

"Heatwave," I said without hesitation.

"That was mine too. I loved 'Groove Line.' Boy, that was the cut."

I jumped up from his lap and started singing and dancing. He quickly joined me.

"Leave your worries behind, 'cause rain, shine, don't mind. We're ridin' on the groove line tonight, oh-oh!"

We sang in unison and fell over each other onto the sofa, laughing. It was the first time in long time that I'd been so happy. I was finally going to meet his family, on his birthday in exactly one week, and then we were going to the Slammin' Seventies Summer Jam Concert the next day. I pinched myself a dozen times to make sure I wasn't dreaming as Wynn and I spent the morning singing, dancing, talking and reminiscing.

I had mostly good memories of the Seventies. For years, Mama's brother, Uncle Sol, entertained me, my brother and all of the neighborhood kids with stories of Never Never Land. Once a year, he'd pack us up, blindfold us and drive us to the outskirts of town where he would dump us in a huge field full of trees, which he and some of his friends had decorated earlier with candy, fruit, money, books and toys.

All of us children would spend the rest of the day pulling a plethora of treasures off the trees and listening to the older men's fabulous tall tales. Even at the age of nine, when I stopped going to Never Never Land because I considered myself "too grown," deep down I regretted staying behind.

For years, whenever my parents responded to my requests for money with the universal parental retort, "Do you think money grows on trees?" I'd always tell them yes. At least it did in Never Never Land.

My uncle and his wife, who died a few years earlier of a mysterious ailment, had never had kids, and that always saddened me because he was so good with my brother and me — with a few notable exceptions. Throughout my childhood, he jokingly called me Half-Pretty Lacy. He did so oblivious to the fact that if half of me were pretty, the other half of me *had* to be ugly. I'd spend hours in the mirror trying to figure out which half of me was which.

Had I not been so enchanted with my uncle, I'd probably still be in therapy today because of the Half-Pretty Lacy nickname given to me during such a critical stage of my development. When I got older, my uncle explained that he called me that because he wanted me to realize there were more important things to focus on in life than looks. I didn't have the heart to tell him that his moniker had the opposite affect. It instead made me focus on my looks almost to the point of obsession.

Growing up, my uncle and I had been extremely close and we still were. I was glad that he, my father, and grandmother — the only living relatives I had that I knew — were going with me to Wynn's birthday party bash.

My family was on cloud nine because on the day after Wynn's birthday, they were leaving for a church conference in Louisiana. I hoped their planned trip would keep their spirits high and prayed that our family's first meeting with the Trust family wouldn't be a disaster like a reunion between the Hatfields and the McCoys.

To say that I was apprehensive about meeting Wynn's family for the first time was an understatement. But as far as I was concerned, this meeting was overdue. Wynn and I had been together for seven months, and I was beginning to get the sinking feeling that I hadn't yet met his family because he wasn't taking our relationship nearly as seriously as I was.

From what I gathered, Wynn's huge family contrasted sharply with my own. My daddy's birth parents, Harold and Sally Foxx, abandoned him when he was two years old. At the age of three he went to live with a foster family that never showed him any love or affection. To the Smith family, my daddy was just a monthly paycheck. They anticipated with bated breath the $400 a month they received from the state and federal governments for putting a roof over his head and food in his belly.

When my daddy turned eighteen, he left Lake Charles, Louisiana, enlisted in the Army and became estranged from his foster parents. He met my mama when he went on leave with his roommate, my Uncle Sol, who was from Kansas City. According to my daddy, Mama was like no woman he'd ever met before. He was completely enamored by her. She blew him away. She was larger than life, just like the women in her family before her. After they married, for the first time in his life, my father felt loved.

My father was a quiet, gentle soul. Mama was just the opposite. When I was young, she seemed free-spirited and moody. Her moods were like a pendulum, swinging her from one extreme emotion to the other. Her moods were actually caused by her bipolar disorder, although she controlled it as best she could with Lithium, Depakote and other psychotropic drugs.

Sometimes when I looked at Daddy, he looked older than he should. He was only fifty, but his years of loving a bipolar depressive made him look older.

The memories I had of Mama's illness were few and far between. I remembered her lying in bed not moving for what seemed like weeks on end. I also remembered not being able to get anything but necessities for more than a year because she had written thousands of dollars worth of bad checks and didn't remember doing it. Plus, I remembered her disappearing periodically, once for as long as a year. When she did this, my brother and I would go live with Bibi.

In a psychology class I took as a high school junior, I learned the truth about the pills my mother was always popping. But the pills hadn't been enough to keep her together when my brother died. Mama and I had always been close, but I knew my brother was her favorite, so it came as no surprise to me or anyone else when she accidentally took a toxic dose of her pills to dull the pain of Gary's death.

On my mother's side, since her grandmother had been cut off from the family, I didn't know any of my relatives, who I assumed lived mostly in Michigan. My great-grandparents had died decades earlier. My great-grandfather, Frederrick Hale, was shot more than a dozen times and then hung by a gang of white men when he bravely attacked them as they tried to rape my great-grandmother. In the end, Eymaleen was raped, she lost an eye, and she barely escaped with her life and the life of her only child, Hannah.

Legend has it that Eymaleen never had a kind word to say about men after her husband was killed and Bibi, for the most part, inherited that trait from her mother.

I didn't know much about Wynn's family, but from what I had gathered, contrary to my own family, it seemed like he had tons of relatives and I couldn't wait to meet them.

A few hours after Wynn announced we were going to the concert, I drove to the YC to pick up some materials I needed for work the following week. As I entered the building, I ran into Trey.

"What's crackin', Li'l Miss Reporter? Whatcha doin' here today?"

"I had to pick up a few things. After I leave here, I have to run some errands, but I need you to do me a favor, Trey."

"Name it."

"I'm going to Sinbad's Slammin' Seventies Summer Jam Concert in a week and to keep me in the mood for the concert, I want you to download onto a CD for me some old school joints off the Internet. I'll pay you twenty bucks an hour if you do this for me. I'm just too busy to do it myself."

"What songs do you want?"

"I'll put together a list and I'll give you my credit card to pay for it."

"Okay, bet."

We walked together to the library. I put together a list of thirty songs I wanted and the artists who sang them. I gave Trey the list, along with my credit card, my business card with a work address, and a couple of CDs.

"I'm just going shopping for a Seventies outfit and I'll be right back."

"Take your time. This is gonna take a minute," Trey said as he sat down at the nearest computer.

I grabbed the papers I originally came for and then left. Two hours later, after finding the perfect Seventies gear, I returned to the YC. Trey was just finishing my CDs when I arrived.

"Here they are. These are masterpieces," he said grandly as he handed me the two CDs. "And just in case you've forgotten the words to the songs, I printed off lyric sheets for each one. They're in the same order as what's on the CDs," he said, handing me the lyric sheets.

"Ah, Trey. You're a sweetheart. Here, let me pay you. I owe you forty dollars, right?"

"No need. I took care of it," he said.

"What do you mean? How?"

"I charged a forty-dollar shirt on seanjohn.com to your credit card."

"What? Who said you could do that, Trey?" I asked incredulously.

"You said you were gonna pay me," he said defensively.

"But saying I'm gonna pay you forty dollars and you charging forty dollars on my credit card without my permission are two different things! A lot of folks would call what you did stealing," I said.

"I'm sorry. You want me to cancel my order?"

"No, no, forget it," I said, remembering I was dealing with a child who had never had much, a child who had struggled all his life. "Just don't ever let anything like this happen again, okay?"

"Okay, okay. I won't."

An awkward silence enveloped us as he handed me my credit card and logged off the computer.

"It's kind of quiet around here for a Saturday, isn't it?" I asked, making small talk while we walked out of the library together and down the hallway.

"Yeah. Most of the younger kids are on a field trip, and the old heads are watching *Rush Hour* for the billionth time," he said, laughing.

"Thanks again, Trey, for the songs, not to mention the debt," I said, once we arrived at the YC's outer doors.

"Ms. Foxx, I promise nothing like that will ever happen again. I promise."

"It better not, Trey. It better not," I said as I walked out the door.

The minute I got in my car, I pulled my credit card out of my purse and dialed the customer service number on the back. When I finally got through to a human being, with more than a tad bit of guilt, I cancelled the card.

SEVENTEEN

A week after the credit card fiasco, I arrived at the home of Wynn's parents with the rest of my family in tow. Unfortunately, my worst fears were realized.

As usual for August, it was a scorcher. I hadn't stopped sweating since getting out of bed. Needless to say, I was dehydrated and not feeling my best. But I felt even worse as I approached the elder Trusts' home.

From a distance, I could tell their residence was even more spectacular than their son's. When I knocked on the huge mahogany front door, Wynn's mother, Elaine Trust, appeared. She was a tall, slender, well-preserved woman whose cocoa-colored face bore the wrinkles of a woman who had raised three kids and led a full life. She was wearing an expensive-looking gray Calvin Klein silk pantsuit. Her short salt-and-pepper hair, styled in pre-weave Halle Berry fashion, framed her face. The unmistakable scent of Jessica McClintock enveloped her.

"Hello, I'm Wynn's mother. You must be Lacy," she said in a friendly nasal tone as she hugged me. "My, aren't you attractive?" she said admiringly while twirling me around like a deformed and ill-trained ballerina.

"Hello, Mrs. Trust. It's so nice to finally meet you."

My diva radar and fraud detector were both in working order, but their alarms never sounded. Mrs. Trust's snooty, upscale look contrasted sharply with her obviously loving, down-home heart. I immediately liked Wynn's mother, even if she did look me over like a slave being examined by prospective owners before being purchased. I half expected her to ask me to bare my teeth or comment on the fact that I was hippy and looked like I was from good birthing stock.

"Mrs. Trust, I'd like you to meet my family," I said awkwardly, feeling like a young child speaking before a large class on the first day of school. "This is Bibi—I mean my grandmother, Hannah Hale, my father, Harold Foxx, and my uncle, Solomon Hale," I said, barely able to get the words out.

"Nice meeting you all. Lacy, why don't you go find Wynn? Don't worry about your people. I'll keep them entertained. You and I can talk later. Everyone around your age is outside. Just go down the hallway and out the back."

I entered the home and was stunned by how beautiful it was inside. From what I could tell, the house—or shall I say mansion—had several levels. There was either marble, solid wood or gold inlays on every inside surface of the house. On the garden level that we were on, a block-long view of their exquisite garden located on the southern side of the home was visible.

Also inside on the garden level, a breathtaking collection of modern art was nicely balanced with antique-looking Queen Anne style furniture and one-of-a-kind light fixtures. Smiling faces of people of various shades, shapes, sizes and ages peered out from an endless selection of ornate picture frames.

Once I finally made it outside, the bright sunlight temporarily blinded me and I failed to notice Wynn walking toward me with two women walking doggedly behind him.

"Hey, sweetness, I'm glad you're here," Wynn said, greeting me with a kiss.

"How's my birthday baby?" I asked as I gave him a bear hug.

"I'm good. Lacy, this is my sister, Nya, and you know Voncile."

"Hi, Nya. I've heard a lot about you. It's nice meeting you," I said, greeting his sister eagerly with an outstretched hand. "Hey, Voncile." *Silence.*

"Hi," a young voice said from somewhere in the vicinity of my kneecaps.

"Hi, Perri with an I," I said, welcoming the tension relief. "Are you having fun, baby?" I asked as I bent down and pinched her full cheeks.

"Yeah, baby, fun?" Perri asked, modeling me.

"Perri, leave folks alone," The Weebil said, chastising her young daughter.

"So, Lacy, you're a reporter?" Nya asked in a disinterested voice.

"Yeah, I am. I'm covering Sinbad's Slammin' Seventies Summer Jam Concert tomorrow, as a matter of fact. It should be one of my more exciting assignments. Are you going to the concert with us?"

"No," she said in a beyond-bored tone. "I'm not as corny as my brothers."

"Lacy, did I ever tell you that Nya majored in journalism in college too?" Wynn asked, eager to help us find common ground.

"So, what do you do now, Nya?"

"I work in advertising and I hate it."

"If you'd like to get into reporting, let me know. I could put in a good word for you at *The Tribune*."

"Print reporting? I would never do that," she said snobbishly. "What I really want to do is work in television."

Snooty witch! I didn't care if she was Wynn's sister. I couldn't stand her.

"Come on, let's go get something to eat," Nya said to The Weebil. The two of them rolled their eyes in our direction and then, with Perri trailing behind them, walked away without as much as a good-bye or a good riddance.

"Babe, what's your sister's problem? She obviously doesn't like me."

"Forget her. She's like that with all my girlfriends. She's friends with Vonnie and she knows Vonnie was interested in me. Don't take it personally. It wouldn't matter if you were Angela Bassett. My sister still wouldn't like you."

"That's nice to know. Can she be bought? Sex? Drugs? Money? Men? What's her pleasure?"

"Know any good plastic surgeons that can make you look like Voncile?" he asked.

"Nope. Can't say that I do."

"Good, 'cause I loves ya likes ya is."

"You better love me, babe. I can't believe you're making me put up with all of this crap. It's pure torture," I said.

"It's just for one day, Ms. Foxx. Aren't I worth it?"

"Ask me in a couple of hours. I'll tell you one thing. You can kiss me good-bye now, 'cause I'll never survive if this is what the rest of the day is gonna be like."

"It'll get better, sweetness. I promise," he said.

Out of the corner of my eye, I saw four burly men wrestling on the ground.

"Who are they?" I asked, amused by the image of four grown men in their twenties rolling around in the grass like children.

"That's the A-Team. They're my cousins, although they're more like brothers to me. All of their names start with the letter A. There's AJ, Aaron, and the twins, Alan and Alonzo. They're Abram's younger brothers. You know, the one that runs the YC. They actually live in St. Louis and just came down for my birthday. Look at 'em, grown fools rolling around on the ground like that. It's a shame," Wynn said with a gleam in his eyes that indicated he thought it was anything but. It was clear he would have joined them in a second had I not been there.

"So, how are you all related? You know, it's amazing we've been together as long as we have, yet we don't know much about each other's families."

"You know my mom had three brothers and two sisters. Her youngest sister, Azella is their mother. She lives in California. She's the one that's sick. Liver cancer. She's an alcoholic. She's one of the reasons I don't drink. Addictive behavior runs in the family. When we were growing up, she was always in and out of rehab. My cousins stayed with us a lot," he said.

"How sad."

"My mom and dad practically raised the A-Team. We all grew up together. That's why we're so close. My mom's oldest sister died of Sickle Cell as a child. My three uncles, who all live on the East Coast, all have four children, and all of their children have three children, and that's just on my mother's side."

"It must be nice being a part of such a large, close family. My father grew up in a foster home and was taken care of by a family that didn't care a lick about him. He ended all contact with them when he turned eighteen," I said.

"And what about your mother's side of the family?" he asked.

"At the age of seventeen, my grandmother's mother was disowned from the family because she married outside of her race. She was full-blooded Indian. She had a twin sister and two brothers, but she was cut off from them. The only family I have that I know of is my grandmother, my father and my uncle."

"I've got enough relatives for us both. I've got tons of kinfolks, and not the kind you just see once a year at reunions and then forget about, either," Wynn said.

"Speaking of relatives, where is your dad? I sure would like to meet him."

"My father? He's at work. Where else?" Wynn said with a hint of sadness.

"Too bad." I changed the subject. "So, where's Édonte? I want to give him a big old son-of-the-birthday-boy hug."

"He's running around here somewhere."

"So, is my honey having a good birthday?" I asked.

"Now that you're here? Yeah, I am. Come on, there's someone I want you to meet. It's my crazy brother," he said, steering me in the direction of a handsome young man dressed in a rust-colored silk short set.

"So, finally I get to meet the extremely sexy brother you've been keeping me away from," I said once we reached his brother's side.

"What can I say? Good looks run in the family," his brother said.

"Too bad they hightailed it past you," Wynn said with a laugh.

"Hi, I'm Eric. Don't worry about him. I'm used to his petty, jealous behind," Wynn's attractive older brother told me, offering me his hand. He looked just like Wynn, only lighter and with more hair.

"Hi, Eric. I'm Lacy Foxx, and I'm used to his behind too."

"Oh, I like her. How come you get all the feisty ones?" Eric asked.

"Maybe because you're married, dear," a melodic female voice said from behind him.

"Uhmmm, here comes the old ball and chain now," Eric said.

"Otherwise known as Kim, his long-suffering wife and the mother of his two children," a pretty, dark-skinned, slender woman with large, expressive eyes and a generous smile said as she greeted me.

"You're so pretty. Are you a model? If you're not, you should be. You should be working in New York giving Tyra and Naomi a run for their money," I said, admiring the tall, thin woman in the colorful, form-fitting sundress.

"Oh, I like her too. Can we keep her, Wynn? Huh? Huh? Huh? Huh? Huh? Can we, please?" Kim asked, teasing.

"That's what I'm planning on doing if you two don't run her off," Wynn said.

"Don't listen to him. It's pretty hard to get rid of me once I'm hooked."

"That's nice to know, seeing as how my brother can't seem to keep a woman," Eric said in mock complaint.

"Yeah, first there was wife number one, Willena Hughes who he married in college. And then there was that witch Jacqui," Kim said.

Tha hell?

Wynn had been married to Willena Hughes? She was a well-known and respected area doctor I had interviewed on several occasions. And she'd participated in his career fair at the YC. I couldn't believe it. This was news to me.

Minus five hundred stupid points!

"Can we not listen to a dissertation on my love life? I'm sure Lacy isn't interested in hearing it," Wynn said nervously.

"Speak for yourself, babe. I'd love to hear all about your first marriage to Willena Hughes, especially since I knew nothing about it before today," I said coolly.

"Oops, looks like someone has foot in mouth disease," an embarrassed Eric said.

"Lacy, we didn't know—"

"Apparently, neither did I," I said before turning to leave.

"Laaaacy!" Wynn yelled from behind me. "Lacy! Slow down. Don't you think we should talk? Why are you getting so upset about this?"

"What do we need to talk about?" I asked, turning around to confront him. "Why I didn't know you were once married to Willena Hughes? What else don't I know about you? Is your real name Wynnton Trust?"

"Willena and I were married briefly. We got married during our second year in college. I was nineteen. It was over by the time we graduated. I had just turned twenty-two. We were both too ambitious. She wanted desperately to be a doctor, and between college, learning the computer industry from the ground up while I ran my company, and volunteering at the Youth Center, I barely had a free moment," Wynn said. "I didn't make time for my marriage."

"Oh, now you want to give me details?"

"Because I was on the road so much trying to drum up business, and because of my desire to learn everything I possibly could about computers, I hardly ever saw Willena. And being a typical clueless man, what little extra time I did have, I spent it at the Youth Center and not with her. As a result, our marriage just died. We were only married for three years."

"That's not the point. How long you were married doesn't matter. What *does* matter is the fact that your marriage to her was a major milestone in your life that I knew nothing about," I said.

"I didn't tell you because I've had two failed marriages and I'm just thirty-two. That's a pretty spotty track record, and I didn't want to scare you away."

"I'm not gonna lie. That is a little scary. But what's scarier is the fact you lied to me," I said.

"I didn't lie. I just withheld a little information. Besides, it's old news."

"Not to me. You know what? It doesn't really matter," I said, fishing for my keys in my purse.

"What do you think you're doing?" he asked, grabbing my hands.

"I'm gonna go get my family and then we're leaving."

"What? Why?" Wynn asked.

"Why do you think?"

"Because of Willena? That's crazy. Do I know about every person you've ever been with?"

"You made me a promise. You told me you wouldn't keep important stuff about your life from me anymore. If I had been married, you would definitely know about it. Besides, it's not just her. Look at us. It's taken you seven months to introduce me to your family. Not five or six months, but seven months! Why is that? What's wrong? Are you ashamed of me? Are you secretly hoping to get back with Willena, or worse yet, Jacqui?"

"No! You know I have a really hard time letting people in. I wanted to take things slow. It's just that my money seems to draw the wrong kind of women," he said.

"I've heard all this before! It's taken you this long to figure out I'm the right kind of woman?"

"I admit, maybe I'm taking things too slowly. But you're here now. That's what's important. So, why don't we forget about this other mess?"

"It's not that simple, Wynn," I said.

"Yeah, it is. Don't lame out on me, sweetness. Let's get back to the party."

"Oh, so now my feelings are lame?"

"That's not what I meant. Lacy, you know I love you. No one else matters to me. You're special. You're my heart . . . you're home. I haven't ever felt like this. What we have is like food, nourishment for my soul, and I need you here. I can't celebrate my birthday without you," Wynn said, encircling his arms around my waist. "I'm sorry for not telling you about my marriage to Willena. But come on. Stay."

"Wynn, no. I can't. I don't feel like I know —"

Before I could finish my sentence, he kissed me in a way that touched the depths of my very core. No more words were necessary. We both knew I was staying.

EIGHTEEN

In Marsha's ever-present quest for ways of improving herself and stepping out of her comfort zone, she decided to take up poetry. I could think of a million things I'd rather do than listen to her spout off some of her nonsensical poems in front of a large crowd on a Saturday night. But being the dedicated friend that I was, I'd agreed to meet her after Wynn's birthday party for a Poetry Slam Jam at the Blue Room, the nightclub for Kansas City's renaissance black folks. And after Marsha was done reciting her poetry, I was going over to Wynn's house to give him his present and to help him finish celebrating his birthday.

Marsha took up poetry the month before, and while she spent a lot of time honing her craft, if you asked me, her angst-ridden poems came off as hollow, insipid, creative overindulgence. How angst-ridden could she be? She had her health, she was gorgeous, she made over fifty thousand dollars a year, she lived in a fabulous condo, and she had a nest egg that she could use to retire and live comfortably, anytime she wanted.

Personally, I think she participated in the poetry readings because of the attention she got from men every time she stood on stage and read one of her poems. This was the third reading she had participated in within as many weeks. She thought it was great therapy, and like any true friend would, I encouraged her as if she were as talented as 18th-century African-American poet, Phillis Wheatley.

Recently, Marsha had gone so far as to hint that she wanted to quit her job so that she could write poetry full-time. The child actually had hopes of getting published. I thought she was crazy. Her poetry stank and she was long overdue for a reality check.

But I kept my mouth shut. If truth be told, I actually loved the Blue Room, and listening to Marsha's awful poetry was a small price to pay for hanging out there.

The Blue Room was nothing fancy. It was simply a small, blue, circular room, but on any given night, an eclectic mix of jazz, old school rhythm and blues, and hip-hop appeased the musical tastes of the club's I-got-ants-in-my-pants-and-I-need-to-dance crowd. Or, if your entertainment tastes were more refined, it was *the* spot for poetry readings, book signings and the like.

Immediately upon entering, I searched for Marsha in the small club. As usual, the Blue Room was a frenetic onslaught of nicely dressed, tryin'-to-impress professionals, creative types, local sports celebrities, television talking heads and related hangers-on. I finally spotted Marsha in the crowd, and like a rat going through a maze to get to a piece of cheese, I deftly made my way toward her.

"Hey, Lace the Ace Band-Aid. Sponsors, three o'clock," Marsha said as I eased into the chair across the table from her.

A sponsor was our term of endearment for the older gentlemen in clubs who foolishly believed they could buy their way into a young woman's heart with a few stale drinks and even staler lines. They wasted their hard-earned cash on women who otherwise wouldn't give them the time of day.

Marsha and I were proud of our euphemism, stolen from the mob movie *Casino*, because a sponsor sounded much more refined than a sugar daddy. We smiled and waved coyly at the two men who were old enough to be our fathers. They smiled and waved back, flattered by our acknowledgement. A few minutes later, a waitress appeared at our table and announced that our two newfound friends would pay for our drinks for the night.

"Oh, I forgot. I'm up first. You know what I want to drink," Marsha said as she rushed off to join the other poets, leaving our waitress and me alone in her wake.

143

"We'll have two Alizé Wild Thugs. Make 'em wet. Plenty of ice," I said.

"I'll be right back," the pretty waitress said.

The waitress returned with our drinks just as Marsha stepped up to the mic. I intently observed the supportive crowd, willing some of their enthusiasm to rub off on me. Once the clapping, barking and catcalls ceased, I focused my attention in the direction of the stage and watched as Marsha spoke.

"Hi, I hope you like this. It's titled '*Trapped*'," she said in a little girl voice.

She stepped up closer to the mic, cleared her throat, and began her diatribe.

> *A little girl trapped in the body of a woman,*
> *no one can hear me scream*
> *My heart, my soul, my spirit are torn.*
> *What does it all really mean?*
> *A little girl trapped in the body of a woman who*
> *lives her life unfulfilled*
> *Always trying to be what others expect,*
> *life has no real appeal.*
> *When my impulses are stymied,*
> *my desires are squelched*
> *My reasoning is scattered; no one can help.*
> *When I'm misunderstood, black and blue,*
> *depressed and lonely, what can I do?*
> *With my every glance, my every step,*
> *my every touch, my every breath,*
> *My every sigh, my every lie, a little girl trapped.*

When Marsha finished, there was more clapping, barking and catcalls.

"So, what did you think?" Marsha asked an hour later as she settled into her seat after having fought off an army of men, all trying to fill her head with nonsense about her . . . uhmmm . . . talent.

"That was great," I said after finishing off my third drink, courtesy of our sponsors.

"Really? You think so?"

"Actually, no. I think that was three minutes of my life wasted that I'll never get back," I said capriciously. "Don't get me wrong. I understood what you were trying to say, but I'm not gonna lie to you. That was pretty awful."

"Don't hate," she said dismissively. "I should have known you'd have a problem with it."

"I had a problem with it a'ight. Just like I do with all bad poetry."

"Yeah, whatever," Marsha said.

"Whatever my behind, Little Miss Trapped."

"What the heck is your problem? I don't have to take your abuse, your vituperation!"

"I don't even know what that means, but my problem is I'm tired of listening to you rant and rave in your poetry about your non-existent problems! Some of us have real problems, ya know!" I yelled.

Heads were cocked and eyes were fixed in our direction. People of all shapes, colors and sizes in the immediate area smiled silent can't-take-a-sistah-out-nowhere-in-public smiles.

I suddenly felt bad. Marsha's poem wasn't that awful. She'd created much worse. It wasn't her fault that I was having man problems. It wasn't her fault that she just happened to be in the wrong place at the wrong time with the wrong friend. At least I hoped we were still friends. From the look on her face, I wasn't so sure. Our waitress hesitantly approached our table and asked us if we wanted to refill our drinks.

I winked at our sponsors, bared a little thigh in their direction, and ordered two Alizé Bleu Bling Martinis while Marsha continued to stare at me as if I'd lost my mind. We sat through two poems worth of tension.

"Say something, Marsh," I said as the silence at our table grew uncomfortable.

"I've gotta get home. Patrick is supposed to call me."

"Come on, Marsh. Have another drink. The night's still young," I said, knowing my attempt would be futile.

"No, really. I have to go."

"Marsh, I'm sorry. I didn't mean what I said. I'm having a bad week. Did I tell you Wynn was once married to Doctor Willena Hughes? That's something he's failed to tell me since we've been dating. I found out purely by accident earlier today. Oh, and have I mentioned that every time I'm with Wynn, whenever I turn around, The Weebil is right there all up in my face? I know they work together and they're good friends, but I'm sick of seeing her all the time."

"So, because you don't like a co-worker and because your man is lying to you, possibly cheating on you and basically acting like a dog, you have to treat me like dog dung? You know what? I don't even care," Marsha said while simultaneously grabbing her purse and standing to leave. "I'm the best friend you have, but my friendship comes with a price. That of respect and appreciation—two things I've seen very little of lately from you, Band-Aid."

"Excuse me if I'm not kissing your ass enough for ya. I'll make sure to set aside some time for groveling and brown-nosing next week," I said snidely.

"Don't bother. Next week may be too late. My advice to you is you better make some changes and soon, or I may not be around. Consider this the crucial moment of truth, the epoch of our friendship," Marsha said before heading to the door.

If she was gonna tell me off, the least she could have done was have the decency to use words I understood. What the heck was an epoch and who cared?

Forget Marsha *and* her dollar-fifty words! I knew we'd eventually make up, but for now I didn't need her when I had my two sponsors and plenty of Alizé to keep me company.

******

Early the next morning, I called Marsha on my cell phone from Wynn's bathroom.

"Rweok?" I asked in a nonsensical way, trying to take the sting off our most recent conversation.

"Do you mean are we okay? What do you think?" Marsha asked with a 'tude.

"I *think* I'm an idiot. I didn't mean what I said last night. Your poem was cool, and I'm just jealous 'cause I couldn't do what you do in a million years. I couldn't put my real self out there like you've done the past three weeks in front of God and everybody."

"Hmmm . . . " Marsha said icily.

"And just in case you care, you were right. Things are kinda shaky between Wynn and me, and unfortunately last night I took it out on you."

"Girl, don't let that man drive you crazy. I got six words for ya. Arsenic. Brownies. Kidney failure. Worm food."

"You're suggesting me and Betty Crocker off him?"

"What? Too extreme?"

"Nope." We both laughed. "Marsh, you ever think some folks weren't built for love? This relationship mess is hard, and I wonder if it's worth it."

"If anybody can make a relationship work, it's you."

"I'm glad somebody thinks so, 'cause I'm not so sure."

"You'll be a'ight. Look, Ace, I'm glad you called. I was gonna call you later and apologize for over-reacting last night. I ain't a poet and I know it. I'm giving up poetry."

"Girl, don't give up your poetry. And for the record, you did over-react a bit. The whole epoch thing knocked my drunk ass for a loop."

Marsha laughed. "You don't even know what it means, do ya?"

"I do now. Thank God for the Internet. But for real, don't let my craziness get in the way of your poetry. Some of the stuff you've created is really good."

"Poetry, smoetry. I'm done with that mess. Takes too much time, and being overly introspective can be a mutha. So, whatcha doin' now? I'm thinking about going to sign up for skydiving lessons. Wanna join me?"

"Tha hell? You've got to stop this whole testing your comfort zone thing."

"Why? Testing one's comfort zone ain't never hurt nobody," Marsha said obliviously.

"I'm almost a thousand percent sure that's not true. Look, I can't go jumping out of planes with you because I have some shopping to do and then I have to get ready for the concert."

"That's right. Sinbad's tonight. Well, have fun, Ace. See ya."

NINETEEN

"Get down, get down, get down, get down," Kool & the Gang encouraged during the course of their hit, "Jungle Boogie", which I was listening to on my stereo as I prepared for Sinbad's Slammin' Seventies Summer Jam Concert.

Getting down was exactly what I planned on doing, and the CDs that Trey put together for me were putting me in the mood to do just that. There was music from Seventies groups like Foxxy, Peaches & Herb, McFadden & Whitehead, George Duke, Taana Gardner, Zapp, Funkadelic, A Taste of Honey, the Brothers Johnson, Con Funk Shun and Parliament, and that was just on the first half of one of the CDs.

As Andy Culchic, one of *The Tribune's* top photographers, and I flitted around my condo practicing our Seventies dance moves, I caught a glimpse of myself in a mirror and laughed out loud. My face looked like a walking neon sign. I had on way too much garish blue eye shadow, iridescent lipstick and sparkling blush, not to mention royal blue nail polish. But as hideous as my makeup was, my clothes were even worse. I was wearing a multicolored, psychedelic form-fitting halter-top, matching hip hugging pants and clunky blue platform shoes. A huge mood ring and a peace sign necklace completed my retro look. Well, almost.

To top everything off, I had achieved the perfect afro-puffs. Instead of purchasing a wig, I'd opted to achieve my own look by washing my hair and curling it with small foam rollers while it was still wet. The result? Two large curly balls of hair now sat in ponytails on both sides of my head, and I was quite pleased with the results.

I couldn't believe it when I did it, but I'd managed to convince the SOB that the concert was worthy of a major spread in the newspaper. He agreed. He assigned Andy as my photographer and told me he wanted complete, in-depth

Seventies coverage: the hair, the clothes, the makeup, the dances, the songs, the politics — the works.

The plan called for Wynn's brother and sister-in-law, Andy, Wynn and myself to meet at the Red Vine Restaurant, a popular hangout before and after black cultural events, located just down the street from the Peach Tree. Andy was going to photograph people in all of their Seventies regalia and I was going to interview them. When we were done, we planned to head to the concert, where Andy and I would use our press passes to get backstage so that we could interview the performers.

I was wiping off some of my makeup and talking to Andy about the sensibilities of the Seventies decade when the phone rang.

"Hello?"

"Hi, sweetness. It's me," Wynn said through the phone.

"Are you on your way to pick up me and Andy?"

"I'll be there at five o'clock, like we agreed. But first I have to take Édonte over to my parents and then I have to stop by the YC and pick something up."

"Babe, why tonight of all nights? We have plans."

He cut me off. "I won't be long. I promise. Okay?"

"Okay. Bye," I whispered seductively into the receiver before returning it to its cradle.

"So, was that your Huggie Bear?" Andy asked, making reference to Starsky and Hutch's black, pimpified sidekick.

"Yeah. He'll be here shortly. Until then, I'm gonna shake my groove thang, yeah, yeah," I sang off-key as I pushed him down on the couch and showed him some more of my Seventies dance moves.

Forty minutes later, Wynn had not arrived to pick us up nor had he called. Since I'd been dating him, not once had he been late for a date. He'd never been a minute late, not even a second late. And although he was just ten minutes late, I was instantly worried. I could tell something was wrong. I could sense he needed me.

I called the Youth Center and let the phone ring ten times just in case he wasn't near it, but there was no answer and the machine didn't pick up. I programmed my high tech phone to redial Wynn's cell phone number every five minutes for the next hour.

After another twenty minutes, there was still no word from Wynn. Andy and I agreed that it was best for him to go on to Red Vine without us. I promised him that we'd meet him either there or at the concert as soon as we could. The minute Andy left, I picked up the phone and called Marsha's brother, Mark, who was a cop.

"Hello? Mark Turner here."

"Mark. Hi, it's Lacy. I need you to do me a favor."

"Sure, girl. What's up?"

"My boyfriend, Wynnton Trust, who is a volunteer at the Greater Kansas City Youth Center, was supposed to meet me nearly an hour ago. Last time we talked, he was on his way to the Youth Center at Thirty-third and Owens and I haven't heard from him since. The man is anal when it comes to punctuality, so I know there's something definitely wrong. Can you have someone drive by the Youth Center to check things out?"

"Lacy, technically—"

"I know. Technically he's not a missing person until it's been twenty-four to forty-eight hours, but I know something's up. We can't afford to wait that doggone long. Something has happened to Wynn. I can tell. I can feel it," I said.

"Okay. There's a unit that normally does rounds in that area around this time. I'll have them check it out and I'll call you back."

"Thanks, Mark. Good-bye."

Twenty minutes later, my phone rang. "Lacy. It's Mark Turner. Are you alone? Are you sitting down?"

151

"Why? What's wrong? You're scaring me, Mark."

"It's your boyfriend. We found him. He's been shot," he said.

With those words, my heart stood still. "Shot? What are you talkin' about? What happened?"

"I had a few of my officers check out the Youth Center and they found your boyfriend, Wynnton Trust, behind some garbage bins in the back parking lot. Apparently he was robbed. Someone shot him twice from behind."

"This can't be. Are you sure it was Wynn?" I asked.

"We found positive identification near the body. An ambulance has already picked him up and taken him to Research Hospital. He's lucky to be alive. According to my men, if we had found him ten minutes later, he would have bled to death there at the scene. You saved his life."

"So, when do you think he was shot?"

"We think it happened about thirty minutes before you called me."

"How is he?" I asked.

"He's unconscious but alive, although it looks pretty bad. Is there anything I can do for you?"

I inhaled deeply. "I've got to get to the hospital. Could you call Marsha and let her know what's going on? I'm supposed to be covering Sinbad's concert. Could you ask her to do it for me?"

"Sure, I'll call her. Are you going to be okay, Lacy?"

"I don't know. I doubt it," I said feebly.

"Do you want me to call anyone else? We've already contacted his family. Do you want me to call your folks and have them meet you at the hospital?" Mark asked.

"No. Bibi, my daddy and my uncle are out of town at a church convention. I don't want to worry them. At least not until I know more."

"Well, if you need anything, just let me know."

"Okay. I will," I said as if I were in a trance. "Thanks for looking into this for me, Mark."

"I only wish I didn't have such bad news," he said.

"Yeah, me too. Bye."

I quickly changed into normal clothes, scrubbed the garish makeup off my face and headed to Research Hospital. I was surprised I made it to the hospital, which was thirty minutes away, in one piece because I was so overcome with emotion. When I arrived, I was told that Wynn was in surgery and that he would be in there for at least an hour. All that was left for me to do was wait.

I had been at the hospital for thirty minutes when Wynn's parents and son arrived. His sister, brother and sister-in-law arrived a few minutes later.

"Thank goodness you're here, Lacy," a distraught Mrs. Trust said, greeting me.

"Lacy, hello. I'm Wynn's father. I'm sorry we haven't met until now," a thin, tall reed of a man told me. He was an older-looking version of Wynn and Eric. He had a nice, kind face and a warm personality that I was immediately drawn to. I liked the elder Mr. Trust instantly, just as I had liked his son when we first met, prior to the alien invasion of his personality.

"How's my dad?" Édonte asked, rushing to me.

I reached down and hugged him. "I don't know much, honey. He's been in surgery for a while. No one will tell me anything specific. One nurse did tell me that Wynn should be out of surgery shortly. She said we'd be able to talk to his doctor then."

"Hey, maybe that's him now," Eric said after eyeing a weary-looking, middle-aged doctor in scrubs who was walking toward us.

"Are you the Trust family?" the doctor asked no one in particular.

"Yes, I'm Wynn Trust, Senior. How is my son, doctor . . .

doctor . . . "

"Doctor Hammond Pryce. Mr. Trust, your son is in serious condition. He took two bullets from behind. One caused little damage, but the other bullet caused quite a bit of tissue and muscle damage. We removed both bullets during surgery."

"Oh my goodness!" Mrs. Trust said as she slumped against her daughter.

"He's in a coma now. He's lost a lot of blood. His body is in shock. But we're optimistic," Doctor Pryce said. "He's pretty bad off, but I've seen much worse. We've stabilized his vital functions and we're monitoring him very closely. The next seventy-two hours are extremely critical. By that time, we'll know if there is any permanent damage."

"Where is my son now?" Mrs. Trust asked between sobs.

"He's in the recovery room."

"Can we see him?" Nya asked.

"In a little while. But be prepared. It's not a pretty sight. He's connected to all sorts of tubes and a life support system. He won't even know you're there. I'm sorry I don't have better news for you."

"It's okay, doctor," Mr. Trust said, acting as the voice of reason. In the space of a few minutes, Mr. Trust appeared to age twenty years.

"I always knew that volunteering at that stupid Youth Center would cause Wynn nothing but trouble," Mrs. Trust said after the doctor left.

"Not now, Elaine. Please, not now," her husband said before falling exhausted into the chair behind him.

"I came as soon as I heard," an out of breath Voncile said a few minutes later as she approached us.

"How did you find out about this?" Mrs. Trust asked, seeming glad to see her.

"Nya called me on her way over here. How is he? How's Wynn?"

"Not good. He's in a coma. The doctor says the next few days are the most critical," Nya said.

"Do they expect him to live?"

"Yeah, but there might be some permanent damage," Kim said.

"So, where's our little girl?" Wynn's mother asked, no doubt referring to Perri with an I.

"I left her with my oldest brother. Maybe I'll bring her by once Wynn is doing better. Is there anything you need?"

"No, I'm fine. Exhausted but fine," Mrs. Trust said.

"How about you, Mr. Trust? Eric? Nya? Kim? Édonte? Is there anything I can do for any of you?"

As usual, she ignored me.

"No, we're fine," Mr. Trust sniffed. I instantly got the impression that he disliked The Weebil as much as she and I disliked each other.

An hour later, a nurse from the ICU came down to take us to Wynn's room. Despite the doctor's warning, nothing could have prepared us for what we saw. Tubes ran in and out of Wynn's body like an overused electricity adapter. Gadgets that blinked, beeped, clicked, flashed and gurgled surrounded the once indomitable Wynnton Trust.

"Dad? Dad? Dad?" Édonte whispered as he hugged me tightly.

"Hey, man. We're here to make sure you're all right," Eric said on the verge of tears.

"Li'l bro', everything is gonna be fine," Nya said, reassuring Wynn and herself.

"Junior, Lacy is here with us," Mr. Trust said to his son. "She's the one that sent the police to look for you. She saved your life. It's no wonder you love her."

"I'm here too, Wynn," Voncile said quietly, not to be outdone.

There was no response. Nothing to indicate that he even knew we were there. Nothing to indicate that he had once been so full of life, vitality and vigor. Nothing. Just more blinking, beeping, clicking, flashing and gurgling from the machines.

We prepared ourselves for our extended vigil. Mr. and Mrs. Trust settled at the head of the bed. The rest of us settled on either side. Second after second . . . minute after minute . . . hour after hour . . . the time slowly passed.

Late the next evening, Doctor Pryce walked into Wynn's room to examine him.

"I see the gang's all here," he said cheerily.

"Where else would we be?" a caustic Nya asked.

"Nya, there is no need to get upset with Doctor Pryce. The man is just trying to do his job," her father said.

"So, Doc, how does it look?" Eric asked, concerned.

"I fully expected him to be responding by now but he's not. It's been a full twenty-four hours," Doctor Pryce said.

He poked and prodded Wynn incessantly. "There's tissue and muscle swelling which is causing paralysis below the waist. But with time, possibly a few months, that should go away."

"What about the coma? When will he come out of it?" Elaine Trust asked.

"That's hard to say. Like I said earlier, I expected him to pull out of the coma by now. He's stabilized. All of his body functions appear to be normal. It's anyone's guess. It could be three days, three weeks, three months or three years."

"That's the best you can do? Three days, three weeks, three months or three years?" Nya asked.

"I'm afraid so," Dr. Pryce said before leaving the room.

"Look, Junior won't come out of the coma any sooner just because we're angry and frustrated," Mr. Trust said, voicing the obvious. "All we can do is hope and pray, pray and hope."

And that's what we did.

TWENTY

After the doctor's pronouncement that Wynn's coma could last three days, three weeks, three months or three years, I asked if anyone needed anything. No one in the family had eaten since they arrived and they all let me know that they could really use some food. The Weebil and I quickly offered to get everyone a bite to eat from the hospital cafeteria.

While we walked in silence to the elevator together, I looked long and hard at The Weebil. Wynn had been in the hospital for more than twenty-four hours, and Voncile had been there the whole time, by his side, just as faithfully as his family and I had been. The minute we stepped into the elevator, The Weebil burst into tears. I tried consoling her.

Big mistake!

"This must be tough on you, seeing the Youth Center's volunteer coordinator in there so helpless."

Silence.

"I know the two of you are really close, and I know Wynn's family appreciates you being here. If Wynn knew you were here, I know he'd appreciate it too."

More silence.

I tried again. "I know you've worked with Wynn for years. He's always talking about what a wonderful employee you are. Don't tell him I told you this, but he's always saying that his cousin couldn't run the YC without you."

"Work, work, work, work, work!" The Weebil yelled at me, catching me off-guard. "I'm not here because Wynn volunteers at the YC. He's the father of my two-year-old daughter, Perri. That's why I'm here! Don't you know anything?"

I knew that I had just used up another thousand stupid points. I knew that all that glittered sure the hell wasn't gold. So what if Wynn was a millionaire? So what if he gave back to the community? None of that could hide the fact that he was a liar and that I didn't know him as well as I thought I did.

"Of course I knew," I said. I had to lie. What was I supposed to say? After a few moments, the silence between us grew unbearable.

"I need to be by myself," Voncile said, stumbling out of the elevator the moment it opened. I was left alone to wallow in my misery. I gave forty dollars to the first orderly I saw and asked him to take some food to the Trust family on the sixth floor. Then I burst into tears and fled from the building.

I couldn't believe it! I felt like I barely knew the man I'd so intimately shared the last several months of my life with. In the blink of an eye, Wynn had become a total stranger to me. All of the hours I'd spent crying and praying had been for a complete and utter stranger. How could he have kept something like this from me for so long? Could it be that he and The Weebil were still fooling around and he didn't want me to find out?

The lies with him had become endless. First, he waited six months before informing me about the extent of his wealth. Then I had to wait another month to meet his family. He had neglected to tell me he had once been married to Doctor Willena Hughes prior to his marriage to Jacqui. All of that, and now this . . . an illegitimate child with a woman I truly hated.

What Wynn perceived as flotsam, unimportant, miscellaneous information, I lionized and desperately needed. How could he be so willing to sacrifice our love by killing it with his lies and omissions?

His lies were becoming the juggernaut that would crush our relationship. He once told me that addictive behavior ran in his family. Could he be addicted to lying? Was he a pathological liar? Could he not help himself?

I racked my brain trying to remember Kansas City's laws on euthanasia. It wasn't his pain and suffering I was worried about eradicating, but my own. I couldn't get away from

Research Hospital fast enough. I quickly found my car, jumped in it and headed south. I needed my faithful shoulder to cry on, and before long, Sebastian was facing me.

"Lace, what are you doing here?" he asked, surprised to see me at his front door. "How did you know where I lived?"

I didn't bother explaining to him that I got his address off of the work order from the movers that came to get his stuff out of the POD at the beginning of the year.

"I need someone to talk to," I said, unable to stop my tears.

"Why? What's wrong?" he asked, embracing me.

"It's my boyfriend . . . Wynn . . . uhmmm . . . you remember . . . Mr. T. The one I kind of mentioned when we . . . uhmmm . . . you know . . . he's in the hospital."

"In the hospital? What happened?" Sebastian asked as he led me to the sofa in his living room. I totally broke down before my behind hit the sofa's cushions.

"We were going to that Seventies Summer Jam Concert, but Wynn had to run by the Youth Center on Thirty-third and Owens to pick something up. He called me on his way there. The police found his body behind the Youth Center and Mark Turner, Marsha's brother the cop, called me. He told me Wynn had been robbed. Whoever robbed him, shot him from behind and left him there to die."

"Are there any suspects or witnesses?"

"Not that I'm aware of," I responded with a heavy sigh.

"He's in the hospital?"

"Yeah, at Research. He's in a coma. His doctor says it could be three days, three weeks, three months or three years before he comes out of it. If he comes out at all."

"I don't know what to say except I'm sorry."

"Sebastian, that's not all. I was talking to the assistant director of the Youth Center and she informed me that she's given him the one thing that I will never be able to give him."

"What's that?" Sebastian asked.

"The same thing I couldn't give you. A child. The child's momma told me today. The two of them have a kid together. That just happens to be one of many things that he's failed to mention to me during the last seven months. I see his daughter at the YC occasionally and I can't stand the child's mother. I feel so selfish for feeling like this, but I'm so mad at him. How could he keep something like that from me?"

"I don't know, Lace," Sebastian said, shaking his head in astonishment.

"What if they're still seeing each other? That's all I thought about on my way over here. God, I feel so selfish for being obsessed with this, especially while Wynn is in a coma, but I can't help it," I said to Sebastian as warm, salty tears continued to roll down my face.

"Hold up! Hold up! Hold up! There's no reason for you to feel guilty about what you're feeling. I doubt they are still seeing each other. If she was as emotional as I imagine she was when she told you about their child, I'm sure she would have told you if they were still seeing each other."

"Yeah, I guess you're right," I said in agreement. "You know, this just makes me wonder what else he's lied to me about or what he's capable of lying about. This whole thing is driving me crazy!" I said, resting my head on Sebastian's muscular chest.

"Do you love him?" Sebastian asked in a barely audible tone.

"Yeah, at least I did. I mean I do. I'm so confused. I don't feel like I even know him anymore. I certainly don't feel like I can trust him. The man lies like he breathes — all the time."

"Well, whether or not you can trust him is a question only you can answer. Give it time," Sebastian said, giving me a bear hug.

"Sebastian, you're always there for me. Thank you," I said in an appreciative tone while looking up into his handsome brown face.

"And I always will be," he said, gently brushing his soft lips against mine.

We looked at each other and kissed again. This time we kissed longer, deeper, harder. "Uhmmm, I'm sorry," Sebastian said, pulling his lips away from mine.

"Don't be sorry. Did you hear me complain?" I asked before climbing into his lap, my mouth hungry for more. After a few minutes, I removed his shirt and slid off his pants and underwear and then my own. I grabbed a condom from my purse, quickly slid it on him and guided him inside of me. My body, which for the last twenty-four hours had been numb, suddenly came alive.

Our lovemaking was over before you could say I-can't-believe-I'm-having-sex-with-my-ex-fiancé-while-my-current-boyfriend-is-fighting-for-his-life. When we finished, we just sat there looking at each other.

"Sebastian, don't say a word. I want you to know that making love to you just now allowed me a momentary sense of control in my otherwise out-of-control life and for that, I'm thankful," I said, sounding more clear-headed than I felt.

"Lace, I didn't mean to —"

"Neither one of us meant to, but I'm not sorry it happened. You shouldn't be either. Now, where's your bathroom?" I asked, gathering my clothes in my arms.

"Right around the corner," he said, stretching out on the couch.

I rushed into the bathroom and wept silently. An hour later, I exited the bathroom, buttoning my blouse just as Charron, Sebastian's girlfriend, walked into the room. Sebastian, who had fallen asleep naked on the couch, was awakened by a backhand to the face.

With that slap, we were both instantly dropkicked back into reality.

"Sebastian! What the hell is goin' on?" Charron asked incredulously. "I can't believe you just had sex with that slut. Tell me that's not what happened here!"

He grabbed her wrists. "Don't you ever in your life slap me again!"

"That's all you have to say to me? Well, let me tell you something! I'm tired of settling for her sloppy seconds! It's always been about Lacy Foxx and it's always gonna be about her, isn't it?" Charron asked, screaming at the top of her lungs.

He stared at her coolly without saying a word, and she turned her anger toward me. "Why can't you just accept the fact that he's with me now? Why don't you just leave him the hell alone?"

"Charron, I'm so sorry. We didn't mean for this to happen."

"Shut up, bee-yotch! Save it for somebody who will believe it!" she snapped before running from their home. I expected Sebastian to follow her but he didn't.

"Aren't you going after her?"

"Nope," Sebastian said without a hint of concern.

"So, what do you say after something like this? Thanks?" I asked with a forced smile as he walked me to the door.

"Take care of yourself," he said, pulling me close, "and keep me posted on how things turn out with you and your boy."

"I will. But only if you promise me you'll patch things up with Charron. My conscience couldn't stand it if you two were to break up over this."

"She and I have been having problems here lately anyway."

"What kind of problems could the two of you be having so soon?"

"The number one problem is she isn't you."

"Sebastian, while there's still a strong connection between us, sometimes I wish there wasn't. It keeps confusing things. It makes everything so hard. You get me and understand me like no one else in my life. You always have and probably always will."

"Maybe there's a reason for that. Maybe God is trying to tell us something."

"I don't think He is. He knows and we know we're better off apart. Sooner or later you and I are really gonna have to let go of us, the past and what we had."

"Lacy . . ."

"Don't, Sebastian. I shouldn't have come over here. I didn't mean to mess things up for you. Go after Charron. I'm your past. She's your future," I said before quietly slinking out the door.

TWENTY-ONE

"Lacy, you're not gonna believe it. Wynn has come out of his coma," a jubilant Elaine Trust said as she greeted me while I was on my way to Wynn's hospital room hours later.

"Oh, really?" I asked with more enthusiasm than I felt.

"He came out of his coma a few hours ago. He's talking to Édonte, or rather listening while Édonte talks, and we think he's been looking for you."

"That's great news. I'm sorry I wasn't here when it happened. I had to run home." I studied her face and body language closely wondering if she knew her son was a liar and I was a cheating fornicator.

"Come on, Lacy. Don't just stand there! I know Wynn is dying to see you. Oops, bad choice of words."

Not quite ready to face Wynn because of my guilty conscious, I tried to buy some time. "This is a bit of a surprise, Mrs. Trust. I just need a moment to gather myself. I want to make sure I don't burst into tears in front of him."

"I understand, dear. Just don't take too long, okay?"

"Yeah, sure. Okay."

I was at once surprised and confused about what I was feeling. I was thrilled that Wynn had pulled out of the coma, although I knew the road to recovery he faced would be a long, hard, treacherous one. But at least he was alive. By the same token, I was still hurt by his lies, his omissions, his betrayal. He'd broken my heart into a million tiny little pieces. I loved him dearly, but his latest omission had been too much for me to handle. It's what led me into the arms and bed—I mean couch—of another man. At least that's what I kept telling myself.

The gig was up. Convinced that no matter how hard I tried to hide it Wynn would instantly know what I had done, I slowly walked into his hospital room. It was overrun with well-wishing family members and friends. Among them was

Trey, who was crying as he sat beside Édonte at the foot of Wynn's bed.

"What's he doing here?" I asked Mrs. Trust with the credit card fiasco still fresh in my mind.

"He's Trey Jenkins. He's one of Wynn's kids from the YC."

"I know who he is. Why is he here?" I asked.

"Several kids from the YC just left. Trey stayed. He said he hasn't been at the YC all week, but he heard what happened. He's worried about Wynn. He's really concerned about whether the police know who did this. He's a sweet boy. Been crying since he got here."

When Trey saw me, he rushed toward me and hugged me. Despite everything, in truth, I was glad to see him.

"Hi, Trey," I said, warmly embracing him. "How are ya? Haven't seen you at the Youth Center in a while."

"I'm okay. How is he? Is Mr. T. gonna be all right? He's not gonna die, is he?"

"I'm sure he will be fine eventually," I said reassuringly.

"Ms. Foxx, I'm so sorry about everything. I'm sorry for what I've done . . . you know, the whole credit card thing."

"Trey, let's just try to move on from that, okay?"

"Yeah. Well, I . . . uhmm . . . I gotta go. It was good seeing you. Take care of Mr. T., okay? And tell him I'm not gonna be at the Youth Center for a few weeks. I'm trying to work out some personal things."

"I'll tell him, Trey," I said while hugging him again. As he walked out the door, Trey looked back at Wynn, who gave him a faint smile.

"Lacy, go say hello to Wynn," Mrs. Trust said rather loudly from across the room.

"She's the one that asked the police to go look for him," someone whispered. Instantly, all eyes in the room were on me, including Wynn's. He feebly beckoned me to his side.

"Hey, babe," I whispered once I made my way to the head of his bed. Suddenly, his lies and my infidelity didn't matter.

All that mattered was that he had survived and prevailed. Now, if only our love could.

"Don't be alarmed by the fact that Junior's not speaking," Mr. Trust said. "He will be able to in just a matter of time. We think he's been looking for you."

"That's what I told her earlier," Elaine Trust said proudly.

Nya and The Weebil grunted.

"Doctor Pryce was just here. He wants Wynn to stay still and quiet until he builds up his strength," Kim chimed in.

"Can he understand me?" I felt him squeeze my hand.

"Every word," Édonte said, beaming.

"I love you." Wynn mouthed the words in my direction. I was instantly overcome by emotion. I put on a brave front.

"You know, if it wasn't obvious before that you needed me, it certainly should be obvious now," I said in a quiet whisper.

He smiled. Despite everything, he still had a beautiful smile.

"You have a lot of people here concerned about you. Don't let us down," I said, choking back tears. "I was so worried about you. But now everything is gonna be all right. I just know it is. You'll be back on your feet, getting on my nerves in no time," I whispered in his ear. "I love you and you've got to get better for my sake, for our sake."

"Come on, Lacy. Don't hog all of my little brother's time," Eric said, rushing to his brother's side with his wife in tow.

"I'll be right here if you need anything," I said, kissing Wynn firmly on the cheek. As I moved to make way for Eric and his wife, it felt like my heart was going to burst. I wondered if in my kiss Wynn could taste *my* lie, *my* omission.

"Lacy, do you realize we've experienced a firsthand miracle?" Mr. Trust asked, pulling me aside to a secluded spot in Wynn's hospital room. "You heard the doctor. He said it could be three days or longer before Junior came back to us, and here he is, out of his coma in a little over twenty-four hours. You should have been here. It's like something jolted him out of that coma. It's like he was claiming back his life."

His life — and his cheatin' and triflin' woman, I thought to myself.

"Truly, it's a blessing," Wynn's father said.

"Yep, that it is," I said in agreement, wiping tears from my eyes. "So, when is he gonna be able to go home?"

"The doctor said possibly in a few weeks. I know my son. He'll want to go back to his house. He won't come to our home and stay with us. However, we're going to keep Édonte until Wynn recovers. I'm looking into getting a home health care nurse for him. Someone here at the hospital recommended a Nadia Stephenson from Mobile Health."

"I plan on helping too. Just so you know, I plan on being with him around the clock until he gets better," I said, hoping that the news was of some comfort. "I'm taking off work for a little while."

"You've been such a good friend to Wynn," Mr. Trust said.

"I love Wynn, and I can't help but be there for him and your family."

"You and Voncile have both done more than enough, although I don't care for her much. I realize she is the mother of my son's child and that she dropped out of college at age nineteen just to have his baby. She'll always be a part of his life to some degree. She'll always be the mother of his child, but that doesn't mean I have to like her or trust her. Because I don't," he said.

Baby mama drama? Now there was something I had tried my hardest to avoid my entire adult dating life, because babies' mamas were a not-so-rare breed of women. Once they snared a man with a child, they never went away.

"Well, she's here to stay. The two of them seem very close," I said.

"A fact which I imagine is tough on you," Mr. Trust said compassionately. "It's really rather shameful the way she

167

chased Junior once his wife left him. He was vulnerable then, just as he is now. But despite her tactics, Wynn stepped up. He pays child support, spends quite a bit of time with his daughter . . . her and Édonte."

I stared at him blankly.

"Don't give up on him, Lacy. He'd probably kill me if he knew I was telling you this, but you're all he ever talks about. I know he can be a real challenge, but he needs a good woman like you to keep him focused and on track."

"Speaking of focused, how long will it be before he fully recovers?" I asked.

"No one knows for sure. As you know, muscle and tissue swelling has caused some paralysis below the waist. They don't think he'll be able to walk for a while, but the doctor says Wynn should be able to walk again, perhaps in a few months. They're still trying to evaluate his condition, but after he's out of the hospital, they think he'll need intensive physical therapy."

Slowly and not so surely during the course of the next week, the number of family members and friends that came by to wish Wynn well began to dwindle. During this time, I stayed faithfully by his side. I read to him, talked to him, bathed him, and helped him with his physical therapy exercises day after day without any verbal response from him. Not that I needed it. I was driven purely by guilt.

After another week, Wynn was released from the hospital. By then, he was eighty percent himself. He could talk up a storm and had regained a lot of strength in all areas of his body — well, almost all areas — and once we were out of the hospital, I had my own ideas on how to remedy that. I took off two weeks from work with plans of spending the time nursing my man back to health.

I knew his road to recovery would be a long, hard one, and knowing what I had to do, the road to recovery for our relationship would be even longer and harder.

TWENTY-TWO

"Don't be fatuous," Marsha said while we made our way around the Country Club Plaza for some shopping shortly after Wynn's release from the hospital.

Couldn't she just tell me to not be childish or silly like any normal person would have?

Known as the Rodeo Drive of the Midwest, The Plaza was a Spanish architecture-inspired shopping and entertainment nirvana. A fourteen-block stretch of fountains and sculptures, upscale shops, five-star restaurants and world-class museums, The Plaza was a hot spot for the most discerning of shoppers. Even the coolness of the early September evening and Marsha's coolness regarding my infidelity couldn't damper the excitement I felt that night shopping on The Plaza.

"I can't believe you're thinking about telling Wynn you slept with Sebastard," Marsha said.

"I have to. And by the way, Sebastian is *not* a bastard."

"I know. Where have you been?"

"If you knew, why have we been calling him that all this time?"

"Because after you two broke up, you said 'he's a bastard,' and the name kind of stuck. Sebastard was born," she said, laughing.

"Well, I was wrong. He's not a bastard, and we're not calling him that anymore."

"Fine. Who told you to sleep with Senonbastard in the first place?"

"I don't need a morality lecture, Marsh." From the look on her face, I could tell what I needed was immaterial to her. "I gotta tell Wynn what happened."

"When you thought Senonbastard was cheating on you, you wouldn't even talk to him, let alone forgive him. And now you're about to ask Wynn to do the very thing that you couldn't? Man, what a kerfuffle."

I laughed. "A kerfuffle? That's officially my favorite crazy Marsha word, even though I don't know what the heck it means."

"It means you have quite a morass on your hands, Ace. You're stuck in the middle of an extremely messy situation," Marsha said.

Ya think?

"So, you don't think I should tell Wynn?" I asked. "He's pretty open-minded. He'll forgive me. He'll understand what I was going through. Trust me."

"Trust this. If you tell that man you slept with someone else while he was in a hospital dying, he'll kick you to the curb so fast, you'll think his name was Pele," Marsha said.

"Do you really believe that? Wynn is a mature adult. He'll be upset and hurt at first, but if he values our relationship, he'll understand and he'll get over it. Besides, he's made betraying me an art form," I said.

"He didn't really betray you as far as Voncile and Willena are concerned."

"In my heart, I feel betrayed. If Wynn wants our relationship to work out, he's gonna just have to understand why I turned to Sebastian. He'll just have to accept it."

"Is that what the men are like in your own personal Crazyland? Ace, do you realize that most men who find out their partners have cheated on them dump them immediately? For men, it's a major ego buster. They're not like women," she said. "They don't hang in there for the sake of the relationship."

"Some men do."

"Hmmm," Marsha said, ignoring my more-the-exception-than-the-rule observation. "Let's go in Saks. They're having a sale on their designer suits."

"So? They'll still be too expensive for my poor behind and yours too," I said while following her doggedly inside.

Within minutes, we reached the Misses department.

"Okay, Ace. I gotta be honest. You're my girl and all, but I think you were totally wrong for cheating on Wynn by sleeping with Sebastian, considering what Wynn was going through. I can't support you on this one."

"I'm not proud of what I did. And by the way, I didn't cheat per se. It was really over before it began."

"All the more reason not to say a word," Marsha said, arguing her point. "We all have our peccadilloes. There's no reason for you to broadcast this one to Wynn."

"What does picking a dildo have to do with this?" I asked.

"Hah, funny. I said 'peccadillo,' you nut. It means— "

"I know what a peccadillo is, Marsh."

Forget her and her stupid vocabulary enhancement program. She wasn't the only one that could use fancy words.

"You better listen to me," she warned. "You'll thank me later."

"I've never cheated before and I've never lied in a relationship before about anything this serious, and I'm not gonna start now."

"Don't lie to him. Omit. I think it's wrong of you to burden Wynn with this just so you can ease your guilty conscience. He should be focusing on recuperating."

"Do you think that's what this is about? Easing my guilty conscience? Well, maybe it is, partially. But doesn't Wynn have a right to know what I've done? Besides, after all that he's put me through, he can't say a thing. Love is all about trials and tribulations. If he is in this relationship under false pretenses, the false pretense being I've been faithful to him, doesn't that make our relationship a lie?"

"Does it, Band-Aid?" Marsha asked as she held up a beautiful beaded lavender suit to examine the price. "You mean to tell me that you're never gonna keep a secret from this man? That's impossible," she said, returning the garment to the rack.

"I didn't say that. I won't sweat the small stuff, but anything that could alter the dynamics of our relationship, I think he has a right to know about. He has a right to choose whether or not he wants to stay in the relationship. And in order to make an informed decision, he should have all the facts."

"Here's a fact. You're gonna be looking for a new man if you tell Wynn that you cheated on him while he was in the hospital. Why insist on torturing yourself and him?"

"My affair will be the prism of our relationship. Everything from this point on will be discolored and distorted by it if I'm not honest with him."

"Karma ain't always instant, but eventually it bites you in the ass, so let's flip the script," Marsha said, relishing her role as devil's advocate. "When—I mean *if* Wynn ever cheats on you, would you want to know? And if he did cheat on you, would you stay in a relationship with him?"

"It depends on the circumstances. Habitual cheating is unacceptable. But we're all human. A one-time fling is forgivable. If he was good to me otherwise and I felt confident he wouldn't stray again, sure I'd stay. Wouldn't you?"

"It's not me you gotta worry about." We discussed the intricacies of infidelity for ten minutes as we left Saks and made our way to my car.

"Oops, I can't leave yet," Marsha said after opening my passenger door. My blank stare prompted further explanation. "I forgot to pick up some baby clothes for my brother's new baby. I have to run by Gymboree before it closes. You go on, Ace. I'll catch a cab home."

Reluctantly, I followed her suggestion and headed in the direction of Wynn's house. The closer I got, the stronger my resolve grew to tell him the truth about my adulterous ways. Once I arrived, I let myself in with the key he had given me when he checked out of the hospital.

"Nadia? Wynn? It's me. Where are you?" I yelled from the foyer.

"Just a minute," I heard Wynn yell back. I walked in the direction of his voice.

There in the middle of the living room was Wynn, standing with a large, silly grin on his face. "Stay right there." He slowly walked toward me. "I've been able to stand for three days and I've been walking short distances for the last two," he said once he reached my side. "Surprise!"

"But the doctors said it could take months! You haven't been out of the hospital long."

"I couldn't wait a few months before I was standing by your side," he said, kissing me long and hard on the mouth. "Watch this!" he instructed me. I watched in silence while he walked at a snail's pace back to his wheelchair.

"Baby, I'm so proud of you," I said, jumping into his lap once he was seated.

"Pretty soon, I'll be back one hundred percent, if you know what I mean," Wynn said, rubbing his nose against my neck. "I can't wait 'til you and I can be together again," he added naughtily. A sea of shame washed over me.

What was I supposed to say? *Speaking of being together, I had sex with my ex.*

"Have I told you how much I love you lately?" I asked as I began to cry.

"Hey, what's wrong, sweetness?"

"Nothing. I'm just so happy to see you walking."

"It's more than that. Talk to me. What's up?"

I took a deep breath and stood.

"There is something I have to tell you," I said slowly.

"What? Let's have it. Did they find the person who did this to me?" Wynn asked with an anticipatory smile.

"No, I wish. This is really, really hard for me. Uhmmm . . . while you were in the hospital, I thought you were gonna die and I really couldn't handle that. There was no one around for me to call and I really needed someone to talk to."

"And?" he asked.

"And I went to see Sebastian, and unfortunately, we ended up having sex."

"You what? You had sex with your ex-fiancé while I was in the hospital dying?" Wynn asked, responding vehemently to my news.

"Let me explain . . . "

"Explain what? Why you're a tramp?"

"Excuse you? What did you just call me?" I asked with my head cocked and my hands on my hips.

"What part of that didn't you understand?"

"Why, you sanctimonious ass! I don't have to take this from you! You don't have any right to talk to me like that!"

We had both broken love quarrel cardinal rule number one—no name-calling.

Unfortunately, neither one of us seemed to notice or care.

"I have every right!" he yelled.

"Well, at least I don't go around having sex with children!"

"What are you talking about, Lacy?"

"Why didn't you tell me that you and Voncile had a child together?"

"I wanted to, but I didn't know how. I didn't want to scare you away."

"How old was Voncile when you got her pregnant? Nineteen? She was barely legal! When exactly were you gonna tell me that Perri was your child? Huh, Wynn?" I asked.

"When I thought you needed to know," he said, coming perilously close to running me over with his wheelchair. "Vonnie is just a friend. She means nothing more to me than that. She helped me get over the break-up of my marriage. Granted, she's my baby's mama, but Perri and Vonnie are not the issue here. The issue is, why were you with another man while I was lying on my deathbed?"

"I thought you were dying. I thought I was losing you."

"And that's how you show you care for your dying boyfriend? By sleeping with someone else?"

"I wouldn't have even gone to see Sebastian if I hadn't found out about Perri the way that I did. Voncile let it slip while we were alone together in an elevator. You should have been the one to tell me, Wynn. Not her!" I said. "Under normal circumstances, I would never cheat on you."

"So, this was a revenge thing? You slept with your old boyfriend just to get back at me for not telling you about my illegitimate daughter?"

"For me, it wasn't about revenge. You don't understand. I haven't told you yet, but I'm barren. I can't have children."

"Oh, so you've been keeping secrets too?" he asked.

"That's not the point."

"When you're wrong, it's never the point!"

"It's been eight months and I didn't know Perri was yours! How long were you going to keep that from me? Until she graduated college or had her own kids? And how exactly have you managed to keep this from me for so long anyway? Now that I think about it, I've never even heard her call you Daddy!"

"You're not around every second. You don't hear everything she says to me. Keeping this from you hasn't been that hard. Vonnie's made it easy. Ever since you and I hooked up, she's been trippin'. She's kept Perri away from the YC and from me. I haven't had time to go to court to sue her for joint custody, but I'm planning to. Not that any of this is your business!" he said.

"Knowing the one person I dislike most in the world has given you the one thing I can't ever give you, devastated me. But what hurts most is seeing that it is so easy for you to deceive me by keeping your little secrets."

"So, because I don't tell you everything, you slept with another man?"

"You know, I didn't have to tell you about what happened. You were in a coma! You would have never known."

"Aren't I lucky? You have a conscience—kind of," Wynn said sarcastically.

I sighed, frustrated by the ugliness of what I was going through. Why hadn't I listened to Marsha? A long stretch of silence elapsed before either of us spoke again.

"Wynn, I don't expect you to understand . . . "

"Good, 'cause I don't!"

"I don't even understand it. It's not like I want Sebastian back. Believe it or not, it's you I love. What happened with Sebastian didn't mean a thing."

"What? Oh boy, then we have a serious problem. At least tell me that it's Sebastian you really love and want to be with. We have ourselves quite a problem if you'd throw away what we had for something that didn't mean anything to you."

"The only thing it meant was that for five minutes, I didn't have to think about my life without you."

"I want you to leave," Wynn said in a voice that was low and threatening.

"Can't we be mature adults and work this out? Didn't I forgive you for not telling me you were once married to Willena? Didn't I forgive you for not being honest with me concerning the extent of your family's wealth? I'm willing to overlook the fact that you didn't tell me you had a child with Voncile, so why can't you forgive me this?"

"I didn't betray you."

"Lies and omissions are forms of betrayal. Sometimes they're even worse."

"You're kidding, right? How could you do this to me? You know what I went through with Jac. Been there, done that. I can't be with someone who doesn't love me, doesn't respect me."

"But I do love you and respect you. I adore you! You know that."

"You couldn't possibly love me and do what you did. You know, there comes a time in your life when you have to decide what's acceptable and what's not. When Jac cheated on me, I decided that infidelity was one of those things I would not accept from someone I loved. And while I may have kept the truth about some things from you, I would never cheat on you."

It was a perverted twist on the "honor among thieves" maxim, yet had I been listening with my ears and not my heart, I may have recognized the truth in what he was saying.

"I don't know what to say."

"How about good-bye? I want you to leave."

"Okay," I said as I slowly walked to the door and left.

I sat in my car and cried for about twenty minutes. Finally, after the tears subsided, I started to drive away. When I rounded the corner, I was so blinded by my grief, I almost didn't notice a familiar car coming toward me.

There she was, right on schedule . . . by his side in his time of need. His baby's mama.

TWENTY-THREE

The road to reconciliation for Wynn and me was a short one. With the unveiling of his big whopper of a lie and my confession of infidelity, both sins seemed to cancel each other out. Within two weeks, we'd forgiven each other and had reconciled, surprisingly easily. Unfortunately, the guilt of having sex with Sebastian never went away. I relived sleeping with him and the ugly breakup with Wynn in my mind daily. During my reconciliation phase with Wynn, perhaps the hardest thing I had to do was admit to him and convince myself that sleeping with Sebastian was strictly a revenge thing.

One of the biggest thrills of our reconciliation came when I received a late Sunday night telephone call from Wynn, exactly one month after his release from the hospital, on one of the few nights we weren't spending together.

"Guess what, sweetness?" I heard Wynn's voice ask through the phone that I didn't remember answering.

"Wynn, baby. D'ya know what time it is? It's after midnight."

"I know. I'm sorry. I've been at the Youth Center all day and then Édonte had a late ball game at the YC and then afterwards the team went out to eat, and I'm just getting home. I couldn't call you before now. But wake up. I've got big news!"

"Okay, okay! What is it? What's your great big news?" I asked, not really caring. I just wanted to get rid of him so I could get back to my dream of Denzel and me on our honeymoon, following the untimely and suspicious disappearance of his wife. I loved Wynn and all, but a woman had to fantasize. Didn't she?

"You're not gonna believe this! The Youth Center's board wants to pay for a trip to send two people to London. Actually, it's a working trip. And actually, a government grant we received for staff education is going to pay for it, but the result is the same. They want you and me to attend a weeklong international youth conference."

"Sounds nice, but why are they paying for me to go?"

"Technically I should take Vonnie, but they said it's okay for me to take you. The only catch is you have to write about the YC's involvement in *The Tribune*. You know, a day-in-the-conference-life kind of thing."

Okay, not a problem. I was speechless.

"We don't have much time. The conference starts next week," he said. "Édonte was supposed to move back home this week but my parents are gonna keep him a little longer, so everything is set."

"The two of us are going to Great Britain? Am I dreaming? What's the weather like over there? What should I pack? What will I do while you're at the conference all day, every day? I have to be at the conference every day too to cover it for the paper, don't I? How long are we gonna be there exactly?" I had a long list of questions.

"I'm going to the conference to make connections, so during the day, I'll be pretty busy. But you'll have me all to yourself at night. And if we go up a few days early, we can have a few whole days together. The conference starts next Monday, and I thought we could fly up on Friday."

"Are you kidding? This Friday?"

"Yep, and if you don't want to spend your days at the conference, I could write guest column articles for your paper. You can just edit them. How's that sound?"

"You mean I don't even have to really work?"

"Not if you don't want to."

"Sounds perfect. I'm in."

"Good. You go back to sleep and we'll talk about everything over dinner this week. I'm swamped 'til Wednesday. Let's get together then. My place. I'll cook. How does French cuisine sound?" Wynn asked.

"Sounds perfect. See ya Wednesday. By the way, do you love me?"

"Maybe . . . just a dab. See you, babe. Sweet dreams."

Just a dab? Tha hell? What had happened to his usual heartfelt confessions of love? I was too excited to dwell on it. I spent the next hour imagining the two of us enjoying romantic romps around London, visiting international landmarks and partaking of tea and other indulgent British customs. Shoot, forget Denzel. I finally drifted to sleep fantasizing about a week in paradise with the man I really loved.

******

"You're going where, Ace?" an apoplectic Marsha asked in disbelief over lunch the next day.

We chose to have a late lunch on Monday at Garozzo's, a dimly lit Frank Sinatra shrine disguised as a popular Italian restaurant in the newly renovated River Market area. Because of the late hour, we'd been fortunate enough to get a window booth following the lunch hour rush.

"You are so lucky. You get to go to London, England with your man. There is nothing more romantic than traveling abroad with your main squeeze," Marsha said wistfully.

"Ain't that the truth?"

How would she know? She'd never done it. But she was obviously stuck in romantic overdrive and was no doubt fantasizing about the romantic getaways she'd one day take with Patrick. Marsha was without question head over heels in love. That much was clear. And with The Troll, no less. At first, she'd been the one to give him that nickname, but nowadays whenever I slipped and called him that, she would get mad—I mean really upset—and stay that way for days.

While she and Patrick first got off to a rocky start, they were now in love, and I couldn't be happier for them. Originally, Marsha was sickened by the short, fat, light-skinned smoker whom she reluctantly admitted turned her out like no other man had ever done before. Since Patrick and Marsha had been together, he had lost some weight and even quit smoking, and while Marsha couldn't do anything about his height, she fell in love with him anyway. She told everyone who would listen that they were going to get married as soon as he asked, if she didn't ask him first.

"You know what you need, Ace?" Marsha asked as our penne arrabiate and seafood lasagna arrived. "You need some kind of translation guide."

She was right. The English had a funny way of speaking. They used words like "bloke," "telly," "chap" and "cheerio," plus they used words differently than we did in the United States. To them, apartments were flats, fags were cigarettes, elevators were lifts, mad meant crazy, chips were fries, crisps were potato chips, soda pop was tonic and crack, which was spelled c-r-i-c-k, meant have a good time.

"You're right. Do you have one?" I asked.

"Do I look like Barnes & Noble?" she asked, irritated. Her envy was showing.

"A little from the back," I joked.

"Are you saying my backside is as big as a building?" Marsha asked with a smile in spite of herself. "I have a friend, Myles Andrews, who teaches high school English in London. We went to college together. He's originally from L.A. I visited him in L.A. a couple of times when we were in school, and he has come here. You even met him once. Anyway, I haven't seen him for a while, but we always talk on the phone. He's a fine white-chocolate brotha. Look him up when you get to London. He'll make sure you have a good time."

"He has better things to do with his life than baby-sit me."

"He won't mind. He's a great tour guide and good people. I'll give you his number when we get back to the office."

"Bet. Will you call him and let him know I'm coming?"

"Just don't let him fall in love with yo' crazy self. He's been known to go a little cuckoo for cocoa. He likes sistahs, and if you're well endowed, which you are, for him, all the better. Call him. You'll be glad you did."

Marsha wasn't getting any arguments from me. A white boy that attended Howard University and he liked us colored girls? He had to be down, and I definitely had to meet him once I hit the streets of London.

"Foxx, in my office. Now!" the SOB's voice bellowed through my phone shortly after Marsha and I returned from lunch.

I walked toward his office, surprised by the lump developing in my throat. Being summoned personally by the SOB was like being called to see the principal. I couldn't imagine why he wanted to see me. I couldn't imagine what I had done wrong. I hadn't exaggerated on any of my expense reports (lately). I'd met all of my deadlines, plus I had actually received positive television and radio exposure for the newspaper because of the work I was doing at the YC.

I actually enjoyed working at *The Tribune* again. I'd recaptured the feeling I had when I first got my job at the paper. It had been just what I needed when I graduated from college. When I first started working at the paper, I was a zealous reporter. I always got the best scoops. The SOB took an instant liking to me. He really helped me hone my skills as a top-notch reporter. And while we weren't friends, there was an unspoken bond of mutual respect between us.

During my years at the paper, I had won several awards for outstanding reporting and received my share of personal notes of gratitude from some big muckety-mucks at the paper, the kind whose names are found on the company letterhead. Hard work and talent were definitely rewarded at *The Tribune,* and the fact that I was African-American didn't seem to matter an iota.

By the time I reached the SOB's office, the uncertainty of what I was about to face overwhelmed me. I was a dispirited and confused bundle of self-doubting nerves, and I had to rely on a power greater than my own to lift what had become the heavy burden of my hand so that I could knock on the door.

"Enter," he barked before I finished knocking.

The SOB occupied a large corner office drenched in midday sun. His office furnishings consisted of an expensive cherry-wood desk and a matching wall-length bookcase unit. A black leather antique chair sat regally behind the desk.

On the far left side of the room was a butter-soft black leather couch and four matching chairs that surrounded an oval, cherry-wood table. Textured gray walls were covered with dozens of awards the SOB had received over the years for his journalistic acumen. A state-of-the-art computer system and a large bank of black metal filing cabinets completed the office's impersonal look.

"I bet you're wondering why I called you in here," the SOB said. My dazed look confirmed his assessment. "When I came back from lunch, there was a message from someone who says she wants to file a complaint against you."

"What? Who has a complaint against me? What are they complaining about?"

"The person didn't give much more information than that. My secretary told her to call back at one-thirty. I want you to hear whatever it is she has to say but you can't say a word. The caller can't know you're listening."

At least he was letting me face my accuser, sort of.

We made chitchat while we waited for his telephone to ring. When it finally did, he answered it via speakerphone.

"Bishop here."

"Mr. Bishop, I have a complaint to make against one of your reporters there at *The Tribune*."

The longer I listened to the voice, the more incredulous I became. *Tha hell?* There on the other end of the phone was none other than the Youth Center's assistant director, Voncile Ford, The Weebil.

"Miss . . . uhmmm . . . I didn't catch your name."

"That's because I didn't throw it. I'm gonna make this short and sweet. I happen to know that Ms. Lacy Foxx is traveling to London to report on an international youth conference and the Greater Kansas City Youth Center is picking up her tab. It seems to me like that's a bit of a conflict of interest, don't you think?"

"That depends," the SOB said hesitantly.

"On what? She agreed to go on the trip and write a series of articles about the conference and the Youth Center. It seems pretty cut and dry to me."

"Ma'am, what exactly is your problem with Ms. Foxx attending the conference? The Youth Center does a lot of good work. If Ms. Foxx writes a few articles about the Center it could do a lot to draw attention to a worthy cause."

"My problem is she's taking the place of someone else who should really be going on that trip."

"Someone like who? Could that someone be you?"

"That's not important. What's important is for you to know that I will go to every media outlet in Kansas City and let them know *The Tribune* is being bought by the Youth Center. That would cast a pretty bad shadow on your newspaper's reputation, don't you think?"

"Ma'am, that's not necessary. We'll see to the matter," the SOB said, his hard-as-nails demeanor suddenly replaced with the contrite why-are-you-picking-on-me-again comportment of a small schoolboy.

"Thank you, Mr. Bishop. I thought you'd see things my way," The Weebil said in a satisfied manner before hanging up the phone.

"That cow!"

"You know her?"

"Yeah. She's the assistant director at the Youth Center. She's been trying to sabotage me ever since I started my volunteer journalism program there."

"Isn't she undermining her own employer? You'd think she would want all the positive free press she could get," the SOB said.

"She's envious of me. She hates me, and she's after Wynn, my boyfriend. She doesn't want us traveling out of the country together."

"Regardless of her motives, unfortunately, she's right. You're dating an official at the Youth Center and they're paying for your trip. That doesn't look good. Besides, who gave you this assignment?"

"No one gave me the assignment. I just knew when I emailed you the articles from London, my writing would be so dazzling you'd feel compelled to run a series of articles."

"Hmmm . . . to be honest, I don't even think this is news. It's definitely not worth the newspaper paying for your trip."

"Of course it's news. A local youth expert is going to be prominently featured at an international youth conference. It's like a youth summit. Experts from around the globe will be there."

"Great. If it's that big of a story, we can pick it up off one of the news wires. Like I said, the newspaper is not going to pay for it, and I forbid you from letting the Youth Center pay for your trip. If you want to go cover it, you'll have to take vacation time and you'll have to pay for it on your own dime."

"But the YC has already purchased my airline ticket."

"You'll just have to reimburse them, okay?"

"No, it's not okay! How can you— "

He held his hand up to halt my further protests. "As far as I'm concerned, this issue is dead. If you cover that conference in London, you're paying for it yourself. Period. And I just want to go on record as saying I'm disappointed in you. Both in your lack of integrity and your lack of sound news judgment. Plus, bringing your personal problems into the workplace is extremely unprofessional. Let's not let it happen again. Now, I have to get back to work. I suggest you do the same."

Within thirty minutes of my conversation with the SOB, the whole office seemed to know about my conflict of interest scandal. After dealing with "concerned" coworkers for more than an hour, I locked myself in a bathroom stall for refuge. I was angry with the SOB for placing my business on the corporate rumormongering grapevine so quickly. Although, after thinking about it for a while, I decided he most likely was not the culprit. His secretary, Barbara, who had a reputation for hearing and talking about things she shouldn't hear and talk about, was most likely the person I had to thank for the leaked news.

After work, I headed straight to the YC for my journalism session. Unfortunately, the members' enthusiasm for learning failed to make an impression on me. I let Trey lead the session and then afterwards, I used the old headache excuse to get out of watching one of his basketball games that I'd promised I would attend. As I was leaving the YC, I encountered The Weebil, who had a big, silly grin on her face.

"How was work at *The Tribune* today?" she asked.

I approached her, getting within an inch of her face. "Don't you ever mess with me on my job again, ya hear?"

"I don't know what you're talking about," she lied.

"Do the words jealous, triflin' witch mean anything to you?"

"Only when referring to you."

"You call my job again with some crazy mess and I'll show you just how triflin' I can be," I said, throwing a check for $1,000 in her face before storming off.

"Bring it, bee-yotch!" she cackled behind me.

As I was walking away from The Weebil, Trey ran up behind me. "Yo, yo, yo, Li'l Miss Reporter, where's the fire? You got a minute? I need to talk to you before my game."

"Yeah, Trey. Sure," I said as I took some deep breaths. "What's up?"

"I need a favor. I need someone to come down and talk to my counselor and my principal. Moms is workin' like crazy and I've been havin' some problems at school. That's kinda why I haven't been around here much."

"What kind of problems are you having, Trey? Whatever it is, I'm sure your mom would take off work to handle things if she really had to."

"Moms can't do it, a'ight! I need *you* to be *her*."

"Trey, I can't pretend to be your mama. What's going on?"

"They want to talk to me about this rumor folks been spreadin'. Haters been tellin' lies. Tellin' teachers and the principal that I'm dealin'. They checked my locker and stuff but they didn't find nothin'. But they still want someone to come down to the school to talk. And I ain't got nobody else but you, Mr. T. and Ms. Ford," Trey said.

"Trey, *are* you dealing?"

"Does it matter?"

"What do you think? Yeah, it matters," I said.

"Why? A brotha's gotta survive. My mom is sick, complications from diabetes. But she's still holdin' it down. She's still working three jobs so we can have a little of nothin'. I gotta help her out."

"You could get a real job."

"Doin' what? Flippin' burgers at Mickey D's for minimum wage? I'll pass."

"There are other ways of surviving. You're smart. You're a good athlete. You got a lot going for you. Remember when we met and you were so disgusted by your older sister and brother who were dealers and on crack. You're on the road to that same life you once hated so much," I said.

187

"Why do you think I'm askin' for your help? You know what? Forget it, a'ight! Just forget it. I should have known I couldn't count on you."

"Trey, you *can* count on me. When do I need to be at your school?"

"I'll meet you here tomorrow at eleven. We should go over to the school together. And don't tell Mr. T. Okay?"

"Trey, I can't keep something like this from him."

"Yeah, you can. If he or Ms. Ford knew what was goin' on, they wouldn't let me come to the YC, and other than my kid brother and sister, this place is the only other good in my life right now."

"Okay, Trey. I won't tell Mr. T., but you gotta promise me you'll straighten up."

"I will," he said, sounding no more convinced than I was.

******

The next morning when I arrived at the YC, Trey was already waiting for me.

"What's crackin', Li'l Miss Reporter? You ready?"

"Yep. Jump in."

"Naw, man. I can't be seen in no Dodge Neon," Trey said, laughing. "Let's take my ride." Trey's "ride" was a souped-up 1955 Chevy 210 Delray. I'd never seen the car before because usually when Trey came to the YC, he either walked or caught the bus after school. When we settled into his car, Trey turned his key in the ignition and rap music instantly started blaring on the stereo.

I turned it off. "Nice car. Collector's item? When did you get this?" I asked, avoiding the more relevant question of how he got it.

"An uncle of mine that lives out of town restores cars. He gave it to me."

"He gave it to you?" I asked in disbelief.

"Yep," Trey said, not volunteering any more information.

For the next several minutes, we drove in silence. Once we got a few blocks from the Youth Center, Trey inexplicably swerved and made a hasty U-turn. "Oh, hell! My P.O. ain't gonna like this shit!" he yelled.

"Trey, what are you doing?" I asked.

"Ms. Foxx, duck down!" he said, pushing me to the floor.

At that moment, I heard what sounded like firecrackers. It took me a moment to realize that what I was actually hearing was gunfire. "Is someone shooting at us?" I asked incredulously.

"Yeah!" Trey yelled. "It's a drive-by! Stay down!"

"Kill that sucka, Trey!" I heard someone yell. "Get that fool! This'll teach his ass to stay out tha South Siiiide!"

Trey floored the gas and sank low in his seat. I stared at him from the floor in shock and said a silent prayer as glass caved in around us and the sound of bullets hitting metal echoed loudly in my ears. After a while, the gunfire stopped and Trey eventually slowed down, but I stayed on the floor.

"You okay?" Trey asked, genuinely concerned. "You want me to take you home or back to the YC?"

"I don't want you taking me anywhere. Let me out!" I yelled.

"What? Ms. Foxx, I'm not letting you out!"

"I'd be safer on the street than in here with you. Let me out, Trey!"

"You sure?" he asked.

"Yes! I said let me out!"

Trey pulled over to the side of the road. I grabbed my purse and got out of the car. When I stood on the pavement, I was shaking all over.

"What was that about?" I asked.

"I don't know. It was a random drive-by."

"There was nothing random about that! I heard them. They were specifically trying to kill you, Trey. And me too!"

"Folks are just jealous . . . trippin'. Brothas can't have nothin' nice without folks hatin' on ya."

"That was not about your stupid car! You know it and I know it. Trey, you need to get right and get back on track or you aren't gonna be around much longer," I said in my outside voice. "And don't bother coming back to the YC anymore. I'm not gonna tell Wynn about this, 'cause he would flip the hell out. But I know he wouldn't want this mess around the Youth Center."

"But—"

"But, nothing, Trey! Don't come back to the YC! Ever! I mean it!"

TWENTY-FOUR

The next day, work was irritatingly busy, and it didn't help that my nerves were severely rattled thanks to my close brush with death the day before. But Wednesday evening, as I drove toward Wynn's home, the ambiance of my surroundings was hard to resist, and in no time, my busy workday and the drive-by were temporarily forgotten.

When I knocked on Wynn's door, I could tell he was good and pissed. So what if I was more than thirty minutes late and hadn't called? He would have to get over it. Wynn absolutely hated it when I was late. He said my flagrant disregard for time was just an excuse to procrastinate and get on people's nerves. He said my persistent tardiness was a sign of passive-aggressive behavior and that I was trying to usurp the power in our relationship. He'd read that in a stupid magazine somewhere. What did he and dozens of researchers and psychiatrists know anyway?

"What's wrong with you?" he said, greeting me at the door, remote control in one hand, 'tude on his shoulder. "You own a hundred watches, so why are you always late?"

I walked past him without saying a word. Obviously he didn't understand the delicate intricacies of my character. Was it my fault he couldn't fully appreciate the contradictions of my personality? I knew that getting back on his good side wasn't going to be easy. That's why I came prepared.

"Even though I'm late, aren't you glad to see me? I asked before giving him a passionate kiss. His response was underwhelming.

"Shhh . . . we have to keep it down. Perri is asleep upstairs," he grunted.

"What is she doing here? I thought we were going to be alone."

"Vonnie asked me to keep her at the last minute."

"Since when did you become a member of the baby-sitting club?"

"Since your behind was late. And don't start with me. She *is* my daughter."

I watched while he turned on the television and planted himself on the couch. Some stupid sports show was on the tube, so I had to act fast. I walked over to him, stood in front of him and slid off my lightweight raincoat to reveal myself pimped out in some of La Perla's laciest and finest lingerie. I began my best imitation of a horny, over-sexed, dancing stripper—bumping and grinding to an unheard syncopated rhythm. He loved it when I acted like a freak.

No response. Nothing.

When I finished my routine, he gently pushed me out of the way. "I told you Perri is here. We can't exactly screw in the middle of the living room."

I stood there naked and dumbfounded. Okay, so this was going to be a little harder than I thought, but I was up to the challenge.

"Why do women always do that?" he asked the air.

"Do what?" I feigned ignorance.

"You know what," he said, not taking his eyes off his precious television. "You always piss us men off and then try to make up for it with sex."

We always do it because it always works. Imbecile! Everyone knew the way to a man's heart was through his libido or his stomach.

"Are you gonna act like a doggone child all night? If so, I can head home now. I know you're mad, but I got stuck at work. It couldn't be helped. I know you hate it when I'm late and don't call, but there was too much going on at work. I was under deadline. I couldn't call. I got here as soon as I could. I'm sorry."

My apology fell on deaf ears. He grunted and shooed me away from the television. I grabbed my raincoat and lingerie and walked out of the room, feeling dejected and hungry. I walked into his kitchen and looked for my portion of dinner. I found it in the trash.

You are who you love. Like draws like. Your mate is your mirror. Isn't that how the sayings went? I hoped that none of them were true because that would mean I was an uncompromising, insensitive louse.

I made myself a peanut butter and jelly sandwich and headed for my favorite room in his home, his bedroom. I climbed into Wynn's king-sized Ikea sleigh bed and within minutes, I'd drifted to sleep. When I woke up from my unfit slumber a few hours later, Wynn was lying in bed beside me with his arms around me.

"I'm sorry. You know how I am about punctuality," he whispered before kissing me gently on my forehead. "Plus, I had an awful day at work. I didn't mean to take it out on you. Let's forget that all of this ever happened, and let's talk about our trip to London."

"I'm not sure that I'm going," I lied. "Earlier this week, someone called my boss and threatened to expose the fact that the YC is paying for my trip. My boss thinks it might be perceived the wrong way. He thinks it's a conflict of interest. Plus, he doesn't think this is newsworthy enough for the newspaper to cover on its own dime."

"Sweetness, you have to go. Forget *The Tribune.* I'll personally pay for your ticket. I want you there by my side the whole time. Please don't let what happened tonight get in the way of what we have. We're entitled to a little disagreement every now and then. Until tonight, things have been going good ever since we reconciled. Come on. Tell me you're still gonna go to England."

"I'll think about it," I said nonchalantly. "And if I do go, I'll pay for my own ticket," I said, failing to mention that I had already reimbursed The Weebil.

"I wonder who called your boss. Did he say?"

"It was The Weebil—I mean Voncile. I heard her with my own ears. My boss had her on the speakerphone."

"Vonnie wouldn't do that."

"That's why I didn't bother telling you when it happened on Monday. I knew you'd think I was lying. When are you gonna realize your precious Vonnie ain't the angel you think she is?"

He sighed heavily. "So, what do you want me to do? Talk to her about it?"

"No, let's just drop it. I've already paid the YC back for my ticket."

"So, you are going? I'll let my board know they're only paying for one." For the next several minutes, he was eerily quiet.

"What are you thinking about?" I asked.

"I wasn't gonna tell you, since things were kinda tense between us, but I heard from Jac today."

"Tha hell?"

"She's living in Chicago. She called because she wants Édonte to come live with her. Not permanently, just for a little while."

"I hope you told her no," I said, surprised and disgusted by his ex-wife's gall.

"I talked to Édonte about it and he wants to go to Chicago. He hasn't seen or heard from her in two years. He needs to see his mother."

"You think that's a good idea?"

"Not really, but what choice do I have? He's leaving after Christmas break. He's going to finish out the school year with her and stay in Chicago 'til the end of summer. After that, we're gonna work out a legal joint custody arrangement."

"So, how do you feel about all of this?"

"How should I feel? This whole thing is killing me. I love my son and don't want her hurting him again. I know I'm gonna really miss Édonte when he's with her, but I guess I've got to learn to deal with it. Regardless of what she's done in the past, she has a right to see her son," Wynn said.

"Does she? I think she forfeited that right when she turned her back on the two of you and abandoned you."

"That's why I'm torn about her being back in Édonte's life. If she flakes out on him again, I'm concerned about how it will affect him. Even though he acts like what's happened hasn't fazed him, at the end of the day, he's just a child that desperately wants the love of his mother," Wynn said sadly.

"I know you'll help him through it. He's lucky to have you as his father."

"And I'm lucky to have you."

"Are ya now? I know something that should make you feel better. Why don't you let me make it up to you for being late?"

"I'm down wit' ya."

For the next hour, passion was in abundant supply. After we finished, Wynn begged me to stay the night, but I told him I couldn't. I found the sudden uneasy peace between us unsettling. I knew that hearing from his ex-wife for the first time in two years had contributed to his earlier bad mood, but lurking underneath the surface was something else. Something else was wrong.

Ever since I'd started dating Wynn, I'd been reciting my favorite biblical verse from childhood dozens of times a day. Matthew 7:7. "Ask and it shall be given you." Well, I had asked for it, and it had been given to me in spades.

Unfortunately, for a long time I overlooked the reverse. "Be careful what you ask for because you just might get it."

Now that I had what I thought I wanted, did I really know what to do with it?

On the drive home, I reflected on my relationship with Wynn. The fact that I was a procrastinator and he was so rigid had become major points of contention between us. But that was just the tip of the iceberg. The fact that he often withheld the truth and was more secretive than I liked was another major issue, but it was one that I was sure would change the longer we were together and the more his trust in me grew.

I hoped our trip to London would help our relationship on all emotional levels.

TWENTY-FIVE

Our hotel room in London was full of inexpensive art and objets trouvés, and faux antiques, including Victorian paintings and old-world furnishings. Not that I noticed. I was in Heaven. I couldn't believe my recent good fortune. I couldn't believe the life I was suddenly living, and I knew that if my friends, family or enemies could see me, they wouldn't believe it either.

Upon entering our room on Friday night, Wynn and I fell straight into bed, both of us suffering from major cases of jet lag.

"Wake up, sleepy head," I said eight hours later as I opened all the blinds in the room. "Breakfast in bed is endearing and romantic, but lunch in bed is just plain triflin' and lazy. It's almost noon, and I didn't come all the way to London to stay in bed with you all day, as fun as that may be. Come on. Let's go eat and then enjoy the sights."

"Give me a few minutes to get ready. I can't believe you're up and dressed."

"I'll meet you in the hotel restaurant in thirty minutes," I said, bending over for a smooch. "Ohhh . . . eye boogers and morning breath! I don't think so," I said, opting not to kiss him. He pulled me to his chest and after some playful wrestling, he made me kiss him anyway.

"I hate you!" I said, wrinkling up my face.

"No, you don't. See ya in thirty," he said, walking into the bathroom wearing nothing more than a smile.

God, he has a beautiful derriere.

******

Wynn plopped himself into the chair across from me in the hotel restaurant exactly thirty minutes later. I'll say one thing for him . . . he was always on time.

"So, what do you have in store for us today?" he asked.

"I can't tell you, babe. It's a surprise," I said mysteriously. "I took the liberty of ordering for you."

He eyed the food on the table appreciatively. I knew my man loved breakfast food any time of day, and I made sure his first meal in London was fit for a king. On the table before us were bacon, sausages, scrambled eggs, a concoction of tomatoes, sautéed potatoes and mushrooms, shepherd's pie, freshly baked croissants, crumpets, Danish pastries, toast served with marmalade and all the tea and coffee we could drink.

"That's my girl. I knew you'd take care of me," Wynn said, grinning broadly.

We ate quickly and hurried outside where we caught a cab. I had a big day planned. I'd never traveled to London before, but I did my homework. I was determined to make our trip to London special. It was an adventure that I couldn't wait to embrace with my whole heart and soul.

We spent the rest of the day touring London by cab and by foot. We toured Royal Albert Hall and visited the House of Parliament and Whitehall. We saw Big Ben, toured Westminster Abbey, and visited St. Paul's Cathedral where Princess Diana and Prince Charles were married. We witnessed the changing of the guard at Buckingham Palace and went to the Tower of London to see the crown jewels. We also visited Kensington Palace where we paid our respects to Princess Diana, England's most beloved princess. We ended the day by shopping at Harrods, the world's largest department store and Hamleys, the world's largest toy store.

As we made our way back to the hotel, we talked about how tragic Princess Di's untimely death was and we talked about the fate of her two sons. By the time we returned to our hotel, it was nine o'clock.

"Where are you going?" I asked Wynn as he started to duck into the hotel.

"I'm bushed. I'm heading back to the room."

"I'm not done with you. You see those people over there?" I asked as we watched several dozen people climb into a bus. "We're going with them."

"What are you up to, Lacy Foxx?"

"The conference had a Murder & Mayhem Bus Tour as one of its activities, and I signed us up."

"That's my girl! I'm gonna go to our room, drop off these toys and clothes for Perri and Édonte, grab some jackets and I'll be right back. Don't let them leave without me," Wynn said as he rushed into the hotel.

When he returned, we climbed on board the bus and heard an eerie monotone voice say, "Welcome to a bus trip to murder. A century ago, notorious Jack the Ripper terrorized the courts and alleyways of the East End. He was never caught and to this day, there is still speculation about his identity. Tonight you will visit the scene of each of his crimes and hear the evidence for yourself. Will you be able to guess who dunnit?"

"Sweetness, you know how much I love this stuff. Thanks for signing us up," Wynn said, punctuating his words with a kiss. He was obviously touched.

No one could tell me I didn't know how to please my man. His love of the macabre was one of many interests we didn't share, but I did love him and I wanted to make his trip to London as memorable as possible.

"What's more," the voice droned on, "we'll visit a real haunted house and you'll hear about many of our other infamous inhabitants such as Sweeney Todd, the demon barber of Fleet Street. So, sit back and enjoy, if you dare."

The next three hours were spent with an overzealous gang of mass murderer groupies. Even though it all intrigued me, I anticipated the nightmares I'd have for the next few weeks. In between tales of murder and mayhem, I interviewed several people attending the conference about their countries' biggest issues regarding at-risk kids. I was going to use their comments as sidebars for Wynn's guest articles.

By the time we returned to the hotel, it was after midnight. Wynn and I hadn't eaten since breakfast and we were starving. The hotel restaurant was full of late night patrons, so I suggested a more scenic dinner locale and Wynn readily agreed.

We dined at an out of the way joint that I'd read about. Once there, I ordered the bangers and mash recommended by our waiter. Wynn, ever the pig, ordered oak smoked Scottish salmon with onions and capers, chateau potatoes, chipolata sausages and two choices of vegetables. To top it off, we had heaping helpings of flaming pudding smothered in a spiced rum sauce.

We returned to our hotel around 2 o'clock in the morning. A few hours later, I woke up to Sunday breakfast in bed. After a leisurely meal and an even more leisurely romp in the sack, Wynn and I set off for some sightseeing, this time planned by him.

We traveled to the other side of town where we bartered for jewelry, clothing and unique handmade crafts in an open-air market amid a backdrop of dope Caribbean beats. Wynn and I purchased items for our families, including plenty of loot for Wynn's kids.

For lunch, Wynn and I dined on fish and chips and afterwards we visited several museums for an artistic look at London. By seven o'clock, we were both tired and impressed.

"Great Britain's ethnic roots run deep," Wynn said as we exited an art gallery that exhibited works by culturally diverse artists.

"I know," I said in agreement. The influences of people of color are everywhere. Hey, if you're not too tired, babe, I was thinking we could maybe go check out a few clubs."

"I'm tired, but not too tired to party with my baaabyyy!"

That night, Wynn and I made the rounds to a handful of clubs where we jammed to reggae, jungle, trip-hop, garage, African and American beats. When we returned to our hotel at four in the morning, we were both bushed. Four hours later, Wynn woke me from a deep sleep.

"Hey, howyadoin'?" he asked, greeting me with a kiss.

"I see you're dressed," I said, encircling my arms around his neck. "I thought we could spend the morning in bed together."

"Sounds tempting, but the conference starts today. I have to show my face in the place. While we were on the bus tour the other night, one of the organizers asked me to participate in a few panels, and he wants me to sit at the head table at tonight's banquet."

"Shouldn't I come too? I'm supposed to be covering the conference."

"Remember, I'm writing the articles. You're just editing them. To switch things up, maybe on the last day, as everyone is leaving, you could interview folks on their impressions of the conference. But for now, don't worry about that. I want you to enjoy some more sightseeing and I want you to have fun."

"Well, I guess I can spare you for a few days. But you have to tell me how much you love me first."

"You know I love you, but just a dab."

"Just a dab?" I asked.

"Okay, okay, you've worked your way up to a couple of dabs."

"Get outta here, funny man."

"Alrighty then. I'm off to help the children of the world," he said with a wink while walking to the door.

"Forget the children of the world. Why don't you come over here and concentrate on helping me?" I said, licking my lips suggestively.

"And wrinkle my Armani suit? You can forget that. Besides, if I get anywhere near you and that bed again, I'll never make it out of here. See ya, sexy," he said, blowing me a kiss from the doorway.

TWENTY-SIX

I had committed the phone number of Marsha's friend, Myles Andrews, to memory, but that didn't keep me from getting nervous when I called him shortly after Wynn left our hotel room.

"Hello, this is Myles Andrews," a breathy west coast accent said through the other end of the phone.

"Myles, hello. My name is Lacy Foxx, and I'm a friend of Marsha Turner's from Kansas City. I'm visiting here in London and Marsha suggested that I contact you once I got here. I was hoping we could meet and maybe hang out together for a little while."

"Okay, Lacy Foxx, Marsha's friend. Would ya mind slowing down?"

"It must be odd having a stranger call asking to hang out with you. I told Marsha to warn you that I was coming, but I see she didn't. See, I came to town on Friday with my boyfriend, who's here for a weeklong conference that actually starts today. And all week he'll be tied up day and night, and while I could join him, I'd prefer to check out London."

"You need to breathe before you pass out, girl. Look, before you get wound up again, do you think maybe I could say something?"

"Sure," I said sheepishly.

"You probably don't remember this, but I met you once in passing while visiting Marsha a few years ago in Kansas City. I'd consider it an honor to hang out with you."

"You sure you don't mind baby-sitting me?"

"Not at all. Where would you like to go? What do you want to do?"

"How about a trip to Bath and maybe Stonehenge? I'm staying at the Chesterfield and I think Paddington Station offers a daily excursion to Bath that leaves in two hours."

"I'll be over in an hour and thirty. Let's meet in the lobby."

"Okie doke."

"Okie doke? Now there's an American expression I don't miss much. It's been a few years since I've seen you, so remind me. What do you look like? What are you wearing?"

"I'll be wearing a purple polka-dotted dress. Plus, I'm African-American and there aren't many of us staying here at the hotel. I'll be hard to miss. What are you wearing?"

"Some jeans and a Miles Davis T-shirt."

"Miles D.? You're a fan?"

"During his heyday, my father was one of his stagehands. Today he's still one of his biggest fans, as my name attests. I guess it rubbed off. I better go. See you soon."

I spent the next hour getting ready. Once I was presentable, I stared for twenty minutes out of my hotel room window, gawking at Buckingham Palace, trying to recall under what circumstances I'd met Myles. Convinced he had me confused with someone else, I gave up and headed down to the lobby to meet him.

Once I laid eyes on Myles, I remembered seeing him before. There was no way I could have forgotten him. He was fine, for a white boy. He was tall with a firm build, thick, dark hair, clear green eyes and a square, determined jaw. He was very easy on the eyes. So easy I couldn't take mine off of him.

"Myles?" I asked, unable to believe my good fortune.

"Lacy?" he responded in kind, hugging me as I shook my head in the affirmative.

"It's great seeing you again."

"You too," I said, struck by how much he looked like a young, pre-*ER* George Clooney.

"Come on. We have to hurry to Paddington Station. It's almost ten," Myles said, grabbing my hand.

By the time we arrived at the excursion pick-up site, the tour had sold out. As our second choice, we opted for tickets to Woodstock and Stratford-Upon-Avon, Shakespeare's birthplace. We boarded the coach just as its doors were closing.

"Made it!" Myles said, pulling me into the seat beside him. Once we caught our breath, we both spoke at the same time.

"So, tell me about yourself," we both said in unison.

"You first," I said. "How long have you been in London?"

"I came here the summer after college, and before I knew what had happened, I'd been here for five years. I'm in no hurry to get back to the left coast," Myles said.

"According to Marsha, you're the ultimate tour guide. My expectations are high."

"I'll try not to disappoint. Speaking of Marsha, how is she? I haven't talked to her for a few months."

"She's doing okay, although I'm a little worried about her."

"Worried? Why?"

"I don't know if she was like this in college, but nowadays she has a penchant for danger. She's attracted to it like a magnet."

"She was like that back in college too. She called it stepping outside of her comfort zone. Me and the rest of her crew called it crazy."

"Well, she's way outside of her comfort zone now. At one time she was talking about taking skydiving lessons, and earlier this year, she got a job covering our paper's crime and drug beats. It's really dangerous stuff. Every time she goes out on a breaking story, I worry that she won't come back."

"Her zest for adventure and danger stems from the fact that she comes from a line of cops. After college, she wanted to go to the Police Academy, but her father wasn't having that. So instead, she chose a career as an investigative reporter. Having the crime and drug beats is her version of being a cop."

"I know all of that, but it doesn't lessen my concern for her."

"Marsha can more than take care of herself. Hey, tell me something. Is she still using outlandish words that no one in America but her uses?"

"Yeah, half the time you need a dictionary to understand what she's talking about. What's up with that?"

"In one of our freshman English classes, a professor wrote on one of her papers that she should try expanding her vocabulary. He wrote that it would help make her a better writer."

"And she's been on a mission ever since."

"You gotta love her."

We rode the next few hours in silence. Actually, we both fell asleep. Our first stop was Woodstock, where we had lunch and wandered around a quaint Oxfordshire village. Then we headed to Stratford-Upon-Avon, where we visited all of Shakespeare's old haunts, including his purported birthplace and the cottage where his wife, Anne Hathaway was born. A big fan of Shakespeare's (albeit a closet fan), I bought all three book versions of *Shakespeare's Insults* in a local gift shop and I also bought a Shakespeare magnetic poetry set.

Next, we visited the fourteenth century Warwick Castle, where for hours we toured magnificent staterooms, dismal dungeons, and the infamous armory that housed a magnificent collection of swords, armor and other assorted instruments of torture.

When we climbed aboard the coach headed back to London, both Myles and I were like giddy schoolchildren.

"What did you enjoy the most?" I asked once we settled in our seats.

"The Warwick Castle. I've seen it at least a half dozen times, but every time I visit it, I'm intrigued by something new."

"More of your conversation would infect my brain," I said, using a quote from *Shakespeare's Insults*. "The Shakespeare stuff was all that."

"Spoken like a true writer and literary buff."

"I took a Willie Shakes lit class in college and I have been hooked ever since. You're a teacher. I'm surprised you didn't like visiting the Bard's old stomping grounds more."

"I guess I'm just a masochist at heart."

The trip back to London was spent poring over my books and talking about our trip. When we arrived back at Paddington Station, we were famished.

"It's only eight o'clock. Why don't we go get something to eat?" Myles said.

"I'm game. My boyfriend is gonna be stuck at a banquet until late, and I'm hungry. Are there any dinnertime cruises on the Thames?"

"One leaves every evening at nine. Let's see if we can catch it."

We caught the cruise boat and spent the next two hours enjoying a leisurely and peaceful cruise down the Thames River. The boat's huge, powerful floodlights illuminated historic sites that included St. Paul's Cathedral, Traitor's Gate, the Tower of London, the House of Parliament, Westminster Abbey, the Tower Bridge and South Bank. I was utterly overwhelmed by the city's beauty. By the time we headed back to the hotel, it was eleven.

"Lacy, I've had a great time. Seeing the sights with someone who hasn't been here before makes you see things that you look at every day, differently. It was really a lot of fun," Myles said while escorting me back to my hotel.

"I had fun too."

"So, what do you want to do tomorrow?"

"I gotta check in with my boyfriend, Wynn, to see what's up, and then I'll give you a call."

"Okay."

When we finally arrived at my hotel room, I knocked on the door.

"Where's your key? Did you lose it?" a concerned Myles asked.

"It's in my purse. I just want to torture my significant other for not spending the day with me. If I'm up this late, I want him up too."

After a few minutes, Wynn answered the door in his boxers.

"Show off. Have you no shame?" I said with mock embarrassment. "Can't you see we have company?"

"Excuse me? Do I know you?" he asked, stifling a yawn.

"Wynn, this is Marsha's friend, Myles. He was kind enough to baby-sit me today while you played conference dunce."

"Nice meeting you, man," Wynn said while groggily extending his hand.

"Likewise."

"I hope she wasn't too much trouble."

"When she got too out of control, I just muzzled her."

"I do a lot of that myself."

"Both of you talk an infinite amount of nothing," I said, quoting Shakespeare impressively.

"Huh?" Wynn asked perplexed.

"Shakespeare. We went to Stratford-Upon-Avon. She purchased all three editions of *Shakespeare's Insults* and a Shakespeare magnetic poetry set, so beware."

"Thanks for the warning."

"Myles, thanks again for everything. I had fun," I said.

"So did I. It was nice seeing you again, Lacy. It was nice meeting you, Wynn. Good night."

"Good night," Wynn and I said in stereo.

"Nice-looking guy," Wynn said while closing our hotel room door.

"Hmmm, I hadn't noticed," I lied.

"Yeah, right. So, did you have a good time?"

"I did, but I know how it could have been even better," I said, pulling him into bed on top of me. After a quick but rousing lovemaking session, we cuddled while watching an Agatha Christie murder mystery on television.

"Sweetness, I have something to tell you. Someone asked me to serve on panels every day this week. And they want me to present awards and speak at each of the evening banquets. I really wasn't expecting all of this attention, and I can't say no. There will be lots of media and influential people at all of the events. It will be a great chance for me to plug what we're doing in Kansas City."

"You gotta do what you gotta do," I said, not at all disappointed that I'd get to spend more time with Myles seeing the sights of London.

******

When I woke up several hours later, Wynn had already left. I called Myles and let his phone ring at least six times before he finally answered.

"Hello?"

"Myles, it's Lacy."

"I almost didn't answer, but then I thought it might be you. I'm on my way out to run some errands."

"Really? Well, come by and get me. Wynn is going to be at that conference again all day and night."

"You want me to come get you so we can run errands together?"

"Yeah. I'm tired of sightseeing. I want to do normal, everyday stuff. So, let's go run some errands."

"Anybody ever tell you you're a wee bit insane? Trust me, you do not want to run errands with me. Look, I'll be free after three o'clock. We can do something together when I get back."

"Great. I think I'm gonna catch an excursion to Bath and Stonehenge. There's one leaving from Paddington Station in a few hours. It doesn't arrive back until six o'clock. Let's get together then."

"Fine, I'll meet you at Paddington Station at six. Have fun."

As expected, I was awestruck by Stonehenge, one of the most spectacular prehistoric sites in England. The mysterious large stone monuments, impressive reminders of Neolithic man, put me in a highly philosophical mood. And Bath, which was popularized by Romans who discovered the city's natural hot springs, was utterly breathtaking.

Yet, as impressive as they were, I was unable to enjoy Stonehenge and Bath as much as I'd hoped. The whole time, I kept thinking of Wynn and how what I had hoped I'd be sharing with him, I was instead having to share with another man.

While I was looking forward to dinner with Myles, I would have preferred having dinner with Wynn. It was weird that a guy who barely knew me was being so nice and wonderful to me, making time for me when my own man wouldn't. Myles was filling the void left behind by Wynn, who, to put it bluntly, wasn't giving me the time of day.

I was proud of Wynn for being so dedicated to Kansas City's kids, but where did his dedication leave me? Where did it leave us? Would I always be last on his list of priorities? Would I always play second fiddle? Would I always be left searching for something or someone to fill his void?

By the time I returned to Paddington Station, I was toying with the idea of leaving London the next day. Myles was waiting for me when I climbed off the coach and he quickly whisked me away to a popular local restaurant where we had a fabulous dinner.

"This may be my last night in town," I said after dinner while Myles and I strolled through Piccadilly Circus, a bustling people hub and home to the world-renowned winged archer statue, Eros, the pagan god of love.

"What? I thought you and Wynn were supposed to be here a full week."

"We are. He'll stay. I'm the one that's going back early. Although he promised me we'd spend our evenings together, it's not working out that way. And that's fine. I understand. He came here for a reason. I'm just here to sightsee, and I've seen all I want to see. Besides, seeing the sights is no fun without him."

"Great, thanks a lot," Myles said.

"Spending time with you has been a lot of fun. Don't get me wrong. But don't you have a life to get back to? Don't you have to go to work?" I asked.

"Didn't I tell you? I'm on a sabbatical. I'm writing the great, all-American, foreigner-in-a-foreign-land novel."

"Even so, I'm sure you don't want to spend all of your free time with me."

"Says who? Have you heard me complain?" he asked.

"No, you've been wonderful."

"So, does Wynn know how you feel?"

"Nope, but I'm gonna tell him tonight."

"Man, he'd be a fool to let you leave. You're in beautiful London, and Paris, one of the world's most romantic cities, is just a stone's throw away. I don't care what he came here for. He'd have to be crazy not to take time out to enjoy all of this with you."

"I couldn't agree more," I said quietly.

"Well, if he doesn't come around, you can always call me for back-up," Myles said, his tone suddenly serious.

His comment startled me, until I remembered what Marsha said about his appreciation for black women.

Myles and Robert De Niro . . . God love 'em!

"Myles, you're so sweet."

"You're easy to be sweet to. Lacy, can I tell you something? Ever since you told me what was going on with Marsha, I've been worried about her. I've tried calling her

211

several times and I haven't gotten an answer. I've left severa
messages, but she hasn't returned any of my calls."

"I'm worried about her too. But I also know she's not
gonna change just because we're worried," I said.

"You're right, but just watch out for her."

"Don't worry. I will. You know, I really have to figure this
thing out with Wynn. You won't mind if we make an early
evening of it, will you?"

"No, not at all. I'll walk you back to your hotel."

"That's okay. I'd like to be alone for a while. I need some
time to think."

"All right. Well, it was nice spending time with you,"
Myles whispered in my ear as he hugged me tightly.

"You too, and if you ever come visit Marsha in Kansas
City, look me up," I said as we parted.

It was ten when I arrived back at the hotel. Wynn, not
surprisingly, wasn't there. I showered, slipped into some
pajamas, ordered a bottle of non-alcoholic champagne from
room service and sat on the balcony, enjoying the view.

An hour later, I heard Wynn's key turn in the door. I rose
from my seat on the balcony and greeted him, determined to
tell him I was leaving the next day. But before I could say a
word, I felt his hungry mouth on mine. In the blink of an eye,
my pajamas were lying on the floor in a heap and I was
standing naked before him.

"Hello to you too," I said, laughing. "My day was fine.
And yours?" He uttered not a word as he carried me to our
bed and laid me on it gently. He undressed before me, his
mouth saying nothing, his eyes speaking volumes, and I
suddenly lost my resolve to tell him I was leaving. After hours
of pleasuring one another, he finally spoke.

"Sweetness, I've been a fool. I'm sorry I haven't spent
more time with you. All I've been able to think about all day is
you. I feel guilty that some other man has been occupying
your time," Wynn said.

"I understand you're here for a reason, and I've tried not to get in the way. You're making my job easy by writing all the articles about the conference. But the simple truth is, kickin' it around London without you isn't all that wonderful."

"Can I just say I've been a selfish jerk?"

"No, you haven't been. You had a job to do and you were just doing it."

"Well, I'm miserable-and-blue-lost-without-you-feelin'-like-a-fool sorry."

"Nooo . . . what you *are* is crazy," I said, touched by his sincerity.

"Well, I'm really, really, really sorry that I haven't spent more time with you. I knew my days would be consumed by the conference, but I didn't think my nights would be too. Now here, I have something for you," he said as he rolled over and grabbed something from the drawer of the nightstand beside our bed.

"What's this?"

"Two tickets to Paris. We're taking a Eurostar train through the Channel Tunnel and we're gonna stay in France over the weekend. It will be just the two of us. The Champs-Elysée, the Arc de Triomphe, the Eiffel Tower . . ."

"What about the conference?" I asked.

"If you could be patient, there's just a few more days left. And then it will just be you and me in France for the weekend. I've already changed our airline tickets and I've called your boss to tell him you won't be in on Monday."

"Just a few more days without you, huh? I guess I'll survive," I said.

"Thanks, babe. You've touched my heart and my soul in a way that no one else ever has before. I'm experiencing intense feelings and emotions that were non-existent for me before you came along. So, I'm glad you're letting me do this for you, for us."

"All of this from a man who claims to love me just a dab?" I asked.

"I told you earlier that you had worked your way up to a couple of dabs."

"Lucky me."

"No. Lucky me," he said. "You've opened up a whole new emotional world for me, and the least I can do is give you as much of the physical world as I possibly can."

We were both right. We were both lucky, although I think I fared better in the deal. Wynn expressed his love for me in ways I'd only dreamed of. It wasn't the trips or constant flurry of activities. It was the little things, like him calling just to hear my voice, surprising me with love notes in unexpected places, and always instinctively knowing what type of mood I was in.

But mostly it was the way he looked at me. When we were together, he looked at me like a lifelong blind person experiencing the miracle of sight for the first time, admiring everything with awe and amazement. I'd often wake to find him gazing at me like a mother taking in the miracle of her newborn or God staring in wonderment at His creation of the Heavens and Earth.

The fact that he loved me was in a way its own miracle. The way he looked at me and cherished me meant everything to me. How could he not know that I already had the only piece of the world that truly mattered?

Him.

TWENTY-SEVEN

"Glory be, chile. Yo' hair is tore up from the floor up," Bibi over-exaggerated while parting my hair to apply relaxer the Saturday after I returned from London.

"Owww . . . owwwch . . . " I whined as she tugged on my tresses.

"How long has it been since you last came over here for a retouch?"

"Uhmmm . . . uhmmm . . . I don't know," I said. My mind had gone blank, burned to smithereens by the relaxer, no doubt.

"It's going on two months, and I know you've been scratchin' like crazy. You always do. I can tell you right now it's gonna burn. And don't say nuttin' to me, chile, if all yo' hair falls out."

My grandmother had been doing my hair ever since I was ten years old, when Mama said I was old enough to switch from a press and curl. I had felt so grown when I got my first relaxer. Never mind that it was just on for two seconds before I leapt out of my chair, screaming bloody murder, convinced my grandmother was trying to kill me.

Ever since that less than ideal experience, no one had ever touched my hair except for my grandmother. That isn't entirely true. Once, I did go to this beautician, and I use the word loosely—who believed in the hair philosophy the shorter the better. She could only do two lengths: short and shorter. I made the mistake of falling asleep in her chair, and when I woke up, I was bald. I had no hair! She slicked down my back and sides and expected me to pay her seventy dollars for making me look like Mr. Clean. Needless to say, girlfriend didn't get paid.

The only other time I went to anyone else was when I let a white friend of mine convince me to go to her hair stylist. I should have known then that I was going to the wrong place. I needed me a beautician, not a stylist. Gay, white Arnie washed my hair, blew it dry with a hand dryer, curled it with a curling iron and then sent me on my way.

I couldn't believe it. What? No passing out from heat exhaustion under a twenty-pound dryer? No two hours of torture? No gooey gels, setting lotions or tons of hair spray to keep my 'do done and in place? The minute I stepped outside in the humid Kansas City weather, I looked like an African bush woman. Gay, white Arnie refunded my money and my grandmother has been doing my hair ever since.

"Lawd have mercy," Bibi prayed above my head while working the relaxer through my thick, wavy roots.

Determined not to be a tender-headed crybaby, I bit my lower lip, hoping that Bibi would soon put out the fire that was slowly burning a hole through my scalp. I gritted my teeth, dug my fingernails into my arms and tapped my feet wildly. Five minutes later, tears were settling in my eyes and my lip was bleeding, but I was still determined to keep the relaxer on for as long as it took to de-kinkify my less-than-luxurious locks.

Amid my silent prayers for relief, I heard a distant hammering.

"That doggone man is always out there making a bunch of racket," Bibi said.

"Who? Mr. Harrison?" I asked, willing myself to pass out.

"Who else? No one irritates me like that man," Bibi growled. I decided to tread lightly. At least the conversation, no matter how unpleasant, would take my mind off the burning bush atop my head. "Why does he get to you so, Bibi?"

"Glory be. I don't know why. He just does!" she huffed. Although Bibi wasn't willing to admit it, she was in the same state most women that I knew were in—*Needaman, USA*. "How his wife stayed married to him for as long as she did is beyond me," Bibi professed out loud, sucking her teeth.

I took the bait. "I don't know. She seemed pretty happy to me. Besides, Mr. Harrison is sweet. I hope to marry a man just like that one day."

"God help ya then, chile."

That was it? Hurricane Hannah didn't erupt? I ventured on. "You know, I think he's perfect for you. Really."

"Lacy Eymaleen Foxx, I know what's goin' on in that little matchmaking head of yours. Don't go gettin' no highfalutin' ideas. That man is crazy as a loon and ornery as a rattler. What would I want with the likes of him?"

"You're not getting any younger," I said, reminding her of the obvious.

"Better over the hill than under it," she sniffed.

"Wouldn't it be great to have someone around that loved and adored you, someone you could spend your twilight years with?" I took a quick breath, determined to finally tell my grandmother how I truly felt about her man-less situation. "I love you too much to watch you spend the rest of your life alone, Bibi."

"Don't worry about me. You need to tend to your own man problems," she said, cutting me to the quick. "Now come on, let's get that relaxer off of your head before your head explodes." She wasn't getting any arguments from me.

Thankful for the relief, I continued on. "For as long as I can remember, men have been coming to the house to court you, but you've never given any of them the time of day. Over the years, you've taught me that you can't expect others to love you unless you love yourself. And while you clearly love yourself, you won't allow others in to love you. Don't you want to be loved?" I asked above the sound of the cool water running in Bibi's kitchen sink.

She paused for a moment before speaking. "When I was younger, after your granddaddy died, I thought there would always be time for love, so I kept putting it off. I had kids to raise, a career to keep on track and a God to serve. Finding love just wasn't at the top of my list. The more and more I put it on the back burner, the more and more time slipped away. You're right. It wouldn't be so bad having a man around, but now it's too late."

"It's not too late. Men from the church still come around the house every now and then," I said, feeling encouraged.

"That's true. It's amazing I haven't run them all off," she said with a chuckle.

"What do you have to lose? Why don't you try being nice to a few of them? Better yet, why don't you try being nice to Mr. Harrison?"

She looked at me skeptically. "Chile, I don't have time for no foolishness."

"Bibi, what are you afraid of exactly?" Before she could answer, her doorbell rang.

"Go answer that," she said, slapping a towel over my head. I walked slowly to the door, imagining the locations of the chemical sores that would sprout up all over my head thanks to Bibi's overzealous relaxing abilities. When I opened the door, Sebastian was standing there in a red-and-white Kansas City Chiefs sweatshirt and baggy jeans.

"What are you doing here?" I asked, unable to hide my displeasure at running into him while not looking my best.

"I asked him to come over and rake the leaves," Bibi said. She pushed past me and opened the door widely so that Sebastian could enter.

"Yeah, is that okay with you, Ms. Foxx?" Sebastian asked facetiously.

"What you do means less than nothing to me," I said in a tone that I hoped sounded blissfully blasé. Bibi cut her eyes at me then directed her attention to Ratboy.

"Sebastian, I seem to have misplaced my rake. Would you mind going to the store to get another one? Also, I need seem extra large trash bags. Lacy, you go with him and show him what kind I use."

"That's okay, Momma Hale. I remember from when I used to rake your yard before. I can go get the rake and bags myself," Sebastian said, rescuing us all from the awkwardness of me having to ask my grandmother if she was on crack.

"Lacy can go with you. She ain't got nothin' else to do. Wait a minute. I'll be right back. Don't you go away. I'm gonna go get you some money."

"That's not necessary, Momma Hale. I'll take care of it," Sebastian said.

"You should know better. You're fighting a losing battle," I said in a half whisper.

"Nonsense, chile. I insist," Bibi said to Sebastian as she retreated to the back of the house. Once she left the room, Sebastian and I just stared at each other.

Subtle!

"So, how are you handlin' the baby's mama thing?" Sebastian asked.

"Fine," I said curtly.

"How's . . . uhmmm . . . Mr. T.?"

"He's been out of the hospital for a few months. He's doing fine. He's fully recuperated," I said.

"Good. Lace . . . about what happened when he was in the hospital . . . "

"I appreciate you being there for me when I needed you, Sebastian, but let's not relive it, okay?"

"A'ight. Let's not. I've got work to do. Tell Momma Hale I went to the store," he said, slamming the door behind him.

"Glory be. What did you do to run him off this time?" Bibi asked when she returned to the living room a few minutes later.

"What did *I* do? Why do you always take his side?"

"Because I know you, chile. Look, you just gave me some advice, silly as it was, and now it's my turn. I'm gonna tell the truth and shame the devil. The plain truth is worth more than a pretty lie. That boy still loves you, and the sooner you get your head out of the sand and stop chasin' that Wynn Trust all around the world, the sooner you'll realize you still have feelings for Sebastian Gamble. You'll realize you still love him," Bibi said.

"I do not still have feelings for Sebastian Gamble . . . Okay, maybe I do a little, but what I feel for him is a far cry from love. Love? Don't make me laugh."

"Ain't no reason to laugh, 'cause I ain't said nuttin' funny. You and that man were together for three years. You two were engaged to be married. It's about time you owned up to the blessing God has given you, girl — true love, a soul mate. I've loved only two men in my life. I spent years loving the wrong man, and later I spent years loving the right man at the wrong time. Don't make the same mistakes I've made," Bibi said.

"All my life you've led me to believe that you never regretted your choices when it came to love. It never seemed to bother you that you never married. Why are you getting all sentimental on me now?" I asked.

"Chile, I am not the sentimental type. I never have been and I never will be. You're right. I don't regret the choices I've made. Personally, I think most men are trouble and I thank the good Lord I never really had one meddling in my life."

"But?"

"But you're not me, and if you were truly honest with yourself, you'd admit that I'm right about you and Sebastian. Mark my words," Bibi said.

"What makes you so sure that Sebastian is the right man for me?"

"What makes you so sure he ain't?" she asked.

"The fact that we can't seem to be in a room alone for more than two seconds without getting on each other's first, second, third and last nerves. Plus, he cheated on me. I could never trust him again."

"That man never cheated on you. You know it and I know it."

"No, I don't know that," I said defiantly.

"Umphf . . . I don't know what you're looking for, but you don't have to look no further than right up under your own nose. What you need more than anything is right here in your own backyard," she said, pointing to my heart.

"Bibi . . ."

"I don't wanna hear it. That man still loves you. When the two of you were together, he adored you. He lived for your happiness. He always put you first, above everything and everyone else. When you find a man that loves you like that, you have to hold on to him."

"Wynn loves me like that."

She glared at me and sucked her teeth in a disapproving gesture. "That Wynn ain't no Sebastian," Bibi said pointedly.

Why, because he doesn't kiss your ass like Sebastian? I thought to myself.

I wanted to explain to her how it made me feel when Wynn looked at me, but she would have never understood. "Love is fleeting. Here today, gone tomorrow. What Sebastian and I had, ended long ago. Things have changed. We've both moved on."

"Glory be. Don't go foolin' yourself. A man doesn't love you like that and then just stop after a few months," Bibi said.

"A few months? We broke up about a year ago!"

"A few months, a year, eight years . . . apparently it don't matter. He's here, ain't he? At least he was here 'til you ran him off. And I guarantee you he didn't come over here 'cause he was dying to work on my yard. I told him you'd be here."

"Mm-hmmm," I said, suddenly bored with the conversation.

"That's all I'm sayin' for now. I'm gonna go lay down. That's a leave-in conditioner, so don't wash it out," she said as she left the room.

"Okay," I said, planting myself in front of her console television. Hours later, midway through the U.S. Amateur

Gymnastic Championships' long floor program, I was proud of my girl Shequita from the Youth Center. She was well on her way to winning first place. I'd tuned in just to watch her. Everyone at the YC was probably watching her too. I hadn't seen much of Shequita since I started volunteering at the Youth Center, because her gymnastics career had become her priority and she spent all her extra time working with her coach. The judges were just about to critique Shequita's performance when there was a knock on Bibi's door.

"I'm all done," Sebastian said, brushing past me to get inside once I opened the door. "So, you're still coming over here to get your hair done, huh?"

I subconsciously wiped conditioner off my forehead. Sebastian looked at me and grinned. His enchanting smile was infectious . . . *almost*.

"Yep. My grandmother is resting. Is there something else you want?" I asked, fighting the urge to lick the beads of sweat off his sexy upper lip. "Do you want something to drink? Something to eat?"

"Actually, yeah. But I'd like to go wash up first."

Overcome by a tremendous urge to be nice, when he returned from the bathroom ten minutes later, I had two BLTs and a large glass of lemonade waiting for him.

"Pour vous," I said with a smile, pulling out a dining room chair for him.

"What? You're showing me kindness? Come on and join me," he said, offering me one of his sandwiches. "I won't bite unless you want me to."

I sat down at the table across from him and laughed. "You're crazy," I said, affectionately scolding him.

"Your grandmother told me you went to London with your boy. How's London in the fall? And more importantly, how are *you*?"

"London was fine and so am I. How goes it with you and Charron?"

"After she caught us together, things were rough there for a minute, but now they're good. Actually, they're great . . . actually, things are more than great. They're wonderful," he said, finally settling on the right word.

"Wonderful? Now there's a word you probably didn't use much to describe us."

"Wanna bet? I used it more than you know," he said while taking a huge bite out of his sandwich.

"I hate it when you do that."

"Do what?" he asked innocently. "Chew and swallow?"

"No," I said, suppressing a grin. "When you're nice to me unexpectedly. When you say ridiculously sweet things like that to me."

"Do you want me to stop?"

"Yeah. Yeah, I do."

"No. No, you don't," he said with a broad smile. "You never could handle a compliment."

"Don't you worry about what I can handle."

"Lace, can I tell you something?"

"I guess," I said, bracing myself for more kind words.

"I never told you this before, but I feel the need to tell you now. I always admired the close relationship you have with your grandmother."

"Really?"

"Yeah. The two of you have a pretty special bond. Despite the differences in your ages, you and your grandmother relate to each other so well. Charron hardly ever talks to her younger sister or her mother, let alone her grandmother. She doesn't have a strong sense of family like you do," Sebastian said. "I miss being around that."

"I think one of the reasons why family is so important to me is 'cause I don't have much family."

"Your grandmother was the most stable adult figure in your life, huh?"

"When I was a child, Daddy was always away at work. He was in the Army and sometimes weeks would go by when I wouldn't see him. Although he was stationed his whole career at the local base 'cause of my mama, he did travel a lot. And speaking of Mama, you know she had her issues. But Bibi was always there. I'd say I lived more than half of my childhood right here, in this house. When you think about it, my grandmother is really the one who raised me," I said.

"I don't remember my grandparents. They all died when I was young. But when you and I were together, your grandmother took me in as if I were her grandchild, as if I were her flesh and blood. She still treats me like that to this day."

"She likes you so much because you remind her of my father when he was courting my mother. That and you always helped her out around the house. Like you're doing now."

"Hmmm . . . your grandmother is a very special lady. She's just like her granddaughter," Sebastian said.

"Stop saying stuff like that. Stop being so nice."

"Like I said, you never could handle a compliment," he said with a wink.

"It's just compliments from you I have a problem with."

"You better get used to hearing them. I have a feeling more of these little surprise meetings are in store for us. That is if your grandmother has anything to do with it. You know she wants us back together, don't you? She's always telling me not to get too attached to Charron."

"Don't listen to Bibi. She's getting senile in her old age," I said good-naturedly. "Besides, you and I hate each other, remember?" I said, reminding him of a fact that we both knew wasn't true.

"Hold up! Hold up! Hold up! Who says? I don't hate you. And why do you hate me?" he asked, turning suddenly serious.

"I was kidding. I don't hate you. I've been so outwardly mad at you the past year because I'm inwardly mad at myself for letting you go. I let a good one get away, and the truth is, I hide behind insulting you and my animosity for you because I'm not comfortable with how I feel."

"And how do you feel?"

"I'm always turning to you for some reason. I'll be honest. I'm having a hard time forgetting about what we had. I have been ever since we broke up. And with Bibi being your biggest fan, that doesn't exactly help. She thinks you're my soul mate," I said.

"She could be right. So, you still love me, huh?"

"I didn't say all that. Let's just say my head and my heart aren't always in synch when it comes to how I feel about you."

"Yep, you still love me."

"In your dreams. I love Wynn," I reminded him.

"There you go hiding again."

"The truth is, I have mixed feelings about you. But I think it's pretty clear there can be nothing between us like there was before. You'd have to be a fool to think we could make it work a second time."

"You'd have to be an *absolute fool* to think that," Sebastian said.

"Yeah ... absolutely," I said unconvincingly. "Look, I have to finish my hair. Just leave your dishes on the table and I'll clean up everything later."

"All right, cool," he said, as he stood to leave. "I'll see you later. It was nice talking to you in a civilized manner for a change."

"Yeah, it was. I'll see ya," I said, following him to the door. Why did I suddenly feel like an absolute fool?

TWENTY-EIGHT

"Wake up and wake the hell up now, Ace."
Click.

That was Marsha's pitiful excuse for a wake-up call. Since I'd returned from London, my internal clock had shut down. I had an awful time waking up in the morning, so I'd begged Marsha to call me at the crack of dawn. I didn't want to be late for an early morning interview I had scheduled with 2Tuff.

Two hours after Marsha's call, I arrived at my destination. Khalil "Razzy" Quest, Tamerek "T-Bear" Landon, and I had agreed to meet at their agent's home for the interview. Their agent was the smarmy Denys Robertson.

Denys lived in the exclusive, resort-like housing community known as Heather Bend. The 1,300-acre gated development had an 18-hole private golf course, a spectacular clubhouse, a 50-acre stocked lake and homes priced from the low $200,000s to the millions, or so I'd heard. Other than Denys, I didn't know anyone who lived in the development, and I'd certainly never made it inside the development's gated walls.

I punched in the necessary code that Khalil had given me a few days earlier and drove through the opening gate as the elderly black security guard ushered me in with a smile. Following Khalil's directions, I easily found Denys Robertson's home on Yuma Court. The huge six-bedroom, four-bathroom house was located on two corner acres of land.

The front door opened before I could get out of my car.

"Hey, Lacy Foxx," Denys said while welcoming me into his home.

"Hey, Denys," I said with as much fake enthusiasm as I could muster. Once inside, Denys hugged me and I tried my best not to cringe. Denys was attractive enough—tall, nice build, medium skin tone, small retro afro, expressive, dark brown eyes—but he was the most arrogant and dishonest person I'd ever met.

Still, I had to give the man his props. He really went the distance for his clients. Over the past year, he had strong-armed me into doing stories on all of his acts. He did what he had to do in order to get them the best gigs and contracts possible, and according to my sources, some of the big boys in the music industry on both coasts feared him, this little black boy from Missouri.

"So, what's poppin'?" the overbearing Denys asked. "Tamerek and Khalil have been talking about this interview all week. They're in the recording studio," Denys said.

He led me through his spectacular home, which was decorated in standard bachelor fashion. There was lots of leather, contemporary art and dark wood, plenty of white and red accents, and enough electronic gadgets to give an electronics junkie a major hard-on. When we finally entered a large rec room located in the bowels of his home, we were greeted by Tamerek and Khalil.

"Guys, this is Lacy Foxx. Lacy, this is 2Tuff," Denys said grandly. "You be nice to my boys," Denys barked before turning to leave.

"Finally, a face to match the name. Nice meeting you, Ms. Foxx. I'm Khalil."

"And I'm Tamerek. What up?"

"From what I've heard, you. I'm glad Wynnton Trust put me in touch with you. It's nice to finally meet you both. So, where do you want to do the interview?" I asked, getting right down to business.

"How 'bout right here?" Tamerek said.

"Yeah, we like this room. This is where we do all of our writing and recording," Khalil chimed in.

The room's walls were covered with pictures taken of, awards given to, and articles written about all of the acts that Denys managed. Although 2Tuff hadn't even gone national yet, the local and regional talent show awards they had won over the years took up half a wall. Surprisingly, there were just a few scant articles written about them.

A matching set of oversized furniture—cream leather couch, love seat, recliner, chair and ottoman—provided ample seating for visitors to the room. Tools of the trade were sprawled out all over: a baby grand, synthesizers, keyboards, guitars, digital samplers, drum machines, multi-track tape recorders, turntables, mixers, microphones, speakers and amps. On the far left wall was a heavy oak door that led to a small recording studio.

Amid the equipment, Tamerek and Khalil looked older than their eighteen years. During the course of the interview, I learned that the two of them got their start at age six, singing in St. Mary's church choir. At one time, they were deemed the city's "Little Angels of Gospel Music."

Well, Kansas City's Little Angels had sure grown up.

Tamerek had a sophisticated, worldly, aristocratic air about him. He had "pretty boy" good looks. He had light skin, golden brown eyes, naturally wavy hair cut close to his head and a lean, muscular build. His musical style matched his enchanting looks. He was a lyrical maven with a melodic voice that would sound just as good singing opera as rap. He had a remarkable vocal phrasing and accenting style that was usually only displayed by old pros who had been in the business for decades.

Khalil had a harder edge than Tamerek. He wore a don't-mess-with-me attitude on his sleeve and on his left forearm he sported a Phoenix rising from the ashes tattoo. He was tall, dark and he had "big ears." I don't mean literally—we're not talking Dumbo. I'm talking about his uncanny ability to play by ear any song he heard. Although he never had any formal training, Khalil could play ten different instruments, including the piano, the saxophone and the guitar.

228

The interview lasted an hour. Like most musicians worth their salt, both Tamerek and Khalil admired artists like the Temps, the Godfather, Stevie, Al, Ray, Marvin, Ella, Billie, Sarah, Diahann, Dionne, Tina, Eartha, Nancy, Lena and Barbra. They had dreams of working with P. Diddy, Jill Scott, Mariah, Missy, Mary J., Babyface, Alicia Keys, Whitney, Wyclef Jean, Timbaland and Dre. From what I could tell, while their dreams of working with the music industry's current hit-makers were lofty, with these two, anything was possible.

Near the end of the interview, Khalil started playing the synthesizer.

"Check this out," he said from the far corner of the room. Soon the room erupted into a mass of thick, dense, catchy beats—a kaleidoscopic mix of hip-hop, house, acid jazz, funk and soul. Tamerek's sleepy, velvety croon joined in with clever, satirical lyrics that were all at once poetic, edgy, beautiful, forceful, truthful, political, seductive and imaginative.

"So, what do you think?" Tamerek asked when they had finished.

"I think you two are amazing. I'm surprised you don't have some major labels beating down your doors trying to sign you. Heck, if I had the money, I'd start my own label and you guys would be the first act I'd sign."

"We have a couple of big labels interested, but they're not coming up with the production, distribution and development deals we want. Once we finish our demo though, there's gonna be a bidding war. You watch!"

"Just make sure I get the first autographed copy of your debut CD."

"Bet," said Khalil. "Shoot, we need to hang with you more often. You're great for our egos."

Ten minutes later, after explaining that I'd send a photographer to visit them within the week, the interview was over. Tamerek and Khalil walked me to my car and I climbed in.

I'd finally found my scoop, and the minute I finished writing it, I was sending it right to *Élan Live*. 2Tuff was on the verge of becoming big, and I'd go down in history as the first reporter to write something substantial about them. I'd be known as the reporter who launched their careers.

TWENTY-NINE

During lunch the day after my 2Tuff interview, I convinced Marsha to skip work for the afternoon and join me at the local visiting carnival. However, the minute we arrived at our destination, she regretted it.

"This is some ghetto, messed-up crap. I can't believe I let you convince me to come to this ghetto carnival."

A sucker for any kind of ride and anything that reminded me of Never Never Land, I corrected her. "It's Kansas City's Soul Carnival."

Marsha shot me a hope-you-get-your-mind-back-soon look and mumbled, "Whatever."

She was right. The carnival was G-H-E-T-T-O. Located on the edge of the inner-city Wal-Mart lot, within a half-block radius were 500 people lined up for two rides—a Ferris Wheel and a Tilt-A-Whirl. When not riding or standing in line, carnival goers had their choice of twenty junk food selections including powdered sugar funnel cakes, fried Twinkies and Oreos, Dippin' Dots, oversized pretzels, cotton candy, corn dogs and kettle corn—all of which could clog their arteries in record time.

We paid our $5 cover charge and prepared to ride, eat and stand in line for the rest of the evening. As we got in line for something to drink, Marsha's whining began anew.

"Three dollars for a Coke? Two dollars for bottled water?" she asked in disbelief. The words were barely out of her mouth when a gang of four teenage boys ran past us, nearly knocking us over.

"Ex-cuuuse you!" Marsha yelled after them. "It's the middle of the day. Shouldn't y'all be in school?" she questioned with a scowl.

As one of the boys looked back at us, I recognized him immediately. "Trey? What are you doing here?" I asked.

"Yo, Li'l Miss Reporter. What's up?"

231

I fought the urge to duck and answered him coolly. "Don't 'what's up' me, boy! Why aren't you in school?"

"School's out. At least it is for me," he said.

"What are you talkin' 'bout?"

"I got kicked out for fighting yesterday. But it wasn't my fault. I was just protectin' myself. You know, self-defense."

"Isn't this the third time you've been expelled from school for fighting this year?"

"Yeah," he said sheepishly. "So, who's your friend?" he asked, changing the subject.

"Boy, don't even. She's old enough to be your mama. Plus, she doesn't have a penchant for death."

"Man, why you shut a brotha down like that?"

"Marsha, this is Trey Jenkins. He's one of the kids— "

"I remember. You interviewed him for the Youth Center Gala article."

"Hmmm . . . so I made an impression on ya, huh?" Trey asked with a sexy smile.

"Trey, honey, don't smile at me like that. I've got clothes and shoes older than you."

"I ain't feelin' no love here, so I'm out. See ya, Ms. Foxx," Trey said as he ran off to catch up with his friends.

"Cute kid," Marsha said as we paid for our Cokes. "What's his story?"

I fought the urge to tell her that Trey, the cute kid, almost got me killed. After the drive-by, I'd vowed not to tell Marsha or anyone else about it because I was afraid I'd break down and be inconsolable if I relived that nightmare again—even if it *was* just to talk about it.

"We're losing him, Marsh. If we haven't totally lost him already."

"Band-Aid, eventually we lose a lot of 'em. We just gotta do the best we can."

Marsha and I headed to the Ferris Wheel, where we easily had an hour's wait ahead of us. We'd only been in line a few moments when we started to feel some droplets.

"What just landed in my hair? Did it come from a bird? Is it raining?" Marsha asked.

"I think it's Sno-Cone juice. It came from up there."

Marsha looked up at the Ferris Wheel and juice dripped down the side of her face. "Bebe, why don't you watch your doggone kids?" she yelled to the woman sitting beside two children who were laughing and pointing. "See, that's why I don't want no rugrats."

I grabbed some paper towels from a nearby junk food stand and handed them to Marsha. "You know you deserved that," I said, trying not to laugh.

Marsha wiped her face then mumbled sheepishly, "Yeah, I know."

We both burst into a fit of laughter, nearly falling over each other. When we were done, we sat down on a nearby picnic bench.

"Okay, so why are we really here?" Marsha asked, unafraid of facing the elephant in the room—or in our case, on the Ferris Wheel.

There were times when I hated my job more than usual, and this was one of those times. Recently, one of the paper's fashion editors had quit, and I had the misfortune of being assigned her duties. Some duties! The National Association of Podiatry had just released a report on the state of America's feet and someone, somewhere in the bowels of our organization thought that the story was newsworthy enough to localize—and localize big.

I'd been assigned a two-page spread to talk about, of all things, feet.

"I hate that I've been assigned that podiatry story. I'm here to look at folks' feet."

"Hmmm . . . want some cheese with that whine?" Marsha asked, laughing.

"Ever since I was assigned that story, it's like I've become this woman possessed. I can't go anywhere without looking closely at everyone's feet. I bought four pairs of shoes in one day based on findings in that stupid report. And last night, I spent an hour examining Wynn's feet. It's freaking me out."

"It should be freaking you out. I have two words for you. Seek help."

I laughed. "And I have four words for you. Mind your own business!"

"No, I'm serious. Your foot fetish is a symptom of a much larger problem. Girl, you got issues."

She didn't know the half of it. My foot obsession wasn't my only problem. Trey almost got me killed—a fact I was still in denial about. And despite our trip to London, I still had trust issues with Wynn, who had kept some important truths from me on more than one occasion. In fact, everything of importance I'd ever learned about him, I'd learned from someone else by mistake. Our relationship was wrought with lying, cheating and trust issues—on both of our parts—and that had me doubting Wynn and myself much more than I liked.

Also, I was worried about the feelings I still had for Sebastian. They were feelings that should have vanished long ago. It didn't help that I was getting pressured by my grandmother to get back with him. And to top it off, my career was going N-O-W-H-E-R-E, as was evident by the fact that I was staring at folks' feet!

"You need a drink," Marsha said. She pulled a bottle of Alizé Wild Passion out of her purse and shook it in my face. "Want some?"

"Alizé saves the day," I said as I grabbed the bottle and took a long swig.

"Dang, it ain't Kool-Aid, Band-Aid," Marsha said, grabbing the bottle back.

She wiped the mouth of the bottle with one of her Sno-Cone juice-soaked napkins. "I don't want any of your cooties."

"You can kiss my cootie-havin'-booty," I said while making an exaggerated kissing sound. I watched her drink for far longer than she should have and then I spoke with as much finesse as I could muster, after weighing my words carefully.

"Tha hell? What's wrong with you, Marsh? What's up with the big-ass bottle of Alizé in your purse, ya lush?"

"Where do I start? Oh, I know where. I hate men," she moaned.

"What are you talking about? Aren't things going well with you and Patrick?"

"Nope," she said, shrugging her thin shoulders.

"Why? What's going on? What's wrong?"

"The question is, what's not going on? He and I have been dating for as long as you and Wynn, but have you seen us go away on a vacation together? The man doesn't know squat about being in a relationship."

"Have you talked to him about how you feel?" I asked.

"Not yet, but I'm calling his sorry behind right now to let him know I'm not putting up with his crap anymore," she said as she dug around in her purse for her cell.

"Slow your roll, girl," I said while grabbing her purse out of her hands. "You're not calling him on my watch. Not while you've been drinking."

I had to protect her from herself. I knew that calling Patrick while she was upset and drinking was a big mistake, and a move Marsha would later regret. But I wondered if it was any more dangerous than Marsha letting Patrick rip her self-esteem to shreds. She was obviously way out of her comfort zone, and as her friend, I felt helpless because there wasn't much I could do about it.

"Band-Aid . . ."

"What? What's the problem?" I asked, concerned.

"Number one, Patrick just received a promotion, and he traipses me around to his boring, funky insurance company functions like I'm some kind of stupid token award. Number two, he may not be as well off as your man, but he does have a little chunk of change, although you'd never know it 'cause he's so thrifty!"

"Thriftiness is a worthy virtue," I said with a laugh.

"I have a surprise for his thrifty tail. Like it or not, he's taking me to Mo Bay and soon."

"Montego Bay? You better watch out or you may be the one that ends up getting the surprise, you gold digger."

"I'm not a gold digger, I just want to be appreciated. Number three, Patrick has started smoking again, and it really bothers me. But whenever I complain about him killing me slowly with his second-hand smoke, he tells me, 'you gotta die of something.' Prick."

I tried not to smile. "Bless his little rotund self. He's just being a man, Marsh. This is typical male I'm-afraid-of-showing-real-emotion bull crap," I said.

"I know that, Band-Aid, but it doesn't make it any easier to handle."

"Well, unless you want to be man-less, you better learn how to handle it."

"Maybe I'd be better off man-less."

"Are you kidding? You need to step away from the crack pipe," I joked.

Marsha without a man? Yeah, right. I wasn't even going there with her. I remembered how she was following her break-up with Joaquan, the cop. That mess was not pretty. She was the devil on wheels, plus she was always horny. Joaquan apparently knew how to throw it on her. He had her whipped, although to this day she'd never admit it.

"You wanna hear something even more pitiful?" Marsha asked in a wistful tone. "While Patrick is the ultimate in bed, we don't even have sex anymore."

"What? Why is that?"

"He works these crazy twelve-hour days as manager of the insurance company, and then he goes and works out at the gym at least an hour every night. By the time I see him, he's worn out. And I haven't even told you the worst part yet."

"There's more?"

"During the time that we've been together, Patrick has only told me that he loves me once. Do you know how much that hurts?"

"What?" I asked softly in disbelief.

"Do you know what it feels like to be with someone who never tells you he loves you?" Marsha asked.

Did I know what it felt like? Yeah, I knew. *Just a dab.*

To tell someone you loved him and for him to not say it back was the worst. To be met with total, utter, self-esteem-shattering silence, or worse yet, flippant indifference, sucked to high Heaven.

"Marsh, I know he loves you," I said.

She interrupted me. "I know it too, but I'm from Missouri, the Show-Me State, and I need for him to show me *and* tell me that he loves me."

"Girl, it's really no big deal. Whenever I ask Wynn if he loves me, he tells me, 'just a dab.' He stopped saying he loved me after he learned I cheated on him."

"And you let him get away with that?" Marsha asked.

I would have never imagined that those three small words—I love you—were so important to tough-as-nails Marsha. She wasn't exactly the most sentimental person in the world. But we both knew being sentimental had nothing to do with it. She, like everyone else in the world, wanted something very basic. She simply wanted to be told she was loved, and the fact that the one person she loved more than anything couldn't tell her what she wanted to hear, affected her deeply.

"Although Wynn doesn't say it in those words, I know he loves me, so it's really not that big of a deal for me," I lied.

"Well, it is for me," Marsha said, her eyes moist. "I guess I shouldn't complain, though. Overall, Patrick and I have a good relationship."

"But sometimes you have to give up your *good* to make room for your *better*."

"Okay, Iyanla, Jr. You know, when I'm with Patrick, I get this strong sense of ennui . . . a weariness, a dissatisfaction. In a way, I feel I should call it quits with him, but I'm not ready to end it. Not yet. At least the relationship I'm in now is better than nothing," Marsha said.

Was it better than nothing? Was it really or was Marsha just in denial? I hated seeing her like this. She deserved so much more than she was allowing herself to have. I hated that she was selling herself short. She didn't have to settle for just any old relationship that came along. Didn't she realize that? Deep down, did I?

"Come on, Ace. I wanna talk about something else, okay? What's up with this foot fetish thing of yours?"

"You want the truth?"

"Abso-friggin'-lootly."

"What if you can't handle the truth?" I asked, doing an awful imitation of Jack Nicholson.

"Look, Jack, I can handle anything."

"Okay, the reason I'm so into this story is 'cause I have such horrible feet."

"You know in all the years that I've known you, I've never seen your feet. I've never seen you barefoot, and I've never seen you in sandals with the toes out."

"I know, and you never will," I said.

"Why? I know you say your feet are awful, but how bad can they really be? Tell me but don't show me. I'm not in the mood for a creep show."

"I have no intention of showing you anything. Do you really want to know how bad they are? Okay, my feet are real long and narrow, and so are my toes," I said.

"So what? A lot of people have long, narrow feet and toes."

"I guess. But I have a complex about mine. As a kid, I grew like a weed, and my parents couldn't afford to buy me new shoes all the time. My shoes were always too small and it caused serious problems."

"Oh, please. Your feet couldn't have grown any faster than anybody else's."

"Wanna bet? By the time I was ten, I wore a size ten shoe. I thought every year that I got older my shoe size would change to match my age. I used to pray that I'd never get any older. It was extremely traumatic."

"Well, don't hate me 'cause my feet are beautiful," Marsha said.

"I have plenty of other reasons to hate yo' behind," I said.

"Hah," Marsha responded wryly.

"Unfortunately, this podiatry report story has opened up some old wounds. I remember everyone in elementary, junior high and high school teasing me about my long, narrow feet. They called me Long-foot Lacy. It was devastating."

"Poor baby," Marsha said with a barely contained wicked smile. "Well, we all have our crosses to bear."

"Ooooh, I forgot! I have to interview this exhibitionist rock group, Bare None. They're playing at the Los Angeles Staples Center in a few weeks and they're playing here at Kemper tonight," I said, gathering my things. "I gotta go."

"A'ight, let's roll, twinkle toes."

"Marsh, have I ever told you I love you, I love you, I love you, I love you, I love you?" I asked, accenting my words with a bear hug.

"Forget you, ya big-foot wench," Marsha said as we walked away from the Soul Carnival laughing.

THIRTY

"I'll be stronger than before, I will love you even more, ohhh, ohhh, ohhh, ohhh . . . I'll take you back, if you come back . . . "

I was definitely in an I'm-every-woman Chaka Khan kind of mood as I sang along to the bad sistah's *I Feel For You* CD on the high-tech stereo Sebastian bought me for my birthday a few years ago. I actually was in more of an I'm-*everyone's*-woman kind of mood. The guilt of sleeping with Sebastian while Wynn lay in a hospital bed fighting for his life still bothered me from time to time. And now the thought of being pregnant by Wynn wasn't helping matters.

So much for using condoms! I know that when a woman is stressed, it can cause her period to come late and result in a false positive home pregnancy test, but I was as regular as clockwork. I'd only been late one other time in my life, and that's when I was pregnant. In my case, EPT stood for "evade possible trouble." I was going to call my doctor when I got a free moment so that I could make arrangements to take a real test.

Here I was again, defying the odds. My OB-GYN told me that after I lost the twins, I would never be able to get pregnant again. She also said that on the off chance that I did ever get pregnant, I'd never be able to carry a baby to term. I would always miscarry.

After I lost the babies, my OB-GYN recommended that I have a hysterectomy. I wasn't a big fan of major surgery, so I chose not to, since it wasn't life threatening. I should have listened to her. If I had, I wouldn't be in the predicament I was now in. The phone rang, snapping me out of my self-pitying mood.

"Ohhh, ohhh, ohhh, ohhh . . . I'll take you back, if you come back, I'll take you anywhere you ever want to be, you're the light inside of me." I sang along as I picked up the receiver.

"Hello?"

"Ace, you're not gonna believe this," Marsha said breathlessly into the phone. "I'm getting ready to cover the largest drug bust in the city's history."

"What?" I felt my heart sink.

"The city's drug enforcement team is about to bust up the largest drug ring in Kansas City. This ring has connections to dealers and drug kingpins all over the country. It's one of the top ten distribution rings in the world. Heroin, meth, crack, reefer, ecstasy, and freebase and powder coke. You name it, they move it."

"Marsh, you can't go. I need you. I think I may be pregnant and I need someone to talk to," I said, trying desperately to sound frantic.

"Puhleeze, you're such a liar. You aren't too upset. I heard you screeching right along with Chaka when you picked up the phone. I'll tell you what. I'll come by after the bust. But it will be late. Gotta go. Love ya. Outtie."

Ohhh, ohhh, ohhh, ohhh . . .

******

Funeral services will be held for Marsha Turner on Wednesday, November 15 at St. Thomas Baptist Church at 11:00 a.m. Marsha was born to Loretta and Gerald Turner. She graduated from high school at Paseo Arts Academy then went on to graduate from prestigious Howard University. Since going to work as a reporter for The Metro Tribune, Marsha has won several awards for outstanding journalism. Marsha was preceded in death by both of her maternal and paternal grandparents. She leaves behind her four brothers, Mark, John, Paul and Brad, parents Loretta and Gerald, and a host of other relatives, loved ones and good friends.

******

The day I learned that my best friend had been murdered while covering a story for *The Tribune*, I marched straight into the SOB's office and demanded that he give me the crime and drug beats. I was determined to make the rat bastards that killed Marsha pay. Buying a gun was next on my list. The SOB told me in a not-so-polite manner that I was off my rocker and I'd been at home in bed ever since.

From my bed, I soaked up every single bit of information that I could about the circumstances surrounding Marsha's death. Details about that night flooded the airwaves although initially there weren't many hard facts, just a modicum of useless information.

A large Kansas City drug bust. . . international connections . . . drugs and money confiscated by police . . . inner-city drug war . . . more dead . . .

Useless, useless, useless. I needed names. The money I was going to use to buy my gun with was burning a hole in my knock-off Hermès Kelly bag. Finally, I got what I needed. It was during a visit from Sebastian. I was surprised I didn't scare him away. I looked like death on a hot plate. I hadn't showered, washed my face or combed my hair in twenty-four hours, but he didn't seem to notice or care. He looked at me like I was a beauty queen, a champion show dog. I hated the way he looked at me, comforted me. I hated that no one would ever look at Marsha or comfort her that way again.

Sebastian was droning on and on about God only knows what, when something on television caught my eye—a face I recognized, a name I'd heard before.

Seventeen year old . . . former basketball star . . . former honor roll student . . . former Youth Center member . . . mother works three jobs . . . brother and sister on crack . . . known drug dealer . . . drive-by shooting target . . . wanted murderer . . . Youth Center robbery suspect . . . Trey Jenkins . . .

"What? Trey robbed Wynn? Trey killed Marsha? Oh my goodness!" I screamed as I slumped into a limp pile in the middle of my bedroom floor.

"Lacy! Lacy!" I heard Sebastian yell. "Are you okay? What's wrong?"

Like a child standing for the first time, I rose unsteadily to my feet. "That man, that boy, it's Trey," I mumbled. "He's a member at the YC. I see him there all the time when I go to conduct my journalism sessions. He actually helps me."

"He's a Youth Center member? Are you sure?"

"Well, he was. I haven't seen him for a while. We were once really close. He even met Marsha! I can't believe he's responsible for her death and Wynn's shooting."

"Well, believe it."

We focused our attention on the small television screen located inches away from my bed. As it turns out, the cops who were making the city's largest drug bust ever feared it would be dangerous, so they convinced Marsha to stay in one of the black-and-white units parked outside of the known drug house.

Trey, who from what I could tell was now a stark-raving-mad-lunatic-crackhead-drug-dealing fiend, walked up on the scene and took Marsha hostage in order to get his buddies out of the house. Trey and company later put a bullet in Marsha's head just for the fun of it, and every single one of them got away. The more I learned, the more I wished I didn't know.

"How can this be? The Youth Center is supposed to be saving kids like Trey. What is Wynn doing? How could this have happened?" I asked, bewildered. "Trey was supposed to be one of the good ones. He had promise. He had potential. He was supposed to make it!" I yelled, not recognizing my own voice, which was now distorted by rage.

"You can't blame Wynn or the YC for that monster," Sebastian said, collecting me in his arms. "We lose young black kids to the streets every single day, especially young black men."

"Stop trying to defend Wynn. Because of him and his stupid failure of a Youth Center, my best friend is dead!" I screamed at the top of my lungs as if the sound of my voice would awaken Marsha and return her to the land of the living.

"We all miss Marsha a lot and yeah, Trey, or whatever his name is, was responsible for her death. But do you realize how many more Treys would be out there on the street if it weren't for places like the YC?"

"Don't give me that cockamamie just-a-few-more-dollars-and-we-can-save-the-world baloney. Save it for the donors and volunteers who don't know any better. I get enough of that from Wynn," I said as I began sobbing uncontrollably.

That was the beginning of my breakdown. I didn't speak or get out of bed for the next three days. Wynn, who was out of town on business, called me every morning. Sebastian called me every night, and Bibi, my dad and my uncle stayed with me at my condo the whole time. At least that's what everyone tells me. I personally don't remember any of it.

When I finally stumbled out of my mourning-induced coma, it was time to say good-bye to Marsha. On the morning of her funeral service, it was a typical gray and dreary Midwest November day. For the last two years in Kansas City, there had not been one sunny day during the entire month of November. It was the time of year when all the industrial plants prepared for their year-end inspections, and the proper maintenance and cleaning they'd forgone all year long took place during one month. The stench of environmental neglect could be detected across the city. I hated the month of November. It was a perfect month for death.

Marsha was buried on her killer's birthday. She would have hated her funeral. It was a circus. She knew and was loved by a lot of people. Politicians, musicians, CEOs, sports figures, common folks . . . they were all there to pay their last respects, as was the television media, with lights and cameras blazing. Didn't they realize that some of us were actually suffering and grieving? Sometimes I hated being a part of the media because my cohorts were, more often than not, a bunch of insensitive predators!

Patrick, Marsha's four brothers and a few cousins were the pallbearers. Sebastian was an usher. I was her flower girl. How ironic is that? I always thought I'd be the maid of honor at Marsha's wedding. Never in my wildest dreams did I imagine I'd be a flower girl at her funeral before her wedding day ever arrived.

People weren't supposed to bury their best friends during the prime of their lives. In a fair world, life didn't work that way. But who said life was fair? First my brother, then my mother, next my twins and now Marsha. I had to face the facts. My old friend death was back for a visit.

The burial service was hardest for me. As they lowered Marsha's coffin into the ground, I had an epiphany. Marsha was gone and she wasn't coming back. She wasn't ever again going to greet me with her big smile and signature "What's up, Lace the Ace Band-Aid" greeting. She would no longer be there to offer me her folksy bullshit advice or call me crazy when I offered her mine. Nor would she be there to confuse me with words not used by anyone but ACT and SAT preparers.

Everyone kept telling me that things happened for a reason—the good, the bad and the ugly—and while I racked my brain trying to find the reason behind Marsha's death, I found none. None that made any sense, none that eased my pain.

"Are you okay?" I heard a male voice ask long after everyone else had left the burial service. In my grief I couldn't make out the voice or the face that it belonged to, not that I tried very hard. "Lacy, are you okay?" the voice asked again.

Through the process of elimination more than the return of my senses, I guessed that it was Patrick Nance, the no-telling-folks-he-loved-'em jerk, talking to me.

"No, Patrick, I'm not okay. I just buried my best friend," I said coolly.

I hoped that my grief and sorrow would overwhelm him. I hoped that he would leave me alone. He didn't. He sat his sallow behind beside me and began to cry.

Great! Now I was supposed to cheer him up?

"I loved Marsha so much," he said between sobs. "I was going to ask her to marry me on Christmas Day. I knew almost from the first day I met her that I wanted to marry her."

"What? Why did you wait to ask her? Huh, Patrick? Marsha spent a lot of time thinking that you didn't love her. At times she was miserable."

"Why would she think I didn't love her?"

"Because you never told her you did. Those three words would have meant a lot. They would have meant the world to her."

"I've never been good at expressing my feelings," he said sadly. "But if Marsha died thinking I didn't love her. . . God, I'd never be able to forgive myself."

"Patrick, in her heart she knew you loved her, and she definitely knows it now," I said with a weak smile. His grief was more than I could handle, especially since I couldn't even handle my own. I stood up, gently patted his heaving shoulders and slowly began walking to my car.

Wynn, who flew into town just in time for the funeral, drove me home, expressing his condolences the whole time. He offered to take me to the Lake of the Ozarks. Feeling desperate to get away, I readily accepted.

We agreed we'd leave together the next morning. Wynn was so wonderful. He didn't push or crowd me. He called me that night to make sure that I was okay and to let me know he was praying for me and thinking about Marsha.

On our way to the Ozarks the next day, I wanted to talk to Wynn about the fact that Trey was responsible for his shooting and Marsha's death, but I was too wrapped up in my sorrow to even open my mouth. Wynn obviously didn't want to talk specifically about Trey either. Instead, he chose to talk about how Marsha was in a better place and while I may have loved her, God loved her more and wanted her close to Him.

He said some other things that were meant to provide me comfort, but his words didn't sink in. During his spiel, I studied his face. I wondered if he realized he was a failure. He had failed Marsha, Kansas City's kids and me. I wondered if he knew that his precious Youth Center was a breeding ground for crackheads and killers. I couldn't tell him that he wasn't really changing the world. He wasn't saving children. He wasn't changing lives. He wasn't making a difference, not really, except for when it came to me.

When we arrived at the Trust family's Tan-Tar-A Estates condo off of the lake, I was overwhelmed by how everything looked. One whole side of the rustic condo was glass overlooking the Lake. Even for November, it was beautiful. Marsha would have loved it.

On our first day there, I just sat on the enclosed deck and looked out at the lake. It was freezing but I didn't care. Wynn asked me if I wanted him to stay with me. I told him I didn't. He went off to explore the surroundings and to go to the store. After he left, I felt bad about shutting him out, and I vowed to treat him better over the course of our stay.

We spent the next three days talking and reminiscing about Marsha, often into the wee morning hours. When Sunday finally arrived, we regretted that we had to go back to Kansas City, but we promised each other we'd return to the lake on our one-year anniversary, which was just a few months away.

Once we returned to Kansas City, my life was an exercise in errant behavior. As Thanksgiving approached, I didn't even notice. What did I have to be thankful for? I had just buried my best friend.

Given all the bad that had happened in our lives, Marsha had always joked that the two of us were nearly indestructible. Bulletproof. We had both proven time and again that we were survivors. But in truth, we were far from bulletproof. We bled, hurt, felt, cried and died just like everybody else.

Following Marsha's death, the only times I found solace were when I was in church, sitting in the same pew that Marsha sat in every Sunday, and when I prayed every night for God to restore my spirit and watch over Marsha's soul.

When I returned to work, I was like a woman possessed. I wrote article after article about death and loss. The articles weren't even that good, but no one at the newspaper had the heart to tell me I couldn't write them, not even the SOB. Everyone at the newspaper tiptoed around me, acting as if I would snap. I was given free reign to mourn publicly. Each day my tears, sorrow and heartache were on display for everyone in Kansas City to see and read.

In what became known as my "death column," I paid homage day after day to Marsha and the loss of our friendship, and night after night I cried myself to sleep, wondering if I'd ever be the same, wondering if I'd ever recover.

THIRTY-ONE

Following Marsha's death, my family, as usual during hard times, was there by my side. As they paraded over the weeks, in and out of my condo, their faces bore grave concern, yet I couldn't discard my pain to ease theirs. They knew, as did I, that eventually my fog would lift. Thankfully, it started lifting just before Thanksgiving with the help of a long-awaited phone call.

"Glory be. Doggone fool asked me to dinner!"

True to form, by the time I picked up the phone, my grandmother was already in mid-conversation. "Hi, Bibi. What's goin' on?"

"That idiot neighbor of mine said we needed to call a truce, and he wants me to come over to his house for dinner this evening. He's actually been trying to call a truce for months."

"So, are you going?" I asked, smiling.

"I may as well hear what the old goat has to say."

"Do you want me to come help you get ready?"

"Get ready? Please! Ain't nobody dressin' up for that old fool!"

"Now, you be nice, Bibi. I don't have any extra money for bail."

"I'll be good, baby. Really, I will. Guess who called me today?" she asked, changing the subject.

"Who?" I asked, regretting that I'd taken the bait.

"Sebasssstian," she said in an irritating drawl. Before I could ask what they talked about, I noticed that the reporter in the cell next to me was motioning that I had an important call on another line.

"I have to go, Bibi. But I'll talk to you later on this evening. You behave yourself tonight with Mr. Harrison, okay?"

"You know I will, baby. Bye."

Yeah, right. I picked up the flashing line.

"This is Lacy Foxx."

"Lacy, hello. This is Renaldo Bidich."

"Forget you, Sebastian. That's not funny."

"No, no, this is Renaldo Bidich, editor-in-chief of *Élan Live*."

"OhmaGod! I know who you are. I apologize for what I just said. You see, I have an ex-fiancé who has made it his mission in life to make me miserable. Anyway, to make a long story short, I thought you were him."

"No explanation necessary. Look, I'm calling because of some articles you wrote recently. We here at *Élan Live* have been really impressed with them. Do you know which articles I'm talking about?"

"Are you talking about the article I did on that drug addict and the story I wrote about the rappers, 2Tuff?"

"Yeah. Heard your story on 2Tuff helped them get a record deal. Nice job."

I grinned like the proverbial Cheshire cat that had just swallowed the big, fat, juicy canary. "Thanks," was the only word I could muster.

"Actually, I've been tracking your work for months. Thanks for sending me your articles. I loved your sexual harassment series and those stories you did about college graduates employed in dangerous professions. And who could forget the corruption scandal articles that landed you in jail?"

I was struck by his knowledge of my oeuvre. "You remember that story?" I asked.

"Sure do. Lacy, we'd like to fly you out to L.A. to talk to you about working for us. How soon can you get here?"

"Is tomorrow too soon?"

"Actually, it is," he said. "I'm leaving tonight to go out of town for Thanksgiving. But how about the day after Thanksgiving?"

"Sounds great!"

"Good. My secretary will call you in a couple of days with all the arrangements. See you soon. Good-bye."

"Okay, good-bye," I mumbled, still shocked by Renaldo's call.

After I hung up the phone, I just sat there stunned. "OhmaGod, OhmaGod, OhmaGod, OhmaGod, OhmaGod." After several minutes, I had to remind myself to breathe.

Normally, I would run to tell Marsha my news, but she was gone, a fact that I still hadn't grown accustomed to. I picked up the phone to call someone, but I was oblivious to the digits I dialed. When the phone rang, I expected Bibi, my daddy, Uncle Sol or Wynn to answer, but the voice on the other end of the phone belonged to none of them.

"Hullo? This is Sebastian Gamble."

"Sebastian?" As much as I hated to accept it, he was the first person I wanted to share my news with. While I hadn't seen him since Marsha's funeral, the truth was I missed talking to him.

Not that I'd ever admit that to him.

"Lace? What's goin' on?"

"You're not gonna believe who just called me. *Élan Live.* They want to fly me out to Los Angeles in a few weeks for an interview."

"Are you kidding? Haven't you been trying to get a job with them for years?"

"Yeah," I said. I was surprised he remembered. When we were together, he never seemed interested whenever I talked about my career.

"I'm happy for you, girl. You're moving into the big time. After everything that has happened, you deserve some good news. So, how does your boyfriend feel about your possible new job?"

"He doesn't know about it yet. I don't exactly have the job."

"Don't worry. You'll get it. So, how have things been between you and him?"

"Things are good, although like all relationships, it's hard work."

"Well, it's like your grandmother always says. When times get tough, just hand all of your worries over to God. He'll set things right for you."

"Hand it over to God? People say that all the time, but what does that mean? Really?"

"It's like throwing a silent wish into the air. If your relationship with Wynn is meant to last, it will happen."

"And if it doesn't happen?"

"If it doesn't happen, it isn't meant to be. It's not God's will and you don't need it. Hey, by the way, speaking of not needing something, did I tell you that Charron and I broke up for good?"

"I thought things were so wonderful."

"They were for a little while. She's still stripping, and the truth is I have a problem with that. She told me she'd quit, but she hasn't. We had some other issues, and I just didn't care enough about our relationship to hang around and work them out. I think I'm gonna do the single thing for a minute. That is unless you want me back."

I laughed. "No thanks, I'll pass. I just wanted to share my news with somebody, and you just kind of popped into my head."

"Well, I'm glad you called. Good luck."

"Thanks, Sebastian. Bye."

Later that evening, I arrived at the Youth Center thirty minutes before my session. After Marsha's death, returning to the YC had been hard, but I couldn't fault the whole place for what had happened. For weeks, a sad and somber vibe embraced the Youth Center like a slow moving fog, threatening to choke the life out of those of us who were left behind.

Since most of the kids at the YC adored Trey, they had a hard time dealing with the news of Marsha's death and Trey's eventual arrest. Wynn paid out of his own pockets to have psychiatric counselors talk one-on-one with the kids, and not surprisingly, a lot of them signed up for the counseling.

After I dropped off my things in the main office, I began my search for Wynn. I couldn't wait to tell him my news. I found him in the rec room with The Weebil. She and I cut our eyes at each other in our usual I-can't-stand-you-so-don't-say-nothin'-to-me greeting.

"Babe, I need to talk to you," I whispered in Wynn's ear as I encircled his waist with my arms.

"Now, sweetness? This is not a good time. I just got here from the office. I'm behind schedule. We're in the middle of a table games tournament, and I'm short on volunteers."

"Well, put Voncile to work for a change. Come on. I need to talk to you now," I whispered in his ear as I tugged on his arm, "in private."

"All right," he said, motioning for one of the few volunteers to stand in for him.

"Vonnie, can you excuse us? I'll be right back."

"There ain't no excuse for your sorry behinds," I heard The Weebil say as we were leaving.

"Simple witch," I mumbled.

"Lacy, stop. The two of you are worse than little kids."

"Why don't you tell her to stop? Dagnabit, I'm sick of her. I know she's your baby's mama, and I know you don't want to disrespect her, especially around the kids, but why do you let her talk to us like that? Respect should be a two-way street."

"Sweetness, let it go," Wynn said in a bored tone.

I rolled my eyes at him as we quickly made our way to the Youth Center's empty library, where he properly greeted me with a big, wet, sloppy kiss.

"I am so glad to see you. For the last twenty minutes kids have been asking me, 'Where's Ms. Foxx? Where's Ms. Foxx?' like they don't know what time you normally arrive."

"You better not be giving my babies a hard time," I said.

"Who, me? Never! So, what did you want to talk to me about, sexy?"

"Earlier today, I got an amazing phone call. The editor-in-chief of this national online entertainment website that I've been trying to get a job with for years, called to tell me he was interested in interviewing me for a position."

"That's great. What will you be doing? Working a Kansas City beat?"

"No. The company is based in Los Angeles. I'll have to move there."

"Move to California? I never knew you wanted to move to L.A."

"Yeah, you did, Wynn. I told you about it on our first date."

"I know, but I assumed that was just . . . talk."

"Excuse me if I'm wrong, but you don't seem to be exactly thrilled. What's wrong, babe? Why aren't you happy for me?"

"Do you want the truth?"

"No, lie to me," I said facetiously. "Of course I want the truth."

"Well, things between us have been going pretty well, and I'm a little surprised that you want to just up and leave."

"Why not? I assumed we could move to California together."

"I hate big cities. I hate the west coast. There is no way I'm moving to that cesspool. Besides, my whole life is here. I have a business to run, my kids are here and I'm dedicated to the YC. The kids really need me here."

"Your business virtually runs itself. You can run it from anywhere. We could fly Édonte and Perri to L.A. on the weekends, during the summers and during school vacations.

And the kids at the YC aren't the only kids in the world who need saving. If anyone needs someone to help them out, it's the kids that live in Lost Angel-less."

"You've given this a lot of thought, huh? The truth is, my cousin and I have turned this place around. We've spent tons of our own money investing it into the YC. I can't just up and leave. Besides, I thought you were growing attached to this place too. He should be back early next year, and I had hoped the three of us could one day run this place together."

"That's a nice dream, babe, but when were you gonna tell me about it?" I asked.

"I'm telling you now."

"When we first went out, I expressed to you how important my writing and my career was to me. Why are you acting so funny now that I'm starting to get ahead in my profession?" I asked.

"Because when we first met, you were a single, lonely female who had no choice but to spend her life devoted to her career. But now you have me. I'm rich, baby. You don't need to work at all, and certainly not in Los Angeles," Wynn said.

"Excuse me, but who is this male chauvinist egomaniac that has taken over your body? No choice but to spend my life devoted to my career? Who do you think you are? Do you think you're the first man who has offered to take care of me?"

How dare he not support me? Stupid points were dropping like flies.

"I didn't say that I was," he said, defending himself.

"I've had plenty of other offers and I chose my career, just like I'm gonna do now. Because when you screw up, which given your history, you undoubtedly will, I still have to get up every morning and face myself in the mirror. I have to face my choices. And by betting on me, I can never go wrong."

"You! You! You! Can't you think about someone else for a change?"

"Someone like whom? You? You? You?"

256

"You're not the only person this is gonna affect. I see us having a future together, but I don't know how that can happen if you move to California," Wynn said.

"It would be so easy for me to get lost in you, in us. But if I give up my dreams, I'll be full of resentment and won't be any good to anybody."

"Same here."

"Besides, it's not like *Élan Live* has even offered me the job yet. It's just an interview. Let's see how that goes first and then if they make me an offer, we'll cross that bridge when we come to it. Deal?"

"I have to get back to the tournament," he said grudgingly as a wave of children filed helter-skelter into the room. I sadly watched him retreat and threw a silent wish into the air.

A few hours later, after my session was over, I headed to the Youth Center's gym. I had promised several of the boys I'd come cheer them on during the basketball tournament. The team had taken a real moral hit once Trey was arrested, and they needed all the support they could get. By the time I arrived, the gymnasium was already packed. Unfortunately, the only empty seat I could find was located next to The Weebil. Swallowing my pride, I sat down beside her and Perri with an I. After concentrating intently on the game for about twenty minutes, I found myself studying The Weebil's profile.

"Looks like you're gonna get your wish," I said. "I may be leaving town soon. I may be moving to California."

"Yeah? And?" The Weebil asked without looking in my direction.

"And that leaves the door wide open for you. You can go after Wynn hot and heavy now, although it's not like you haven't been."

"Trust me. If I wanted your man, I could have had him by now," The Weebil said without taking her eyes off the game. "Look, I don't like you. You don't like me, and sometimes I can't stand Wynn. But it ain't that type of party."

257

"Cut the bull, Voncile. Sometimes I feel like I'm dating you. I see you as much as I see Wynn. You aren't fooling anybody. You and I both know you've been eyeballin' Wynn for a long time."

"You need to remember one thing. He and I have a child together. We have a history, and contrary to what he may have told you, seducing him wasn't all that hard to do in the first place. It wasn't hard then and I guarantee you, if I wanted him, it wouldn't be hard now."

"That's what you think."

"No, that's what I know," she said, looking me dead in the eyes for the first time in days.

THIRTY-TWO

I had been in Los Angeles for all of an hour and I had yet to be impressed.

It didn't have to do with the fact that I was jaded and unable to be affected by L.A.'s big-city panache, although that would be understandable since I traveled there often because of my job. No, my inability to get excited about Los Angeles had to do with the fact that while on the plane I slid into an unyielding abyss when I came to the realization that my life wasn't crap—or that my life was crap, depending on how you looked at it.

As I walked through the airport, I couldn't think straight. I had too much on my mind. The most immediate of which was why I had decided to travel in four-inch high heel stilettos. And why on earth had I chosen to wear an off-white pantsuit, knowing I was overdue for a visit from Aunt Flow, who finally arrived several thousand feet in the air.

So much for my pregnancy. I was so relieved when I learned at the doctor's office that I wasn't pregnant. According to my OB-GYN, my two missed periods were most likely just the result of mega-stress.

Although I was in a daze, I somehow managed to make it to the American Airlines baggage claims area at LAX to retrieve my bag. Watching the luggage make its way around the carousel reminded me of my life, going around in circles and not getting anywhere.

Wynn and I had long exited the honeymoon phase of our nearly yearlong relationship, and we were now deeply entrenched in the forget-what-you-want-I'm-doing-what-I-want phase. He didn't want me to come to California for my interview, and he made it perfectly clear that he wasn't interested in moving. Heck, he didn't even drive me to the airport to catch my flight. Ole Faithful—my new name for Sebastian—had been kind enough to do that.

I was depressed about losing Marsha, with whom I'd normally be sharing this adventure. And to make matters worse, the fact that the limo promised to me was not waiting when I arrived at LAX, really helped me spiral toward a desperate, enervating low.

While waiting in the baggage claims area, I was flipping through an old issue of *Essence* for the second time when I was paged to the Transportation Services desk. When I arrived, I was handed a message that stated Renaldo Bidich was picking me up at the airport himself.

By my calculation, he was thirty minutes late.

When Renaldo finally arrived, my black mood matched the cheap, ebony-colored garment bag I bought for $19.95 after eyeing it in a Wal-Mart circular the night before.

Élan Live's editor-in-chief appeared amidst plenty of pomp and circumstance, created mostly by his purple-haired, designer clothes-wearing companion, a flamboyant homosexual with the deportment of a circus clown reject. Renaldo Bidich, on the other hand, was an Italian Stallion. He was a class act. He had dark, straight, ear-length hair that was combed back from his face to accentuate mesmerizing brown eyes, strong cheekbones, a firm chin, and a large crooked nose.

Both men were dressed in Armani suits and despite my foul mood, I couldn't help but smile when I heard Barney-head yell at an airport worker who accidentally bumped into him. "Hel-lo! Armani wrinkles!"

"Chaz, butch up!" I heard Renaldo snap at his winsome companion.

Things were definitely starting to look up.

******

"So, Lacy, tell me about yourself," Renaldo demanded.

We had decided on an early dinner at an upscale restaurant located on the city's west side in a nondescript, two-story, beige stucco eyesore of a building. On the inside, the tony restaurant was the hallmark of chic with upscale furnishings, a well-crafted menu that was an ingenious mix of fresh ingredients and fat-gram consciousness, and an elevated "buzz" in the air created by a well-heeled crowd of beautiful people.

I rambled on about myself while eating my charcoaled tuna steak and nicoise salad, painfully aware of the fact that at any given moment portions of food could get stuck between my teeth, thwarting my chances of getting the job at *Élan Live.*

Renaldo attacked with unconcerned vigor his ostrich napoleon and grilled veggies smothered in mushroom sauce. Our dinner companion, Barney-head, otherwise known as Chaz Epperton, had fallen asleep, his head cocked precariously above his grilled veal chop, steamed vegetables and couscous.

"Am I that boring?" I asked Renaldo while observing Chaz.

"Heavens no. Chaz has narcolepsy. Whenever he's not the center of attention, which isn't often, he just falls asleep."

"Don't they have medications for that?"

"Yeah, he takes Tofranil and Vivactil, but he ran out a few weeks ago. Now he's trying to beat this thing the natural way, through diet and a change in his sleeping patterns. As you can see, it's not working. Tomorrow, I'm personally taking him to get his prescriptions refilled," Renaldo said.

"How long have the two of you been, er, friends?"

"You mean how long have we been an item? We've been together about six months now. But you know, I like women too," he said with a sly, seductive wink.

Was he hitting on me? Teasing me? I let myself imagine being a willing conquest of the seductive, enigmatic man sitting across the table who would hopefully become my boss.

"So, why don't I tell you a little about what I have planned for you at *Élan Live*?" Renaldo said, snapping me out of my sexual harassment fantasy.

"I'm all ears."

"Your primary duties will be to act as the online editor of *Élan Live.* You'll also contribute to our cable broadcasts. I'm interested in you because I need someone who is versatile. I need someone who can write about the business side of entertainment and someone who can write about the creative side of it too," Renaldo said.

"Cool. That sounds exactly like what I want to do."

"I need you to be our Jackie of all trades. You'll be responsible for reviews, in-depths, profiles, kiss-and-dis interviews, and calendar mentions. You'll cover music, movies, books, fashion, television, the fad of the month, the whole bit. You'll be totally responsible for the online content and a large chunk of the cable content. We want to give *E! Entertainment* a run for its money. Sound interesting? Think you're up to it?"

"Of course! I believe you have to get in where you fit in, and what you just described sounds like a perfect fit for me. I hate being pigeonholed. I love variety, it's the spice of life."

"So they say. I like your attitude. This job is as varied as jobs come. Now, why don't I tell you about the lay of the land? As for my management style, people say I'm moody and humorless, but that's baloney," he said rather moodily and humorlessly.

"Renaldo, may I ask what drew you to the field of journalism?" I inquired, relieved to deflect some of the attention from myself.

"Well, you're not gonna believe this, but while I was in college, I took an aptitude test that led me to believe I was headed for a career as a beautician."

"So, what happened? You obviously aren't doing hair."

"I opted instead for a career in print journalism. I worked for my college's newspaper and yearbook. I toiled away for years at small, medium and large newspapers and magazines. I covered every beat imaginable. Finally, after ten years of paying my dues and many years of doubting whether or not I chose the right career, I landed at *Élan Live*. I've been there for four years and couldn't be happier."

"Four years in one place? For a journalist, that's a lifetime."

"I know. Look, Lacy, I'd like to extend a job offer to you. Since we're paying to relocate you, there's a six-month probation period you have to go through, but if you still like us and we still like you at the end of the six months, the job is yours. You can start after the first of the year. We'll start you out with a hundred thousand dollars a year and an unlimited expense account. We also have a relocation package that's worth about twenty thousand. What do you think?"

"I think I'm moving to L.A.," I said, unable to contain my enthusiasm.

"Great. We're having a creative editorial staff meeting tomorrow at nine. Can you make it?"

"Sure. Wouldn't miss it."

"Good. I'll send a car for you," he said, motioning for the waitress to bring us our check.

"I'll be there. My plane doesn't leave until three. Will Chaz be there?"

"No, he doesn't work for *Élan*. He's a P.B.S."

"He's at PBS?" I asked in disbelief.

"No, he's a P.B.S. A professional bullshitter. He basically lives off of me."

"Oh." We laughed in unison when Chaz started snoring loudly, as if on cue.

******

263

The next morning, I met Renaldo in the lobby of the building that housed *Élan Live*. We exited the elevator on the eleventh floor and after maneuvering a tricky maze of sharp corners and even sharper stares, we arrived at our destination. The room where the creative editorial meeting was being held was a small, cramped, sparsely decorated shoebox of a room that didn't exactly inspire creative thought.

"Come on I want you to meet the team before we begin," Renaldo said, grabbing me by the hand before slowly making his way around the room with me. He led me to a group of four bored-looking twenty-somethings who were hovering at the back of the room near the coffeemaker.

"Lacy Foxx, this is Brianna Tate, our fashion editor; Mave Clark, our music critic; Dean Alexander, our political columnist; and Pike Elders, our social conscience. They do stuff for the site and the cable network. Guys, meet Lacy Foxx. I just hired her away from *The Metro Tribune* in Kansas City."

"Nice to meet you," Brianna and Dean said in unison.

"Welcome aboard, Lacy," Pike, a fine but obviously gay brother said while extending his hand. He seemed to be thrilled by the fact that *Élan Live* had chosen to darken its employee ranks.

"Kansas City?" the short-shorn, six-foot-tall Mave asked. "What was the last big entertainment story you covered there?" she sniffed. "Billy Bob's backyard hoe-down?"

"Actually, Mave, she managed to get an exclusive with Bare None when they performed in Kansas City, which is something you couldn't seem to do when they came here to L.A. to perform," he informed her.

Hah!

I smiled graciously at Renaldo. "What was that about?" I whispered in his ear after we walked away from the group.

"You know how you women get when you feel your territory is being encroached upon. Come on. There's someone else I want you to meet," Renaldo said, leading me to the other side of the room. "September Oldrite, I'd like for you to meet our newest staff writer, Lacy Foxx. She'll be heading up *Élan Live's* website."

"Oh, so you're *Élan's* newest flavor of the month?" the entertainment reporting legend greeted me with an outstretched hand. The frozen smile on my face began to thaw. I was sick of Los Angelinos. They were rude and obnoxious. I hadn't been in the room five minutes and I had already been insulted twice. Had Marsha been there, she would have gone straight ghetto on them all.

September Oldrite was a legend at the top of the entertainment reporting game. She was as big a star as the entertainers she immortalized with her pen. She was a bony, ferret-like nervous ball of energy. Cigarette smoke oozed from every pore of her being. Her sunken face, which was aging into a permanent scowl, was topped by frizzy, bleached blonde hair with roots long-neglected. I had heard that September had never been married, and that she had no children. Her life-long disappointments were etched in the fine lines of her face like hieroglyphics entombed in rocks thousands of centuries old.

Never before had I met a person whose name so aptly fit them. It was common knowledge that September Oldrite was sixty years old and she looked every bit of her age, plus some. She dressed like she was in a 1970s time warp. She wasn't doing the popular retro fashion thing. It was evident that she just hadn't visited a mall since the dawning of the Age of Aquarius. I immensely disliked the old bat, and the feeling appeared to be mutual.

As we walked away, Renaldo apologized for September's rudeness. "I don't know what has gotten into the women that work for me. All of a sudden, they're like the Devil's spawn. The only female that acted like she had a lick of sense was Brianna, and she's the youngest one in the bunch."

"It's like you said earlier. It's a territorial thing."

"It won't be this way for long. I'll see to that," Renaldo said sincerely. "Come on, gang. Let's get started. Today's editorial meeting is going to be short and sweet," Renaldo said to the group, which now included an additional ten people who had just casually strolled into the meeting as Renaldo took his place at the head of the long, mahogany table in the center of the room.

Renaldo's idea of short and sweet was nearly three hours, and for the most part it was a hodgepodge of heated debates. Toward the end of the meeting, when Renaldo announced that he needed a lead online story for March, I quickly raised my hand.

"How about a story on feng shui?" I said.

"Oh, yeah, that would be awesome," Brianna chimed in.

"Hmmm . . . doing something on how you can harness energy, enrich your environment and create balance in your life, simply by redecorating. That could work," Renaldo said in an approving tone.

"Yeah, lots of city planners, architects and designers use it in their work. Maybe we can find someone locally who's a real expert on the subject. Maybe we can have the expert analyze *Élan's* workspace and do an extreme makeover. Or maybe they could analyze and makeover the living quarters of a reporter," I said.

After Sebastian and I broke up, I had my condo in Kansas City analyzed and was told my love, career and wealth corners needed work. *Big revelation!*

"Hmmm . . . it's new age and hip. Folks, I think we have our March lead story for both the website and cable. Lacy, call me from K.C. and we'll flesh out the piece. The feng shui thing has been done before, so let's find some new angles. Perhaps we can do something interactive with visitors to our site."

"Maybe they can e-mail us photos of their living and working spaces and we can have them analyzed by experts online," I said.

"Sounds like a winner. That's a great idea, Web Queen. That will surely draw traffic. Call me so we can work out the details. Okay, gang, that's a wrap."

The story meeting seemed to go fast because it was so interesting, but by the time it was over, it was almost noon and I still had to pack and get to the airport to catch my flight by 3 o'clock. I was about to rush from the room when Renaldo grabbed my arm.

"Don't you want to see your new working quarters?" he asked.

"I can't. I have a plane to catch. But as long as it's a corner office that's twice the size of yours with two windows, I'm fine with it," I said, laughing.

"Will a cubicle near the bathroom do instead?"

"That's fine too," I said while shaking his hand. "Thanks, Renaldo. Thank you for everything."

"No problem, kiddo. Glad to have you on board. See you in a month."

"Yeah, I'll see ya," I said, stepping into the elevator.

THIRTY-THREE

There had to be a Murphy's Law that read: when you need traffic to move fast, it grinds to a halt—a law I was now living. A trip that had previously taken twenty minutes now took nearly an hour. When I arrived back at my hotel, it was almost one. I only had two hours to pack, check out of the hotel and get to LAX.

I packed quickly—if you call throwing items in a suitcase packing—and checked out of the hotel in record time. Traffic was extremely heavy on the way to LAX, causing me to arrive breathlessly thirty minutes prior to my flight's departure. After stepping out of the cab, I eyed a sexy Jamaican airport worker who took pity on me and agreed to help me catch my flight. I didn't bother checking my bag. We arrived at my gate just as a perfectly coifed American Airlines flight attendant near the door announced the final call for Kansas City. I handed her my boarding pass, generously tipped my knight in shining armor and boarded the plane. I found my seat near the back of the aircraft, strapped myself in and took a deep breath.

I rudely thwarted attempts at conversation made by the portly man in the seat next to me, so that I could reflect on my brief but enlightening time spent in California. I was amazed that Renaldo was so enthusiastic about my first story idea. Unfortunately, my elation about my new job and securing a major story was short-lived. The prospect of a major story didn't mean anything to me without the love and support of my man. And last time I checked, Wynn had been anything but loving and supporting.

I drifted to sleep, formulating ways to convince Wynn that a move to L.A. now would be the best move either of us could possibly make. The captain's sexy, baritone voice stirred me from my slumber several hours later.

"Ladies and gentlemen, we are about to land in Kansas City, where it is a balmy forty degrees. We thank you for flying American. We realize you have a choice, so the next time you fly, please choose us, your friendly guide to the world."

Once on the ground, I made my way to the taxicab pick-up zone. An hour later, my taxi pulled up to Wynn's front door. I asked the driver to wait for me, just in case Wynn wasn't home. Once he agreed, I walked to the door, inserted the key Wynn had given me and began my search for my man.

Not finding him on the first floor, I inched my way quietly upstairs, hoping he'd be in bed naked and waiting for me. When I stepped into his master bedroom, what I saw froze me in my tracks. There were Wynn and The Weebil — together.

I mean together! I watched for what seemed like hours as her creamy, light-skinned, chunky body took in his silky smooth blackness. I watched his big, strong hands draw her to him. I listened as their staccato breathing grew louder and louder. In their pleasure, I found tremendous sadness. When I turned to leave, the hardwood floors in his bedroom cried out in the pain I had yet to express.

"Oh no! Lacy! Wait!" I heard Wynn yell as I ran from the room.

I raced down the stairs, trying desperately to get out of the home that I had once loved and had hoped to share with him. Now all I wanted to do was burn it to the ground with the two of them in it.

"Lacy! Lacy! Wait!" I heard Wynn yell again, only this time his voice was closer. Just as I reached the front door, I felt his hands on me. He grabbed me from behind and turned me around to face him. The Weebil stood naked behind him.

"Sweetness, what you saw . . . it's not what you think!"

"Are you kidding me? If it wasn't screwing, then what the hell was it?"

"She came over to get her child support check and things got out of hand."

"How do you go from 'here's your money' to 'now let's have sex'? Oh, I get it, you've got your very own prostitute whore."

"Who you callin' a whore?" The Weebil yelled at me.

"If the shoe fits—no, make that if the condom fits. Or does your triflin' behind even bother with a condom?"

She approached me menacingly, but one look from Wynn stopped her.

"I . . . I don't know what to say," Wynn said in a pathetic, I-wish-I-hadn't-got-caught tone.

"How about I'm the scum of the earth? How could you do this to me? And of all people, why with her?" I yelled, beating on Wynn's chest as hard as I could with both fists.

"Go ahead, sweetness. Do what you need to do in order to deal with this."

"What? I don't need your permission to deal with this! Why don't you tell me the truth? How long has this been going on behind my back, Wynn?"

"There was just one other time. She and I were together right after you confessed to me that you had slept with your ex. I called her and asked her to come over. We ended up sleeping together. It was an accident."

"What? An accident? You just accidentally fell inside of her?"

"You and I had already broken up."

"Yeah, just barely. You expect me to believe that you've only had sex with her twice and that both times it was an accident?"

"You could consider us even. The reason I took you back so easily when you cheated on me with your ex was because I cheated on you when I found out. You needed comforting so you slept with him. Then and now, the same is true for me!"

"Don't you *even* try to turn this around! This is not the same thing! I thought I was losing you."

"So did I," Wynn said pointedly.

"This is different. I'm not dying. You're not losing me. You sleeping with her is like you sleeping with the enemy. To me, it's the ultimate betrayal."

"Why are you trippin'?" The Weebil asked. "You're moving out of the state. You move, you lose. It's not like the two of you belong together anyway."

"Really? Well, whom do you think he *does* belong with? You?"

"As a matter of fact, I think he does. I ain't gonna lie. I've been determined to get him back, and once I set my mind on something, there's no stopping me," The Weebil bragged.

Her cockiness apparently surprised even Wynn, who looked at her as if he were just seeing her for the first time.

"No stopping you? He's a grown man. He could have stopped you anytime he wanted. It's not like you were holding a gun to his head."

"In a way I was. Wynn was mad at you for going away to California, and he told me that he couldn't get the thought of you and your ex together out of his mind. Those were the only weapons I needed. I knew it would only be a matter of time before he came around and gave in."

"You planned this?" Wynn asked, struck dumbfounded by her revelation.

"Yeah, I planned it. She's shown you time and time again that she doesn't want you, love you, or respect you. Why should she end up with you? She doesn't really appreciate you. Not like I do."

"Vonnie . . . "

She ignored him and continued. "I dropped out of college to have your child. I'm the one that needs you. Perri needs you. *She* doesn't! She's always too worried about herself to please you. She don't care a lick about you, Wynn. She would never put you first like I have," The Weebil screamed at him, near tears.

"Vonnie, this is crazy," Wynn said, finally relieving himself of his rose-colored blinders.

"I don't expect you to understand. My brothers and I were raised by a single mother who latched on to every man that looked her way, so that she could get a father for her kids. I don't want to be like that. I want you, Perri and me to be a family. I want us to raise our daughter together."

"Voncile, save the Cosby-family-white-picket-fence drama for your mama," I said callously.

"Lacy, not now. Vonnie, can you leave us alone for a minute?" She grunted, rolled her eyes and ran up the stairs two at a time.

"You have yourself a real winner there," I said sarcastically.

"Will you stop with the insults for a minute? Enough is enough!"

"You're absolutely right. Enough is enough, and I've had enough of the two of you. I can't stand the sight of either of you. Why don't I just leave now so you two can continue your freakin' lust fest?"

"Wait! Can't we talk civilly? Just the two of us?" he asked as he approached me.

I shot him a look that stopped him cold. "I know you ain't standin' there with another woman's bodily fluids drippin' off yo' triflin' ass, talking 'bout let's be civil. "

"Lacy . . . "

"Someone I once respected and thought was wise once told me, 'There comes a time in your life when you have to decide what's acceptable and what's not.' Your cheating on me is not acceptable. Not that it matters anymore. I got the job in L.A. and I'm moving after the first of the year, so you can screw Voncile all you want with a totally clear conscience," I said before running from his house.

Death by brownies! I should have taken Marsha's advice months earlier.

272

After catching Wynn with Voncile, I never went back to the YC, not even to get my stuff. And while Wynn called me every day for weeks, I never answered or returned any of his calls. He even dropped by my house and the office unexpectedly on several occasions, but I always made sure I was unavailable.

Despite the measures I went through to avoid Wynn, the truth was I still loved him. I thought about him every day, and that wasn't just because he was stalking me. But even stronger than my love for him was the fact that I'd had it! I was tired of being a drama magnet. I'd dealt with more crap in my life than a person my age should have to deal with. I had to try to put an end to it—starting with my relationship with Wynn.

While Wynn and I were together, I thought I had found all that I *wanted* in a man. He was rich, smart, talented, generous, committed to the black community and drop-dead gorgeous. But in reality, Wynn couldn't offer me what I *needed* from a man—respect, loyalty, honesty, and trustworthiness. We were, once and for all, done.

Ding, ding, ding. Minus one thousand stupid points. Game over.

THIRTY-FOUR

"I knew it, I knew it, I knew it, knew it, knew it. Bibi is getting married, Bibi is getting married," I sang like a little kid from the backseat of my father's car.

Actually, that wasn't entirely true. I didn't know it. I never saw it coming. I was too wrapped up in my own sad, pathetic and neurotic world to notice that my 70-year-old grandmother had suddenly fallen in love. The news of my grandmother's impending nuptials after I returned from L.A. a few weeks ago hit me hard and officially sent me careening into a tailspin. Coming on the heels of the end of my relationship with Wynn, Bibi's good fortune had me questioning everything, including love, life and even myself.

Bibi and Mr. Harrison had gone from hate to love—one extreme end of the relationship spectrum to the other—in record time. While I was thrilled for them, I couldn't help but wonder why that kind of 'til-death-do-we-part love was so elusive for me. Instead, with Wynn, I'd been left with the 'til-you-get-caught-cheating-do-we-part kind of love.

From Bibi and Mr. Harrison's first "date" just before Thanksgiving until their wedding day, only a month had passed. In the two weeks before the wedding, when I wasn't trying to avoid Wynn's phone calls and his drive-bys, I had a major pity party for myself where I did more than a bit of drinking. Every night, with a bottle of Alizé nearby, I watched every happy-ending matrimonial movie I could find, and after watching them, I cried myself to sleep. I skulked around the city for hours spying on unsuspecting men and women in love. In some cases, I was brazen enough to actually interview the couples. Plus, I interviewed so-called "experts" on love under the guise that I was writing a series of articles on the subject for *The Tribune*.

In the face of all that research, I still didn't have a clue as to how Wynn and I got so terribly off track. I loved Wynn—

cherished him even. We were the black couple that made other Blacks proud – Beautiful, smart, successful, happy, healthy, positive, in love. That was us, or so I thought. Yet it hadn't been enough.

Despite my newly failed relationship, I was determined to not let it ruin my grandmother's wedding day. "Bibi is getting married, Bibi is getting married, Bibi is getting married."

"Lacy Eymaleen Foxx, why on earth are you bouncing around like that back there?" my daddy asked, eyeing me in his rearview mirror.

"Because Bibi is getting married, Bibi is getting married, Bibi is getting married," I sang.

My Uncle Sol turned to face me in the backseat. "I can't believe it. What's my mother thinking? It's all happened in a little over a month. That's too doggone fast, if you ask me. But you act like you knew this was gonna happen all along."

"I did. I didn't buy that 'I hate my neighbor' crap for one second. Call it female intuition, but I knew all along there was something between the two of them. It just took them a little while to realize it. In that sense, it hasn't been so fast. I think they've secretly loved each other for years."

"That's scary. Hey, I just realized something. We haven't seen your rich boyfriend since Marsha's funeral. Is everything okay? Is he coming to the wedding?" my daddy asked.

"He can't make it to the wedding, but he said he'd try to make the reception," I fibbed. Now was not the time nor place to get into a discussion about Wynn's virtues or lack thereof.

"That's good. I'd like to see him again. He's not like Sebastian, though. When you two were together, we saw more of him than you. But Wynn seems like a nice young man. I think your mama would have liked him."

Nice young man, my behind. "He a'ight," I said, rubbing my mother's watch.

Bibi had decided to get married on Christmas Eve. I expected the church to be empty because after all, Christmas

Eve was a special night most people spent with their families. I couldn't have been more wrong. When we arrived at the church, other people were also arriving, and the wedding didn't start for another hour. It turns out the marriage of 70-year-old Hannah Hale was about as big a Christmas miracle as you could get.

Once Daddy parked the car, I floated into the church, well ahead of him and my uncle. The excitement I felt for my grandmother was overwhelming. I was so thrilled that she had finally found the love and happiness that she deserved after all these years.

The service was being held at the Baptist church my family belonged to on the northeast side of town. Since its early days, St. Thomas had been the preferred place of worship for all of the city's hip and happenin' Christians. Growing up, I spent many Sunday mornings on the hard, wooden pews of St. Thomas. Eventually, time passed and so did the church's stalwart older members. In recent years, hundreds of younger parishioners had moved into the community (thanks to that side of town's revitalization). They'd joined St. Thomas Baptist Church and had been passed the torch by the handful of old members still left. Once the younger generation took over, the church's attendance rosters had tripled, nearing 1,000 members.

In my haste to find my grandmother, I collided with the pastor of St. Thomas. The 70-year-old, soft-jowled Reverend Phillip Lee was a short, proud, slightly wrinkled, light-skinned man.

"Lacy Foxx, long time, no see. Slow down, girl."

"Reverend Lee, it's not every day my grandmother gets married," I said, hugging him.

"No, I guess it's not," he agreed, laughing heartily. "But when praises go up, blessings come down, and this is truly a blessing."

"That it is."

"So, when will you be making your way down the aisle, Ms. Foxx?" the good-natured Reverend asked.

When Hell freezes over, I wanted to say, but thought better of it since I was talking to one of God's right-hand men. Besides, it was a question I anticipated hearing a lot during the course of the day, and now was as good a time as any to come up with an answer that didn't make me sound too pitiful.

"I'll make my way down the aisle just as soon as I find the right man," I said respectfully, "but for now I need to find my grandmother. Have you seen her?"

"I sure have. The smile on her face is illuminating the church like a 3,000-megawatt bulb. You can't miss her. She's in the large meeting room downstairs."

"Thanks, Reverend Lee. I'll see you later."

"Not if I see you first," he said, laughing.

Old folks . . . so cute and corny.

"There you are!" I said a few minutes later when I burst into the room where my grandmother was undergoing her transformation into a beautiful bride.

"Glory be. You scared me, chile," Bibi said, grabbing a robe to cover her scantily clad body.

"Puhleeze, we're family. You don't have anything that I haven't seen."

"You know, speaking of unseen things, do you realize that Cyrus has never seen me naked?"

"I like what you've done with your makeup," I said, changing the subject.

"Do you realize in less than twenty-four hours I will be on my honeymoon with my husband doing the wild thing?" My eyes nearly popped out of my head.

"This is crazy. Bibi, I can't believe you're talking to me about sex in church. I don't want to hear this."

"I haven't had sex for several decades. I need some advice."

"Not much has changed since you were younger and sexually active."

"But aren't there new positions?"

"Who cares? Just do what feels natural, whatever makes you both feel good. That's all that matters."

"How did I get a granddaughter who is so wise?"

"I guess it runs in the gene pool," I said, hugging her.

"I feel so silly about this, but Cyrus insisted we have a big wedding. I'm too old for all of this nonsense."

"Oh, Bibi, please. This is your special day. As a little girl, didn't you dream of a large, beautiful wedding?"

"I haven't been a little girl for nearly three quarters of a century."

"Well, when it comes to love and weddings, we're all little girls."

"So, you don't think this is silly?"

"Would I be here if I did? I'm just so happy for the two of you. Be honest. Did you ever dream you'd be marrying Mr. Harrison?"

"The truth is I've probably secretly loved the man for years. It's just that I had been friends with him and his wife for so long and when she died, my feelings for him didn't seem natural. I felt like I was betraying her."

"So, for five years you acted like you hated him when you really loved him? Just think of all of those years wasted. You could have been with him five years ago if only you hadn't been so proud."

"I know. Well, now I'm planning to make up for lost time. And I hope you have learned from my mistake. I don't want you wasting time like I did, when it comes to love."

"I think it's so romantic. And his proposal . . . Tell me again how he proposed to you. I think it's all so sweet."

"Glory be. Lacy Eymaleen Foxx, you've heard this story a million times."

"I know, and I never get sick of hearing it."

"Well, I'm sick of telling it."

"No, you're not. Come on, Bibi. Tell me."

"Okay, fine. It was four o'clock in the morning and all of a sudden I heard this banging noise coming from the direction of Cyrus' house, from that doggone storage shed, to be exact."

"The one you complained about him working on at four o'clock in the morning, right?"

"You know good and well that's the one. Anyway, at first I tried to ignore the banging, thinking that he would eventually stop."

"But he didn't."

"No, he didn't, so I threw on some boots and my winter coat over my pajamas and I headed to the shed, prepared to give him a piece of my mind. Only when I walked into the shed, he said, 'Hannah, before you give me what for, look at the wall behind you.' 'You fool,' I said to him. 'Don't you know I got better things to do than look at stupid walls at four o'clock in the morning?' And he said, 'Hannah, hush and just look.' So I looked."

"And?"

"And there, strung up in multi-colored blinking Christmas lights were the words 'marry me'."

"Ahhhh . . . how romantic."

"Romantic nothing. I could have caught pneumonia or been mugged messin' around with that fool, Cyrus."

"Yeah, but you didn't and you weren't. So, then what happened?"

"You know what happened."

"Humor me, Bibi!"

"Then he said, 'So, will you marry me, Hannah?' And I told him, 'Not on your life! You're a nut, and I've had my share of nuts.' And he said, 'Hannah, I've loved you for the last five years of my life, and I've been too proud to let you know it. If you think I'm a nut, so be it, but without you, I'll be a crushed nut.'"

"Ahhhh . . . how sweet."

"That's when I took pity on him and told him I'd marry him."

"And that was earlier this month, shortly after I came back from L.A., right?"

"I know it's all happened fast, but I'm old and I don't have time to waste."

"How did you pull this all together so quickly? The church is packed with people and everything looks absolutely beautiful."

"The ladies from church helped, and of course Mary has been a godsend."

"I wish you would have included me more in the planning, Bibi."

"You had plenty going on in your own life, what with Marsha's death, that trip to California and *that* man," she said scornfully.

"You don't seem to like Wynn much. Why?"

"It's not that I don't like him. I just like Sebastian more. You two were meant to be together. Just like me and Cyrus." Before Bibi could elaborate, Mrs. Mack and a swarm of busybodies entered the room and swept her away.

I quietly left the room and began my search for my father and uncle. I found them sitting on the back pew of the sanctuary with Mr. Harrison's now-grown grandchildren. Glad to see the four of them, I hugged them all and we spent the next twenty minutes catching up on each other's lives. In the midst of our reunion, I caught a glimpse of Sebastian approaching us.

"What is he doing here?" I asked my uncle.

"You know he's tight with your grandma. He's a groomsman. One of Cyrus' groomsmen got sick at the last minute and Cyrus asked Sebastian to replace him," my uncle said.

"Didn't your grandmother tell you? He's walking you down the aisle," my daddy said with an amused look on his face. Before I could protest, Sebastian, who was now standing in front of me, kissed me smack dab on my lips. Too stunned to say anything, I stood there with my mouth wide open.

"Hi, Mr. Hale. Hello, Mr. Foxx. Samuel. Collin. Andrea. Pascha. Lacy."

"Howyadoin', son?" my daddy asked, standing up to shake Sebastian's hand. "Glad you could make it. Aren't we, Lacy?"

I pinched my daddy's leg.

"I wouldn't have missed this for anything in the world," Sebastian said respectfully.

"I don't think any of us would have," my uncle said in agreement with a chuckle.

"I saw Mr. Harrison a few minutes ago. He wanted me to tell you that we're about to get started," Sebastian said.

"How can that be?" I asked with an attitude. "They haven't even finished decorating the sanctuary."

"Hold up! Hold up! Hold up! Don't kill the messenger. I'm just telling you what I was told."

After saying a short prayer for Bibi and Mr. Harrison, I followed my daddy, my uncle and Sebastian slowly into the vestibule. Mr. Harrison's grandchildren moved to one of the church's front pews. While waiting for Bibi and Mrs. Mack, I inhaled deeply and eyed Sebastian suspiciously.

Mrs. Mack and Bibi finally appeared ten minutes later, looking like two giddy schoolgirls. When the signal was given, the ushers, two young boys from the church, opened the doors leading into the sanctuary. I was amazed at the breathtaking transformation that had taken place during the ten short minutes since we'd left to wait in the vestibule.

The sanctuary was awash in candlelight. Two six-foot tall, thirteen-taper candelabras stood on either side of the pulpit, illuminating the altar. Large votive candles, their holders decorated with gold-mesh ribbon, sat in the church's windowsills, playing off the large, multicolored stained-glass windows. Strings of miniature, twinkling white lights hung strategically from the rafters. Floral swags, organdy ribbons, tulle and poufs of netting hung above the doorway that led into the sanctuary, below windowsills, on the end of pews, and atop six large column pillars.

Dozens of simple white and peach roses adorned the altar, and for the finishing touch, opalescent glitter was sprinkled on the ivory aisle runner that trailed through the center of the sanctuary. I was so overcome by the beauty of it all that Sebastian had to literally pull me down the aisle.

I beamed broadly as Mrs. Mack and Mr. Harrison's brother, Clark, followed behind Sebastian and me. Mrs. Mack looked as uncomfortable as I felt in our twin dresses, which were tea-length peach concoctions with flared georgette skirts, jeweled velvet bodices accented by four small rhinestone buttons, unflattering empire waistlines and matching velvet scarves.

I looked on proudly as my grandmother made her entrance to "Amazing Grace," flanked by my daddy and uncle on both sides. They were both dressed like Mr. Harrison, his brother and Sebastian. They wore gray double-breasted tuxedos with satin-ribbed lapels, simple white shirts and gray bow ties and cummerbunds.

Bibi looked adorable in her soft, cream-colored lace and sequined jacket with sheer stretch lace sleeves and a chiffon drape from shoulder to shoulder. The jacket topped a sweeping, tiered, tea-length chiffon skirt. I began to cry before Reverend Lee uttered his first word. The ceremony was elegant and heartwarming. I cried through most of it. Two hours later, after shaking hands with a hundred well-wishers in the reception hall, Bibi announced to the wedding party that she was ready to toss the bridal bouquet.

"Lacy, I want you right up front. I'll throw it directly to you."

"No, you will not! I'm not about to sit up here and maul or be mauled by my fellow single sisters as part of an antiquated custom for an institution I'm not even sure I ever want to be a part of."

"Translation, she can't catch," Sebastian said with a laugh.

"Well, here," Bibi said, handing me her bouquet of peach and white roses. "That solves *that* problem."

"Are you kidding? You can't just hand me the bridal bouquet. You'll have every single woman in this place ready to kill me."

"C'est la vie. Let's dance," she said, grabbing the hand of her beaming hubby.

"Congratulations! You're getting married next," Sebastian said before making a beeline for the food. He returned shortly with two plates and sat in a chair across from me at the table reserved for the wedding party.

"Lace, I haven't seen you for weeks. How have you been?" he asked, handing me a plate.

"That depends. Do you want the short, pretty lie or the long, ugly truth?"

"How about both?"

"Okay. The lie is everything is fine," I said. "The truth is I just accepted a job in a city I don't particularly like. And did I happen to mention I just broke up with my boyfriend because I caught him having sex with a woman I can't stand? My grandmother is lucky. I can't get a man to look at an aisle, let alone walk down one with me," I lamented while sucking on a chicken bone.

"I was willing to walk down the aisle with you," Sebastian said.

"You don't count. You're certifiably insane," I said with a nostalgic smile.

"Okay, if you're through complaining, it's my turn. The water heater in my house isn't working, and my car needs a paint job." I laughed at his feeble attempt at misery. "I'm glad to see you haven't lost your sense of humor," he said.

"This is Bibi's day, and I'm not gonna spoil it by being in a bad mood because of my problems with Wynn. Out of guilt after I confessed to him that you and I slept together, I let him get away with much more than I would have ever let you or anybody else get away with. But those days are over. By the way, no one in my family knows about me and Wynn, and I want to keep it that way for a while, okay?"

"They won't hear a thing from me. I'm going back for seconds. Want anything?"

"Yeah, I'd like a huge, heaping helping of a happy, normal life."

"If they don't have that, will another piece of chicken do?"

I answered him by throwing a grape at him, which bounced off his nose. For the rest of the evening, Sebastian took it upon himself to cheer me up. We were inseparable. We danced, partied and had one heck of a good time. It reminded me a lot of when things were good between us, back when we were really a couple. And for a few hours, we were able to go home again, defying the popular belief that it couldn't be done. Seven hours later, Sebastian was still hanging around the reception hall, long after all the other guests had left.

"This was fun. Would you thank your grandmother for including me?" he asked earnestly.

"Yeah, I will."

"You've sure loosened up today. You're not as hostile toward me as usual."

"How could I be mad at you on a day like this that's so full of love? Besides, we're facing a new year, and I want to turn over a new leaf. Life is too short to hold on to all the crap I've been holding on to. I'm gonna try to let go of my self-righteous ways and get rid of the anger I've been feeling toward you since your affair and our break-up."

"I did not cheat on you!" he said, shaking his head.

"Would you give it a rest? When it comes to that, you are so sensitive. I was just playing. Actually, a part of me believes you. I guess a part of me always has. You may not have cheated on me at the time I accused you of it, but with the way I was acting, you would have eventually. The truth is, I wasn't ready for where things were heading for us. After I lost the babies, accusing you of cheating was my way out."

"So basically, you're nothin' but a big ole scaredy cat?"

"Basically. I'm scared of commitment, so I do all I can to push folks away when things get too serious. Unfortunately, it's a pattern I keep repeating."

"It's nice to hear you finally admit it, although I suspected that was the problem all along," he said. "Now, let's change the subject. I got a question for ya. What are you doing on New Year's Eve? If you don't already have plans, why don't the two of us get together and go out?"

"This isn't a pity invitation, is it? Just because I broke up with my boyfriend doesn't mean I don't have a life."

"I just thought it would be a good idea. You know, two old friends bringing in the New Year together. Can't a brotha just be nice and considerate without being accused of having some ulterior motive?"

"You're right. I'd love to spend New Year's Eve with you."

"Great. I'll pick you up at eight."

"Okay, I'll see you then," I said before kissing him lightly on the cheek.

I watched him walk out of the church, realizing I'd received the best Christmas gift I could have ever wished for.

Two old friends bringing in the New Year together . . . indeed.

THIRTY-FIVE

If someone had told me a year ago that I would be spending New Year's Eve with Sebastian, I would never have believed them.

In typical Sebastian fashion, he was late picking me up. When he finally arrived, he immediately began babbling off one excuse after another.

"Sebastian, be quiet! You have exactly ten seconds to tell me how incredibly beautiful and sexy I look," I said, desperately fishing for a compliment.

I was wearing a red sequined Bolero jacket with sheer sleeves that topped a low-cut, curve-hugging beaded dress with spaghetti straps and a flirty, lace-edged hem. He was wearing a black, double-breasted suit, with a maroon shirt and a cute but tacky blinking Happy New Year's tie.

"You look incredibly beautiful and sexy," he said admiringly.

"And you don't look half bad yourself," I said, stepping outside.

"Hey, what's that?" Sebastian asked, reaching over my head.

"What's what?" I asked, looking up at the doorway. "Aren't you clever? It's mistletoe and you're about a week too late," I said, pushing him away.

"It was worth a try," he said, laughing. "You know, that dress you're wearing looks like an I-want-you-back dress if ever I saw one."

"Dream on. It's more like an I-hope-he-don't-get-on-my-nerves-tonight dress, although it doesn't appear to be working," I said.

"Give me time. The night is still young. I'm a little rusty," he said with a wounded look on his face.

"So, where are we headed?" I asked, sashaying past him.

Like a true gentleman, he opened the car door for me. "Always the reporter. Can't you just sit back and enjoy? You're always asking questions."

"Admit it. That's what you like about me."

"Yeah, right," he said sarcastically.

We drove to our destination, listening to KPRS, the #1 all-black station's Top 100 Hits of the Year countdown. We joined in and sang terribly off-key to most of the familiar tunes.

We arrived twenty minutes later at Bar Natasha, a popular downtown spot. The place was packed, and we waited in line outside for nearly an hour. Once inside, we approached a couple we saw standing behind a table.

"You leaving, partner?" Sebastian asked just as the woman threw her drink at her date. The man looked at us sheepishly. "I am now," he said, following the woman out of the club.

Sebastian immediately motioned for a waitress who cleaned up the mess. When she was done, we requested the advertised two free noisemakers and two free glasses of non-alcoholic champagne.

"So, what should we talk about?" I asked.

"How 'bout us? Hmmm, there's a great title for a song," Sebastian said, making reference to one of our favorite make-out songs.

"How 'bout us?" I asked, taking the bait.

"Do you remember how we used to bring in the New Year every year?"

"Yeah, no matter where we were, we had to stop whatever we were doing and make love at midnight. We had sex in some pretty wild places," I said fondly.

"Remember that year in the bathroom stall at Ruby's Supper Club?"

"And how about that time in my grandmother's bedroom? After that, I couldn't look her in the eyes for weeks."

Sebastian laughed. "Neither could I! So, how about it? Right here, right now?"

"Puhleeze!"

"Okay, if you won't have sex with me, at least come and dance with me."

We spent the next thirty minutes gyrating to most of the songs we had just listened to on the car radio.

"So, tell me, Lace. Have you made any New Year's resolutions?"

"Just one. I'm not falling for anymore lying, cheating, deceptive men."

"Is that what you think I was?" he asked.

"I'm not talking about you. I'm talking about you-know-who."

"Oh. Any other resolutions?"

"Yeah. Although I don't like L.A., I want this job at *Élan Live* to work out, and I'm gonna do everything in my power to make that happen."

"When do you leave?"

"The day after tomorrow. January second. I start my new job the following week. I'm excited and scared. As you know, this is something I've dreamed about for years. It's really kind of scary when your dreams actually come true."

"Well, no one deserves success more than you do. I'm really happy for you. I hope it all works out for the best," Sebastian said sincerely.

"I'm just really, really lucky."

"It's not all luck. You've worked hard to get this far. So what does your family think about the new job?"

"They're happy for me, but of course they're sad about me leaving. So, how about you? Any interesting resolutions?"

"Just one. This will be the year I marry the woman of my dreams."

"Wow, let me be the first to congratulate you and Charron."

"Charron? Who said I wanted to marry her? We haven't got back together."

"Have you been holding out on me? Are you dating some terrific woman that you haven't told me about?"

"Actually, you know the lady I plan on marrying quite well. Her name is Lacy Eymaleen Foxx."

"Hah! Funny! Oh, oh, oh, there's our song," I said, pulling him out on the dance floor so we could slow dance to Campaign Lyrics' song, "How 'Bout Us."

We danced for another twenty minutes and then the countdown began. "10-9-8-7-6-5-4-3-2-1, Happy New Year!"

Sebastian and I were oblivious to our surroundings as we lost ourselves in the warmth of each other's eyes. We looked at each other for a long time, cocooned in a comfortable silence.

"Happy New Year, Lacy Foxx."

"Happy New Year, Sebastian Gamble," I said as he bent down to kiss me.

A few seconds later, once the embarrassment of our heartfelt kiss wore off, he spoke. "Last year was a pretty busy year, huh?"

"It was a pretty awful year. Marsha died and Wynn lied to me repeatedly."

"There were some good times, though. You traveled to London and to the Bahamas. You got a wonderful new job, and your grandmother fell in love and got married," Sebastian said.

"Looking back on it now, it seems that in some way or another you were right there with me going through it all."

"Oh, there's one other really good thing that we totally forgot about."

"Oh yeah? What's that?"

"That you and I are here . . . together . . . now," Sebastian reminded me, ever the optimist.

I leaned into him for a hug and smiled.

THIRTY-SIX

"Daddy? Did you bring more boxes?" I yelled from the sofa when I heard my doorbell ring. I put down my reading material and ran to answer the door. To my surprise, standing before me wasn't my father. I was facing Wynn, whom despite several attempts on his part, I hadn't seen or talked to since we broke up several weeks ago.

"Wynn, come on in," I said, after we untangled ourselves awkwardly from each other's arms. "I'm surprised to see you. How are you?"

"I'm good. Call me crazy, but are you reading a dictionary?" he asked, after observing the large reference guide on my coffee table.

"Yep. I figured now was as good a time as any to try and figure out what Marsha's been talking about all these years."

He laughed. *God, he still has a wonderful laugh.*

"Do you want something to drink?" I asked once he settled on the sofa.

"Yeah, water is fine."

"So, what's up? How ya been?" I yelled from the kitchen, trying unsuccessfully to hide my surprise at seeing him. "How is Perri with an I and Édonte? Has Édonte left for Chi-town yet?"

"They're both fine. And no, Édonte isn't going. Jac and I decided not to pull him out of school. He's staying here in Kansas City 'til the end of summer. In the meantime, me and his mom are gonna work out a legal joint custody arrangement."

"That's good. Tell Perri and Édonte I said hello."

"I will," Wynn said awkwardly. "Lacy, I know you're leaving for L.A. soon, and I just really wanted to see you."

"Oh?" I asked when I returned with his water. "Does Voncile know you're here? She loves you, ya know."

290

The pained look on his face immediately made me want to take back my comment.

"Since you brought her up . . . I've decided I'm gonna pay for Vonnie to go back to college. I can afford it. I want the best for my daughter, and that includes a mother who is well educated. She's planning on attending the University of Missouri-Kansas City. She starts school in a few weeks."

"That's a pretty selfless act."

"I don't want you to think I'm paying for her to go back to school because I love her or anything, 'cause I don't. You're the one I love. You're the one I'll always love."

"We've been down this road before and it didn't work for us, remember?"

"We can make it work this time. Since we broke up, I've been miserable. You won't return any of my calls. You won't answer your door when I come by to visit. You're never available when I come by your job. Are you planning on avoiding me forever?"

"It was too soon. I couldn't have talked to you then like a sane and civil human being," I said, trying to justify my avoidance techniques.

"I understand that. But with time, I forgave you when you told me you cheated on me with Sebastian. Why can't you forgive me now? Will you ever be able to forgive me?"

"It's not a matter of forgiveness. I just can't forget. To be totally honest, I just don't think we belong together."

"How can you say that?"

"Don't you think there's something wrong with our relationship if we're both so quick to turn to others for comforting? Sexual comforting at that?"

"Our relationship is still young."

"Still young? We were almost together for a year."

"Well, we *almost* got it right. We just need to communicate better, that's all," Wynn said resolutely. "I'm ready and willing to try it again if you are."

"Are you?" I asked while looking at him skeptically. "Why? I'm leaving for California tomorrow. I know it's just a trial run and I could end up right back here in six months with my tail between my legs, but God willing, I want this job in L.A. to work out. How do you feel about that?"

"You know how I feel."

"There you have it, then. Personally, I don't think either one of us would be any good in a long distance relationship."

"Just hear me out. I'm still not willing to move out of town with you, but maybe we could do the commuter thing, and after a while you'll be so indispensable, your new employer won't care what city you live in."

"Yeah, nice dream, but it's a dream all the same."

"Sometimes dreams come true." He smiled the sweetest of smiles that turned my heart to jelly. "You didn't answer me before. Are you ever gonna forgive me for the numerous omissions, the lies and the cheating?"

"I've already forgiven you. There was a time when I doubt I would have ever been able to say that, but so much has happened during the last year. If this had happened two years ago, I probably never would have forgiven you. I was a little overly self-righteous then. But while I've forgiven you, I'll never forget what's happened."

"Hmmm . . . I see," he said, although it was clear he didn't.

"We're approaching a new year, and I have a birthday coming up. Now is a really good time for change. I don't want to spend the rest of my life with our past hanging over my head. I guess I've learned to let things go. Marsha's death and Bibi's new lease on her love life have taught me how to be still, be observant, be forgiving, be open to God's lessons and blessings and let bygones be bygones. Life's too short to hold grudges. You're looking at a new and improved Lacy Foxx. I'm a kinder, gentler version."

Wynn studied me in silence. "There was nothing wrong with the old Lacy Foxx," he said.

"That's sweet, but it's not true. The last year has been one big wake-up call from God as far as I'm concerned. I'm taking some time off from relationships with men. I'm gonna find a nice church home in L.A. and spend some serious time working on my relationships with God and myself."

"I wish there were room in there for me."

"Wynn, don't."

"You don't have to tell me twice. I'm not a big fan of repeated rejection."

"Most of us aren't."

"Hey, guess what? I ran into Patrick a few days ago. He misses Marsha a lot. He talked about her the whole time we spoke. Did you know he was planning to ask her to marry him? He really loved her."

I smiled, knowing Marsha was cheesing up in Heaven.

"Laaaacyyyyy!" I heard Bibi screech from outside.

"Look, your family is here to help you pack, and there are tons of things I need to do today, so I better get going," Wynn said, rising to his feet.

"You don't have to go."

"I think it's best. Hey, do you need a ride to the airport?"

"I'm not sure. I'll call you in the morning and let you know."

"Okay, good-bye, Lacy," he said, brushing his soft lips against mine.

"Glory be. Even empty, these things are heavy!" Bibi said loudly. She brushed past Wynn and I and headed to the dining room, her arms full of boxes. "Where do you want these? Your dad, uncle and Cyrus are on their way with plenty more."

"Why don't you put them in the kitchen?" I said.

"Here, let me take those," Wynn said.

"Bibi, you remember Wynn, don't you?"

"Yeah," she said less than enthusiastically.

"Here, let me take those for you, Ms. Hale," Wynn said again.

"It is Mrs. Harrison now, and I can handle these boxes by myself, thank you," Bibi said brusquely. She walked into the kitchen after giving me a disapproving nod.

"I can see I'm not her favorite person."

"Don't worry about her," I said. "Look, I have to get back to my packing."

"Okay. Don't forget to call me," he said, blowing me a kiss from the doorway before turning to leave.

"Happy New Year, Wynn," I whispered as I closed the door behind him.

From the other side of the door, I heard him whisper back, "Happy New Year, sweetness. See ya next lifetime."

As a result of Wynn's unexpected visit, I knew I had to make an important decision that night, and an equally important phone call in the morning.

THIRTY-SEVEN

The ride to the airport was one of the longest trips I'd ever taken. He was quiet and self-absorbed. I was just confused. The man I'd spent a good chunk of my recent life loving, was sitting next to me, and suddenly, I didn't want to leave him. Fear of the unknown had me wanting to hold on to my old life, a life that I had once shared with him.

He parked his car and helped me carry my luggage inside to the American Airlines ticket counter. He watched in silence as I checked my luggage and got my boarding pass. The silence was killing me, us. "You really don't have to do this. I'm not a kid. I can handle a trip out of town all by myself," I said.

"There's something I have to say. You know you don't have to go. We can make things work between us."

"You don't have to stay. Come with me. Let's start fresh in California."

I knew he wouldn't come. We both knew it would be better if he didn't.

We walked in silence to my gate. People were already boarding.

"Final call . . . final call . . . American Airlines Flight 219, Kansas City to Los Angeles," a monotonous voice droned over the intercom, rushing me to a destiny I wasn't yet ready to face.

I reached for him, hugged him, and slowly walked to the boarding line. I used every ounce of strength I had not to turn around. I couldn't look at that nose . . . that mouth . . . that body which I had long ago memorized and could see so clearly even with my head turned.

I had to use all of my self-control to keep from getting out of line and running back to him. It's not that I wanted him back. I just wanted to hold on to what he represented — security, safety, comfort, the familiar. After being apart for a little over a year, there was still a huge soft spot in my heart for him, but I was smart enough to know, finally, that what I felt for Sebastian was no longer love.

Nor was I in love with Wynn. My relationship with him had merely been the stepping-stone I needed to help me distance myself from Sebastian. But there was no denying it. In both Sebastian and Wynn, I had good friends that I would always cherish for the rest of my life.

Although it would have been easy for me to stay with Sebastian, I didn't. I had a new life ahead of me in Los Angeles. A new job, new friends, and new experiences awaited. I had just finished a very important chapter of my life, and I was now ready for the next leg of my life's journey.

Moving forward, I was determined to embrace love with my whole heart. I'd learned the hard way that *almost* truly didn't count . . . and the next time, for me, just a little dab wouldn't do.

BULLETPROOF SOUL READING GUIDE

1. What does the novel's title mean to you? When it comes to hardships in our lives, we've all had a few. Each of us have our own "bulletproof soul" stories — life events that have given us clarity, redefined who we were, and/or drastically changed our worlds without destroying us. Identify the "bulletproof soul" moments of the various characters in this novel. What about your own?

2. Starting over is a key theme in this novel. For example, at the beginning of the story, Lacy entertains the idea of starting over with her ex, Bibi starts over with a new outlook on love, and later Lacy debates reconnecting with a past love. What's the significance of returning to where one began as a way of healing and moving forward?

3. Death and loss are two other common themes throughout the novel. What is the significance of the loss and "lack of life" themes? Examine the various physical deaths and near-deaths, as well as the relationship/emotional deaths in the book. How does each affect Lacy? How do you think she manages to go on? In your life, what deaths have you had to deal with and how have they affected you?

4. The relationship between Lacy and her grandmother is a close one. How does this relationship shape Lacy's beliefs and opinions about love and life?

5. Lacy's father and uncle play subdued yet important roles in her life — reminders of the fact that good, positive men do exist. How does their constant presence help or hurt Lacy as she navigates the rough terrain of her love life?

6. The relationship Lacy has with Sebastian is contentious, yet he's always there for her during crucial moments in her life. Is this realistic or a flaw in the story? Should it be hard for people who are no longer dating to remain friends? Do you have ex-loves that are always there for you? How have friends, family and other lovers dealt with the closeness between you and your ex-love(s)?

7. Lacy and Marsha's feminist "women can do anything" views seem to be undermined by the fact that they both appear so needy when it comes to men. How realistic is this? How common is it to see women who "have it together" in most aspects of their lives, not have it together when it comes to love? Why do you think this is? For women who do seem to "have it together" when it comes to love, how are they different from those who don't?

8. How are the issues of friendship, trust, love, betrayal and infidelity handled in the novel? Examine these issues in the context of Lacy's relationships with Sebastian, Wynn, Voncile, Marsha and Trey.

9. When dealing with their respective relationships, what do you think about the advice Marsha and Lacy give each other? Is it thoughtful, helpful, hurtful? What advice do you give your girlfriends when it comes to relationships? Is the advice you receive from girlfriends different than the advice you get from male friends?

10. During a difficult phase in her life, Marsha writes a poem called "Trapped." In some ways it defines how many women feel at some point in their lives. Identify times when you have felt trapped by your life. What did you do to overcome this feeling?

11. How do the characters in this novel use preferences, patterns and obsessions to deal with life or avoid facing it head on? Use as examples: Lacy's obsession with feng shui and redecorating her condo after breaking up with Sebastian. Also look at Wynn's obsession with the Youth Center and how it might relate to his childhood. Plus, examine Marsha's dedication to her dangerous job. What patterns, obsessions and preferences do you have that help you cope?

12. The importance of language is a theme that is focused on throughout the book. Marsha takes up poetry and practices a vocabulary enhancement program. Not to mention both Lacy and Marsha are journalists and they regularly use lingo as shorthand for certain aspects of their lives: (SOB-their boss, Stephen Olin Bishop; their AIDA Plan of Love, etc.) What are some of your own language eccentricities? Why do you think language is stressed so in the novel?

13. Someone close to Lacy has a near-death experience. Could this experience represent a part of the relationship with Lacy that is dying? What part of the relationship do you think that is? Could it be Lacy's blind faith and trust in this person? Does this near-death experience adequately foreshadow the outcome of their relationship? Have there been foreshadowing incidents in your own relationships that hinted of things to come? Did you ignore them or stop and pay attention?

14. In the end, Lacy makes an important, somewhat surprising decision. What overall message do you think the author was trying to get across based on Lacy's ultimate choice?

15. What's your favorite moment in the novel? Why?